Acclaim for EMPIRE

'A damn fine read . . . fast-paced, action-packed.' Ben Kane

'Stands head and shoulders above a crowded field . . . real, live
characters act out their battles on the northern borders with an
accuracy of detail and depth of raw emotion that is a rare
combination.' Manda Scott

'Riches has captured how soldiers speak and act to a tee and
he is very descriptive when it comes to the fighting. It is a novel
full of power, lust, envy, violence and vanity. The very things
that made Rome great and the very things that would lead
to its downfall. If you like historical novels, read this book.'
NavyNet on *Arrows of Fury*

'With *Wounds of Honour* Anthony Riches has produced a terrific
first novel that focuses on the soldiers of the Roman Empire in
great detail. He vibrantly portrays the life in an auxiliary unit.'
Canberra Times

'This is fast-paced and gripping "read-through-the-night"
fiction, with marvellous characters and occasional moments
of dark humour. Some authors are better historians
than they are storytellers. Anthony Riches is brilliant at both.'
Conn Iggulden

EMPIRE

Wounds of Honour
Arrows of Fury
Fortress of Spears

About the author

Anthony Riches holds a degree in Military Studies from Manchester University. He began writing the story that would become the first novel in the *Empire* series, *Wounds of Honour*, after visiting Housesteads Roman fort in 1996. He lives in Hertfordshire with his wife and three children.

Find out more about his books at www.anthonyriches.com

The Leopard Sword

Empire: Volume Four

ANTHONY RICHES

HODDER

First published in 2012 by Hodder & Stoughton
An Hachette UK company

First published in paperback in 2012

3

A CIP catalogue record for this title is available from the British Library

ISBN 978 1 444 71184 4

Typeset in Plantin Light
by Palimpsest Book Production Limited, Falkirk, Stirlingshire

Printed and bound by Clays Ltd, St Ives plc

Hodder & Stoughton policy is to use papers that are natural,
renewable and recyclable products and made from wood grown in
sustainable forests. The logging and manufacturing processes are expected
to conform to the environmental regulations of the country of origin.

Hodder & Stoughton Ltd
338 Euston Road
London NW1 3BH

www.hodder.co.uk

For Robin

ACKNOWLEDGEMENTS

The writing of *The Leopard Sword* was at one point proving to be something of a challenge, with the book half-written but stubbornly refusing to progress beyond a knot in the plot from which I couldn't tear myself free. At the low point of this increasingly panicked situation an old friend, on hearing of my plight on a rugby pitch touchline one Thursday night, uttered the words that were to reinvigorate my writing life: 'Just come down to my office and write.' So I did. No internet (critical that, nothing with which to fluff about in endless prevarication), just cups of tea and the occasional chat, that and a blazing eight or nine hundred words an hour. It was like going from dial-up to super-broadband in one step. Lesson learned, I now rent a converted henhouse on a local farm – no internet there either – and when I'm not doing 'real' work I commute a few miles to write in blissful peace and without any opportunity to do anything but write. So to you, Eddie Hickey, go the biggest thanks of all this time round. Let's hope my new-found regime will see me turning out two books a year with perfect equanimity.

Apart from that I have to offer all the usual but heartfelt thanks. To Helen for encouragement and occasional strong direction (and tolerating the last touches being put to the script in the south of France); to the kids for putting up with it all; and when the pressure notched up a bit the dogs for providing the alternative perspective of lives bounded by the need to get walked and fed. My agent Robin was his usual urbane self, and Carolyn the editor sat on her hands pretending to be calm while I struggled over the line.

On the subject of Hodder & Stoughton it's worth mentioning

that my publisher remains a delight to work with, so thanks to Francine, Nick, Laure, Jaime, James, Ben and everyone else whose name I'm too scatterbrained to have remembered. Clare Parkinson did an amazing job on the copyedit and rescued me from several embarrassing errors, taking all that gore and unpleasantness in her stride. Well done. John Prigent also read the original manuscript, and made more than one telling comment, as ever!

Lastly, and as ever, thanks to everyone else that's helped me this time round but not been mentioned. To use that old cliché it's not you, it's me. Those people that work alongside me will tell you how poor my memory can be, so if I've forgotten you then here's a blanket apology. Where the history is right it's because I've had some great help, and where it's not it's all my own work.

Thank you.

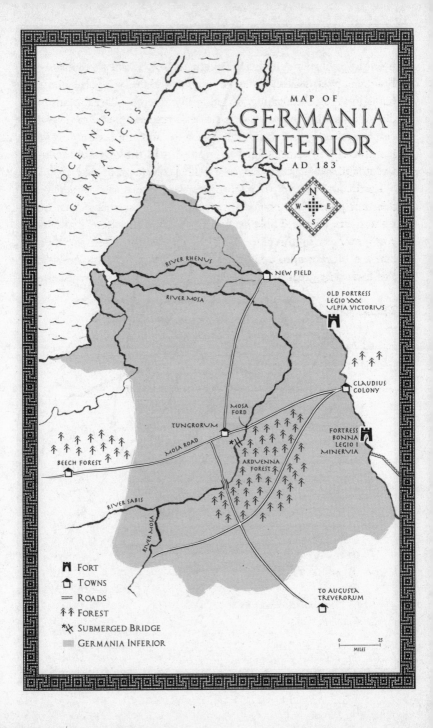

MAP OF
GERMANIA INFERIOR
AD 183

OCEANUS GERMANICUS

RIVER RHENUS

RIVER MOSA

NEW FIELD

OLD FORTRESS
LEGIO XXX
ULPIA VICTORIUS

CLAUDIUS
COLONY

MOSA
FORD

TUNGRORUM

MOSA ROAD

FORTRESS
BONNA
LEGIO I
MINERVIA

ARDUENNA
FOREST

BEECH FOREST

RIVER SABIS

RIVER MOSA

TO AUGUSTA
TREVERORUM

Fort
Towns
= **Roads**
Forest
Submerged Bridge
Germania Inferior

0   25
MILES

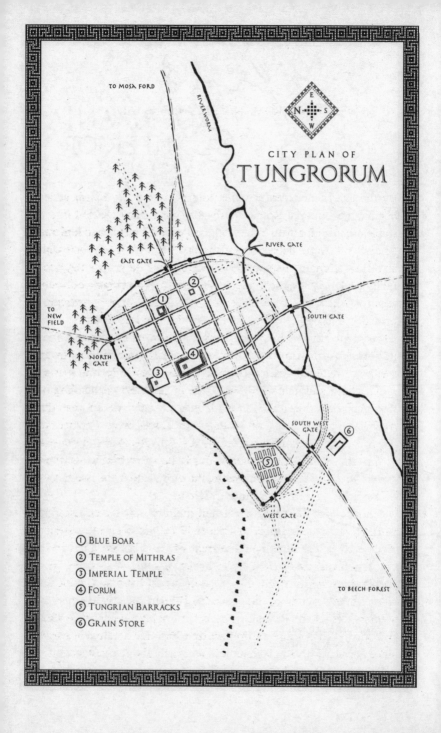

CITY PLAN OF
TUNGRORUM

TO MOSA FORD

RIVER WOLD

RIVER GATE

EAST GATE

TO NEW FIELD

SOUTH GATE

NORTH GATE

SOUTH WEST GATE

WEST GATE

TO BEECH FOREST

① BLUE BOAR
② TEMPLE OF MITHRAS
③ IMPERIAL TEMPLE
④ FORUM
⑤ TUNGRIAN BARRACKS
⑥ GRAIN STORE

THE ROMAN ARMY IN 182 AD

By the late second century, the point at which the *Empire* series begins, the Imperial Roman Army had long since evolved into a stable organization with a stable *modus operandi*. Thirty or so **legions** (there's still some debate about the 9th Legion's fate), each with an official strength of 5,500 legionaries, formed the army's 165,000-man heavy infantry backbone, while 360 or so **auxiliary cohorts** (each of them the equivalent of a 600-man infantry battalion) provided another 217,000 soldiers for the empire's defence.

Positioned mainly in the empire's border provinces, these forces performed two main tasks. Whilst ostensibly providing a strong means of defence against external attack, their role was just as much about maintaining Roman rule in the most challenging of the empire's subject territories. It was no coincidence that the troublesome provinces of Britain and Dacia were deemed to require 60 and 44 auxiliary cohorts respectively, almost a quarter of the total available. It should be noted, however, that whilst their overall strategic task was the same, the terms under the two halves of the army served were quite different.

The legions, the primary Roman military unit for conducting warfare at the operational or theatre level, had been in existence since early in the Republic, hundreds of years before. They were composed mainly of close-order heavy infantry, well-drilled and highly motivated, recruited on a professional basis and, critically to an understanding of their place in Roman society, manned by soldiers who were Roman citizens. The jobless poor were thus provided with a route to both citizenship and a valuable trade, since service with the legions was as much about construction – fortresses, roads, and even major defensive works such as Hadrian's

The Chain of Command
LEGION

LEGATUS — LEGION CAVALRY (120 HORSEMEN)

BROAD STRIPE TRIBUNE

5 'MILITARY' NARROW STRIPE TRIBUNES

CAMP PREFECT

SENIOR CENTURION

10 COHORTS
(ONE OF 5 CENTURIES OF 160 MEN EACH)
(NINE OF 6 CENTURIES OF 80 MEN EACH)

CENTURION

CHOSEN MAN

WATCH OFFICER   STANDARD BEARER

10 TENT PARTIES OF
8 MEN APIECE

The Chain of Command
Auxilary
Infantry Cohort

Legatus

Prefect

(or a Tribune for a larger cohort such as
the First Tungrian)

Senior Centurion

6-10 Centuries

Centurion

Chosen Man

Watch Officer   Standard Bearer

10 tent parties of
8 men apiece

Wall – as destruction. Vitally for the maintenance of the empire's borders, this attractiveness of service made a large standing field army a possibility, and allowed for both the control and defence of the conquered territories.

By this point in the Britannia's history three legions were positioned to control the restive peoples both beyond and behind the province's borders. These were the 2nd, based in South Wales, the 20th, watching North Wales, and the 6th, positioned to the east of the Pennine range and ready to respond to any trouble on the northern frontier. Each of these legions was commanded by a **legatus**, an experienced man of senatorial rank deemed worthy of the responsibility and appointed by the emperor. The command structure beneath the legatus was a delicate balance, combining the requirement for training and advancing Rome's young aristocrats for their future roles with the necessity for the legion to be led into battle by experienced and hardened officers.

Directly beneath the legatus were a half dozen or so **military tribunes**, one of them a young man of the senatorial class called the **broad stripe tribune** after the broad senatorial stripe on his tunic. This relatively inexperienced man – it would have been his first official position – acted as the legion's second-in-command, despite being a relatively tender age when compared with the men around him. The remainder of the military tribunes were **narrow stripes**, men of the equestrian class who usually already had some command experience under their belts from leading an auxiliary cohort. Intriguingly, since the more experienced narrow-stripe tribunes effectively reported to the broad stripe, such a reversal of the usual military conventions around fitness for command must have made for some interesting man-management situations. The legion's third in command was the camp **prefect**, an older and more experienced soldier, usually a former centurion deemed worthy of one last role in the legion's service before retirement, usually for one year. He would by necessity have been a steady hand, operating as the voice of experience in advising the legion's senior officers as to the realities of warfare and the management of the legion's soldiers.

Reporting into this command structure were ten **cohorts** of soldiers, each one composed of a number of eighty-man **centuries**. Each century was a collection of ten **tent parties** – eight men who literally shared a tent when out in the field. Nine of the cohorts had six centuries, and an establishment strength of 480 men, whilst the prestigious **first cohort**, commanded by the legion's **senior centurion**, was composed of five double-strength centuries and therefore fielded 800 soldiers when fully manned. This organization provided the legion with its cutting edge: 5,000 or so well-trained heavy infantrymen operating in regiment and company sized units, and led by battle-hardened officers, the legion's centurions, men whose position was usually achieved by dint of their demonstrated leadership skills.

The rank of **centurion** was pretty much the peak of achievement for an ambitious soldier, commanding an eighty-man century and paid ten times as much as the men each officer commanded. Whilst the majority of centurions were promoted from the ranks, some were appointed from above as a result of patronage, or as a result of having completed their service in the **Praetorian Guard**, which had a shorter period of service than the legions. That these externally imposed centurions would have undergone their very own 'sink or swim' moment in dealing with their new colleagues is an unavoidable conclusion, for the role was one that by necessity led from the front, and as a result suffered disproportionate casualties. This makes it highly likely that any such appointee felt unlikely to make the grade in action would have received very short shrift from his brother officers.

A small but necessarily effective team reported to the centurion. The **optio**, literally 'best' or **chosen man**, was his second-in-command, and stood behind the century in action with a long brass-knobbed stick, literally pushing the soldiers into the fight should the need arise. This seems to have been a remarkably efficient way of managing a large body of men, given the centurion's place alongside rather than behind his soldiers, and the optio would have been a cool head, paid twice the usual soldier's wage and a candidate for promotion to centurion if he performed well. The century's third-in-command was the **tesserarius** or **watch officer**, ostensibly charged with ensuring that sentries were posted and that everyone know the watch word for the day, but also likely to have been responsible for the profusion of tasks such as checking the soldiers' weapons and equipment, ensuring the maintenance of discipline and so on, that have occupied the lives of junior non-commissioned officers throughout history in delivering a combat-effective unit to their officer. The last member of the centurion's team was the century's **signifer**, the **standard-bearer**, who both provided a rallying point for the soldiers and helped the centurion by transmitting marching orders to them through movements of his standard. Interestingly, he also functioned as the century's banker, dealing with the soldiers' financial affairs. While a soldier caught in the horror of battle might have thought twice about defending his unit's standard, he might well also have felt a stronger attachment to the man who managed his money for him!

At the shop-floor level were the eight soldiers of the tent party who shared a leather tent and messed together, their tent and cooking gear carried on a mule when the legion was on the march. Each tent party would inevitably have established its own pecking order based upon the time-honoured factors of strength, aggression, intelligence – and the rough humour required to survive in such a harsh world. The men that came to dominate their tent parties would have been the century's unofficial backbone, candidates for promotion to watch officer. They would also have been vital to their tent mates' cohesion under battlefield conditions, when the relatively thin leadership team could not always exert sufficient presence to inspire the individual soldier to stand and fight amid the horrific chaos of combat.

The other element of the legion was a small 120-man detachment of **cavalry**, used for scouting and the carrying of messages between units. The regular army depended on auxiliary **cavalry wings**, drawn from those parts of the empire where horsemanship was a way of life, for their mounted combat arm. Which leads us to consider the other side of the army's two-tier system.

The **auxiliary cohorts**, unlike the legions alongside which they fought, were not Roman citizens, although the completion of a twenty-five year term of service did grant both the soldier and his children citizenship. The original auxiliary cohorts had often served in their homelands, as a means of controlling the threat of large numbers of freshly-conquered barbarian warriors, but this changed after the events of the first century AD. The Batavian revolt in particular – when the 5,000-strong Batavian cohorts rebelled and destroyed two Roman legions after suffering intolerable provocation during a recruiting campaign gone wrong – was the spur for the Flavian policy for these cohorts to be posted away from their home provinces. The last thing any Roman general wanted was to find his legions facing an army equipped and trained to fight in the same way. This is why the reader will find the auxiliary cohorts described in the *Empire* series, true to the historical record, representing a variety of other parts of the empire, including Tungria, which is now part of modern-day Belgium.

Auxiliary infantry was equipped and organized in so close a manner to the legions that the casual observer would have been hard put to spot the differences. Often their armour would be mail, rather than plate, sometimes weapons would have minor differences, but in most respects an auxiliary cohort would be the same proposition to an enemy as a legion cohort. Indeed there are hints from history that the auxiliaries may have presented a greater challenge on the battlefield. At the battle of Mons Graupius in Scotland, Tacitus records that four cohorts of Batavians and two of Tungrians were sent in ahead of the legions and managed to defeat the enemy without requiring any significant assistance. Auxiliary cohorts were also often used on the flanks of the battle line, where reliable and well drilled troops are essential to handle attempts to outflank the army. And while the legions contained soldiers who were as much tradesmen as fighting men, the auxiliary cohorts were primarily focused on their fighting skills. By the end of the second century there were significantly more auxiliary troops serving the empire than were available from the legions, and it is clear that Hadrian's Wall would have been invalid as a concept without the mass of infantry and mixed infantry/cavalry cohorts that were stationed along its length.

As for horsemen, the importance of the empire's 75,000 or so **auxiliary cavalrymen**, capable of much faster deployment and manoeuvre than the infantry, and essential for successful scouting, fast communications and the denial of reconnaissance information to the enemy cannot be overstated. Rome simply did not produce anything like the strength in mounted troops needed to avoid being at a serious disadvantage against those nations which by their nature were cavalry-rich. As a result, as each such nation was conquered their mounted forces were swiftly incorporated into the army until, by the early first century BC, the decision was made to disband what native Roman cavalry as there was altogether, in favour of the auxiliary cavalry wings.

Named for their usual place on the battlefield, on the flanks or 'wings' of the line of battle, the cavalry cohorts were commanded by men of the equestrian class with prior experience as legion military tribunes, and were organized around the basic 32-man **turma**, or squadron. Each squadron was commanded by a **decurion**, a position analogous with that of the infantry centurion. This officer was assisted by a pair of junior officers: the **duplicarius** or **double-pay**, equivalent to the role of optio, and the **sesquipilarius** or **pay-and-a-half**, equal in stature to the infantry watch officer. As befitted the cavalry's more important military role, each of these ranks was paid about 40 per cent more than the infantry equivalent.

Taken together, the legions and their auxiliary support presented a standing army of over 400,000 men by the time of the events described in the *Empire* series. Whilst this was sufficient to both hold down and defend the empire's 6.5 million square kilometres for a long period of history, the strains of defending a 5,000-kilometre-long frontier, beset on all sides by hostile tribes, were also beginning to manifest themselves. The prompt move to raise three new legions undertaken by the new emperor Septimius Severus in 197 AD, in readiness for over a decade spent shoring up the empire's crumbling borders, provides clear evidence that there were never enough legions and cohorts for such a monumental task. This is the backdrop for the *Empire* series, which will run from 182 AD well into the early third century, following both the empire's and Marcus Valerius Aquila's travails throughout this fascinatingly brutal period of history.

Prologue

'Fucking rain! Rain yesterday, rain today and rain tomorrow most likely. This bloody damp gets everywhere. My armour will be rusting again by morning.'

'You'll just have to get your brush out again, or that crested bastard will be up your arse like a rat up a rain pipe.'

The two sentries shared a grimace of mutual disgust at the thought of the incessant work required to keep their mail free of the pitting that would bring the disapproval of their centurion down on them. The night's cold mist was swirling around the small fort's watchtower, individual droplets dancing on the breeze that was moaning softly across the countryside around their outpost. The blazing torch that lit their section of the fortlet's wall was wreathed in a ball of misty radiance that enveloped them with an eerie glow, and made it almost impossible to see further than a few paces. Shielding their eyes from the light as best they could, they watched their assigned arcs of open ground, with occasional glances into the fort below them to make sure that nobody, neither bandit nor centurion, was attempting to creep up on them.

'I don't mind the polishing so much as having to listen to that miserable old bastard's constant stream of bullshit about how much harder it was in "the old days": "When the Chauci came at us from the sea, well, that was real fighting, my lads, not that you children would recognise a fight unless you had a length of cold, sharp iron buried in your . . ."'

He fell silent, something in the darkness beneath the walls catching his attention.

'What is it?'

He stared down into the gloom for a long moment, blinking his tired eyes before looking away and then back at the place where he could have sworn the darkness had taken momentary form.

'Nothing. I thought I saw something move, but it was probably just a trick of the mist.' Shaking his head, he planted his spear's butt spike on the watchtower's wooden planks and yawned widely. 'I hate this time of year; the fog has a man jumping at shadows all the fucking time.'

His mate nodded, leaning out over the wall and staring down into the mist.

'I know, sometimes you can imagine—'

His voice choked off, and after a moment's apparent indecision he slumped forward over the parapet and vanished from view. While the other sentry goggled in amazement a hand gripped the edge of the wooden wall, hauling a black-clad figure over its lip and onto the torchlit platform; the intruder's other hand was gripping a short spear whose blade was running with the dead sentry's blood. The attacker's boots shone in the light, the flickering illumination glinting off the heavy metal spikes that had carried him up the wall's sheer wooden face. The sentry stepped forward, dimly aware of shouting from another corner of the fortlet, and raised his spear to stab at the attacker even as the other man flicked his hand as if in dismissal, sending a slender shank of cold iron to bury itself in his throat. Coughing blood, he staggered backwards and stepped out into thin air, plummeting to the hard earth ten feet below.

Lying half asleep in his small and draughty barrack, the detachment's centurion heard the unmistakable sounds of fighting as he dozed on his bed, and he was on his feet with his sword drawn from the scabbard hanging from the room's single wooden chair before he was fully awake. Thanking the providence that had seen him lie down without removing his boots, he pulled on his helmet and stepped out through the door with a bellowed command for his men to stand to, feeling woefully under-equipped without the reassuring weight of his armour. A shadowy figure came at him out of the darkness to his right, the attacker's spear shining in the light of the torch fixed to the wall behind the centurion, and with a speed born of two decades of practice he swayed to allow the weapon's thrust to hiss past him before stepping in quickly to ram the gladius deep into his anonymous assailant's chest. Shrugging the dying man off the blade to lie gurgling out what was left of his life on the damp grass, he advanced towards the fortlet's gate, pausing to pick up a shield left lying alongside the broken body of one of the wall sentries. A throwing knife protruded from a bloody hole in the dead man's throat, and the centurion scowled at the ease with which his men's defences seemed to have been compromised.

As the centurion advanced cautiously down the wall's length, in hopes of making out the detail of what was happening around the fort's entrance, his heart sank. The gate was already open, and a flood of attackers was pouring through it with their swords drawn. Sheltering in the palisade's deeper shadow he watched as they overran the few men who still stood in defence of the fort, battering them brutally aside in a brief one-sided combat. Having already made the decision to slip away and report the disaster to his tribune in Tungrorum, the centurion shook his head, turning away from the sight of his command's destruction just in time to spot a dark-clad figure coming at him out of the darkness with a short spear held ready to strike. Smashing the weapon aside with the shield, he punched hard at the reeling assailant's face with his sword hand, catapulting the other man back against the wall. The intruder's head hit the unyielding wood with a dull thud and he slumped slackly to the ground, his eyes glassy from the blow's force. Kneeling to dimple the fallen attacker's throat with the point of his gladius, the centurion hissed a question into the stunned face, the one question that had been on the lips of every soldier in the province for months.

'Obduro? Who is Obduro?'

The dazed man simply looked up in mute refusal to reply.

'Tell me his fucking name or I'll stop your wind!' Desperation lent the words a lethal menace that left the victim in little doubt as to the sincerity of this threat.

Regaining his senses, the fallen intruder cautiously shook his head, his eyes fixed on a point behind the vengeful centurion. He spoke quietly, his voice almost lost in the din of the one-sided fight: 'More than my life's worth.'

'Fair enough.'

Nodding slowly, his face hardening with the realisation that they were not alone, the centurion stood, and as he turned to face the men behind him he casually pushed the sword's point through the helpless man's throat, putting a booted foot on his victim's heaving chest to hold the man's body down while he withdrew the blade with a vicious twist. Half a dozen of the fort's attackers were standing in a loose half circle around him, all but one with spears levelled at him. Their black clothing, clearly intended to provide them with concealment in the moon-less night, gave no clue as to who they might be, although more than one face seemed distantly familiar. The sixth man was armed only with a sword at his waist, but the centurion took an involuntary step back at the sight of the Roman cavalry helmet that completely hid his features. Its thick iron faceplate was tinned and highly polished, the mirror-like surface broken only by a pair of black eye holes and a slit between the thin, cruel iron lips. It reflected a distorted version of the centurion as he raised his shield to fight.

'You wanted Obduro? Then here I am. And that was an unneces-sary death, Centurion, given the fact that your men are already scattered and beaten; and he was a good man, one of my best. You *know* I can make you pay heavily in lingering torment for that brief moment of revenge, and yet you still chose to pay that price for a fleeting moment of satisfaction. How amusing . . .' The words were muffled to the point of being made barely audible by the helmet's faceplate, and the voice was distorted enough to be unrecognisable, despite the rumours as to the wearer's identity that were the stuff of soldiers' gossip across the entire province. 'Tonight we are taking prisoners, Centurion, recruiting men to join us in the deep forest. You could still live, if you'll drop the sword and shield and bend your knee to me and promise faithful service. Or you could die here, alone and uncelebrated, no matter how brave your death might be.'

The centurion shook his head, hefting the sword ready to fight.

'Send your men at me, then, and let's see how many I can put down before they stop me.' He spat on the cooling corpse at his feet in an attempt to goad the masked man to a rash move. 'I'll cost you more than your boyfriend here before you kill me.'

The masked man shook his head in return, then drew a long sword from the scabbard at his waist in response. The blade's surface seemed to ripple in the torchlight, its intricate pattern of dark and light bands giving it an unearthly quality.

'I do believe you're right, Centurion, and I'll not waste good men when there's no need. I'll take you down myself.'

He bent to pick up a discarded shield before stepping forward to face the centurion, lifting the patterned sword to show his opponent the weapon's point. They faced each other for a moment in silence before the soldier shrugged and took the offensive, stamping forward and hammering his sword into the masked man's shield. Once, twice, the gladius rose and fell, and for a brief moment the centurion believed that he was gaining the upper hand as the other man stepped back from each blow, using his shield to absorb its force. Raising his sword again he stepped in closer, swinging the blade with all his strength. Halting his retreat, the masked man met the descending gladius with his own weapon. The two blades met with a rending screech, and in a brief shower of sparks the patterned sword sliced cleanly through the iron gladius's blade and dropped two-thirds of its length to the ground in a flickering tumble. The centurion stared wide-eyed at the emasculated stump of blade attached to his ruined weapon's hilt. Allowing no time for the shocked soldier to get his wits back, the masked man attacked with a pitiless ferocity. He hacked horizontally at his enemy with the seemingly irresistible sword, carving cleanly through the centurion's shield. The layered wood and linen fell apart like a rotten barrel lid, leaving the soldier clutching the lopsided section of board in one hand and his sword's useless remnant in the other. He threw the sword's hilt at his opponent, clenching his fists in frustration as it bounced off the polished faceplate with a metallic clang, then hurled what was left of the shield after it, only to watch as the other man sliced the flying remains cleanly in two with a diagonal cut. Taking another step forward, the masked man dropped his shield and raised the patterned blade in a two-handed grip.

'And now, Centurion, you can pay that price I mentioned.'

Looking at his reflection in the helmet's polished facemask the centurion saw defeat in his own face and, enraged by the very possibility, he gathered himself to jump at his enemy with a snarl of hatred. Attacking with a speed and purpose that matched the soldier's berserk leap, the masked swordsman swung his sword in a short arc to slice into the centurion's abdomen, pulling the blow rather than cutting him cleanly in two, and grinding the weapon's ferocious edge across the centurion's spine as he ripped it free. The eviscerated soldier dropped to the ground in a gout of blood and intestines, his eyes flickering as his brain absorbed the sheer scale of the destruction wrought on his body. Bending as if to speak to the dying officer, the swordsman cleaned his blade on a fold in the other man's tunic, then slipped the sword into its scabbard. He lifted the helmet's faceplate to allow the cold night air to cool his sweating face. Looking down at the dying soldier he smiled bleakly, nodding his respect.

'Well done, friend. You died like a man. And now you are on your way to meet your gods, once we give you the coin with which to pay for your crossing. In reality, of course, given where you are, you will only be meeting Arduenna. And trust me, Centurion, she is a spiteful, vindictive bitch.'

He turned away, only to find his leg held in a firm grip. The dying centurion was using the last of his strength to clamp a trembling hand around his ankle.

'*You . . .?*'

He stared down into the fading light of the dying man's eyes.

'Yes. *Me*. It does come as a bit of a shock, doesn't it?' He pulled his leg free and watched blank-faced as the last vestige of life left the centurion's body, then closed the faceplate over his features. 'Bring his corpse over to the gate. I want as many of them as possible to join our cause and encourage their comrades in the city to do the same, and having him laid out for inspection ought to be all the encouragement they need.'

I

'It might be your homeland, Julius, but I think it's a shithole.' The heavily built young centurion pulled his thick woollen cloak tighter about him, grimacing at the cold mist surrounding them on all sides. The fog, which muffled his voice and reduced visibility to barely fifty paces, gave the impression that the small party was being enveloped by thick grey walls. 'The weather's no better than in Britannia, the food's worse than in Britannia, and the beer's just piss.'

One of the other two officers marching alongside him flicked water out of his heavy black beard and snorted, wincing as the movement allowed a trickle of water to run down his back.

'The last time I saw this place, Dubnus, was when I was fifteen. My memories of Tungrorum are so bloody dim that I doubt I'll even recognise it when we get there. If we ever find it in this bloody murk.'

One of the three barbarians walking behind them snorted his own particular disgust.

'Some fool told me that we were headed for Germania. All the time I was puking my guts up crossing the sea, and then when we were shivering in those freezing, louse-infested barracks through the winter, I consoled myself that I would soon be close to the land of my people, the land of the Quadi. A land of forests and rivers, teeming with game and watched over by my father's gods. Instead of which –' he lifted his hands to encompass the gently rolling land to either side of the road's arrow-straight course – 'I find myself trudging across interminable farmland populated only by gangs of listless slaves and wreathed in vapour. This is *not* Germania; this bloody province is just one big field.'

The centurion marching on Dubnus's left turned round to face the barbarian and walked backwards, an amused smile on his angular, hawkish face.

'As it happens, Arminius, you've hit the nail squarely on the head. This part of Germania Inferior is just like Gallia Belgica to the south; it's almost entirely turned over to farming for corn. Good soil, or so my old tutor told me. If it wasn't for this province, and the farmland to the south, there'd be no legions based on the River Rhenus to keep the German tribes in check, because there'd be no corn to feed them with.'

The barbarian shook his head in disbelief.

'Only *you*, Marcus Valerius Aquila, only you could take a complaint and turn it into a lesson on the workings of the empire.'

Julius kept marching, but his tone when he spoke was peremptory.

'Just stick to the name he's using now, Arminius, that or call him "Two Knives" like the soldiers do. Let his past sleep where it lies, because if you prod it hard enough it'll only wake up in a bad temper and give us all more grief. Our brother in arms is Marcus Tribulus Corvus, and we'll use that name whether we might be overheard or not. You know as well as I do what the penalty would be, were we found to be harbouring an imperial fugitive, in Britannia, in Germany or in any other part of the empire you'd like to mention.'

Another of the barbarian trio chuckled darkly, his one good eye winking at the subject of their discussion. With the wound that had ruined the other eye now healed he had dispensed with any attempt to hide the fresh, angry pink scar that cut the heavy brow into two separate parts. The eye socket itself was empty, a permanent reminder of a blood-fuelled night of revenge on his tribe's oppressors.

'Aye, especially a fugitive with such aristocratic blood.'

'And so says the only member of royalty actually present, eh, *Prince* Martos?'

The one-eyed man shook his head briskly at Dubnus's jibe.

'I forfeited my tribal rank when I turned away from the Dinpaladyr and marched south with you, just as you did when you turned away from your people to become part of the *civilised* world. Besides, my tribe has no need of my presence, not with a Roman garrison posted to watch the Fortress of Spears until such time as my nephew is ready to rule without their assistance. I'm better employed helping you keep this one –' he tipped his head at Marcus – 'out of the public eye.' Clenching one big fist and watching with a grin as the heavy muscle of his arm rippled in response, he shot the equally muscular Roman a lopsided smile. 'As if anyone's going to spare him a second glance when a one-eyed warrior built like one of your legion bathhouses is anywhere nearby.'

The third barbarian, taller than the other two by a full head, and with a heavy iron-beaked war hammer resting across one slab-like shoulder, gave a snigger of amusement so quiet that it might have passed unnoticed. The prince turned his head to focus his one good eye on the bigger man, a fierce scowl creasing his face as he snapped out a question in the language their two tribes shared.

'What's your problem, Lugos?'

Martos had yet to fully accept the giant as a member of the cohort's unofficial scout century, formed by the remnant of his Votadini warriors after their defeat by the Romans the previous year. Their capture had been a consequence of betrayal by the hulking tribesman's king, the leader of the Selgovae tribe, and Martos's view of the big man remained unmistakably jaundiced, but Lugos was clever enough to bide his time with the Votadini leader.

'There is no problem, Prince Martos. I simply listen, and in doing so I learn.'

Martos gave him a hard stare, but the giant's innocent look dampened his temper before it had the chance to boil over. Waiting until the prince had given up his fierce scrutiny, Lugos shot Marcus a swift wink. The Roman raised an eyebrow in return and turned back to face the direction of their march, catching a conspiratorial glance from Dubnus as his friend resumed his attempts to goad Julius.

'How far to the city now, Julius, do you think?'

The older man gave him a sideways look of disbelief.

'Five minutes less than the last time you asked, I'd say. Why, do you need to empty your bladder, or is that spear wound playing you up again? You should have gone before we . . .' He stopped, and put a hand on the hilt of his sword, pointing at the ground dimly visible to the right of the road's path. 'Do you see that?'

Out in the mist, at the point where distance made the movement nearly impossible to discern, something had risen from the mud surrounding them. As they watched, another figure rose from the ground close to the first, a human figure daubed liberally with mud. Dubnus shook his head, staring hard at the apparitions, then pointed into the fog on the other side of the road.

'More of them!'

While the Romans stood and stared, a dozen and more of the unidentifiable figures rose to their feet around them, seeming to climb, wraithlike, straight out of the ground into the mist's murk. Lugos broke the spell, stepping forward with his hammer gripped in two white-knuckled hands, barking out a single eager, angry word.

'*Bandits!*'

The Romans looked at each other and drew their swords, Marcus pulling a long cavalry sword from the scabbard on his right hip to join the shorter gladius already held in his right hand. The gladius's gold and silver eagle-head pommel gleamed dimly in the fog's pale light. Dubnus pulled a throwing axe from his belt, tossing the weapon into the air and catching it by the handle's base, ready to let it fly. They watched in silence as the figures moved closer, gradually taking on solid shapes as they closed their circle around the bemused group. Looking about him, Marcus saw that they were indeed men; their garments were worn and filthy, but each of them carried a sword or spear whose blades appeared well cared for.

'Close enough, unless you want to find out what the point of my sword feels like as I slide it between your ribs!'

Their gradual advance stopped at Julius's challenge, a single man stepping forward from their encircling line. What Marcus had taken for features set in stony resolution resolved themselves into the dull iron lines of a cavalry helmet, and when the man spoke his voice was distorted by the close-fitting face mask.

'We are three times your strength. Lay down your arms and surrender your coin, and nobody gets hurt. Try to fight us and we'll slaughter you like cattle.'

Julius stepped forward, sliding his gladius back into its scabbard and reaching into a pouch on his belt.

'You're right; there is a better way of settling this.'

Marcus and Dubnus exchanged knowing glances, and behind them Lugos growled softly, barely restraining himself from wading into the bandits single-handed. The centurion raised his hands, a flash of silver glinting in the swirling mist, and the masked bandit relaxed slightly, holding up an open hand to keep back his fellow robbers.

Julius's face hardened into a predatory smile as he moved closer. 'No, really, there's no need for any of *us* to get hurt. You, on the other hand, should run. *Now.*' He lifted a hand to his face, putting a shining whistle to his lips while the bandit leader scowled and raised his sword to fight. 'No? I warned you . . .'

After blowing a single piercing note he dropped the whistle and ripped his dagger from its sheath, stepping in to attack the masked bandit with the weapon held low. His assailant swung his sword in a clumsy diagonal cut, aiming for the junction of the Roman's head and neck, but Julius spun to his right and ducked under the blow, pushing his weight off his right foot and springing onto the bandit, bearing him to the ground and breaking his grip on the sword's hilt. He rammed the dagger's foot-long blade up into the bandit's exposed left armpit and then, as the other man screamed with the agony of his wound, snapped his head down to deliver a crunching butt with his helmet's brow guard, smashing a deep dent into the cavalry helmet's iron face mask. Pushing himself off the bandit's inert body he jumped back to his feet and swept his gladius from its scabbard again, turning to the nearest of the bandits with a broad smile.

Unable to contain himself any longer Lugos had already stepped off the road to confront two of the robbers, raising the hammer as if to bring it down on the nearest man's head, but then changing the attack at the last minute and sweeping the weapon's heavy iron beak into their legs. One of the pair dropped to the ground in crippled agony, forcing the other to jump back sharply. Pushed off balance by the sudden move the robber tripped and fell head-long backwards, his arms splayed out to either side. The huge barbarian hoisted the hammer over his head, swinging its vicious hooked blade down in a whistling arc to bury it deep in the fallen man's chest with a sickening crunch of splintering bones. As Martos and Arminius advanced to either side of him, the German swiftly finishing off the bandit felled by his first swing, the giant Briton put a foot on the dying man's stomach and tore the hammer's blade loose in a scatter of rib fragments, his eyes searching the mist for his next victim.

Marcus and Dubnus moved quickly to join Julius as he advanced into the throng of bandits, Dubnus hurling his axe in a spinning arc that ended with a wet, crunching thump of iron into flesh and bone before dodging a spear thrust from another man. He gripped the weapon's extended shaft to drag his assailant off balance, then, drawing his gladius, he thrust the blade deep into the spearman's thigh. Wrenching the weapon loose in a spray of blood he tore the spear from his victim's faltering grip, spun it a half turn over his head to present the blade and then stamped forward, slinging the spear to transfix another of the bandits edging towards them. Marcus took on a pair of swordsmen, feinting towards the first to back him up before spinning to attack the other head on. He steered the robber's sword aside with the gladius, then hacked the longer spatha in his other hand deep into the defenceless bandit's side. His opponent convulsed in agony as the cold iron sliced into his body, slumping to the ground as the Roman swung back to face the other man, the bloody spatha pointing at the robber's chest as he backed slowly away. The bandits were looking at each other in silent amazement now, not yet willing to run from their intended prey but afraid to take the fight to them, given that so many of their own number were either dead or wounded.

For a moment silence ruled the open field, aside from a distant, rhythmic sound so faint as to be at the limit of audibility but rapidly gaining in volume, a metallic ripple that pulsed through the fog like the gnashing of a million tiny iron teeth. Julius smiled even wider, spreading his hands and turning on the spot to encompass them all as he spoke.

'You hear that? That, my friends, is the sound of your death rushing towards you! I'd say you've twenty heartbeats left, thirty at best, before a huge armoured monster comes out of this fog and tears you all to pieces. Either run now or make your peace with your gods.'

He paused, theatrically putting a cupped hand to his ear. The sound was swelling now, hardening, its distinct rhythm starting to disintegrate into one long clattering rattle. Marcus stared at the filthy, exhausted bandits around him, seeing every man's face reflect the same urge to run that they were all feeling. With a visible start one of the robbers realised what was happening; he turned to flee just as the first soldiers came out of the mist at the forced-march pace, their heads back to suck in the damp air. Marcus recognised the centurion running alongside the four-man-wide column as Clodius, at the exact moment that his colleague raised his drawn sword and bellowed an order at his men.

'Third Century, take them down!'

The bandits scattered in all directions, and the centurions watched in bemusement as the column's ordered ranks broke into organised chaos in the space of an instant, individual soldiers choosing their victims and going after them like hunting dogs. Each of the desperate men suddenly found himself pursued by half a dozen soldiers eager for blood, and the mist filled with the shouts and screams of hunter and hunted. One zealous soldier ran at the three barbarian scouts with his spear raised, mistaking them for robbers in the heat of battle. A moment later he was staggering backwards, clutching his face, as Arminius, his face dark with anger, stepped forward to stop him dead with a swift jab of his massive fist. The unfortunate Tungrian fell onto his backside with blood streaming down his face.

'You've broken by dose!'

The German shook his head contemptuously, gesturing back at his companions.

'And whose fault is that? Just count yourself fortunate it was me and neither of these two that put you right. The prince would have gutted you like a fish, and the big lad would have taken off your head with the same punch. Now go and bleed somewhere else.'

Clodius walked across to his brother officers with a raised eyebrow, pulling off both his helmet and its padded linen liner, allowing the cold air to get to his grey-streaked hair. He watched as his men dragged the corpses of their victims back across the muddy fields.

'I should have known you three would find some kind of trouble.'

Dubnus wiped his sword clean on the greasy fabric of a dead man's tunic and sheathed the blade before replying.

'It found us.'

Clodius grunted morosely.

'Nothing new there. How's your wound, young Dubnus? Still giving you problems when you get down on your knees for a . . .' Catching a movement in the corner of his eye he half turned and then snapped out an order. 'Third Century, stand at attention!'

Tribune Scaurus strolled into the knot of centurions with First Spear Sextus Frontinius in close attendance, returning their salutes while his deceptively soft grey eyes took in the scene about them.

'I know we're here to kill bandits, gentlemen, but given that we haven't even reached Tungrorum yet this all seems a little keen, even by your standards.' He looked around him at the litter of scattered corpses and the few groaning survivors of the swift fight. 'And that, I have to say, seems to be that. Normally I'd be of the opinion that since we killed them we'd best burn or bury them, but under the circumstances . . .' He turned to Frontinius with a questioning look. 'What do you say, First Spear?'

The senior centurion limped across to the fallen body of the robbers' leader, pulling the cavalry helmet from the corpse's head to reveal the dead man's smashed face; the blood that had streamed from his broken nose was stark against the pale grey of his skin.

'I'd say he didn't find this helmet at the side of the road. I'd say he's probably killed enough good men that his death will please our gods. And I'd say that we leave him here to rot with the rest of his gang.'

Scaurus pursed his lips and nodded.

'Agreed. Strip them of their weapons and anything else of value, and load the survivors onto the supply carts. I'd imagine the authorities in Tungrorum will be happy enough to receive a few captured bandits for some public punishment.' He half turned away, then swung back to Frontinius with a swift nod. 'And that'll be enough of these gentlemen walking out in front of the cohort for one day. I don't mind losing officers in battle as long as they have the good grace to die expensively, but given we're already short of good centurions I won't risk making our problems any worse by tempting fate like that.' The 1st spear nodded, giving the three officers a significant stare. 'And what happened to him?'

A bandage carrier was fussing over the soldier whose nose had been broken by Arminius. The German stepped forward, nodding to Scaurus.

'He seemed set on putting his spear through me, so I changed his mind for him.'

The tribune raised an eyebrow at his bodyguard.

'You seem to have done rather too good a job of it, from what I can see.' He tapped the hapless medic on the shoulder, eliciting a flustered, bloody-fingered salute from the man. 'Either you get that back in place now or you can deal with it at the end of the day. We've no time to be standing round in the mist while you work it out.'

The bandage carrier spread his wet and bloodied hands in apology.

'Sorry, Tribune, I just can't get a grip on the bone.'

Arminius pushed him aside without ceremony, putting a hand on the terrified soldier's shoulder to prevent him from rising.

'Stay put, you. This won't take a minute.' He grasped the soldier's nose, rubbing it briskly between finger and thumb to gauge the break's location. While the soldier was still squawking in pain at this rough treatment, the German took a handful of hair to hold his head in place and quickly manipulated the bone back into place. With a shrill scream of agony the soldier passed out, his weight suspended from the German's grip on his scalp. Shaking his head, Arminius pushed him into the bandage carrier's arms. 'It's done. He'll have a pair of black eyes for a week or so. It might teach him to pick his targets with a little more care.'

First Spear Frontinius nodded to his tribune, a wry smile touching his lips.

'It seems that your man has a way with mending broken bones, Tribune. Perhaps Centurion Corvus's wife might do well to recruit him for her clinic?'

Scaurus shook his head, watching the German walk away.

'I think not. He's more than a little lacking in the delicate approach required of a medical man. He's been that way ever since I saved him from the sword back in the war with the Quadi, and I can't see him changing now.' He turned to look at the road ahead, still wreathed in drifting curtains of mist. 'Well, then, shall we get these cohorts back on the road? I'd estimate there's still another ten miles to the city, and there'll be no respite from this cursed drizzle until we get there.'

As the leading centuries formed back into their marching column Marcus noted that Julius was scanning the ground around the corpse of the bandit group's leader.

'Lost something?'

His friend nodded, keeping his eyes on the ground.

'My whistle. It was a nice one too.'

Glancing about him, Marcus caught Dubnus's eye, and saw that he was pointing ostentatiously at his own belt pouch and grinning smugly. Giving up the search, Julius turned back to his colleagues to find Dubnus apparently searching the ground at his feet with exaggerated interest.

'I could do with a nice whistle; mine sounds like a castrated cat.'

The older man shook his head in disgust as the 3rd Century, set to lead the long two-cohort-strong column of march, started to move again at Clodius's bellow of command.

'Very funny, Dubnus. I suppose that's the price I have to pay for being first into the fight. As per *fucking* usual.'

He stamped away to join his own 5th Century, leaving the two friends to wait for their men to march past.

'How long will you hold onto it?'

Dubnus shrugged at Marcus's question.

'Until he's bought a new one? I'll sneak it back into his pouch once he's laid out some coin for a replacement.' He frowned at his friend's sudden solemnity. '*What?* It's not like I've lifted his purse!'

Marcus shook his head.

'No, it's me. I was just thinking how funny Rufius was going to find this.'

Dubnus put a spade-like hand on his friend's mailed shoulder.

'I know. I miss the old bastard almost as much as you do, but life, as Morban keeps telling anyone that will listen, is for those left around to profit from it. And here come your boys now. Go and cheer up Qadir with the story of our colleague's whistle. You know he always turns grumpy when it's too wet for his lads to play with their bows.'

After another four hours of marching, all of it through an afternoon made into premature twilight by the swirling mist, even Marcus was ready for the day's journey to end. Marching alongside his chosen man, Qadir, at his century's rear, he noted that the usually imperturbable Hamian's demeanour became grimmer as the day progressed.

'I'm going up to the front to make sure Morban's not bullying the trumpeter too badly.'

The Hamian grunted in reply, his eyes locked on the gloomy landscape fitfully revealed by the mist's drifting grey curtains.

Marching up to the century's head, the Roman found his standard bearer, a twenty-five-year veteran famed for both his acerbic wit and his prodigious appetites for gambling, drinking and whoring, in reflective mood on the subject of their colleague's unhappiness.

'I tried to cheer him up at the lunch stop with a few jokes, but he wasn't having any of it. Perhaps he's starting to realise what him and his mates tossed away when they decided not to stay with the Hamian cohort back on the Wall. Carting around half their weight in iron can't be much fun when they're more used to prancing round the forest wearing next to nothing and shooting the occasional animal for the pot.' Oblivious to his centurion's icy stare, he ploughed on. 'And now here he is, freezing cold, water dripping from the end of his nose and his bow hidden away for days on end for fear of the glue rotting. No wonder the poor bastard's feeling miserable. Not like us, we're used to this.' Marcus stared out into the mist, shaking his head slightly at the realisation that Morban's view of what might be affecting Qadir's mood could just as easily be applied to his own situation. 'Anyway, we'll be tucked up in this new place's barracks soon enough, with a few logs in the stove and all this nastiness behind us. And if dear old Qadir can't take a joke then perhaps he shouldn't have—'

The standard bearer's sentiment was interrupted by a shout from further up the column, which promptly came to a halt in a succession of shouted commands from each centurion down the cohort's column. Hearing the century in front of his own being told to halt Marcus shouted the same command to his men, then barked a terse order to Qadir to watch the ranks and walked forward to see what was happening. He passed the back of the leading century and the reason for the unscheduled halt became clear: a twenty-foot-high stone wall loomed out of the mist. A group of bemused centurions were gathered around a pair of massive wooden gates set in an imposing stone archway that barred the cohorts' route into the city. The first spear was craning his neck to call up to a pair of soldiers who in turn were peering down into the mist with looks of deep suspicion.

'Just open the bloody gates and we'll worry about the paperwork later. I've got two full cohorts of soldiers slowly freezing their balls off out here, and I want them in barracks before dark.'

Julius, who was standing behind the senior centurion with a grim look on his dark, bearded face, shook his head at Marcus.

'This isn't going to end well. Those are legion troops if I'm not mistaken, and whenever the road menders get involved there's usually grief.'

Another soldier appeared on the walls, this one wearing the feathered and crested helmet of a legion chosen man. He spoke to the guards for a moment, then leaned out and called down to the auxiliaries gathered below.

'I'm sorry, Centurion. I'm under strict orders not to open the gates without permission from my own officer. I've sent one of my men to find him, but until he gets here there's no way I can let you in.'

He spread his hands to convey his helplessness with the situation, and then disappeared from sight to leave the first spear fuming with anger.

'Was that segmented armour I saw before that man went to hide from the wrath of an infuriated first spear?'

The centurions turned to find Tribune Scaurus standing behind them with a questioning look on his face. Frontinius nodded grimly, his face creased with anger.

'Yes, Tribune. It would appear that the regulars have got here before us.'

Scaurus looked out into the swirling mist for a moment.

'And I suppose that if we leave this to take its apparent course, the men could be standing around here for quite a while.'

Frontinius nodded again, the angry lines of his expression softening as he turned a quizzical gaze on his superior.

The tribune nodded at him, cleared his throat, and shouted up at the apparently deserted wall.

'*Chosen Man!* Show yourself!' After a long silence the chosen man looked over the wall again, his face falling when he saw the tribune staring up at him. Scaurus lifted his cloak, showing the other man his finely wrought bronze plate armour, sculpted to resemble a muscled torso. 'Have a good look, Chosen Man! You'll observe that I'm not a centurion but the commander of these cohorts, and not without influence, or an understanding of how things work. Which legion might this be that I'm talking with, I wonder? Either the "grunts" or the "scribblers", I'd guess. Which is it, Chosen Man?'

The chosen man sprang to attention.

'First Minervia Faithful and Loyal, Tribune!'

Scaurus smiled, muttering quietly to himself.

'*Got you.*' He looked up at the chosen man for a long moment before speaking again. 'The "grunts", then. First Minervia, Faithful and Loyal. A proud name for a proud legion. Tell me, Chosen Man, is that sour-faced old bastard Gladio still First Spear of the Third Cohort?'

The chosen man squinted down at him, clearly wondering just how much influence this unknown tribune might have with his own officers. His answer was carefully balanced to avoid giving any potential offence.

'Yes, sir. He's still as cheerful as he ever was.'

Calculating that the moment to attack had arrived, Scaurus raised his voice to an enraged bellow.

'Well, if I'm not through those fucking gates before I've counted to thirty, you'll soon find out that I'm a good deal less sunny of character than he is, and a good deal more vindictive! Do you understand me?' The chosen man nodded unhappily. 'Good. Then let's get on with it, shall we? Or do I actually have to embarrass us both by starting to count?'

After a few seconds of silence the chosen man turned and

disappeared, and a moment later the gate's man-sized wicket gate yawned open. Shooting a glance at his first spear, Scaurus stepped forward.

'I'll go and get this sorted out before the cohorts freeze to death.'

Frontinius pointed to the group of centurions, gesturing them forward with a jerk of his thumb.

'Centurions Julius, Dubnus and Corvus, you can provide the tribune with an escort. There's no telling what sort of person's running around behind those walls, given that there's a legion involved.'

The men guarding the gate made to close the man-sized door as Scaurus stepped through it, but a firm shove from Julius held it open, while his fierce glare dissuaded them from any thought of objecting to the presence of the tribune's escort. The hulking Tungrian stared about him with a curled lip before addressing the chosen man.

'If you toy soldiers are supposed to be keeping the city safe you're not doing much of a job of it. We've got several wounded men on wagons out there, all that's left of a score or so of bandits who tried to ambush us on the road. You might want to bring them in for medical attention before they die of cold and deny the people of this city the chance to watch them being executed.' Shaking his head he turned away, staring unhappily into the mist that wreathed the ground inside the city's wall; it was just as impenetrable as it had been outside. 'Now, which way to the headquarters building?'

The chosen man waved his men back to the warmth of their guard house before pointing down the road that continued from the gate into the city's murky interior.

'That way, Centurion. But don't be looking for a headquarters. This is a civilian settlement, not a fort. Go down there for a quarter mile or so and you'll come to a crossroads. The big building on the right is the forum, and, at a guess, you'll find the officers there, in the basilica.'

The three centurions formed a protective cordon around

Scaurus as the party walked forward. Dubnus put a hand on the hilt of his sword, muttering nervously as he stared out into the fog.

'Four hundred paces to the middle of the city? That would make this place bigger than the Sixth Legion's fortress at Yew Grove. It's . . .'

'Enormous?' A gentle smile was playing on Scaurus's face as he looked with interest at the buildings looming out of the fog on either side of the road. 'This is a provincial centre, Centurion. There are perhaps eight or ten thousand people inside these walls, or at least there would have been before the plague came. There are at least a hundred times as many in Rome, and yet Rome's walls are only three times as long. Which makes you wonder what they're doing with all the space.'

In the murk ahead of them a pair of blazing torches indicated the entrance to the forum, with a pair of sentries standing guard in front of the high archway. Before the tribune had any chance to explain their presence to the surprised soldiers a legion centurion walked out of the courtyard beyond them, stopping with a start of surprise when he saw the newcomers. Staring with narrowed eyes at the three centurions' unfamiliar armour and crested helmets, he was further taken aback when he realised who it was they were escorting. Scaurus allowed the silence to play out for a few seconds, watching the calculation in the legion officer's face before speaking in an acerbic tone designed to communicate his status.

'Yes, Centurion, this is a senior officer's uniform, and yes, Centurion, you're supposed to have your hand in the air some time about now.'

The other man saluted quickly, his face reddening with embarrassment, while the sentries worked hard but not entirely successfully at keeping the smirks off their faces.

'I'm sorry, Prefect, it's just that we weren't expecting to receive any reinforcement.'

Marcus looked at Julius, wondering if his colleague was going to correct the legion man's mistaken identification, but his questioning gaze was answered only by a slight shake of the big man's head. Scaurus nodded to the centurion, looking over his shoulder at the dimly visible administrative building on the other side of the forum's open courtyard.

'That's perfectly understandable, Centurion, because we're not reinforcements. If you'll show me to your tribune . . .?'

The centurion led them across the forum's wide, paved expanse, around which the city's merchants would gather to tout their wares in better weather, and into the warmth of the basilica. Realising that he was on the back foot, he made a belated effort to regain some sense of the dominance to be expected in the relationship between a legion and its supporting auxiliary cohorts.

'And now, gentlemen, if I might ask you to leave your weapons here before you go through for your interview with the tribune—'

Scaurus cut him off in a flat tone, looking about the entrance hall at the rich wall hangings and an elaborate mosaic of Mercury stretched out across the floor.

'No, Centurion, you might not. I've neither the time nor the patience at the moment.'

He walked past the astonished officer and through the hall, his hobnailed boots rapping harshly against the mosaic's delicate surface, and after a second's hesitation his centurions followed in a clatter of iron. Dubnus winked at the disgruntled legion centurion, and muttered from the side of his mouth.

'Just be grateful you're not left holding his cloak like a uniformed doorman.'

Pushing open the doors at the entrance hall's far end, the Tungrians walked into a high-ceilinged chamber dominated by a massive table, around which were sitting several men in the crisp white tunics of legion officers and two civilians dressed in togas. They looked round curiously at the unexpected entry, and the youngest of them got to his feet with a look of annoyance on his face, tapping the senatorial stripe adorning his tunic. The Tungrian centurions snapped to attention and saluted

crisply, while Scaurus fiddled with his cloak pin, tossing the
thick woollen garment onto a chair and revealing his finely
wrought breastplate. The young tribune flicked his eyes across
the centurions' mail armour, and his mouth tightened fractionally in response to his prompt assessment of the newcomers.

'You're auxiliaries, I presume?' he said. Scaurus nodded tersely,
looking back at the man with a level gaze. 'Which would make
you a prefect? And I have a tendency to insist on the finer points
of military etiquette, *Prefect*. Such as the expectation that even
officers should salute their seniors.'

The young tribune's voice was reasonable enough, but he spoke
in a manner which indicated he had grown accustomed to being
listened to more than he listened. To Marcus's trained eye he
appeared the model of a legion senior officer, a man in his mid-
twenties with fashionably long hair, his beard grown thick and
bushy in emulation of the imperial fashion but nevertheless glossy
and neatly trimmed. His eyes, hard with their challenge to the
unknown officer standing before him, were set close above a clas-
sically Roman nose, down which he was looking with an expression of sorely tried patience. Scaurus looked at him with a level
gaze for a moment, reaching into his satchel and pulling out a
scroll. When he spoke his voice was dry and without any hint of
recognition of the other man's professed superiority in rank.

'I heartily agree, *colleague*. I was saying just the same thing to
a young legion tribune of senatorial rank only a few weeks ago,
when he happened to come under my command, and before he
died nobly in battle beside me.' Watching the legion officers,
Marcus noted their various widened eyes and intakes of breath,
the signs of men hearing the unexpected. Scaurus shook his head
slightly, holding the scroll loosely in one hand. 'You don't believe
in getting your facts straight before you open your mouth though,
do you, colleague?' The other man turned pale, but as he opened
his mouth to speak again Scaurus walked around the table and
went face to face with him, his grey eyes suddenly stone hard,
and his voice a low murmur that forced the other man to listen
intently to make out the words.

'This is that interesting, perhaps life-defining, moment, Tribune, that we all encounter when we least expect it, that moment of truth when the pit opens up before us, and we have only to step forward to be in it up to our neck. Do you have any questions you might want to ask me before we get down to the good old-fashioned contest to see which of us has the bigger cock? Any doubts as to which of us might end up raising his hand in respect at the end of that conversation?'

The legion tribune shook his head, clearly holding onto his rage by a fine thread.

'I am Lucius Domitius Belletor, Military Tribune commanding the Seventh Cohort of Imperial Legion First Minervia, on detached duty to safeguard the city of Tungrorum. I have orders from my legion's legatus to command the services of any and all suitable forces that come within my reach. Which means you, and your men, *Prefect*.'

He raised an eyebrow at Scaurus, who, holding his gaze, replied in a louder tone than before, ensuring that all of the men around the table could hear him.

'Very well. I am Military Tribune Gaius Rutilius Scaurus, commanding the First and Second Tungrian Cohorts and on detached duty from the army of Britannia to seek and eliminate bandits, deserters and rebels from the province of Germania Inferior. I have orders from the governor of Britannia not to allow my force to fall under the command of any other officer unless I deem this to be in the interests of pursuing my given orders. Perhaps he foresaw just such an eventuality as this one.' Belletor opened his mouth to speak, but Scaurus held up a hand. 'I can see I haven't yet convinced you, and I see nothing to be gained from our discussing this matter in public. Perhaps we ought to ask our colleagues and these other gentlemen to leave us alone for a few minutes?'

Belletor nodded slowly and turned back to the legion centurions, who were, to a man, gaping in silent amazement at the drama playing out before their eyes.

'Leave us.'

The officers rose and headed for the door through which the Tungrians had entered, followed after an embarrassing pause by the two civilians. Julius, last to leave the room, closed the heavy oak doors and, spotting a thick curtain clearly designed to improve the privacy of the room, drew it across them.

'I'm guessing you're the senior man here?'

He turned to face the speaker, a grizzled man with broad shoulders and big hands, his face riven by a heavy scar that ran from his right eyebrow down across his upper cheek, bisecting his lips and reaching down to the point of his chin. Julius braced himself for the expected torrent of abuse, and both Dubnus and Marcus shifted their stances fractionally, subconsciously positioning themselves to fight. The speaker raised his eyebrows and lifted his hands to forestall any argument although he didn't, Marcus noted, step back from the challenge.

'No, there's no need for you to feel threatened. We're all on the same side here. I'm Sergius, First Spear of the Seventh Cohort.' He put out a hand, and Julius shook it without hesitation. 'Whatever's going on in there probably has to be said between the two of them and then forgotten, so it's best we're out of earshot, right?'

Julius nodded, finding himself starting to warm to the other man despite the unfulfilled expectation of hostility.

'I'm Julius, Centurion, First Tungrian Auxiliary Cohort, and these two are Dubnus and Corvus. Our first spear's waiting at the west gate with the rest of the men. Any chance we could get them inside before it gets dark?'

Without the restrictions of an audience of their subordinates, Belletor promptly went on the offensive, putting his finger in Scaurus's face and spitting a stream of fury at him.

'How fucking *dare* you speak to me that way in front of my officers?'

The older man smiled into his anger, shaking his head.

'You brought it on yourself, *colleague*. A simple quiet question or two would have shown you the real position of status between us, rather than what you'd like it to be. But let's ignore your inability to ask questions before throwing your weight around.'

'My legatus will hear about this soon enough! I'll have you—'

Scaurus stepped forward, his face white with anger, putting his face inches away from the other man's and making him take an involuntary step backwards.

'That was the wrong choice of words, Tribune! Any sorting out between us is going to be done here, *between* us. Put any idea of using your legatus to deal with me out of your mind, because I'm here and he *isn't*! I've dealt with *your* type of officer before, and I've learned that allowing your type of *officer* to delude yourselves only brings more grief than shattering your illusions nice and early. The days when even the least capable man with senatorial rank could tell veteran field commanders with equestrian rank what to do are dying away, Domitius Belletor. And as far as I'm concerned, in this particular small corner of the empire they may as well never have existed.'

He picked up the scroll from the table in front of him.

'First, Tribune, my orders, which were handed to me by my provincial governor, *insist* that I operate independently of any other command unless I choose to do otherwise. Secondly, Tribune, the facts are that you've less than half my strength in spears and you've been given the Seventh, one of the tradition-ally weaker cohorts in any legion. Your command is highly likely to be packed with raw recruits and boys barely out of the first year's training. And thirdly, *Tribune*, my perceptions of your achievements, if I'm being blunt, are that you've done little more since you got here than line the walls of this city with your troops. My officers were assaulted by a score of bandits little more than ten miles from these walls, and none of them showed any of the fear for our uniforms that I would have expected if your men were patrolling with anything like the necessary vigour. My two cohorts are hardened from recent battle in the barbarian uprising across the water in Britannia, and I have no intention of wasting their abilities by allowing them to sit around and go soft under your command.'

Belletor shook his head decisively, still refusing to concede the point, his lip curling in amazed contempt.

'I am a *legion* tribune! That automatically gives me the right to command you, a mere auxiliary! Anything else is simply—'

To his obvious fury, Scaurus had turned his back and walked away from him, his boots rattling against the floor's flagstones as he examined the murals decorating the walls. He replied without turning to face the other man, his voice rich with irony.

'A *legion* tribune? I've stood in your boots as a *legion* tribune, but that was years ago, in the wars against the Quadi. I know how much power a broad-stripe tribune has, Domitius Belletor, hemmed in between the legion's legatus and the more experienced narrow-stripe tribunes and their senior centurions, all of whom expect the right to tell you what to do. I've been fighting for the empire for the last ten years in one province or another, and I've earned my *second* tribunate the hard way, with this.' He tapped the hilt of his sword. 'So, far from being your subordinate, Tribune, I consider myself at worst your equal, and, in terms of my command's strength and abilities, my own training, and my combat experience, clearly your superior. You're free to play the big man with the local officials to your heart's content, and you're probably wise to keep your men behind these nice thick walls and out of harm's way, but if you lift one finger to impede me as I go about ridding this province of the men preying upon it you will find me a very dangerous enemy indeed. You choose.'

Sergius nodded to Julius's request, and before resuming the conversation he sent one of his colleagues to deal with the matter of getting the Tungrian cohorts inside the city's walls. The two civilians were keeping themselves to themselves in one corner of the entrance hall. The taller of the two, well built and with a haughty look about him, was talking intently with his colleague, a leaner man with a look of sharp intelligence.

'Our boy's got a bit of a temper, I'm afraid.'

Sergius's knowing smile betrayed his feelings on the subject, and Julius found himself warming to the legion officer.

'Ours too, but we hardly ever see it.'

Sergius chuckled quietly, his voice low to avoid it being carried in the lobby's quiet to the men at the door.

'Which makes you pay attention when he displays it, eh? Whereas we're all worn down by Tribune Belletor's incessant rages, to the point where he's become something of an amusement to the cohort.'

Julius frowned.

'So what's he doing here?'

'Can't you guess? Tribune Belletor's daddy is very well connected, and very rich. That's how his lad got a legion tribunate, and that's why our legatus has to tolerate him, if he knows what's good for him. The orders to send a cohort down here provided the big man with the perfect excuse to get a bit of peace and quiet.'

Julius's face took on a pained expression.

'But the Seventh Cohort? Surely this isn't a job for raw troops?'

'I couldn't agree more, but you wouldn't find the legatus signing up to that point of view. First Minervia's still under strength, what with all the men that died of the plague and the lack of young lads to replace them, given the number of civilians that died at the same time. We've already had to send three cohorts off to reinforce the army in Britannia after some idiot managed to lose the best part of a legion . . .' The look on Julius's face stopped him in mid-flow. 'What?'

'We were there, First Spear. And it wasn't pretty.'

Sergius shrugged.

'It never is. I was a green centurion when the last war with the Chauci started, and it took a lot less than a year for me to go from being desperate to get into the fight to being happy if I never saw another dead barbarian, as long as I didn't have to watch any more of my men die. Anyway, three cohorts to Britannia, another two sent to the coast to help the "scribblers" keep our boot on the Chauci's throat . . .'

'Scribblers?'

'The Thirtieth Legion, Ulpia Victorious. Our sister legion in this province. When the call goes out for men to help with manual work it usually gets directed our way, whereas they seem to get all the reading and writing work. If the governor's office needs twenty clerks to sit around scratching their arses they get the job, and if there's a forest that needs cutting down they call for us. They call us "grunts", and we call them "scribblers", and it's been that way for as long as I've served. So, we're five cohorts down before we consider upkeep on the fortress, men on leave and the usual long list of malingerers, which means that a cohort was all our legatus could spare. Even with that small a loss of manpower the legion will be deep in the shit if the hairy boys that live on the other side of the Rhenus decide to come across in any numbers. So he sent us, as fine a collection of half-trained soldiery as ever hid behind a shield, and he was probably happy to see the back of us. And Tribune Belletor.'

Julius conceded the point.

'Understandable. But surely five hundred of you ought to be able to scare the bandits back into their holes?'

Sergius glanced at his brother officers, a wry smile lighting up his face.

'And that's exactly what we thought when we got here six weeks ago. Send a couple of centuries out to garrison the roads and they'll soon enough wind their necks in, but . . .'

The doors to the chamber opened and Scaurus pushed his way through the curtain.

'Right, gentlemen, let's go and get our soldiers bedded down for the night.' Pausing to fasten his cloak about him before stepping back into the cold air, he spoke to the civilians in passing. 'My apologies, gentlemen, for rushing off so quickly, but it seems the available barracks are all full of the legion's men, and so I must find a spot inside your walls to pitch my cohorts' tents. I'll be back here early tomorrow morning though, and then we can discuss how to start dealing with the thieves that have made life so awkward for you these past few months. That and what I'll need from you to feed and shelter fourteen hundred fighting men.'

*

'How long can we keep the men in these conditions? In this weather?' First Spear Frontinius pulled a thoughtful face. 'Days. A week at best. The tents have taken a bit of a beating already, and with this much moisture in the air they'll start falling to pieces sooner rather than later. We need to get the men into proper barracks, stone built for preference, but wood will do if there's nothing better. Perhaps the legion will help us? After all, aren't First Minervia supposed to be good at that sort of thing? Their tribune may not be cut from the finest cloth, but the officers sound experienced enough, from what Julius told me earlier.'

Scaurus took a sip of his wine before answering his first spear's musing. He made a point of consulting the older man most nights, having found him a source of sound advice in the months since taking command of the Tungrians. His thin face was set in contemplative lines.

'Perhaps they will help us, but I won't be pinning my hopes on it. As for the officers, this Tribune Belletor is an idiot, pure and simple, the sort of man that gives the aristocracy a bad name. His centurions seem a decent enough lot, but I don't see much fire in their guts. They've seen battle, but not any time recently. I don't know about you, but I've found that combat experience has a tendency to make or break the man. It can make him stronger, and bring his best points to the fore, or it can just as easily blunt his edge. The First Minervia hasn't seen a decent fight in ten years now, and that's a long time for a man to brood on the things he's seen and done. I think I'd be a bit happier if Tribune Belletor was commanding a few centurions with less friendliness but more recent scars, if you know what I mean. Anyway, it is what it is, so we'd better make the best of it. At least the governor managed to send us to a place where the name *Aquila* isn't on every man's lips. With a little luck it'll have thrown any more imperial agents off the scent for the time being, and we can forget about that particular risk.'

The first spear raised his cup.

'I'll drink to that. As, I'd imagine, would Centurion Corvus.'

Scaurus drank, and then sat back in his chair, stretching wearily in the light of a pair of oil lamps.

'Speaking of Corvus, did the doctor manage to keep alive those bandits we captured?'

'She managed to keep some of them breathing, four at the last count. Another two died from their wounds on the way here.'

The tribune's gloomy expression lightened a little.

'Good. That'll give me something to lighten the mood when I upset the municipal authorities in the morning.'

'This is simply outrageous, Tribune Scaurus! You have absolutely no right to commandeer private property in this way! I shall be writing to the governor about this, and when I've finished he won't be in any doubt as to the sort of officer with which the authorities in Britannia have saddled Tungrorum. You are rapacious, unprincipled, and no better than the bandits who are bleeding us dry from outside our walls. At least we can keep *them* out! This city is only just getting off its knees after the plague killed a third of its inhabitants, we're still not taking enough in tax to satisfy the empire's requirements of my office, and now you march up demanding that a civilian population of seven thousand people should feed nearly two thousand soldiers. All of whom seem to eat like gladiators, if I'm to judge from this supply requirement of yours! *No!* I simply cannot agree to these demands!'

Procurator Albanus scowled across the wide table at Scaurus, his bearded face contorted with righteous anger, and he slapped his hand down on the table with a loud crack before turning away in apparent fury. Scaurus glanced across the table at his colleague Belletor, noting that the other man was unsuccessfully attempting to suppress a smirk. Belletor's senior centurion, Sergius, was stone-faced alongside his tribune, while the procurator's clerk was avoiding Scaurus's eye, his head bent over his tablet as he sat in his place at the procurator's left hand. On Albanus's right sat his colleague of the previous evening, a wiry man with a thick mane of dark brown hair, who was wearing a long-sleeved tunic, his face shaved smooth in defiance of the prevailing fashion and his eyes hard stones in a face which seemed to be blessed with a talent for complete immobility of expression. Introduced by Albanus in a perfunctory manner as Petrus, he appeared to be the procurator's deputy, although he had made no contribution to the discussion, apparently happy to sit and watch as the meeting played out.

The last man at the table had slipped into the room and taken a seat between the two sides of the debate just after Albanus had started his tirade of complaint at Scaurus's requirements five minutes earlier, and was yet to be introduced. His cloak, discarded over the back of the chair next to him, was flecked with mud, and his damp and muddied leggings bore further witness to his having recently arrived from elsewhere. As he glanced around the table with a questioning look Scaurus noted that one of his green eyes had a slight squint, an effect he found vaguely disconcerting. Shaking his head slightly the tribune got to his feet, the sound of his hobnailed boots muffled by straw matting laid out over the complex mosaic. He reached out a hand to the newcomer.

'Before I reply to Procurator Albanus I ought to introduce myself. Rutilius Scaurus, Tribune commanding the First and Second Tungrian Cohorts.'

The other man smiled, taking the offered clasp.

'With passions running so high I doubt anyone will think to introduce me, so I'll return the favour myself. I'm the governor's prefect with responsibility for ridding the province of bandits, on detachment from Fortress Bonna. Quintus Caninus.' He shot a meaningful glance at Albanus, who was looking at him disdainfully. 'Procurator Albanus has a low enough opinion of me, and I've only got thirty men to feed and house, so it's no wonder he's got excited at the sight of two more full cohorts inside his walls.'

Albanus snorted his derision.

'Thirty men I can live with, and even the horses we have to feed and stable. A cohort of legionaries at least provides us with security against the thieves that the army seems unable to control. But two more whole cohorts to feed? And now this . . . *gentleman* . . . is demanding that we also build barracks for fourteen hundred men! I find myself—'

Scaurus, having picked up his first spear's vine stick from the table where it rested in front of him, and with a look of apology to Sextus Frontinius, smashed it down onto the flat surface with a terrific bang. He stared hard at the shocked procurator for a long moment of complete silence, ignoring the incensed glances that Belletor was shooting at him.

'Is that it?' The procurator goggled at him in silent amazement, while his colleague Petrus stared up at the angry tribune with a look of interest. 'Good! Thank you, Procurator Albanus, for making your views on the subject so clear. You've made a most lyrical defence of your desire not to provide my men with either shelter from the elements or food in their bellies, despite the fact that they've been sent to protect *you* and your people from the bandits who have been preying upon them for months. And now I think it's time we heard from someone other than a *coin counter*! Prefect Caninus, I'd be grateful to hear your views on the subject of exactly what it is that we're facing.'

Caninus got up from his place at the table, pulling a hanging curtain aside to reveal a detailed map of the area around the city painted onto the wall behind it.

'Very well, Tribune, this is my assessment of the current position with regard to the bandit threat to this part of the province. First, consider the geography of the area. Tungrorum is here, right in the middle of everything that matters for the province.' Frontinius frowned, and Caninus raised an eyebrow. 'You have a question, First Spear?'

Frontinius nodded, pointing at the map with his vine stick.

'Where I come from, ground is only important if it allows the man that holds it to control something. What makes this place so important?'

Albanus raised his eyes to the ceiling, but Caninus continued, warming to his subject.

'A good question. What makes this city in the middle of nowhere of any interest to anyone? There's a simple answer, First Spear. Roads. Look, I'll show you.' He pointed to the map. 'To the west, the road runs across easy ground to Beech Forest, the Nervian capital, and from there down into Gaul. And it runs through miles and miles of fertile soil, fields of grain for as far as the eye can see.' He indicated a spot on the map to the east of the city. 'From Tungrorum that same road runs east for a half-day's march to cross the river at Mosa Ford, and then continues all the way to Claudius Colony on the River Rhenus. From there the road runs along the river's western bank to all of the major towns and fortresses on the river.'

He stopped speaking and looked at Frontinius, who was studying the map with fresh understanding.

'So the grain from Gaul is shipped up the road to Tungrorum, then on to the fortresses on the Rhenus?'

'Exactly, First Spear. The journey's too long for carters in Gaul to go all the way to the Rhenus, so they bring the grain here to the grain store –' Albanus snorted again, but the prefect continued speaking without any sign of having heard him – 'where it can be collected and shipped to the east. Without grain from Gaul the fortresses on the Rhenus would be unsustainable, and without the legions camped on the river the Germans would be across the border and raiding deep into our land in no time.'

'And without Germania Inferior the whole of Gaul would be wide open. Not to mention the road to Rome.'

Caninus smiled broadly.

'You've a sharp mind, First Spear. As you say, without the supply of grain to the fortresses on the Rhenus, the empire's entire north-western flank would be wide open to barbarian attack. Within fifty years they'd have settled Germania Inferior and be knocking on the door of Gaul. Not to mention the fact that not defending the lower stretches of the Rhenus would put the defences along the upper reaches of the river under threat of attack. Tungrorum is absolutely critical to the maintenance of control over the German tribes. And Tungrorum is under a threat whose severity Procurator Albanus seems determined to under-estimate in favour of commercial concerns.'

He looked directly at the procurator, waiting for him to deny the accusation, but the administrator stared intently at the table, clearly determined to ignore the provocation. Scaurus waved a hand at the wall.

'Tell us about the bandit threat, Prefect. I'm curious to know why it hasn't already been stamped out, if the supply route to the frontier is of such critical importance.'

Caninus pointed to the map again, indicating an area to the south and east of the city.

'March to the east for ten miles and cross the River Mosa, and you'll find yourself confronted with a vast forest that rises from the river's edge to form a range of hills. It's impossible ground to police, riven by deep river valleys and covered with dense woodland where the light of day barely reaches the ground. When it's not raining the hills are wreathed in mist, and it's as cold as the grave at this time of the year. And that is the root of our problem, Tribune. The locals call it the Forest of Arduenna, after their goddess of the high woods. She rides a boar to hunt, they say.'

'A German Diana, then?'

'Yes, Tribune, apart from her association with high ground. The forest is littered with shrines to her name, hunters invoking her good favour in the main, although there are rumours of a darker side to her worship. Human sacrifices . . .' He paused, touching an amulet that hung from his right wrist. 'Not that we've found any sign of the kind of sacrificial altars you'd expect if the rumours are based in fact, but . . .'

Scaurus nodded, his face set hard.

'When we had men captured in the war with the Quadi it wasn't unusual for the tribesmen to sacrifice them to their gods, usually slowly, and often within screaming distance of our camps. Let's hope your amulet brings you protection. So, tell me, what have you achieved against these bandits?'

Albanus jumped to his feet, suddenly livid at the question.

'Nothing! Exactly nothing at all! We house these men at the governor's request, we provide them with stabling, and yet—'

'*Procurator!*' Scaurus's voice was cold, and his tone not that of a man likely to brook any argument. The civilian looked at him, his mouth open. 'I promise you, in fact I swear to Mithras Unconquered, that if you interject your nonsensical gabbling into this conference one more time I will have you ejected from the room. Keep your mouth shut, so that those of us who have to go *outside* these walls and hunt down the men putting the empire's entire northern frontier at risk can work out what is to be done!' He held the administrator's gaze until the other man looked away, while his clerk stared with even greater intensity at his notes. Petrus, the first spear noted, didn't so much as flicker an eyelid; he simply watched Scaurus with the same closed expression. The tribune waited another moment to make sure his point had been made, then gestured to the waiting Caninus. 'Prefect? Do please continue.'

Caninus looked at the map in silence for a moment, shaking his head ruefully.

'You want to know what we've done? Everything we can, given our resources, but nowhere near enough. We patrol the roads as frequently as we can, capturing and killing the occasional small band of robbers, but the real threat is still out there. And why, you ask? Why haven't we already ground them into the mud of the flat open fields that border the road for as far as the eye can see? There are two reasons, and if I have your measure you already know very well what the bigger of the two has to be.'

Scaurus nodded.

'I think I know the first of them as well, but please continue.'

'The first is simple enough. All the way through the war with the Marcomanni and the Quadi, a war which only really ended two years ago, no matter what the victory coins might have said before that, this province was bled of men and gold to fund the campaign's insatiable appetite for blood and treasure. The legions on the lower Rhenus are stripped to the bone, capable of little more than guarding the frontier; and the farm owners are taxed to the hilt to make up the financial shortfall caused by the plague, so they drive their slaves like animals. As a consequence of these problems the number of army deserters and escaped slaves swells the numbers of those committing the crime of robbery faster than I can bring them to justice with only thirty men. As you expected, Tribune?' Scaurus nodded, his expression thoughtful. 'And your guess as to the second problem?'

The tribune stood, stretching his back before walking across to the map. As he stared intently at it a tense silence filled the room, broken by the slap of his hand on the wall.

'Simple. You have two different types of bandit at work here. There are opportunists like those we killed yesterday, escaped slaves for the most part, running from the harsh conditions imposed on them by their masters, who are, as you say, desperate to make a profit despite the heavy taxes squeezing them dry. After all, most of them owe money, and the lenders aren't traditionally known for their patience. This first type of bandit stays close to the road, and preys on the weak and unprepared, but keeps well away from the grain convoys. You are escorting the grain across the province?'

'Yes. We meet the convoys twenty or so miles to the west and escort them to the city. The convoys from here to the legions on the Rhenus we accompany as far as the Mosa to the east. It's the most that we can do with the strength we have, and the carters are sufficiently well armed to fight off most of the smaller bands of robbers.'

'But here –' Scaurus slapped the wall again, indicating the forest's sprawling mass – 'here's your bigger problem. The forest is less than a day's march from the road, and provides a sanctuary that you'll never be able to penetrate. There's a major band operating from the forest, at a guess?'

Caninus laughed ruefully.

'More like an army. There were already at least two hundred of them before the auxiliaries sent to hunt them down decided to mutiny and join with them last autumn. A century sent to man an outpost fort on the road south was attacked after dark and those that decided to resist were slaughtered to the last man. When their bodies were discovered, the rest of the cohort decided they'd be better off siding with the bandits. They killed their prefect and deserted, and it was only by good fortune they weren't actually in the city when it happened or there would have been a bloodbath. The band in the forest must be at least five hundred men strong now, and that many mouths take a lot of feeding.'

Scaurus stared at the map for a moment.

'Which puts the grain convoys at constant risk. I see the size of the problem.' He turned away from the map, his hard stare raking across the faces of the men sitting around the table. 'First things first. Now the magnitude of what we're facing has been made clear, my first priority is to get my men under solid roofs, with proper food and stoves to cook it on. Once that's achieved, you, Prefect Caninus, can show us the ground we'll be operating across. And so, gentlemen, to business. I need enough wood, nails and tools to build barracks for fourteen hundred soldiers, plus stabling for thirty horses, and my food supplies for both men and beasts will have run out by the end of tomorrow. So are we going to work this out with the professionalism the empire expects from us, or am I going to have to show you all my teeth?'

2

'It's not much of a market, is it? I remember this place from when I was a boy, with every wall lined with traders, and all of their stalls loaded with fruit and vegetables. But this . . .'

Julius stood with his hands on his hips and looked about the forum's thin population of traders and their limited variety of produce, shaking his head slowly. Marcus and Dubnus had volunteered to come with him on the task to which he'd been appointed by Frontinius, and the two men exchanged a glance. The state of the city's housing had also become apparent to them in the daylight. There were empty houses in every street, many of them falling into sad disrepair and at least one with a sapling sprouting through an open window.

'The city's population seems to have been slashed in size from those days, by the plague, I suppose. And since the whole province appears to have been turned over to growing grain, from what we saw on the march in, perhaps a shortage of meat and vegetables is the price they have to pay. There doesn't seem to be any shortage of bread though.'

The big man nodded at Marcus's observation.

'Which is one small mercy, but I wonder where the meat and vegetables to feed two cohorts of big strong lads are going to come from if this is the best they can do. Anyway, forget the food, what we're looking for is someone that'll sell us something to wet our—'

He stopped talking abruptly, drawing curious glances from his colleagues as he stared in silence at a small party walking past them through the forum, a woman flanked by two burly men who could only be bodyguards, to judge from their size and demeanour.

'Come on, Julius, stick to the job in hand. You're not going to get what Uncle Sextus sent you out for by ogling every good-looking floozy who walks past.'

If their colleague had heard Dubnus's jocular comment he didn't acknowledge it, and he strode out into the forum without a backward glance, his attention locked on the woman's back. His friends exchanged baffled glances, Dubnus frowning irritably after his colleague.

'We'd better go with him. Those two have the look of men who'll reach for their knives rather than waste time on pleasantries.'

When he was a half a dozen paces behind the small group Julius called out a single word to the woman.

'Annia?'

She stopped walking and turned to face him, and to Marcus's eye her expression was a combination of hope and dread. At close quarters he realised that she was a beauty, her features enhanced by cosmetics of a quality and subtlety that he hadn't seen since leaving Rome the previous year, her black hair artfully arranged to frame a face that, if it wasn't in the first flush of youth, was still strikingly handsome. Her eyes narrowed on seeing the big centurion standing before her, and her lips tightened. Marcus guessed that her frown of recognition wasn't the reaction for which Julius had been hoping. The men to either side of her moved quickly, stepping forward to intercept the Tungrian without any sign of deference to his uniform. With a tight smile one of them, a bulky man, put a firm hand on Julius's chest, dropping the other onto the hilt of his knife. His hair was cropped close to his skull while a bushy moustache bristled under a nose which had clearly been broken more than once. The other man, whip thin and with a dark, brooding look to him, reacted with equal professionalism, taking a quick step to one side and putting his hand to the handle of a long blade, clearly ready to unsheathe the weapon if necessary. If they weren't military trained, they clearly had enough experience of their roles to perform them competently.

'That's close enough, soldier boy. The lady doesn't want to be bothered by the likes of you.'

The bodyguard's harsh voice was hard-edged with the promise

of force to back up his words, and Marcus felt the hairs on the back of his neck rising as the familiar urge to fight made his nostrils flare and his eyes widen. The second bodyguard, alert to the situation's potential for violence, noticed as the young officer rose slightly onto the balls of his feet, unconsciously poising himself to fight, and he shook his head in caution. His voice was more reasonable than his colleague's, if no less confident in his abilities.

'The lady doesn't want to be disturbed, sonny. Better if you were to go and bother someone else, eh?'

Julius turned to his friends and momentarily bowed his head as if accepting the bodyguards' rebuttal, then struck without warning, grabbing the hand that was still planted on his chest and bending it back with savage force, twisting it to his left to put the man off balance before using the bodyguard's instinctive resistance to heave him to the right, shoving him into his colleague hard enough to put them both on the ground. The bodyguards leapt to their feet to find three hard-faced centurions ready for them with their swords drawn, and looked at each other in consternation. From the corner of his eye Marcus saw a man turn and leave the forum at something close to a run, and realised they only had a matter of moments before reinforcements arrived to back up the angry bodyguards. Julius lowered his gladius, putting up a placatory hand.

'Steady, boys. Don't make the mistake of biting off more than you can handle. All I want is a quiet conversation with the lady, and then you can go on your way with no more damage done than a bit of embarrassment. Or we can fight, and when Tungrians fight it's all or nothing. So don't say I didn't warn you.'

While the bodyguards were still pondering Julius's words, their faces reflecting their confusion, the woman stepped forward and lifted her hand.

'It's *my* decision who I speak with, not yours.' She gave the two men a pointed stare before turning back to Julius. 'And not yours either, Julius. That *is* you, isn't it, behind the beard and the hard words?'

He nodded, bowing his head.

'I'm sorry. Your men were a little too quick to give offence.'

'And you were more than ready to take it. Just as you were fifteen years ago, as I recall? So here you are, back in Tungrorum after all this time. I'll assume you didn't come back to find me, and that this is just a coincidence?'

Marcus heard a note enter Julius's voice that he'd not heard in all the time they'd served together.

'I meant to come back for you, Annia, but you never answered the messages I sent with the men who came back here to retire. I supposed that you'd met someone else.'

One of the bodyguards smirked, and Marcus's eyes narrowed as, in a sudden flash of insight, he worked out what it was about her that had been bothering him. The woman's hollow laugh confirmed his guess.

'I met a few other men, as it happens. Look at me, Julius, look properly.' She raised her arms and performed a twirl on the spot. 'Does nothing bother you about what you see? The toga I'm wearing, for example? I know it's not made of the prescribed floral pattern, but it's still quite a giveaway. Or perhaps you've noticed my lack of footwear? The city authorities are quite strict in enforcing that nice little rule.'

The centurion stared at her for a moment before realisation dawned.

'You're a . . .' He shook his head and tried again. 'I – I mean, you've become . . .'

'Yes, I've become a whore. And, as I'm sure you can tell from the quality of my clothing, not to mention the men paid to make sure I'm not bothered when I walk through the city, really quite a good whore. Your precious love of all those years ago turned to servicing men for money to survive. I didn't have much choice in the matter, not with my father dead, and my mother and I dependent on whatever money I could bring in.' She shook her head in dismissal of the memory, her voice hardening. 'So, here we are, the soldier and the whore reunited after all these years. What stories we could tell each other. But perhaps it's better if we leave it there, and try to forget what might have been, if only you hadn't felt compelled to join the army and leave me here to rot.'

The big man stood aghast, and the man he'd disarmed opened his mouth to make some cutting remark, only to close it again as Dubnus caught his eye with an extravagant glare.

'Why didn't you write and tell me? I would have sent you money, all my money . . .'

'And how would I have done that? We didn't have enough to buy what little we needed to survive, never mind paying someone to carry a message to Britannia. I've done well, all things considered. I'm well looked after, and I'm in partnership with a local businessman who supplies the city with grain and fresh provisions. We have an arrangement that ensures I'm left to run my house without fear of harassment, and a dozen girls working hard can turn over more money than you'd think, even with a healthy percentage for protection. I'm a wealthy woman compared to most people in Tungrorum.'

'And that, I think, is enough.' The moustached bodyguard stepped forward with his confidence rediscovered and his expression painfully close to being one of mockery, jerking his head to indicate several men approaching them across the forum. 'The lady needs to be on her way, and this reunion, touching though it's been, is over.' Julius nodded with a faraway look on his face, and Marcus tensed himself to strike if the bodyguard made any move to take advantage of the centurion's distraction, but the lady's escort did nothing more than shake his head disparagingly and mutter an insult under his breath. '*Cunt-struck prick.*'

Dubnus bristled with anger and made to step up to him, but stopped with a frown as Marcus put out a hand to restrain him. Sheathing his sword, Marcus then moved forward and put his face within a few inches of the bodyguard's, speaking in quiet but fierce tones.

'I'd be a little more careful who you insult, if I were you. And when you're done with trying to get yourself killed, you can take a message to your employer. Tell him that there's a customer looking for enough wine to keep twenty thirsty centurions happy for a month, and quickly. We're camped on the empty ground by the west gate, and he needs to ask for First Spear Frontinius. The good stuff, mind you, and we're paying in gold.'

Unabashed, the bodyguard raised an eyebrow at his mate, a slight smirk on his face.

'In gold, is it? We'll pass your message on, soldier. *Fresh* gold's always welcome here.'

He turned away, putting a proprietorial hand on the lady's arm and leading her towards one of the market's exits. Julius watched them walk away across the forum, his expression still wistful as he addressed his colleagues, ignoring the newly arrived bruisers who closed ranks behind Annia's bodyguards to deny the Tungrians a chance to follow her.

'And that, brothers, was my first love. The blows that life deals you just when you least expect them, eh?' He sighed, his voice hardening as he regained control of himself. 'Feel free to mention this meeting to anyone you like, but be prepared to sleep with one eye open if you do.'

To his surprise Dubnus, usually the first with a quip at his expense, shook his head dourly.

'It wouldn't be funny, brother. Forget you ever laid eyes on her, and we'll do the same.' He winked at Marcus, tapping his pouch with a significant stare at the back of Julius's head. 'And if you ever want someone to cheer you up, I'm your man. All you have to do is *whistle*.'

The view to the west from the top of the Tungrorum city wall was less than impressive, Qadir decided, its monotony made all the worse by the frequency with which the 9th Century's Hamians were being allocated the duty of standing watch over the open fields beyond them, while the two Tungrian cohorts were on construction duties. Half of the century, and among them all of the twenty-odd Hamians who had elected to stay with the cohort, were dispersed along three hundred paces of the wall's eastern length, while the rest were hard at work with the other centuries below them. The sounds of hammering and sawing were an incessant accompaniment to their vigil, as the soldiers below laboured, sweated and bled to erect the wooden barrack blocks required to house their numbers. Empty fields that receded into the featureless grey had been intriguing to the Hamian members of the century at first, but their interest in the open ground's potential for archery had quickly palled with the continued presence of the bitterly cold fog that wreathed the landscape beyond the city's walls.

'There!' The man at his side started and pointed into the mist, his voice lowered to avoid spooking the cautious animal. Following his arm Qadir saw the outline of a magnificent stag advancing slowly out of the murk, bending its heavily antlered head to pick carefully at the sparse grass. The soldier shrugged the bow case from his shoulder, raising an eyebrow at his chosen man. Qadir looked long and hard at the animal, calculating the amount of meat that his men's skilled hands would strip from its carcass, before regretfully shaking his head and putting a restraining hand on the man's arm.

'Our goddess will not look with favour upon the man who looses an arrow at such an easy target. That animal was made to be hunted with skill and stealth through the great forest, not to be shot down for straying into this unnatural wilderness of empty land. Spread the word: the man that shoots a single arrow at the beast will suffer my displeasure, and likely that of Our Lady the Deasura too. Go.'

The soldier nodded and turned away to pass Qadir's command to his fellow Hamians. The big chosen man was a placid individual for the most part, but every man in the 9th Century was only too well aware that they crossed him at their peril, such was his temper when eventually roused. Qadir watched with satisfaction as the soldier walked down the wall's broad fighting platform, taking pleasure from the fact that he had spared an innocent creature of the forest from an ignoble death.

'That's a fine-looking beast. Plenty of meat on those bones, I'd guess?'

The chosen man turned, rolling his eyes in mock disgust.

'Still you have the ability to ghost your way to my shoulder, Centurion. I stand abashed at your skills.'

He opened his arms in a slight bow of respect, and Marcus nodded in return, his face creased by a wry smile.

'So we're not hunting today?'

Qadir shook his head, watching the stag as it turned and slid back into the mist.

'It would not be fitting. Such a prize needs to be taken in a true hunt, not like the target on a practice ground. As long as he is under my men's bows, he will have the protection of the Deasura herself.'

Marcus shrugged easily, still smiling.

'In which case he's lucky to have encountered the only leader of men with your eastern philosophy for a hundred miles or more.'

They stared out into the empty fog in silence for a moment before Marcus found the words for which he had been groping.

'You've been a different man of late, Qadir. Morban thinks you've realised what a mistake you made in deciding to stay with us.'

The Hamian stared out into the mist.

'An easy assumption to make, I suppose. The easterner comes to his senses when he realises that most of the infantryman's life is nothing more than rain, marching, boredom and more rain.'

Marcus laughed.

'And that the other small part is nothing but blood, terror and death?'

The Hamian smiled slowly.

'In your company, Centurion, it does seem that way.' He turned to look at his friend. 'But in all truth, none of that bothers me. I am troubled by a different fact.'

He fell silent again and turned back to the mist, his face bleak in the morning's cold light. And just when Marcus thought that the subject was closed, the Hamian sighed and turned to face his friend again.

'My continuing black mood, Centurion, is the result of your near death at the hands of imperial killers before we left Britannia. And I'm not the only man that feels this way. If not for three unwashed barbarians and a centurion still recovering from a serious wound, both you and your woman would have suffered the fate they had planned for you. We are all ashamed to have allowed those Roman animals to have taken you from the cohort without any attempt at rescue.'

Marcus smiled gently at his words.

'You couldn't have saved me even if you'd been aware of what had happened, which you weren't. Nobody but Arminius, Martos and Lugos could have run fast enough to arrive in time, not with all the weight we all carry in weapons and armour. And since it worked out well enough in the end, let's have an end to this intro-spection, shall we? There'll be plenty of other chances for you to pull my grapes out of the press.'

The Hamian looked into his face, his weary expression brightening.

'Very well. I will put the failure behind me, and consider only how best to provide you and yours with the protection I have sworn to deliver.'

'Sworn?' Marcus's expression turned quizzical. 'You mean an oath to the gods?'

'Just one goddess, Our Lady the Deasura. And I'm not the only one. You're unjustly accused, every other member of your family has been murdered, and only you, your woman and her unborn child stand between the empire and the final destruction of your name. None of your friends will allow that to happen, not without challenge.'

The Roman shook his head, his eyebrows raised in amazement.

'I'm speechless, Qadir. I . . .'

'There is no need for you to comment. We need neither your approval nor your assistance in this matter. Simply accept that you have friends who will fight to see you survive this injustice, and go about the duties that accompany this new identity you have chosen knowing that we watch over you.'

They looked down over the wall onto the ground below, and at the wooden frames that were being erected to form the basis for the barracks. At length Marcus spoke again.

'Thank you. And to avoid embarrassment for all concerned we'll speak of it no more, although I remain quite astonished.' He took a deep breath, and waved an arm at the scene below. 'It's going more slowly than the first spear hoped.'

Qadir nodded.

'We are none of us carpenters. Everyone below us is skilled with a sword and shield, but few have any skill or desire to wield a saw. Perhaps if the legion were helping the job would go more smoothly?'

Marcus laughed softly.

'Perhaps it would. But I fear that the word "if" is most likely to stay the case. Speaking of which . . .'

Two hundred paces to the north of their place on the wall the city's west gate had been opened, and a column of soldiers was marching out in full armour. The two men watched as the legionaries poured out of the city at the march, both of them counting the soldiers until the last rank cleared the gate. Qadir raised an eyebrow, watching as the marching column was swallowed up by the drifting fog.

'Two centuries. It seems that the legion's tribune has changed his mind about the need to patrol outside the city.'

Frontinius and Scaurus watched the building work from the doorway of the tribune's tent, the first spear standing in silence while his superior officer listed the progress made in getting the two cohorts properly supplied.

'So we have enough food to see us through another week, although I'm concerned as to the impact of our presence on the city's grain stocks. What with our two cohorts and Belletor's men that's another two thousand mouths to feed. Hungry mouths too, ones not used to going without their full ration.'

Frontinius scratched his head, looking critically at the dirt that came off his scalp under his fingernails.

'Gods, but I could do with a proper bath. I used to think the bathhouse at the Hill was a bit draughty and poky, but I'd give my left ball for a good long sweat right now. What about that great big grain store outside the gates? Surely there's enough corn in there to feed everyone and to spare?'

Scaurus raised a sardonic eyebrow.

'That grain, First Spear Frontinius, belongs to the empire. Why else do you think it was built outside the walls, but to keep temptation from overcoming the citizens of Tungrorum? You'll have noticed that our colleague Belletor has soldiers posted around it to dissuade the populace from any idea of getting at its contents? It seems that Tribune Belletor and Procurator Albanus are aligned on that much, at least. No, we'll have to keep a close eye on the city's food stocks. I won't have civilians going hungry to feed the men who are supposed to be protecting them. Doubtless those men that delivered our wine already have a strong grip on the supply of scarce items at inflated prices, so it'll be the poor that suffer if we turn a blind eye. It appears that Albanus's deputy, Petrus, is the merchant in question, so I doubt the city authorities will be taking much of an interest in the event of our causing a shortage.'

He looked down at the tablet in his hand.

'As to shelter, how long do you think it's going to take to complete the construction?'

Frontinius scratched his head again.

'The best part of a week, based on their current progress. We don't have enough of either the right tools or the skills to go any faster.'

Scaurus shook his head, his face hardening.

'Not fast enough, First Spear. You'll have to find a way to get it done quicker. I want these men out in the countryside hunting down bandits, not developing their building skills inside these walls.' Frontinius grimaced, but nodded his understanding as his tribune scowled down at his tablet. 'Anything else?'

'Yes, Tribune. Bathing and drinking.'

'Ah . . . I see.'

'My thoughts exactly when Julius pointed it out to me earlier. The men haven't seen the inside of a bathhouse or a beer shop since we marched away from the coast. Bathing shouldn't be too hard to arrange, although we'll have to agree a rota with the legion boys to avoid the inevitable friction; it's the drinking that worries me more. There are several likely looking establishments in the city, and that's before we get to the unlicensed beer shops that any soldier worth his salt will find for himself soon enough.'

Scaurus nodded, his face creasing into a knowing smile.

'Quite so. And if we try to stop the men from using them we'll just end up with them sneaking about the camp after dark, and risk someone getting speared by a sentry who doesn't know him and doesn't like the look of him. No, we'll have to organise some sort of rota for that as well. Since Julius came up with the point he can follow it through, especially as he knows the city better than anyone else. Have him organise a schedule that allows the men enough time to enjoy themselves, but not so much that they'll end up roaring drunk and starting fights. While he's at it he can have a chat with the owners of the taverns to warn them that they'll be getting some extra custom, and perhaps he could discuss the timings of our boys' visits with First Spear Sergius too. It wouldn't do our image with the locals much good for Tungrians and legionaries to end up in the same hostelries at the same time, eh?'

Frontinius looked over his shoulder, raising an eyebrow.

'It looks like we'll be able to tell Sergius in person.'

Scaurus swivelled, frowning at the sight of 1st Minervia's senior centurion approaching from the legion's barracks, a crowd of thirty or so men following him in tunic order, most of them carrying leather bags. Sergius saluted Scaurus smartly, nodding his greeting to Frontinius.

'Greetings, gentlemen. It's a fine morning for a patrol, or at least that's what Tribune Belletor said as he was mounting his horse all nicely wrapped up in his cloak. I'm not sure what our first and second centuries will think about it, but either way they're out for the day.' He turned to look across at the labouring Tungrians. 'Your boys are well stuck in, I see, but I'm ready to bet good money that you're going slower than you'd like. Knowing Procurator Albanus I'm pretty sure that the city authorities will have provided you with a smaller number of tools than you need, and low-quality stuff at that. And, with no disrespect intended, your men don't look like it's coming naturally to them either.' He turned back to them, finding both men staring at him with quizzical expressions. 'And no, I've not come to gloat, but to do something a good deal more constructive than my tribune would find acceptable, given the poor start to your relationship.' He waved a hand at the legionaries behind him. 'All of these men are skilled builders, and they have their tools with them. I've no shortage of either, but what I *don't* have are enough trained soldiers to get a grip of the cohort's large number of new recruits. You know how that works best, eh, colleague?'

Frontinius nodded knowingly, seeing where the other man's line of reasoning was taking them.

'One experienced soldier for every four or five recruits. Any more than that and he can't keep a close enough eye on them to spot what they're doing wrong and correct them while they're doing it. Thirty such veterans of a few nasty fights could train two centuries at a time.'

'Exactly. And in return, thirty skilled builders would be two for each of your barrack blocks. Not enough to throw them up in a day, but it would make a big difference to the speed and quality of the build to have men who knew what they were doing pointing out the mistakes as they were being made.'

Both men turned to Scaurus with questioning looks. Raising his hands, he shook his head and laughed out loud.

'No, gentlemen, the less I know the better! The pair of you can work out whatever shady deal it is you think will best meet the needs of your respective cohorts while I go and root out our cavalrymen. Since they're lucky enough to have found empty stables for their beasts, they can make themselves useful rather than sitting round getting fat. Mind you . . .' He turned back to face them with a conspiratorial look. 'Mind you, given that we wear red and your men wear white, it might be a good idea for your men to swap tunics while they're doing each other's jobs. Just a thought.'

Marcus and Qadir were still looking out at the foggy landscape when a horseman rode up to the wall's rear and called for them. Eager to be out of the city, the sturdy animal pranced about on the spot as its rider waited for the officers to appear over the parapet.

'Decurion Silus's compliments to you, Centurion. He was wondering if you and your chosen man would care to join the mounted squadron for a look-around? It's been approved by the tribune.'

Marcus looked along the wall's fighting platform, spying the bulky figure of his standard bearer a hundred paces distant. Morban was talking animatedly with a group of soldiers and as Marcus watched with narrowed eyes he slapped palms with one of them.

'Another wager made, no doubt. The man's incorrigible. Remind me to have a discussion with him about his grandson when we get back. *Morban!*'

He beckoned the standard bearer to him, waiting with a tapping foot while the veteran soldier waddled up the stretch of wall between them, snapping to attention when he reached his centurion.

'Centurion?'

'Is Watch Officer Augustus still helping with the building work?'

'Yes, sir, the one-eyed old bast—' Catching a hardening of Marcus's face, he quickly rephrased his reply. 'Yes, he is, Centurion.'

'In that case you're in command of the Ninth until we come back from patrol. Silus has a couple of empty saddles, from the look of it.' Morban saluted again, adopting a determined expression. 'And I'd lose the frown, Standard Bearer. It makes you look as if you're struggling with a particularly difficult bowel movement.'

Marcus and Qadir hurried down from the wall and headed off towards the west gate, while Morban gestured to the soldiers with whom he'd been speaking before.

'Time to pay up, gentlemen. As predicted only a moment ago, I am now in command of the Ninth until that nice young gentleman decides his arse is sore and he comes back from playing with the donkey wallopers. Thank you.' He took a coin from each of the soldiers, dropping his winnings into a heavy pouch on his belt. 'Rest happy in the knowledge that your pay will shortly be making a powerful impression on the whores of this fair city.'

Marcus and Qadir found the mounted squadron waiting for them at the gate, and the young centurion threw a mock salute at their decurion.

'Greetings, Silus. Your messenger said you had a pair of horses too flighty to be ridden by anyone but myself and my chosen man?'

Silus grinned slyly at him, extending a welcoming hand to indicate a pair of horses without riders.

'Indeed, Centurion. Qadir is well known for his discernment with regard to horses, and his consummate skill in the saddle. With that in mind I have reserved the very best of our horses for him.' He gestured to an empty saddle, raising an eyebrow at the Hamian whose sour mood had clearly lifted on seeing the horse in question. 'You remember this beast, I presume?'

The Hamian threaded his way through the throng of horses, stroking muzzles and patting flanks until he reached his mount, a magnificent chestnut mare he had last ridden in Britannia. He nodded his thanks to Silus and jumped into the saddle with the practised grace of an accomplished horseman. Silus smiled at the sight of horse and rider reunited, leaning out of the saddle to mutter conspiratorially to Marcus.

'I do like to see man and beast so well matched.' Marcus raised a sardonic eyebrow, knowing what was coming next. 'And no more so than in your case. For you, Centurion, I have an animal which we already know can match your quick temper and restless desire for a fight.'

He raised his arm and indicated a big rangy grey stallion waiting impatiently alongside his own horse. Marcus shook his head wryly then walked round to greet the animal, which responded by nudging at him with its muzzle.

'You see, dear old Bonehead remembers you! He knows that he has only to put his ears back and you'll happily allow him his head, certain that he'll take you straight into the deepest shit available. I've never seen a horse and rider more made for each other.'

Marcus shook his head in mock disgust, climbing into the saddle and accepting a spear and shield from the cavalry officer.

'Let's be away, then, Decurion. I'll do my best to remain in control of this high-spirited animal, although Mercury himself may struggle to stay with us if he spots a deer. You, I fear may be left far behind, given that your poor animal's carrying all that extra weight.'

The men guarding the gate opened the massive wooden doors, and the squadron trotted out into the thinning mist.

'Tribune Scaurus wants us to scout away to the west, as far as the point where the road forks to the south to cross the Mosa at Arduenna Bridge.'

They proceeded at an easy trot, allowing the horses a pace that wouldn't overtax them. Silus led the way with the squadron's standard bearer riding alongside him. The dragon standard's long cloth tail hung limply in the damp air, droplets of moisture forming on the bronze head's highly polished surface, much to its bearer's disgust, and the occasional gust of air rippled the mist and elicited the faintest of moans from the reed concealed within its fiercely fanged mouth. Silus upped their pace to a brisk trot, and within a half-mile's progress the rear of the legion centuries' column appeared out of the mist before them. The decurion extended his arms to either side, his hands held out rigidly like blades, and he called back over his shoulder loudly enough to be sure that the infantry's rearmost ranks would hear him.

'Pass to either side, and ignore any comments that might come our way. Just content yourselves with the fact that they'll be tramping through mounds of horseshit soon enough!'

The legionaries launched a barrage of insulting and occasionally witty comments at the horsemen as they trotted past the marching column, and, as was equally traditional, the riders kept their gazes fixed on the direction of travel and their faces set in expressions of utter disinterest. One wag in the leading century bellowed out the first line of a song beloved of foot soldiers across the empire, and his comrades joined in with all the gusto expected of them.

> The cavalry love buggering sheep,
> In various bogs and ditches,
> When they've done the flock they all suck cock,
> Those dirty sons of bitches!

The squadron rode on, the final rider turning in his saddle with a smile of glee as the horse in front of him lifted its tail to deposit a long trail of droppings in the marching column's path.

Silus raised a hand to signal the canter, and the riders spurred their mounts to the faster pace, their clattering hoof beats rattling dully across the empty fields. After ten minutes of riding Silus frowned, peering forward into the light mist. A man was running towards them, staggering along the road's cobbles in a manner that suggested he was close to dropping from exhaustion. Reining in his horse, the decurion jumped down from his saddle and caught the runner by his arm as he slumped to the road's surface.

'Bandits . . . attacking . . . carts . . .'

He pointed back into the mist from which he'd staggered, his chest heaving, and Silus, half carrying him to the side of the road, barked a terse question at him.

'How many?'

The hapless carter shook his head.

'Mist . . . too many . . .'

The decurion looked up at Marcus.

'No telling how many of them might be waiting for us. We should probably wait for the infantry to catch up.'

His friend hefted his spear.

'Probably. And probably lose them as a result. They'll vanish off into this murk with their prize as quickly as they appeared from it.'

Silus nodded grimly.

'Very well, we'll go after them alone, but ride on the verge rather than the road. Let's not give them any warning. Lower that standard too, or they'll hear it howling from miles away once we get up some speed. *Ride!*'

Tribune Scaurus found Prefect Caninus in his headquarters, a small building tucked away behind the forum. The prefect's men were hard at work preparing their gear and sharpening their weapons as Scaurus walked between them to the office at the building's rear, and he felt their eyes on his back as he knocked at the office door. Inside, by the light of the lamps that had been lit to compensate for the shuttered windows, the prefect was standing at a map of the area around Tungrorum painted on the wall behind his desk, an exact copy of the one they'd discussed in the basilica the previous day. The diagram was littered with hand-painted annotations, each one consisting of three lines of text beside a small cross to indicate a location. The crosses were for the most part aligned with the main roads to east and west, and the notes that accompanied each one were abbreviated in the official style. The tribune put down the bag he was carrying and shook his colleague's hand before turning to examine the map with him.

'You keep a record of bandit activity, then?'

The prefect nodded, waving a hand at the map.

'That which is reported to my office, yes. I'm trying to spot a pattern. Something to give me an idea of where they might be hiding themselves, so that I can get on the front foot for a change, rather than just reacting to their attacks. It also gives me a clue as to how many of them are out there, and where they might be hiding. Look here . . .' Smiling grimly he pointed to a tight cluster of a dozen crosses ten miles or so to the west of the city. 'There's one group of robberies, more or less where you ran into that band of thieves on your way here. Perhaps we'll hear no more from them.'

Scaurus examined the map for a moment.

'So we have clusters of robberies here . . .' He pointed to the east, on the road between the city and the small settlement at Mosa Ford, ten miles distant from Tungrorum. 'Here . . .' His finger moved to indicate the road to the south, passing within a few miles of the forest of Arduenna in its path to Augusta Treverorum, the city of the Treveri tribe. 'And here, on the main road to the west.'

Caninus nodded, slapping a finger into the middle of a group of twenty or so crosses.

'Exactly. That's where they've been attacking the grain convoys, seven times this year, and always when we're elsewhere, as if they have some inside knowledge of my men's movements. They always strike in force, never less than two or three hundred strong, and that means the carters never have enough men to hold them off. Especially since they managed to subvert the auxiliaries sent from the frontier to hunt them down.'

Scaurus shook his head.

'That's been puzzling me ever since you first mentioned it. What happened to make a whole cohort of trained soldiers throw in their lot with a gang of bandits? Why abandon any hope of becoming a citizen for a life of constant uncertainty and a good-sized chance of a violent death?'

Caninus waved a hand at his chair.

'Take a seat and I'll tell you.' He paced across the office before turning back, his face bearing the look of a troubled man. 'It's the band that is operating out of the forest that's most of the problem here. The rest of them are disorganised, slaves and deserters trying their luck, and taking advantage of the fact that we're overstretched. If that was all there was to it I could probably keep a lid on things with the men I have, but the fact is that the man in control of that gang is undisputedly good. Almost supernaturally lucky, or skilled. Or both. They must have some sort of hiding place deep in the woods, somewhere off the usual hunting tracks, because I've not found any trace of them in the months we've been searching the forest, which we do whenever I can spare the manpower. I know, it's not enough to explain the desertions . . .' He rubbed his face wearily with one hand before continuing.

'It's their leader. He seems to have them all convinced that they're not bandits, but rebels against the empire. He tells them that it was the imperial army that brought the plague back from the east, and that it's the emperor's fault we all lost friends and loved ones. He's got them believing that they're freedom fighters, rather than the thieving scum they really are. Worse than that, they seem to believe that he's invincible. He wears a cavalry helmet with one of those flashy reflective face masks whenever he thinks he's running the risk of being seen, so nobody has any idea of who he is, or where he's come from. He carries a sword made of some strange metal which is reputed to have the strength to cut through just about anything, including, believe it or not, iron sword blades. And he's utterly ruthless.'

Scaurus shrugged slightly.

'I've seen a lot of hard men in my time. What do you mean by ruthless, exactly?'

Caninus was silent for a moment before speaking.

'You asked me why a cohort of auxiliaries would desert. Well, it wasn't a full cohort; it was three centuries of Treveri soldiers.'

Scaurus shook his head unhappily.

'Some idiot sent men recruited in the Treveri lands, which are, what, fifty miles to the south of here, to deal with a local banditry problem?'

Caninus nodded.

'You've guessed it. The legatus at Fortress Bonna, clearly a man without much understanding of local history, detailed the Treveri cohort's prefect to take four centuries and clear this particular gang of bandits from the forest. If he'd been any kind of student of recent history he would have known that the Treveri have had a mixed relationship with the empire ever since their initial cooperation with the Blessed Julius in defeating the Nervians. The very fact that they threw in their lot with the Batavians when they decided to revolt should have been enough of a clue, but I suppose that after a hundred years the memory's become a bit distant. All the same . . .'

He raised his eyebrows at the irony of it all, sharing a moment of dark amusement with Scaurus, who sat and waited for him to continue.

'Anyway, nothing much went amiss until they sent a century out on outpost duty to guard the road to Claudius Colony. The bandits overran it one dark night, slaughtered every soldier who raised a sword to them and took the rest prisoner. They then put the centurion's head on a spear. It didn't take whoever *he* is – the local nickname for him is "Obduro", by the way – to work out where the men of the other three centuries were from. He surrounded their camp the next night and called on them to kill their officers and join him in the fight for "their people's" independence in the name of the goddess Arduenna. And so they did. Her name has a powerful magic for men raised in the shadow of the forest.'

Scaurus opened the bag at his feet, fishing out the dented cavalry helmet.

'This won't have been his, then, from the sound of it?'

Caninus picked up the helmet and examined the face mask, badly dented from the impact of Julius's brow guard.

'Sadly not. It would have solved most of our problems if it had been – cutting the snake's head off, so to speak – but this is far too shabby to have been his. I presume that you took this from one of the bandits that attacked you during your march here?' Scaurus nodded, and Caninus spread his hands, palm upwards, in a gesture of frustration. 'You see the man's influence? Even the dimmest of common robbers has worked out that the myth of Obduro can work for him too.'

'Why "Obduro"? Why call yourself "hard"?'

Caninus smiled wryly.

'Oh it's not his choice. That's the name the people of the town gave him when his modus operandi became clear, after the first couple of times his men overran a guard post, or a detachment of soldiers. He has them killed, as I said a moment ago, almost literally to the last man. Nothing protracted, but no mercy shown either, except to the few men he takes back into the forest, presumably for the purposes of sacrifice to their goddess, and the one man he chooses to bring the news of his latest victory to me.'

Scaurus frowned.

'Specifically to you?'

The prefect grinned at him without humour, his expression suddenly bleak.

'Oh yes, *most* specifically to me. He's developed something of a determination to see me dead, it seems. He mocks me with every fresh message that we receive from him, making sure that the survivor seeks me out and tells me in graphic details what will happen to me when I'm captured. He tells them that he'll know if they don't pass the message exactly as he tells them to, and that he'll visit the same fate he has planned for me on them unless they follow his instructions to the letter. He tells them to do it publicly, not in private, so that the people around me hear everything.'

'Which implies he has some good sources of information close to you?'

The prefect stared at his boots for a moment.

'Yes, that thought had occurred to me, but whoever it is must be either terrified or utterly devoted to him. Someone with a family member taken hostage, perhaps, or just a loved one who's an easy target. Don't forget that a score of travellers pass through Tungrorum every day, on their way along the main road from Beech Forest to Mosa Ford. Any of them could be one of his people, sent to deal out the threats he's made to ensure obedience from whoever it is he has close to me.'

He leaned back against the wall, shaking his head wearily.

'Most of my men have family in the city, and every one of them presents an opportunity for threats and coercion to a man as ruthless as he is, so any one of them might be his agent, willing or not. The only answer that I can see is to find this Obduro and remove his head from his shoulders in the time-honoured fashion, and to do it in such a way as not to show the dice I'm rolling until they hit the table.'

The tribune stood and walked across to the map.

'And given that I'm the commander of the only battle-experienced unit that's available to help you, I think we'd better start coming up with ways to impose ourselves on this particular gang's freedom of action. As you say, you've been reacting to him for the last few months, and searching for him without any result. I'm guessing that my fourteen hundred men have much more chance of finding him than your thirty.'

Caninus pointed at the forest's dark mass, dominating the southern half of the map.

'The only place to take the fight to him is in there. But be careful, Tribune. Arduenna has a justifiable reputation for being dangerous for the unprepared, especially at this time of year. It may be spring, but winter can return to the forest in an instant.'

He touched the amulet on his right wrist in a reflexive gesture, and Scaurus nodded solemnly.

'I see you are a believer in Mithras Unconquered. I'd be grateful of a chance to worship alongside you, if the city has a temple? And you needn't worry, colleague. I'm not going to set a single foot into that maze of trees without your advice to guide me. And now I'd better go and see how my men are progressing with their building work.' He picked up his cloak and made to leave, but turned as he reached the door. 'By the way, you mentioned that you were sent here from Fortress Bonna. Is that where you were raised?'

Caninus shook his head, pointing to the spot on the map that was Tungrorum.

'No, Tribune, I'm a local boy, born and brought up here in the city. I travelled away from Tungrorum for several years in the imperial service, but when the chance came to return to my birthplace I jumped at it. Although, with hindsight, perhaps my decision would have been different had I known what I was stepping into.'

Scaurus nodded in sympathy.

'Never go back, eh?'

The prefect shook his head slowly.

'No, Tribune, it wasn't the coming back that was the mistake. My error was in having any expectation of the place being as I'd left it.'

The squadron parted to either side of the road, their hoof beats muffled by the soft ground as they cantered quickly to the west, their shields and spears held ready to fight. For long, anxious moments they rode steadily forward into the murk, unsure of what they might confront at any second, and with every moment the tension mounted. Marcus was starting to believe that they had missed the bandits in the mist, when a sharp-eyed rider on the right-hand side of the road pointed at the fields and shouted a warning to his decurion. Almost invisible in the fog, the indistinct shape of a grain cart was just discernible, with the figures of several men gathered around its rear apparently attempting to free a wheel from the track's thick mud. Marcus wheeled the big grey to face the bandits, swinging the spear's head down from its upright carrying position. The horse needed no further encouragement once it saw the weapon's wicked iron head drop into its field of vision, and it sprang forward across the field's heavy clay soil toward the robbers at the gallop, clods of earth flying up in its wake.

Faced with a wall of cavalrymen charging down on them out of the mist the bandits wavered for a moment and then turned to run, their attempts to flee reduced to little better than a stagger by the field's thick mud. Marcus picked a runner as the men scattered in all directions and rode him down, the cold iron blade stabbing brutally into the small of the man's back and punching him to the ground with a grunt. Tearing the blade free Marcus turned the horse in search of another target. He heard a horse's scream of distress and the sound of a rider hitting the ground hard, followed an instant later by a bellow of victory underlaid by a gurgling, agonised groan. Riding towards the noise he barely had time to react as a shaven-headed swordsman charged at him from out of the murk, a bloody blade held high and ready to strike at the horse's long nose. Stabbing out with the spear, Marcus rammed the weapon's iron head into the attacker's face, sending him reeling into the mud with both hands clutching at his shattered, bleeding features.

Having kept his seat by clinging to the enraged animal's neck, Marcus trotted the grey forward past another three grain carts, steering the horse around the bodies of dead and dying bandits. At the head of the short line of carts he found a tight knot of ten or so bandits in the middle of a circle of horsemen whose spears were lowered and ready to stab into them. Silus caught sight of him and rode over to speak face to face, keeping his voice low.

'Not bad with only one man down. I've given orders for him to be placed in one of the wagons, and perhaps if he lives long enough your woman can work her healing magic on him. As to this sorry collection of cut-throats, what do you think? Should we kill them here, or take them back to Tungrorum?'

Marcus grimaced.

'First things first, I'd say. We need to find out what they did with the carters, and where they were going with that grain. There may be more of them waiting for this lot to return, in which case . . .'

'We could clean out that nest of snakes as well. Good idea.' Silus turned to his men, bellowing an order to his deputy.

'Double Pay! Disarm them and get them kneeling in a line beside that cart, hands tied behind their backs and their knees hobbled.' He dismounted, and Marcus followed suit. 'You do realise that getting information out of them is going to get unpleasant?'

The Roman nodded, preoccupied with sliding the tip of his

dagger into a sack of grain and putting the grains that spilled from the small hole under his nose, recoiling slightly from their odour.

'*Qadir!*'

The chosen man led his mount across the field, kicking at the cart's wooden wheel to dislodge some of the mud clinging to his boots.

'Centurion?'

Marcus offered the grain to him, then watched as the Hamian put his nose to the kernels and breathed in slowly. Grimacing, he took one and popped it in his mouth, chewing it briefly before spitting the fragments out with a look of disgust.

'Tainted. Mould, I'd say. And with mouldy corn it's a coin toss as to whether you can eat it safely or not, never mind the foul taste. Get it wrong and you'll be sick for days, weak as a baby and rolling around in your own faeces. I'm surprised that any farmer would bother shipping this to Tungrorum. There's no way that an experienced buyer is going to give them anything for it.'

Marcus nodded his head to the tethered captives.

'And we may never know why they were bringing it to the city, unless one of these men can take us to any survivors of the robbery.' His chosen man raised an eyebrow. 'I know, it's not very likely, but . . .'

He led the Hamian across to where Silus was waiting for him, sword drawn and face appropriately grim as he stared up and down the line of terrified-looking bandits.

'Not so bloody brave now, are you? Well, I can make it worse for you, much worse. You've got a choice to make, you scum. You can either die here, nice and quick, or you can choose to tell us what we want to know.'

One of the bandits looked up at him, his face twisted in defiance.

'What, and then you'll let us go, will you?'

Silus smiled broadly at him, walking across to his side.

'Excellent. There's always one man that wants to go first.' He nodded at the cavalryman standing in front of the line of kneeling men, and the soldier stepped forward, grabbed the defiant bandit's hair and used it to pull his head down, baring his neck for the sword. Silus put his spatha on the exposed flesh, sawing the rough sharpened blade backwards and forwards, the sword's weight exerting enough pressure on the skin to start a thin line of blood trickling down the helpless man's throat.

'Of course I'm not going to let you go, but at least you'll get to survive today, and who knows, if you sing loudly enough perhaps the procurator will spare you for assisting us?'

'Spare us? More likely he'll—'

Silus whipped up the blade, taking a quick breath with the upstroke before hacking down into the exposed neck with enough power to partially sever the man's head from his shoulders, then lifted the sword again to finish the job. The headless corpse toppled forward, blood still pumping from the stump of the dead man's neck. It sprayed the soldier with a hot jet that made him drop the man's head and fumble to wipe his eyes clean. Bending, Silus picked up the head by the hair, scowling at the man whose job it had been to hold it. He raised the bloody, mud-spattered trophy, giving the other bandits a good long look at their comrade. The faces reflected fear, hate, but mostly the numb realisation that they would face the same fate soon enough. Marcus watched from the side of the line, his thoughts racing as he considered the murder of the helpless prisoner.

'So, one man wanted to die here, in this muddy field, with no one to spare him a coin for the ferryman. Does anyone else feel the same need to leave this life here and now? Or would any of you like to talk, and spare the rest of us having to go through this ritual until you're all dead? No?'

He nodded to the soldier, who gripped the next man's hair and turned his face away while the decurion braced himself with a two-handed grip on the weapon's hilt and inhaled quickly. The sword rose and fell in one clean blow this time, and Silus nodded to himself.

'It seems I'm getting the hang of this. Anyone want to talk? No? Very well.'

He stepped up to the next man down the line, raising the blade as the soldier once again took a grip of the victim's hair. Tensing himself for the downstroke the decurion took another quick breath of air, but held off from delivering the fatal blow as the helpless man beneath his sword let out a creaking moan of desperation and audibly soiled himself. Silus grinned at the terrified bandit, wrinkling his nose at the sudden stench of terror.

'Nobody wants to die on an empty stomach. Perhaps I'm not being fair.' He looked sideways at the man on the far side of the first bandit to die, watching as the colour drained from his face. 'After all, I started in the middle of the line; perhaps I should have chosen the man on the other side to go third.' He beckoned to the soldier holding down the bandit's head to raise it, allowing him to see the victim's face. 'What do you think? Fairer to go the other way for a bit?' The captive goggled up at him wordlessly, almost unable to comprehend his desperate circumstances, and Silus stroked his chin as if deep in thought. 'It does seem a bit lopsided.'

The decurion turned away from the bandit, beckoning his assistant to follow him, and the soldier released his grip on the prisoner's hair. Reprieved, the helpless man fell forward into the mud and started to cry like a baby, watching as the decurion moved up the line. He gestured to the soldier, who grabbed his new victim's copper-hued hair and dragged him forward, ready for the killing stroke. Silus lifted the sword, and stood over the man, waiting patiently for some reaction. After a moment his victim turned his head as much as he could, given the harsh grip on his hair, and snarled at his executioner.

'Get it done!'

The decurion looked down at him with a gentle smile.

'Now there's a man with a pair of balls I can respect. You're not going to shit yourself any time soon, are you? I can't kill this man; he deserves a better exit than a quick hack in a muddy field. No, let's go back to the other one.'

His original victim, still lying in the field's cold mud, gave out a shrill squeal of horror.

'No! No, not me! I'll tell you anything you want to know! *Anything!*'

The redhead spat his anger into the soil.

'Shut your mouth! There're good men will die if you betray them, and we're dead whatever happens, here or in some—'

Silus whirled around, hacking off his head in one swift movement before turning back to the weeping bandit with a tight smile.

'No one likes to be interrupted when they're speaking. You were saying . . .?'

When the legion column arrived on the scene, Tribune Belletor found Marcus and a handful of soldiers stacking the dead bandits by the roadside, the badly wounded Tungrian having been wrapped in his cloak and laid in the rearmost cart for transport back to the city.

'What's happened here, Centurion. Some sort of battle?'

Marcus briefed him on the short action, watching as the tribune looked about him at the carnage wrought upon the bandits with an expression of mixed horror and distaste. The senior officer's glance chanced upon the three headless victims of Silus's interrogation, and his face creased into an unhappy frown.

'Those men appear to have been beheaded?'

Marcus nodded, his face impassive.

'Field interrogation, Tribune. The remainder of the squadron is running the rest of the band to ground based on the information gained.'

'That's *not* acceptable, Centurion.' He shook his head angrily, and Marcus waited for him to continue, wondering if the legion officer was a more humane man than his reputation indicated. 'Look at their arms!' Marcus realised that Belletor had spotted the slave brands on the dead men's arms. 'No, each of these men is someone's property. My father farms a large estate in Italy, so I know the value of good slaves.'

'Good slaves, Tribune?'

Belletor, missing the acerbic note in the young centurion's voice, smiled tightly at him.

'Fit men, good for decades of hard work if managed the right way. It's not the army's job to bring judgement on these animals; that's a job for their masters. A good overseer will make such a man pay for his crimes in manifold ways, and deliver his value to the farm. That's got to be better than just hacking off his head and leaving him to rot in the mud, eh?'

Marcus nodded quickly, recognising an argument he could not hope to win.

'Indeed, Tribune. Now if you'll excuse me, I'll get these carts on the road to Tungrorum.'

Belletor's response was suddenly hard-edged, brooking no argument.

'No need, Centurion. First Minervia will escort this cargo back to the city's grain store. And you can get that soldier out of the rearmost cart. I'll not have the emperor's grain spoiled by a dying man's blood.'

Marcus spun back, fighting to keep a hold of his temper at the harsh words.

'Tribune, I've taken a sample from each cart. My family used to deal in grain, which led me to examine the contents of the bags. I found that the grain is already useless, spoiled by mould. Also, I believe that my man may live long enough to reach our doctor if I keep him on his back, and the only way to do that is to—'

Belletor shook his head.

'Unacceptable, Centurion. Your man will have to take his chances on horseback. I *will* have this grain away to the store before any other brigands decide to have their way with it.'

He turned away to his own men, bellowing orders for the march to their centurions. Marcus clenched his fist and tensed himself to put a hand on Belletor's shoulder, but found himself restrained by a firm grip on his sleeve. He turned to find Qadir standing behind him, the Hamian shaking his head in admonishment. He leaned close, speaking quietly in the Roman's ear.

'Since your friend Rufius died you have lacked a man to restrain you from those dark impulses that will be the ruin of everything you have left in this world. In the absence of a man with whose opinion you will readily agree, allow me to present the next best thing.' He bowed slightly. 'Your friend, who would rather see you grow to your full potential in the shadows than burn fiercely for a short time, but in doing so attract the attention of powerful men. And not only to himself.'

The Roman nodded slowly, his anger subsiding to a dull ache in the pit of his stomach.

'Thank you. The tribune wants our man off the grain cart. Do you think he'll . . .'

'Our man is already dead. The wound was too severe. I have placed the coin between his lips, and asked our comrades to place him upon his horse with whatever dignity we can give him.'

A wan, wry smile touched Marcus's lips momentarily.

'As well that you restrained me, then. I would have chinned that aristocratic fool to no purpose.'

Qadir smiled back at him darkly.

'"Chinned?" I'll wager you didn't learn that at some philosophy tutor's knee.'

His friend shook his head.

'No, I was gifted the term by the freed gladiator my father employed to train me to fight with bare knuckles, in readiness for that time when there's no other choice. Every fallen son of privilege should have had one. Now, let's gather our dead and get back to Tungrorum.' He opened his clenched fist, revealing a handful of the tainted grain. 'I think Tribune Scaurus is going to be interested in this.'

3

Forewarned by a rider sent on ahead by Marcus, Scaurus was waiting at the west gate with Julius when the small party of riders led by his centurion shepherded their captives into the city.

'More prisoners for your cells, eh, Procurator? We'll have to have a meeting as to what to do with them all.'

Albanus snorted derisively.

'You can crucify the lot of them here and now as far as I'm concerned.'

Marcus climbed down from his horse, allowing a soldier to lead the big animal away. He snapped out a smart salute to the two men, giving Scaurus a significant look as he reached into his pouch for a tablet.

'Excuse me, sir, but I carry *instructions* from Tribune Belletor. The tribune is following us in with four cart loads of grain that these bandits intercepted eight miles to the east of the city, presumably from one of the local farms although most of the men who were bringing it here were murdered by the bandits. Most of it seems to have been spoiled by mould. He instructed me to escort these prisoners to the city's slave quarters and place them under guard there, to await being claimed by their owners.'

Scaurus raised an eyebrow at Albanus.

'Does that sound right to you, Procurator? These men are bandits. They were caught in the act, I presume, Centurion?' Marcus nodded. 'And therefore their lives are forfeit. I find my colleague's idea that the protection of private property should come before the administering of justice more than a little surprising.'

Albanus shrugged, as if the matter was of little interest to him.

'Their lives are indeed in the empire's hands, Tribune. Whether the empire then chooses simply to take their lives or return them to their rightful owners for a lengthier punishment is a topic for further discussion. For the time being you must do with them whatever you feel best. My priority now is to ensure the safe receipt and storage of the recovered grain.' He turned to Marcus. 'Tell me, Centurion, were there any survivors from the carters from whom the theft was made?'

'One sir. He managed to escape the initial attack, and then ran for his life.'

The procurator pursed his lips.

'Just one? A lucky man, I'd say.'

Scaurus raised an enquiring eyebrow.

'So you'll be keen to speak to him, I expect? You'll want to know who to pay the fee to for the corn that's been recovered.'

Albanus shook his head.

'Not if it's mouldy. I'll have it quarantined to prevent any fool from trying to sell it or feed it to an animal, but there'll be no payment made for inedible grain.'

Scaurus nodded his understanding at the other man.

'Commendable, Procurator; no payment for food that can't be consumed. Although that does tend to make me wonder why anyone would be bothering to bring four carts of the stuff here when there was no way they were going to get paid for it. Come on, then, let's have a look at this rather impressive grain warehouse of yours. I must admit that I'm curious to see such a magnificent building. You won't mind if I bring these two officers along for a look, will you?'

'You've never seen anything half the size! It was huge! The whole of our fortress at the Hill would fit inside it, and the walls were lined with granaries each twice the size of a barrack block. And half of them full of grain sacks. Enough grain to feed a legion for a year, or so that oily civilian bastard was saying.'

The other men in the tent had learned over the years to treat everything that the soldier they knew as Scarface said with a degree of caution, but the story he was telling them had every man's attention. They stared at him in the dim lamp light, although not every face was entirely friendly. The tent party's other veteran soldier, Sanga, a man with whom Scarface had sparred for unofficial leadership of the group over the course of several years, was sneering at him from the other end of the enclosed space.

'So while we was working ourselves into the ground putting up barracks, you was skiving off "with the tribune". There wasn't a certain centurion wearing two swords involved, by any chance, was there?'

One of the two Hamian members of the eight-man tent party giggled into his hand. After the decision by a number of Syrians to stay with the cohort, Marcus and Qadir had decided to fully integrate them with the existing members of the century rather than have any hint of 'them and us' between the veterans and their new comrades. Scarface snorted his derision, poking the Hamian in the chest with a scarred and calloused finger, although not hard enough to give genuine offence.

'Less of your tittering, pretty boy, else I'll have to give you a slap. I was detailed to escort the officers along with three other blokes standing guard on the wall. And yes, as it happens, both Latrine and Two Knives were there.'

He stared hard at the older man, but if his comrade was intimidated there was no sign of it, and his reply dripped with scorn.

'Of *course* Two Knives was there. What was it that Latrine called you when we took the Fortress of the Spears? Oh yes, I remember; he said you was "following *him* round like a love-struck goat herd". I reckon Centurion Corvus must wonder whether it was the doctor he married or you!'

Scarface raised an eyebrow at him, injecting a note of disappointment into his reply.

'That miserable bastard Julius was just annoyed 'cause we got to go up the hill and see the dead Selgovae that the one-eyed barbarian hacked the cocks off, and he didn't. That's why he had a go at me. And you've forgotten our agreement, have you, then? Us veterans, the front rank, the cream of the century? Didn't we agree to keep an eye on that young gentleman and make sure he don't come to no harm? Or are you too good to honour your promise, eh, Sanga?'

Called on his oath, the other soldier prevaricated.

'I ain't forgot it, I just ain't so sure that young gentleman needs much looking after. If it came to swords and boards he'd have you *and* me face down in the dirt double quick, and not even be breathing hard when it was done. And he got his woman with child, what'll give him a reason to wind his neck in. This watching of his back might have run its time, I reckon.'

He put out his chin defiantly, waiting to see how Scarface would jump. His tent mate shook his head, reaching for his sharpening stone and picking the dagger from his belt order.

'Not the way I see it. You fought alongside me at the battle of the rebel camp, so you saw how bad he took it when poor old Rufius got his head stuck on a spear. You've seen his face when the rage takes him.' He bent over the dagger, running the stone along its blade with a slow, satisfying rasp. 'Once something's got him that angry he don't stop to work out the odds, or wonder if he might be best backing off; he just jumps in with them swords flying. I ain't so sure that him being married to the doctor or her having a kid's going to change that. So are you still in, or when the shit starts flying am I going to look around and find you ain't there?'

The other man nodded slowly, his gaze fixed on Scarface, and their audience breathed out a collective breath with the confrontation's apparent relaxation.

'I'll be there, but to back *you* up, mate, not to look out for an officer with a death wish.'

'Good enough for me. So, this grain store, see, it's huge. The size of—'

'Yes, bigger than the Hill, you said. Big long walls lined with granaries.'

'And yet . . .' Scarface paused, ostentatiously waiting for any further interruption. 'And yet once we get inside, the tribune, the centurions and me, well, the tribune, he whispers something to the centurion. And Two Knives, he walks off down the length of the store nice and slow. Like he's after having a nice quiet look at the place without wanting it to be obvious, while the tribune starts asking the civilian questions about the place. But our young gentleman only does twenty paces before the old bloke that runs the place is after him like a dog on a rabbit, going on about needing felt overshoes over his hobnails to go in the granaries, and how they ain't got any to spare, begging the officer's pardon. So our boy just turns round and comes back as sweet as you like, and him and Latrine and the tribune, they look at each other like they've got the result they were looking for. Though what it was beats me.'

In the large tent that he shared with his wife, Felicia, Marcus was slumped in a camp chair while Felicia unlaced his muddy and blood-spattered boots, tossing the first of the pair onto the pile for cleaning. His mail shirt and weapons were already piled in one corner, awaiting the attentions of Lupus, Morban's grandson. 'Get that tunic off and I'll put it in cold water. It's a good thing it's not your nice white one.'

She slyly glanced up at him to gauge his response, but found him staring at the tent's wall, his expression dulled by whatever was happening behind his eyes. After a moment he realised that she was silent, and started guiltily.

'I'm sorry, I was miles away. What were you saying?'

Felicia tossed the second boot aside and slowly stood up, her pregnancy now a visible bulge in her stola.

'Your tunic.'

She held out a hand, waiting while he stripped it off to reveal his pale torso, the muscles finely sculpted by the unremitting daily exercise of carrying his armour and equipment.

'Put this one on.'

He raised an eyebrow.

'The white one?'

'It looks good on you, and all the others are still damp. You can't hide it away just because it's your best.'

He smiled at her and stood, pulling on the garment and adjusting its belt to ensure that the hem was above his knees, then took her in his arms.

'I hide it away because it's the one I wore when we got married.' She smiled back, poking at a faded stain in the pale wool.

'As if we'll ever forget, since we have the evening's wine to remind us.' He winced, remembering the raucous carousing he and his brother officers had enjoyed that night, after Felicia had gone to bed and sent him back to join them. She smiled again, tugging his ear affectionately. 'You had a lot of bad memories to deal with, and if the price of doing so was a few stains on a tunic I'd say it was good value.'

'I killed again today.'

Her smile softened.

'I know, my love. I can always tell, whether there's blood on your armour or not. You may be a natural with your swords, but you're not hardened to the results of using them, are you?'

Marcus shook his head.

'Not only did I kill today, but I watched while Silus murdered three men in cold blood to make the fourth tell us where the rest of their gang was camped out. Yes, I know –' he raised his hands to forestall her response – 'they were bandits, and they'd murdered a farmer and his men not long before, so they deserved their fate. And yet . . .'

'And yet it seems you're gradually becoming hardened to this life? Even if you could not kill a man in cold blood yourself, you watched another man do so without intervening? You fear that in becoming strong enough to defeat your enemies, you will perhaps become so like them that you risk losing that part of yourself that your father sought to make strongest? After all, you've told me often enough how he always stressed decency to your fellow man when he spoke to you about how a man should live.'

Her husband nodded, looking to the tent's roof as he sought the memory of his father's words, spoken in the precious days before imperial scheming had seen the senator and his family murdered, and their estate confiscated by the jealous and grasping men arrayed behind the young emperor.

'"Dignity, truthfulness, tenacity, but above all, whenever you are able to exercise it, mercy." That's what he used to tell me whenever our conversation turned to the ethics that a member of the senate should live by. Slowly but surely I feel my grasp on his teachings sliding away from me. With every enemy I put to the sword I am a little less of the man he raised, and a little more like the men who destroyed our family.'

Felicia hugged him again, whispering in his ear.

'I'll never allow you to become anything like the men that performed those dreadful acts, and nor will your friends. But you will only survive this nightmare if you can harden yourself to do whatever you must to stay alive, and to protect those close to you.'

The tent's flap opened, and Arminius put his head through it. Seeing the couple in each other's arms he raised a hand and started to back away, but Felicia beckoned him to come in.

'Exactly what my husband needs: a friend to take him for a drink and listen to the story of his day.'

Arminius squeezed through the flap, pushing the boy Lupus in front of him then bowing to the doctor and grinning at his friend.

'The drink we can probably manage, eventually. The tribune sent me to fetch you, Centurion. There's a ritual being held in Prefect Caninus's temple tonight, and we're respectfully invited to attend. I'd suggest you wear your cloak though; there's a bitter wind out here that will cut you to the bone without it. And *you*, boy . . .' He tapped Lupus on the shoulder as the child stood staring in dismay at Marcus's soiled equipment. 'You can get stuck into this lot. I want to see it all gleaming when we come back, and make sure you get every speck of blood off those rings. Don't forget that it's your birthday in a few days, and if you keep the centurion's gear in the right condition you'll see the benefit soon enough. Do a good job of it and we'll practise with sword and shield in the morning, make a proper fight of it.'

The boy nodded glumly and sat down among the pile of gear, pulling the rags and brushes he needed from his bag, resigned to the usual nightly routine of cleaning armour and polishing boots that was the price of his morning training sessions with the German. Marcus pulled his cloak around him, picking his vine stick up from the bed.

'Very well, let's go and see what sort of temple to Our Lord Tungrorum boasts. It'll have to be something special to match the one at Badger Holes.'

Arminius laughed, shaking his head.

'Just like a soldier. Everything you people have just has to be the best, doesn't it? You get more like Julius every day.'

Marcus shrugged, pinning his cloak into place.

'There are worse men to emulate.'

The German smiled wryly back at him.

'Just as long as you don't go off into town at night with a pocket full of gold on the hunt for paid company. He was heading out as we walked past the Fifth Century's tents, looking cleaner than I think I've ever seen the man. He's even trimmed his beard.'

Marcus frowned at the German.

'How do you know about Annia's profession?'

Arminius smiled in reply.

'I didn't, until you just told me. You must be tired to have let that slip. No . . .' He shook his head to forestall his friend's irritation. 'It'll stay between us. So the good centurion has a friend from his former life here, does he?'

Felicia raised an eyebrow at him.

'And you'd deny him the opportunity for a little happiness?'

Arminius shook his head.

'Never. But love and money don't mix, in my experience. Your friend may be taking a path that ends in disappointment. And he's not a man that responds well to not getting his own way.'

Julius found the brothel without much trouble, following the directions he'd been given by the men delivering the centurions' mess wine ration. Their foreman had smiled knowingly at the big

Tungrian when he'd asked the question, nodding and agreeing that he knew the establishment the gentleman had in mind, but adding that he'd best bring a heavy purse if he intended sampling the Blue Boar's merchandise.

He paused down the street, watching quietly from the shadows as a pair of men knocked on the door beneath the brothel's flickering lamps, spoke briefly to whoever was behind it and then stepped inside, the heavy wooden door closing swiftly behind them. The sound of bolts sliding home echoed harshly in the otherwise empty street. Tempted to walk away, and to pretend the chance meeting with his former love had never happened, the big man gritted his teeth and strode forward into the light, knocking firmly on the door's stout timbers with his vine stick, the only thing approximating to a weapon he'd carried with him from his tent. A viewing slit protected by iron mesh, slid open, and appraising eyes appeared in its opening, a familiar grating voice speaking after a short pause.

'Well, now, look who we have here. Brave of you to come to this door, soldier boy, given that one word from me would set a gang of the ugliest bastards you've ever seen loose on you. Still carrying your sword?'

Julius shook his head, keeping his face free of any hint of irritation at the bodyguard's air of superiority.

'I was a bit quick to react in the forum, so I've come to make my peace. With the lady, and with you and your mate. I just want to drink a cup of wine and have a talk with her, for old time's sake, and I'd be pleased to extend the same courtesy to you. There was no need for me to treat you so harshly, when all you were doing was what you're paid for. Officer or not, I'm not too proud to admit when I'm wrong.'

The bodyguard regarded him through the slit's stout iron mesh for a moment, then stepped back and slid the door's bolts from their recesses, whistling sharply as he did so. When the door opened there were three doormen waiting for him, all with the professionally expressionless faces of men disappointed with life's inability to prevent the brave and the foolish from presenting them with challenges that were only to be met with swift and brutal violence. The man he'd bested in the forum beckoned him inside, then opened his hands in the universally understood gesture to prepare for a search, and Julius stood patiently while the bodyguard's colleagues ran their hands over his body in a swift, competent and comprehensive search. They stepped back, and the thin man from the forum confrontation shook his head with a vague air of disappointment.

'Nothing, not even a small knife strapped to his dick. Unless he's got a spear hidden up his arse, this one's spotlessly clean. Although I'm not sure I like the look of that stick.'

Julius smiled, raising his vine stick and shrugging.

'Wherever I go, it goes. There're plenty of disrespectful young fucks in my century would like nothing better than to find this and hide it away, or burn it in a brazier, to get back at me for all the times I've beaten some respect into them with it. This one's been with me all the time I've been a centurion, and seen me through three battles with barbarians in the last year, so I've become attached to it. But I'll surrender it, if you like?'

The bodyguard laughed, shaking his head and waving his comrades away.

'There's more than enough of us to manage one soldier, and we've got every weapon ever invented hidden away around the place. I don't think a length of wood is going to trouble us too much. You, Baldy, go and tell the mistress that her friend from the forum's come to visit.' He leaned close to Julius, his breath smelling of wine and spiced food. 'Now then, Centurion Julius, your apology was a good one, and I accept it, so welcome to the Blue Boar, the best, the most expensive and the most exclusive whorehouse in Tungrorum. Behave nicely with the mistress, drink your wine like a gentleman, buy some time with one of the girls if you like, but just remember I'll be watching you. One sign of trouble and your apology will go up your arse, along with that fucking stick. You're a hard man, that's clear, and I can see your scars all right, but I'll have you dealt with right harsh if there's any bother, right?'

Julius looked the bodyguard in the eye and held out his hand.

'Right. I may be stupid and hot-tempered, but I never make the same mistake twice. You'll have no trouble from me. Might I know your name?'

The bodyguard nodded slowly, taking the offered clasp in a firm, cool grip.

'I go by the name of Slap. Been called it so long I almost can't remember what my old mum actually called me when I fell out of her.'

'Slap?'

'On account of what I do when it gets late in the evening, and the wine starts to do the talking and makes the customers do things they'd never normally consider. I'm the slap man, the one that gives them a gentle tickle with this.' He held up a big fist, the knuckles liberally decorated with scars. 'And it usually calms things down right quickly. And if not, there's always my mate, Stab.' He tipped his head to the thin man, who stood with a smirk on his face in front of the curtain that Julius guessed led into the brothel. 'He's the one who grabbed your cock to make sure you weren't carrying iron, although I think he secretly just likes grabbing cock.'

Julius shook his head, unable to keep a smile from his face.

'Slap and Stab, eh? I'll have to introduce you to my mates Knuckles and the Badger. You'd get on like a house on fire. Oh, and my "name" is Latrine. You can probably work it out.'

The underground temple was already almost full of worshippers when Marcus and Arminius walked down the steps and into the chamber's torchlit gloom, having first passed inspection by the Raven-grade initiates at the top of the stairs. Flicking back the cloak hood that had protected his anonymity, as required by the ritual, Marcus looked with interest at the temple's crowded space. Nearly thirty men were packed into the chamber's tight confines, and Arminius had to crane his neck to spot Scaurus through the press. Driving a politely insistent path through the crowded subterranean room the muscular, long-haired barbarian nodded and smiled at the other worshippers, hiding his amusement behind a blank expression as they shrank out of his way. Marcus followed him, keeping an eye on both sides of the big man's path and watching as the disturbed worshippers, clearly men of money and reputation for the most part, cast angry glances after the German, their muttered asides clearly not complimentary. One or two of them caught Marcus's eye, and most of them averted their gaze on seeing his frosty expression, although one man in particular returned the stare impassively, a gaze the young Roman found hard to read.

He looked down the rectangular room, catching a glimpse of an impressive stone frieze fully six feet high and the same in width. The two-inch-thick slab of marble was sculpted with the familiar image of Mithras slaying the bull in the cave into which he had carried it at the end of his long hunt, the main scene surrounded by lavish carvings of the images associated with each of the religion's seven grades. Scaurus turned as Arminius and Marcus reached his side, and, as was always the case in temple, clasped the two men's arms as equals, any hint of their formal relationship put aside in the worship of their god. Scaurus's brow was decorated with the laurel wreath befitting his status as a Lion, the fourth most senior of the religion's ranks. Prefect Caninus echoed the gesture of greeting with both men, his smile of welcome reassuring amid the congregation's obvious hostility.

'You're just in time, my brothers. The priest is about to start the ceremony. Here, we've saved you both a space.'

Marcus looked about him, realising that most of the worshippers were either men in late middle age or boys barely old enough to shave. He leaned closer to Scaurus, not wanting his remark to be overheard.

'A different congregation to that I'd expected.'

The tribune nodded, his reply equally subtle in tone.

'Our colleague Caninus tells me that the city has been somewhat underdeveloped in commercial terms ever since the plague killed a third of its inhabitants. Any bright young lad that wants to get on tends to head west to Beech Forest, or east to the fortresses on the Rhenus. What you see here are the men that have managed to build successful business, and their sons, plus a few senior people from the municipal authorities. First Minervia have their own temple, of course, which is why these men are all looking at us like men who've trodden barefoot on cold dog faeces. They're not happy to be worshipping alongside the men who're bleeding their city white, even if we are brothers in Our Lord, and despite the fact that we're here for their protection. Ah, there's our good friend Procurator Albanus, and the stone-faced character to his right is Petrus, his assistant. I'm still working out which one of them is the real—'

'Gentlemen, please take your places! The ritual is about to begin!'

The temple's pater stood in front of the magnificent stone frieze with his arms outstretched to either side, while his acolytes moved out into the room to darken the chamber, as demanded by the ritual. The worshippers settled down onto the stone benches that lined both long sides of the temple, reclining horizontally and propping themselves up on their elbows as the pater watched his assistants take the torches down from their iron wall loops and walk them away up the temple's steps, the light receding up the stairs in bright haloes until the only remaining source of illumination was a single small lamp which an acolyte, almost invisible in his dark red garments, placed reverently in the priest's hands. After a moment of utter silence, the only sound that of his congregation breathing in the darkness, the pater raised the pinpoint of flame to illuminate his face, his eyes closed against the flame's brightness. He blew out the lamp, and the temple chamber was plunged into complete darkness. Marcus's keen ears picked up a faint rustle from behind the frieze, and then a soft halo of light appeared to surround the marble slab. A point of light rose into view; it came from a small lamp carried by an acolyte, and as he deposited it before the frieze the tiny flame breathed gentle life into the picture it portrayed. The temple's pater spoke again, still invisible in the darkness.

'Beloved brothers, and welcome visitors from beyond our city's walls, we now join in the ritual of our beloved Lord, Mithras the Unconquered, who spilled the eternal blood of the bull at the command of Sol, God of the Sun, to save us all. Let us pray that he looks down on us from his place in the heavens with the Sun God, and give thanks for all the wonders he has given us.'

'You took a big chance coming here, Centurion. It's a good thing I suspected you'd appear at our door sometime soon, and persuaded my business partner's men to go easy on you if you did. Or would you have taken them on with your bare hands and that stick?'

Annia nodded to Julius's vine stick, laid carefully on the table before him, and the big man smiled ruefully.

'Probably not, given the size of them.'

He tipped his head to Slap, standing in the room's corner and carefully positioned to be within listening distance whilst giving the illusion of some privacy, and the big man smirked back at him. Annia shook her head at him with a gentle smile.

'Exactly. Although you never were a man for thinking through the consequences of your actions, were you? But you're here, so let's see if we can't entertain you. Girls!' She snapped her fingers with the manner of a woman who was used to having her commands obeyed, and a line of five women emerged from behind a curtain where they had clearly been waiting for the evening's customers. Eyeing them appreciatively, Julius found himself hardening despite having no intention of sampling the brothel's wares. Annia smiled knowingly, leaning forward to stroke his erect manhood through the tunic's fine wool. 'Well, some things never change. If anything I'd say that's got a little bigger. Clearly some things do improve with age. Will you partake of a little enjoyment, Centurion, on the house, of course? It must be a long time since you've had the opportunity to ride anything quite as soft and eager to please as my girls.'

Julius surveyed the line of women for a moment, noting with a smile how neatly any and every taste was catered for. From a skinny girl scarcely old enough to be considered fit for her role, her apple-sized breasts barely hidden beneath a skimpy shift, to a mature woman in the last flush of her beauty, ripe and sultry with heavy breasts and a face that promised a lifetime's experience, any age of female company a man might desire was paraded before him. He swallowed, painfully aware of both his own arousal and the woman's cool, amused eyes upon him.

'I came to talk, Annia, not to . . .'

'Not to fuck? You're a collector's item, Centurion, an outright rarity. We have the occasional men that pay simply to have the company of a pretty girl, but they tend to be the older men whose cocks have lost their bounce, not fighting bulls like you with their pricks standing at attention. I'll bet you wouldn't last thirty seconds in the hands of Helvia there.' She gestured to the oldest of the women, who winked on cue and slid a finger down into her vagina's hairy cleft with a winsome smile. Julius's face must have been a picture, for Annia burst into a peal of uncontrollable laughter. For a moment he was fifteen years old again, with that same laugh thrilling him as she climbed on top of him in one of their hiding places. She reached out and squeezed his penis again, and watched with a smile as he fought to retain control. 'See. You very nearly released yourself into that nice tunic, and all you've had so far is a wink and a gentle squeeze. So . . .?'

She gestured to the line of prostitutes again, and with a feeling that he was going to regret the decision he shook his head firmly.

'Thank you, but I really did come to talk.' Taking a purse from his belt he opened its drawstring neck, rattling the heavy coins within. 'I can afford to pay for the privilege.'

Annia shook her head, pushing the purse away and ignoring the intake of breath from the bodyguard behind her.

'There'll be no need for that. I'm not given to fucking the customers these days, not unless they're queuing out of the door, and even then I charge an eye-watering sum for the pleasure. Ownership does have some benefits, and mine is being able to be choosy as to when and with whom I get on my back. So, what would you like to discuss? Just what is it that you think we have to talk about, given the way we parted, and the fact that we've not laid eyes on each other for fifteen years?'

Julius shook his head sadly, and when he spoke his voice was that of a man utterly lost.

'I don't know.'

One of the temple's Raven initiates walked solemnly down the double line of reclining worshippers, bowing deeply to Scaurus in honour of the laurel wreath that decorated his brow.

'Forgive me, brother Lion, but there is a man at the temple door who claims he is one of your officers. Apparently there is some trouble in the city.'

Scaurus nodded to his companions and stood up, abandoning his half-eaten ceremonial meal and bowing to the expectant priest who had appeared at the Raven's shoulder.

'You must forgive me, Pater, earthly matters demand my attention. I will spend an hour in prayer to repay our Lord Mithras for this early departure.' He slipped a leather purse into the priest's hands. 'A gift, Pater, a small contribution for the maintenance of your most impressive temple. The reversible altar relief is quite masterful. You must have a generous and devoted congregation.'

The priest nodded with a quiet smile, used to visiting worshippers' amazement when the heavy stone relief depicting Mithras's triumph over the bull was rotated on the circular turntable on which it rested to reveal its equally skilfully depicted reverse, a carving of Mithras and Sol feasting on the dead bull's hide.

'My pleasure, brother Lion, and my regards to your companions. Mithras is a soldier's god, and I feel certain that he will indulge your need to restore order in the earthly realm above us. Please do grace us with your presence again, and bring that young man with you. Perhaps we can advance him a grade in the ordeal pit?'

Scaurus smiled in return, inclining his head in agreement.

'Indeed so, Pater, although when he took the hood last winter, while we were confined to camp by the snows, he threw himself into his studies with such gusto that he has already advanced to the rank of Bride, and his demeanour in the ordeal of ice brought great dignity to our Lord.'

The priest raised his eyebrows, apparently genuinely impressed.

'A man to watch, then? He'll join you in the fourth rank and become a Lion in no time. And now that's enough politeness, my son. Away with you. Who knows what mischief your children are up to while their father worships down here?'

Scaurus bowed to the priest again, muttering a brief apology to Caninus before leading the other two men away up the stairs behind the waiting Raven. Arminius paused at the foot of the steep flight of stone steps and flicked a glance around the room, noting with interest the look that the pater seemed to be sharing with Petrus, then he turned to follow his master, pulling a set of heavy brass knuckles from a pouch on his belt.

'Who do we have out on the town tonight?'

Arminius grinned at the tribune's question as they walked quickly down the road between shuttered houses, hearing the faint sounds of men fighting echo between the closely packed dwellings.

'That's the best bit. The lottery came up with the Third and Eighth Centuries.'

Marcus groaned, shaking his head in resigned disgust.

'The first two centuries allowed out, and one of them is stuffed full of Dubnus's bloody legionaries? This is going to get sporty.'

The bitterly cold wind was still whistling through the city's streets the next morning when all three cohorts paraded outside the walls to watch punishment being meted out to the captured bandits.

'There'll be some thick heads out there this morning. Serves the bastards right for getting the first evening in the city.' Marcus ignored Morban's morose grumbling, watching with amusement as Dubnus marched his century into position next to the 9th, his face still dark with anger at the previous evening's events. 'Perhaps now *he's* having second thoughts about having let a half-century of legion morons join up with us.'

His centurion shook his head in exasperation.

'Would those be the *legion morons* that saved my wife's life last autumn, Standard Bearer? Perhaps your bitterness is rooted in the fact that you didn't think to lay odds on there being a fight in the city last night, despite the two centuries most likely to—'

He stopped speaking when he saw the smug look on Morban's face, and walked away with a look of disgust on his face. The Tungrian auxiliaries still regarded the men of Dubnus's 'detachment Habitus' with the ingrained jaundice that traditionally came to the surface whenever legionary and auxiliary came into close contact. He strolled down the line of the 9th Century's front rank, catching his friend's eye as the angry centurion stalked along the 8th's line, looking for any excuse to further berate his men. Dubnus raised a gloomy eyebrow and tapped his open palm with the vine stick gripped in his other hand, raking a meaningful stare across his soldiers, none of whom appeared to be meeting his eye. Marcus was forced to smile at the memory of his colleague, a man more used to finishing fights than starting them, laying about him with gusto when the brawling between his century's former legionaries and the men of the 1st Minervia had recommenced the previous night. The friends met at the junction between the two centuries' ranks, and Dubnus nodded glumly, speaking loudly enough for his men to hear.

'Thanks for your help last night. These fucking idiots would have taken on every bloody legionary in the city if we'd not given their chains a good jerk. One or two of them want to be careful they don't end up taking the places of those poor bastards.' He tipped his head at the small group of captured bandits awaiting their punishment under the watchful eyes of twice as many guards. Glancing across the lines of soldiers Marcus could see more than one man with a reproachful look on his face, and it was quickly clear that an incensed Dubnus had spotted them too.

'Don't be giving me the cow's eyes, you pricks! One insult, one little fucking jibe at your expense, and you thin-skinned idiots are up on your toes and ready to mix it with ten times your strength. And no, "they were taking the piss out of the cohort" does not get you off the hook, because it was you they were taking the piss out of – *you*, for deciding to serve with a bunch of uncivilised, shaggy-bearded barbarians in armour! You shat in your own beds and now you can bloody well lie in it, you collection of half-witted . . .'

He turned back to Marcus, shaking his head angrily. From somewhere within the century's ranks a quiet voice muttered the word 'Habitus', and half a dozen other men repeated the battle cry under their collective breath. Dubnus spun round to stare at them in fury, but found his men standing with their backs straight, their battered faces staring defiantly at him from between the cheek pieces of their helmets. Waving a hand at them in disgust he returned his attention to Marcus, barking a command over his shoulder.

'Shut the fuck up and wait, in silence, while I have a word with my colleague here. His men, you'll note, haven't said a bloody word since he dropped them into position. They're yours, Titus, so keep them quiet unless you want my undivided and very personal attention once we're off parade. And try not to start any more fights!'

His chosen man shot him a wounded glance from the century's rear, but wisely kept his mouth shut. For all that he'd been trying to separate the two warring groups of soldiers when the cohort's centurions had arrived on the scene, it was widely reported that he'd been one of the first men in the 8th Century to bridle when the legion troops had discovered their origins and started showering them with abuse for leaving legion service to fight with the Tungrians.

'You've created a monster, Dubnus. They won't back down from a fight for anyone, or so it seems, and you've only yourself to blame. It was you that took a half-century of men who'd run from their first fight and gave them their pride. You gave them a name to defend, and you told them to fight to the last man to preserve its honour. You can't be too disappointed when they take what you've told them and apply it literally. And the rest of your century got stuck in beside them.'

His friend nodded almost imperceptibly, turning back to stare bleakly across the sea of battered faces facing him and shaking his head at the black eyes and split lips liberally scattered across the ranks.

'I can't let them see it, but I'm proud of them for it. Three full legion centuries facing up to forty-odd men and they didn't back down. Mind you, I've got to respect the rest of the century, and the Badger's boys from the Third; they piled in alongside the Habitus lads without a second's hesitation. It was a good thing we got there in time, or there'd have been blood on the cobbles the way it was heating up. Anyway, what are you grinning for?'

Marcus started, suddenly aware of his lopsided smile.

'I was just thinking back to the way that our quiet and shy Selgovae tribesman dived into the fight last night. He's another one to watch out for.'

'He's a big arrogant bastard, that's for sure, but I've no room for complaint on that front. And he did put that little squabble to sleep in no time flat.'

Half of the cohort's centurions, led by Tribune Scaurus and accompanied by Arminius and the giant Lugos, who had appeared at their side unbidden, had been forced to wade into the unbalanced fight between auxiliaries and legionaries, which had quickly swelled to fill the narrow street outside one of the city's seamier drinking establishments. Fighting to drive a wedge between the two sides, to force them apart and stop the fight, they had applied their vine sticks without restraint, literally beating apart the two halves of the brawl with brute force. As the two sides of the argument had seethed at each other across the thin line of authority represented by the centurions, Lugos had taken a legion soldier caught on the wrong side of the line of furious officers, held him by the scruff of his neck and literally hurled him bodily into the mass of his comrades. Shrugging off his cloak he'd turned to tower over the legionaries, his tattooed arms rippling as he'd clenched his massive fists and bellowed out a hoarse-voiced challenge that had silenced the bedlam of the encounter in an instant.

'You want fight? You fight me! *I fight you all!*'

His snort of disgust, and the disdainful way he'd turned his back to retrieve his cloak when not one of the legionaries had risen to the challenge, had signalled the brawl's end and left the bemused centurions to pick up the pieces.

'It's a shame that Martos still isn't accepting him on equal terms.'

Dubnus grimaced.

'I honestly don't think the big lad's all that bothered, do you? Besides, if the brother of the man that killed your father turned up here would you be quick to make him welcome? Lugos's people made a right mess of the Votadini, one way and another.'

They stood and watched as the remainder of the Tungrian centuries marched onto the parade ground, and after a few minutes Dubnus nudged Marcus, tipping his head at the senior officers standing to one side of the condemned men.

'I'll bet that's an interesting conversation after last night's excitement.'

Marcus laughed hollowly.

'You wouldn't even get Morban to take that bet.'

The senior officers stood in a small group watching the soldiers make their way onto the parade ground, the two tribunes side by side, while Procurator Albanus and Prefect Caninus stood a discreet distance from their colleagues in the well-founded expectation that the two military men had plenty to discuss after the events of the previous night. The two first spears and the civilian officer's various deputies and aides gathered in a group behind them, Albanus's deputy, Petrus, prominent amongst them, while both Frontinius and Sergius were treating the other members of the party with a hint of shared military disdain. Tribune Belletor watched the Tungrian centuries marching up with a mixture of envy and irritation, his face set hard as he turned to speak to Scaurus, who was watching his men's crisp precision with a quiet smile.

'It's all very well for you to smile, colleague. I've got several men in the hospital this morning because your animals don't understand the limits of off-duty behaviour. I'm told that your men were fighting with coins between their knuckles!'

To his indignation, Scaurus laughed tersely in the face of his colleague's anger.

'Then you can be thankful that *my* officers managed to calm it all down before it got to the point where knives were drawn, colleague. Your legionaries clearly need to learn not to take liberties with men who've seen the ugly face of battle all too recently.'

Belletor seethed with anger.

'I beg to differ. If you can't restrain your men then I suggest you keep them in their barracks. Or do you presume to tell me that my legionaries have to make allowances for your men's inability to differentiate between savages and citizens?'

Scaurus spoke without taking his eyes off his men, his voice perfectly level despite his obvious irritation.

'Oh they can tell the difference between blooded fighting men and tiros, of that you can be sure, because if they couldn't we'd be burying men this morning. And, since you don't seem to see the need to control the number of your legionaries that are allowed into the city each night, I'm going to have to keep everyone, your men and my own, in barracks after dark. We'll have to come up with a rota to determine which centuries are allowed to spend their money getting drunk, and when.'

Belletor stared at him in dumbfounded silence, taking a long moment to find his voice again.

'By *what* right . . .?'

Scaurus smiled at him thinly.

'If you think I'm going to keep two cohorts of men who've all seen battle in the last few weeks, who've all killed, and seen their comrades die in agony, confined to barracks so that a collection of raw recruits and time-expired veterans who should know better can get pissed every night, you've even less intelligence than I'd supposed to be the case. Between us we have twenty-six centuries, your six and ten in each of my . . .' He paused, shaking his head at his own error. 'Twenty-five centuries, since I had one of mine destroyed to the last man in Britain. So we'll allow one-fifth of our strength into the city every night, which will let them all have a beer every few days. We'll segregate them by cohort, so your six centuries will get one night in five and half of each of my ten-century cohorts will get the same.'

Belletor shook his head.

'And what if I refuse to accept this outlandish proposal?'

Scaurus shrugged.

'I'd be more interested in the "why" than the "what". Why would you even consider rejecting something so eminently sensible, and equitable for that matter? Are you frightened of losing face with your officers? Or is it just a question of your own expectations of what a man of your rank ought to do, under the circumstances?' Belletor stared at him in silence. 'I see. So even you're not really sure. As to what happens if you choose to reject this perfectly sound piece of advice, that's simple enough. I'll be forced to use my military seniority and declare the city off limits to all military personnel, with a strict rotation of off-duty privileges which will be enforced by *our* centurions. I'll have no repeat of last night's stupidity, and the best way to ensure that is to avoid any off-duty fraternisation until our respective cohorts know each other a little better. You can have until the end of this salutary demonstration of imperial justice to make up your mind whether this will happen as a tactic we agree between us, or as something that I enforce. And now I'd say it's time for the show to begin. *Prefect?*'

Caninus stepped forward, his face impassive despite the obvious tension between the two military men.

'Tribune?'

'All three cohorts are paraded, so I'd say it's time to get this necessary unpleasantness over with.'

Caninus nodded briskly and gestured to his deputy, a tall, lean man with a flat, expressionless face.

'Let's get to it, Tornach. Bring out the prisoners and prepare them for execution.'

He strode out in front of the waiting cohorts, turning to look at the small gathering of civilians who had decided to brave the cold for a sight of the condemned men's last moments. Behind him Tornach led out a party of prisoners, each man with his arms bound behind his back and his ankles hobbled, each one with a pair of Caninus's men in close attendance to prevent any last-minute attempt to escape the harsh justice remorselessly bearing down on them. The prefect coughed, then raised his voice to address his audience.

'Citizens of Tungrorum! Soldiers of the First Minervia Legion and the Tungrian First and Second Auxiliary Cohorts! These men before you have been caught in the act of attempting armed robbery on the empire's roads, some of them with fresh blood on their hands. The penalty set by the state for their crime is death. It is a penalty which I have no hesitation in carrying out, given the fact that they are believed to have killed on multiple occasions in the recent past. Citizens, some of you may have lost property or loved ones to their rapacious acts of theft. The empire will now exact retribution on your behalf. Are the prisoners ready for punishment?'

His deputy barked an order at the armed men escorting the prisoners, who were now arrayed in a rough line facing the fascinated citizenry. One man of each pair kicked their prisoner in the back of the knees, forcing him to kneel, while the other took a grip of his hair to hold his head down, bared for the executioner's blade. Tornach looked up and down the line before responding to his superior's question, and then picked up a heavy-bladed axe from the ground beside him.

'Ready, Prefect!'

Caninus signalled his permission to proceed with a grim-faced nod, and his deputy walked forward to the first of the eight prisoners with his face set in hard lines. He placed the axe on the helpless man's neck, ready to deliver the killing stroke, but waiting for a second before raising it above his head and looking to Caninus for his final instruction.

'Carry out the sentence!'

The axe flashed down, cleaving the prisoner's head from his shoulders. It hit the damp ground with a slight bounce, rolling to stare lifelessly at the paraded soldiers.

In the 9th Century's ranks Morban muttered a word, loudly enough for the men around him to hear it.

'One.'

Marcus turned from his place in front of the century and raised an incredulous eyebrow at him, but the standard bearer's face remained impassive. The executioner walked swiftly to the next prisoner, placing the axe on his neck before lifting it to deliver the lethal blow. The head bounced once, landing with its face away from the soldiers, and Morban remained silent, ignoring Marcus's searching stare. The prisoner waiting beyond Tornach's next victim started to shout, his voice shaking with desperation at his impending execution. He ignored the increasingly vicious blows to his head that his guards were raining upon him, the words tumbling out of him like beads cascading from a broken necklace.

'*Not me! I had no choice! There are men here with more blood on their hands than me!*'

Marcus swung to face his men, whose surprise at the new development was quickly turning to whispered discussion.

'Silence in the ranks!'

Up and down the cohorts' lines centurions were issuing similar cautions to their men, one or two wielding their vine sticks to silence the miscreants. The prisoner was screaming louder now, as the third man's head fell to the ground with a dull thump. Fighting the grip on his hair that locked his head in place, he strained his gaze sideways to stare at the small group of senior officers.

'*Him! He's the one they're all terrified of! I know! I heard his . . .*'

The man gripping his hair released his grasp, smashing a fist into the back of his head, and before the stunned prisoner had time to recover from the blow Tornach was upon him, swinging up the blade as he stepped briskly over the headless corpse of his latest victim. Seeing his death approaching the desperate prisoner shuffled on his knees, turning his head away as the axe fell in a bloody arc. His last words were a gabble of terrified incoherence, abruptly silenced by the axe's blade. Silence hung over the parade ground for a moment, broken only by the prefect's stern command, his face white with anger.

'Continue the punishment!'

Marcus heard Morban speak again, his voice lowered in disgust. 'A shouter. *Why* didn't I lay odds on a shouter?'

With all of the prisoners beheaded the Tungrians were marched off parade, and they went back to their various tasks. First Spear Frontinius was keen to get the construction of their barracks completed, and to end their reliance on the increasingly dilapidated tents. He gathered his centurions about him, detailing their duties for the day.

'The usual routine, Centurions: two centuries to guard duty, the rest to building. Let's get these barracks finished today, shall we? Centurion Dubnus?'

The big man stepped forward from the group of his brother officers.

'First Spear.'

Frontinius fixed him with a hard stare.

'I've a word from the tribune for you. You can tell your ex-legionaries that they'll be *ex-Tungrians* if there's even a hint that they've been looking for trouble with First Minervia again. On top of that, Rutilius Scaurus assures me that he *will* hand them over to his colleague Tribune Belletor for administrative punishment and whatever duties he feels are worthy of their position as former legionaries. I wouldn't have thought that your men would find that entirely to their liking, would you?'

Dubnus suppressed a smile, the corners of his mouth twitching slightly.

'No, First Spear, I'd say they'll be keen not to have that happen.'

'Then pass the word along, Centurion. They've had their last chance. The next time any one of detachment Habitus steps over the line it's going to feel like they bent over in the bathhouse at the wrong moment. Dismissed.'

Marcus caught Julius's eye as the officers headed away to chivvy their men to work, raising an inquisitive eyebrow at his friend.

'Arminius tells me you went into the city last night?'

The muscular centurion nodded, shooting a quick glance at

Dubnus's receding figure as their colleague headed back to his men. Dubnus walked with the swift and purposeful stalk of a man whose day would be spent drumming home his tribune's warning with all the vigour for which he was famed throughout the cohort.

'Between us, brother? If you tell Dubnus what I was about last night I'll never hear the end of it.'

Marcus nodded.

'Between us. Did you find her?'

Julius stared at his boots, shaking his head.

'Yes. She's the mistress of an establishment called the Blue Boar in the north-eastern quarter of the city, a smart place with all the usual comforts, you know, soft couches, expensive drinks, and girls the likes of which we can usually only dream. She offered me a free ride with any of them that took my fancy, but, despite having a hard-on like a two-denarius blood sausage, all I could see was women like she must have been fifteen years ago, forced to do something she must have found hateful as the price of putting bread on her plate. So I told her I just wanted to talk, which was a lie, of course. All I really wanted to do was undo the mistake I made in leaving her here when I took the military oath. We talked for a few minutes like strangers, which is what we are, I suppose, but it was mostly her talking about how her life went after I left, while I just sat there red-faced and made cow's eyes at her, and her bodyguards sniggered at me behind my back. When even that got too much for me I made my excuses and made to leave . . .'

He fell silent and closed his eyes, shaking his head.

'And?'

Julius sighed, then a faint, embarrassed smile played on his lips.

'She got up, took me by the hand and pulled me into a curtained alcove. Her smart-arsed bodyguard, who now regards me as his personal property from the look of it, told me they call it the "Quicky Cubicle". She drew the curtain, put a finger on my lips and then stuck her hand up my tunic and pulled me off in about as much time as it takes to tell you. Then she gave me a quick peck on the cheek, called for a cloth and sent me on my way. Which is why I missed all the fun with Dubnus's boys.'

Marcus regarded him levelly for a moment.

'And where does all this leave you?'

His friend shook his head again.

'I don't know. Part of me knows I just need to walk away and forget the whole thing, put it down to the choices we make that can never be undone, but all I really want to do is take that fucking place apart with my bare hands and try to make amends to her.'

'And you think that's what she'd want?'

Julius smiled wanly.

'What do you think she'd rather be, a centurion's woman, never knowing which rainy shithole fort she might find herself in next, or independent, and the mistress of her own destiny?'

Marcus raised an eyebrow.

'I've no idea. But then neither do *you*. Have you considered asking her?'

Marcus left Qadir organising the 9th for their day's labour, which consisted of carrying building materials to the more skilled workers, and sought out Arminius. He found the German sparring with Lupus, by turns attacking the child and pushing him to defend himself, then falling back in defence to coach him in the use of his sword. Marcus stood and watched, nodding approval at the boy's slit-mouthed determination as he went forward against his instructor, his wooden training sword ceaselessly seeking an opening in the German's defences.

'How's the boy doing?'

The German turned away from the child to ensure that he wouldn't be overheard.

'Better than I expected. He's quick with the sword, he's got natural footwork . . . I'll turn him into a warrior, given a few years. Perhaps he'll even be good enough to spar with me on even terms.'

Marcus looked at the child speculatively.

'Would you say it's time for him to have some proper equipment? I believe your agreement with Morban was based on his finding the money to provide his grandson with whatever he needs?'

Arminius grinned wolfishly.

'I take it that your statue waver has just managed to make himself a profit of some kind?'

Marcus shrugged indifferently.

'I've no idea, and the agreement is for you to enforce as you see fit. I just found it interesting that he was counting the number of heads which fell facing us this morning. It was the kind of concern a man like Morban might have if he were running a book, *if* you take my meaning. You might find him more amenable to making a purchase for the boy now than he would have been yesterday. Or, for that matter, more amenable than if you wait until he's had a chance to scatter the contents of both his purse and his manhood across the city's entertainment establishments.'

Later that evening, when tribune and first spear took their usual cup of wine to discuss the day's events, First Spear Frontinius found his superior in reflective mood.

'So Tribune Belletor agreed to the new rules for allowing the men into the city?'

'Oh yes. Well, he didn't have very much choice in the matter, as it happens, a fact I made very clear to him earlier today.'

'And yet, Tribune, you seem strangely distracted this evening. Is there something troubling you?'

Scaurus raised an eyebrow.

'Is there? I don't know. Everything seems to be pretty much as it should be. Eight of the barracks are more or less complete, and we'll have them all built and weatherproofed in a day or so. Order has been restored in the city, and any fighting that happens now will be a matter for you or First Spear Sergius to sort out internally, so there's a source of strife removed. It's just . . .'

'The execution today?'

'That's perceptive of you. Yes. The man that started shouting.'

Frontinius shrugged.

'There's often one man who can't meet his end without letting everyone within earshot know how he's feeling about it, you know that. Not everyone's a stoic.'

He regarded Scaurus over the rim of his cup, and to his relief saw that the other man was shaking his head in bemusement at the comment.

'It wasn't the fact that he was shouting that bothered me, Sextus Frontinius. They could all have begged for mercy at the top of their voices and I wouldn't have turned a hair. What was of concern to me was what he was shouting.'

Frontinius raised his eyebrows in question, sipping at his wine again.

'I wasn't really listening, if I'm being totally honest, Tribune. I recall he was trying to tell us all about his innocence though.'

'In point of fact, he was apparently trying to tell us that we had by far the greater perpetrator in our midst. First of all he shouted, "There are men here with more blood on their hands than me!" and he followed that up with, "He's the one they're all terrified of! I know! I heard his . . ." But we'll never know what it was he heard, since Caninus's overzealous deputy promptly silenced him. I heard our colleague ripping into him afterwards for silencing the man in mid-revelation, but done is done. The fact remains, however, that in that moment of utter clarity some men get just before their death, that condemned robber was trying to tell us that we have an enemy within. He couldn't point out the man he was accusing, but he was looking squarely at the senior officers and the men around us while he was shouting the odds. Which leaves us with two questions.'

'Who he was looking at?'

'Yes. That, and exactly what he meant by "He's the one they're all terrified of".'

4

'Right, that's one apiece for keeping your mouths shut about this.' Morban handed every man in the new barracks' cramped room a coin, staring into each pair of eyes as he did so. 'If anyone asks you where I am, tell them I've gone to find some new boots.'

One of the soldiers crowded around him pulled a face at the single coin resting on his outstretched palm, making no effort to pull his hand away and claim the payment.

'I'm not sure one sestertius is enough. What if the duty centurion comes looking for you? If we get caught lying to cover up for your whoring we'll find ourselves on the business end of the scourge, with some big crested bastard striping us all up as the price of *your* fun.'

Morban glared at the speaker, shaking his head in disbelief.

'You just stick to blowing your trumpet when you're told to, sonny, and leave those of us with a head for business to enjoy the fruits of our hard work. After all, this is really just a scouting expedition I'm going on. I go out and spend *my* money working out where the best whores are to be found, and then when we have a pass into town I can take you straight to them. The way I see it, everyone's a winner.' He smoothed his tunic across his ample belly and then reached for his cloak, pinning the heavy woollen garment about him. 'Be good now, lads, and don't do anything I wouldn't . . .'

As the standard bearer opened the barracks door to leave, he found his exit blocked by a shadowy figure that towered over him in the unlit street outside. He recoiled, one hand going to his purse and the other reaching under the cloak for a small blade hanging round his neck. The other man was faster, clenching a big fist around both hand and weapon.

'It's never wise to pull a knife on a man twice your size, little man, especially when he's on your own side.'

Morban puffed out a quick breath, shaking his head in a mixture of irritation and relief.

'What do you want, Arminius? I've no time to bandy words with you.'

The German grinned down at him, planting himself firmly in the standard bearer's path and folding his arms.

'I thought as much. A good friend told me that you were running a book on the results of today's executions, and clearly I've arrived just in time to stop you wasting your winnings in your usual bull-in-a-field-of-cows fashion.'

Morban's face screwed itself up into his customary expression of incredulity. With his eyes narrowed and upper lip raised in a disbelieving sneer, he opened his hands in front of him in a shrug of bemusement.

'What? I made a modest profit by providing a service to my fellow soldiers; it isn't as if I've been dipping my fingers in the burial fund.'

The men behind him nodded sagely. Morban was known to be scrupulous in his handling of their savings. Arminius snorted derisively.

'I made no such accusation, so stop trying to change the subject. Even you're not stupid enough to risk what these men would do to you if they discovered so much as a hint of embezzlement.' The soldiers nodded again, exchanging knowing looks of agreement, but before Morban could respond Arminius leaned forward and whispered in his ear. 'But then you're more than sly enough to have fooled your comrades in other ways, aren't you? As I recall it, you took a lot of bets as to where your cohort's next posting would be before we were shipped over here, and almost none of that money was wagered on the cohort leaving Britannia, was it? A cynical man would wonder if you hadn't managed to find out where we were being deployed next before you opened the book, and I seem to recall some hard words on the matter at the time, even if nobody could prove you had inside knowledge. How do you think your comrades would react to the news that you had actually over-heard the first spear discussing the subject with your centurion, and in that way learned what you needed to know to make a swift and risk-free profit?'

Morban hissed his reply in a tone of disbelief, his eyes widening with fear.

'There's no way you can prove any such thing.'

Arminius smiled widely, delivering the killer blow to any resist-ance from the standard bearer.

'Who said anything about me? I think you'll find that the person who will be doing the telling will have a good deal more credibility than I do. He's a good man, quite young and he wears a crested helmet.'

Morban's eyes slitted in disbelief.

'You're bluffing! He wouldn't . . .'

Arminius nodded his head.

'Yes, he would. He and I knew that we'd need some leverage to persuade you to deliver your promise to equip young Lupus when the time came. And that time has most definitely come. If you don't agree to honour our agreement then you may find your future sources of revenue somewhat more limited than you like. Nobody likes a crooked bookmaker, do they, Morban?'

The standard bearer stared up at him with an expression that combined disgust and resignation.

'How much do you want?'

'Not *me*, Morban. How much does your *grandson* want? There is an armourer in the city who has agreed to make the boy his own sword and mail. Good stuff, mind you, as good as ours if not better.'

'And how much does this glorified blacksmith want in return for selling me a mail coat that will fit the boy for only a year?'

'He'll do the job for a mere one hundred . . .' Morban's face brightened slightly, and Arminius twisted the knife. 'Denarii, that is.'

The standard bearer blanched.

'A hundred in silver? Four hundred fucking sestertii! Are you mad? I can't . . . I mean, I haven't got that sort of money!'

Arminius grinned in the darkness, a swift dart of his hand plucking the purse from the other man's belt. Effortlessly holding off the enraged standard bearer with one hand he hefted the purse with the other, squeezing the top open and turning it to the light of the lamps inside the barrack.

'Really? This does seem to be quite a generous sum you're carrying, and most of it in gold as well. Shall we tip it out for counting?'

Morban, recognising that his guile had met its forceful match, shook his head dejectedly.

'No need. Here, I'll count it out for you.'

Arminius laughed at him, turning his back and tipping out the purse's contents into his broad palm.

'No, no, it'll be *my* pleasure! Here we go! I'll take it in gold to make things nice and simple. One, two, three . . .' He shook the bag to dislodge the last coin. 'Four gold aurei. There we are, all done. Now that didn't hurt too badly, did it?' He peered into the leather bag, pulling an impressed face. 'My word, Morban, you have been busy! Here –' he tossed the purse back to the anguished soldier – 'here's what's left of your treasure. Off you go and enjoy yourself, with that nice warm feeling that comes from having done the right thing. Even if you had to be helped to do so.'

Morban shook his head bitterly, turning to face the men staring at him in the barrack and replying in an affronted tone.

'I've lost all appetite for an evening with the city's ladies. Robbery with the threat of violence will do that to a man.'

Arminius smirked at his back, pulling a small coin from his pocket.

'More like robbery with the threat of blackmail, I'd say, but no matter. Hey, Morban!'

He flicked the coin at the standard bearer, who'd turned round in response to the call and caught the spinning coin in mid-air.

'A sestertius? What's this for?'

The German was already walking away, and called his answer over his shoulder.

'That should be enough for a flask of some of that rough Iberian cat piss you like so much. Have it on me, as a consolation.'

'Well, now, if it isn't the soldier boy again . . .' With a clatter of bolts the Blue Boar's door unlocked, and Slap appeared in the opening to look at Julius with an expression that combined puzzlement and pity, of a sort. 'You're a glutton for punishment, mate, unless you've got a hard-on for humiliation and hand jobs. Haven't you realised what sort of woman she is yet?'

The Tungrian shrugged helplessly.

'She's a bit hard-edged, but that's understandable given what she's been through.'

The disbelief in the bodyguard's answering laughter was enough to put his teeth on edge, but Julius held on to his temper with an ease that he was starting to find more than a little depressing.

'Hard-edged? She's razor-edged, soldier boy, sharper than any iron you've ever carried. She's too smart for this profession, see, and she knows it, but she was forced into it anyway, without the choice, and you were a big part of that. She'll be polite enough to you, but the odds of you getting past that ain't big from what I've seen. In you come.'

Julius spread his arms to be searched, but the doorman waved away the gesture.

'You've got more sense than to bring a weapon here. I think you know the truth of it all right, that you may be the emperor's hard man, but on our ground we're the professionals, and you're the amateur.' He jerked a thumb over his shoulder. 'In you go. I'll send word up to her that you're here. Let me know when you've had enough.'

Julius stepped into the brothel casting a wary eye around the main room's softly lit expanse. An elderly man was sitting in one corner with a pair of girls in close attendance; one sat on his lap squealing with simulated enjoyment while he toyed with the other's breasts in a half-hearted, vaguely embarrassed manner. Apart from that the place was empty. The barman held up an empty wine cup, remembering him from his previous visit, and Julius nodded gratefully, dropping a coin on the counter. He sat at the bar and sipped at the wine, watching as the two whores jollied their elderly customer along to keep his money flowing.

'Have you come to drink, or was there something more you wanted?'

He turned to the staircase that led up to the rooms where the establishment's entertainment was conducted, his heart jumping at the sight of Annia halfway down the wooden steps. She was dressed in a diaphanous gown that did little to conceal her body, and he shifted uncomfortably while she smiled down at him archly.

'I came . . . for you. I mean . . .'

She shook her head in apparent despair, beckoning him up the stairs.

'I told you this isn't going to work, Julius, but for old time's sake I'll take your money just this once. You do have money?' The look on her face was enough to have him on his feet without conscious thought, just the way it always had in days when they were little more than children discovering each other in the secret places where they'd taken refuge from the world around them. Draining his cup, he walked up the stairs to meet her, raising his eyebrows at her outstretched hand.

'How much.'

Her face softened into something close to sadness.

'I'm the most expensive woman you'll ever enjoy, Centurion. A gold aureus for one hour, but it'll be an hour to live in your memory for a long time. I've had a lot of practice since you took my virginity.' He handed her the coin and she tossed it down to the waiting barman, who dropped it into the cash box beneath the bar. 'Good, now that we've got that slightly sordid transaction out of the way, let's see what we can manage by way of entertainment.' Taking him by the hand she led him up the stairs and through one of the doors around the first-floor landing, closing it behind him and putting a finger to his lips, whispering in his ear almost inaudibly as she nuzzled at his neck. 'Don't say anything; these rooms are watched by my associate's men. Touch my breasts like a man who wants to get his money's worth . . . that's it. Once you're on top of me put your hand under the pillows and you'll find a key for a secret door on the east side of the building. The lock's hidden behind the shrine to Venus Erycina set into the wall. It leads to my private quarters, but you must only use it after dark. Come tomorrow night.'

She pulled away from him, opening her gown to reveal her naked body and running her hands over nipples that were already stiff from his attentions before dropping to her knees in front of him. Her voice was loud when she spoke, loud enough to be heard by any hidden watcher.

'Now lift that tunic and let me give you pleasure. Let's make sure you get your money's worth.'

'It's nice stuff, all right, I'll give you that.'

Arminius was holding a mail shirt up to the morning light that was falling through a thin window, examining its thick iron rings with a critical eye. The armourer came out from behind his counter and folded his meaty arms; they rippled with knots of muscle and were criss-crossed with the burns and scars of decades spent working with hot metal and sharp iron. He raised an eyebrow at the barbarian's apparently lacklustre praise.

'I told you when you came here yesterday that it's better than nice; it's the best you'll find this side of the River Mosa. Even the legion smiths up on the Rhenus don't make their gear to my standards. Look at that mail coat properly. The best leather backing, cut from top-quality hide and not split to make the leather go further, mind you. The rings are twice as thick as the ones in your standard-issue mail, thick enough to stop a thrown spear, and there isn't a sword blade made that could cut them, with only two exceptions. You put the boy in my gear, you're providing him with the best protection there is.' Arminius raised an eyebrow at the man's sales pitch, and the armourer spread his arms. 'I'm just saying that you have to pay for quality. Look, here's the deal we discussed: four hundred sestertii to arm and armour the boy here. Look at this.' He fished under the shop's counter, pulling out a bundle of equipment. 'See, a mail shirt made for a lad not much bigger than the boy, made to my usual standard and with room for him to grow into it, and a helmet, *and* a two-thirds size sword. Look at the sword's quality.' He passed Arminius the weapon, and the German held it up to the light. 'Don't touch the blade, it—'

The German gave him an amused look.

'I know. Sweat will make the blade rust. It's nice work though. Look at this, Marcus.'

He passed the sword to the Roman, who looked up and down its length with an approving eye, testing its weight with an expression of surprise.

'Very nice, armourer. How did you make this?'

The smith smiled knowingly.

'Ah now, you can't be expecting me to reveal the secrets of my trade to two men I barely know, can you? But I can see you have an eye for a blade, Centurion, so I'll let you see something even better.'

He ducked behind the counter and came up with a full-sized weapon in a dull metal scabbard, pulling out the weapon to reveal its blade. Marcus reached out and took the sword from him, looking closely at the sword's edge while the smith proudly watched in silence.

'This pattern . . .'

The armourer nodded.

'The pattern reveals the secret of the blade's strength. It is made from a mixture of finest-quality steel from Noricum on the River Danubius, combined with good iron. They are heated together to make them workable and then folded together time after time after time until the resulting sword has many layers of the two. This weapon took me more hours than I'd care to count, heating and cooling, and always forging the two metals together, and then I spent another week polishing it to bring out the pattern you can see along the blade. It will cleave an iron sword in two if you swing it hard enough, and there is no mail made that can resist its blade. It is my masterpiece.'

Marcus looked at the sword, and instantly knew he had to possess the weapon.

'And your price for this sword?'

The smith started.

'In truth I've never thought to sell it. It is of incalculable value to me.'

The Roman raised an eyebrow.

'That would be a first, a tradesman unwilling to sell his work.'

The armourer protested, raising his hands and shaking his head.

'It is my finest work, Centurion, the perfect blade. I could never—'

'And you'll keep it behind that counter for the rest of your days, rather than allowing it to be used for the purpose for which it was forged? Name your price.'

The other man's face furrowed as he thought for a moment.

'The price, Centurion? For a month of my life, for the best materials to be had, even if their expense was ruinous? For my life's labour and experience poured into one blade? I couldn't take less than fifty gold aurei . . .'

Marcus smiled. The price was astounding for a sword, and was more than likely intended to scare him away.

'Done.' The smith's eyes widened in amazement that the Roman was willing to spend so much money on a weapon. 'I'll be back this afternoon with the money. I'm assuming that you'll throw in the child's equipment as a gesture of good will at that price?'

The armourer dithered.

'I'll halve the price, Centurion. Two aurei for the child's gear will close the deal.'

Marcus nodded, then pointed to a shelf above the man's head.

'Before I leave, I'd like to see that helmet you have there, if I may?'

The smith reached up and pulled down a gleaming cavalry helmet. He passed it to Marcus, who looked with interest at its finely tinned face mask.

'Sixteen layers of iron and steel, Centurion, each one hammered so flat that the mask is still as light as a feather, but it'll stop an arrow loosed from twenty paces. Should I name a price for you?'

Marcus shook his head with a smile.

'I'm probably in enough trouble with my wife already, thank you. It's a nice piece though.' He turned to leave, only to find Dubnus and a jaded-looking Julius in the shop's doorway. They walked in, and Julius looked with a professional interest at the racks of weapons around him.

'Qadir said we'd find you here. We're under orders from Uncle Sextus to find you and then go to the bathhouse and get cleaned up. We've got an interview with the tribune this afternoon, and he doesn't want us smelling like a pack of badgers when we turn up, apparently.'

He turned back to the door, only to find Dubnus indicating a small item on one of the shelves behind the counter.

'Didn't you lose a whistle on the way here, Julius?'

Dubnus kept his face admirably straight while Julius stared back at him, winking at Marcus and raising his eyebrows in unspoken warning once the older man's back was turned.

'Yes, I did, now you mention it. I'm surprised you remembered. How much for the whistle, smith?'

'Over there, next to that shifty-looking type, there's a space.' Marcus turned to follow Julius's hand and saw the open bench his friend was pointing out. 'You go and take possession, and I'll see what's taking Dubnus so long. He's probably threatening the bloody cloakroom attendants again.'

He stepped back into the bathhouse's undressing room to find the muscular young centurion pressing one of the bathhouse slaves up against the room's cold stone wall.

'. . . and if any of our gear mysteriously goes missing while we're bathing you're going to wish your mother had never laid hands on your dad's cucumber when I get hold of you, and the same goes for all your fucking—'

Julius tapped him on the shoulder, and nodded his head towards the warm room.

'That's enough of that. If the pricks are stupid enough to lay a finger on our gear then they'll take what's coming. Now come and join me and Two Knives in the warm room, before we lose our bloody seats.'

The two men walked back into the baths to find Marcus surrounded by a group of irritated locals. He was smiling serenely at the men standing around him while they gesticulated furiously at the empty spaces on the stone bench on either side of him. His hands were behind his back, as if he were stretching his spine, but Julius noticed with a practised eye that his right foot was resting against the bench's stone pedestal, ready to thrust him up into their faces at any hint of the debate turning physical. He tapped the closest of them on the man's bare shoulder and then folded his scarred, muscular arms, fixing the man with a hard-eyed stare before looking down ostentatiously at the eagle tattooed on his right shoulder, with the characters COH I TVNGR inked beneath it.

'For those among you that haven't learned to read yet, I'll translate. This says "First Tungrian Cohort". So I suggest you lot stop waving your dick beaters around like a bunch of Gaulish housewives and fuck off now, before you start to irritate me.'

For a moment it looked as if the local men might argue the point, but the sight of an even bigger specimen appearing at Julius's shoulder, and showing every sign of being a man in search of a fight, was enough to turn them away, grumbling but clearly outmuscled. The two centurions took their places next to Marcus, Julius groaning in pleasure as he settled back onto the warm stone.

'Oh yes, that's much better. I'm going to sweat out a bucket of dirt today, and no two ways about it.' He looked down at Marcus's hands with a raised eyebrow, as his younger colleague brought his right hand out from behind his back, opened his fist and waggled the fingers, dropping a handful of coins into his left palm and passing them to his friend. 'A well-brought-up boy like you knuckling up for a fight like a common soldier? You'd better not let the tribune catch you doing that.'

Marcus shrugged.

'There were five of them, and they weren't looking happy at being beaten to the last seats in the room.'

'And you were just working out which one to put down first, weren't you, you bloodthirsty young bugger?' Julius shook his head with a wry grin. 'And there's the difference between the three of us, I'd say. Dubnus, when he's not busy threatening the bath slaves with what he'll do to them if his new cloak brooch goes missing, would just have grabbed the nearest man, banged his head on the wall, dropped him and scared the rest of them off with a smile. I, believe it or not, would rather just face that sort of idiot down, and let the scars and tattoos do their job. But you, the well-educated son of a senator and in theory the born peacemaker of the three of us, you'd have come off that bench like a whorehouse bouncer, wouldn't you?'

Marcus shifted uncomfortably.

'I can't argue with you, Julius; you've seen me lose my temper too many times. I just can't . . .'

He shrugged helplessly, shaking his head, and his friend ruffled his hair affectionately.

'I know. If there's a confrontation to be had you can barely hold yourself back, and when that last tiny bit of self-control is flicked away by some idiot's careless words, or even the wrong look on a man's face, you can't stop yourself from attacking with any weapon that's to hand. I saw it the other night, when we were dragging Dubnus's boys off those legionaries. When everyone else was staring at Lugos and his "I fight you all" act, you were busy putting your vine stick into the guts of anyone that got in your way. I counted four of them on their hands and knees in your wake, and I doubt that most of them even saw you coming.' The older centurion shook his head with a good-natured laugh. 'You're a good man for war right enough, but what will you do when the fighting ends, I wonder? Men like us find peacetime hard enough when they've got used to a regular diet of blood, but men like *you* . . .' He paused. 'Marcus, you can work out what will cause the most damage to a man given the tools at hand faster than anyone I've ever met, but you don't have the restraint that sometimes only comes to a man after years of bitter experience, or sometimes never comes at all. I was the same at your age, all knuckles and fight, and it wasn't until I was ten years in that I started to calm down, and learned to send men away with a look rather than breaking their faces. I never had your speed, or your fearsome temper; I was just a fight looking for someone else to join in. But you're something else, something much more dangerous, because there's nothing restraining you . . .' He looked the younger man up and down. 'I'd say there's not much call for men with your particular mindset – call it a blessing or call it a curse – once the fighting stops and the boredom of a peacetime routine settles on us all like a cloak made of woven lead.'

Marcus raised an eyebrow.

'Peace? And you think we'll see that any time soon?'

His friend stuck out his bottom lip and shrugged speculatively.

'There are only so many tribes. By the time we've found this Obduro and sorted him out the Britannia legions should have the Brigantes whipped into place. It'll be back to the days of drill and route marching for us, and what will you do for a fight then, eh? And you with a family to care for? My advice to you, brother, is to learn to wind your neck in for the sake of those who love you, and for fear that you might leave them alone in the world without your protection. Can you do that for them, if not for me?'

Marcus returned his gaze, his face expressionless.

'I can, but not simply for them. I have a score to settle in Rome, a blood debt with a man so powerful that I'll only get one chance at getting it repaid. And keeping that in mind will be enough to help me stay out of trouble in the meantime. It wouldn't do to miss my moment with the Praetorian Prefect and a sharp blade, for the sake of a few witless fools like them.'

He smiled down the room at the glowering locals, opening his hands in a gesture of goodwill. Julius gestured to a wine vendor, raising three fingers in the universal signal.

'I'll drink to that. Let's use those knuckledusters of yours for their intended purpose and buy ourselves a cup of wine and something to eat, and then get into the hot room for some oil and a scrape. The tribune's expecting us to be nice and clean for tonight's briefing, and I don't intend to—'

He stopped talking, watching as a familiar figure stepped into the warm room and looked about him until he spotted the Tungrians, then walked across to join them.

'Greetings, Marcus, and greetings to you all, gentlemen of the First Tungrian Mule Cohort.'

It was an old joke, but never seemed to wear thin as far as Silus was concerned. Julius nodded, a wry smile twisting his lips.

'Greetings, Silus. I was just saying to Marcus that I could smell horseshit, and then in you came.'

Silus tipped his head to acknowledge the retort, then looked about him again.

'This place is full enough. I suppose the good citizens are getting their bathing in early, before your horrible soldiers take the place over once they're off duty. Not that I blame them. And now, I suppose, you're wondering what I'm doing here, given the place is off limits to all soldiers until sunset?'

Julius shook his head.

'Not at all. Our assumption was that you've been told to come and get clean as a mercy to all those men that don't live for the smell of month-old sweat, stale horse piss and fresh manure.'

Silus smiled, briefly and patently insincerely.

'No, I'm here for the same reason I reckon you are. There's a briefing with the tribune tonight, and your first spear wants me there in my best tunic and with polished boots. A bath was suggested, and in a manner which didn't make it sound optional, so here I am. Old Frontinius didn't say as much, but since you three are also here and busily ignoring the locals' indignant stares, I'm going to presume that you got the same marching orders. And, given the looks you boys are getting from the men sitting next to you, it's not a moment too soon.'

Dubnus swivelled his head to look at his neighbour, whose

affronted gaze flicked away from him just a moment too slowly. He shook his head, standing up and stretching his heavily muscled body, then he bent to put his face inches from the now thoroughly alarmed civilian's.

'Didn't your dad teach you that it's rude to stare at soldiers in the bathhouse? Not to mention dangerous, because if I catch you looking at my cock one more time I'm going to bang your stupid fat head on that wall behind you.' Shaking his head in disgust he turned back to his brother officers. 'Right, let's go for a sweat, shall we, and upset some more of these sheep?'

'The contents of this briefing are utterly confidential, gentlemen, and are not to be shared with anybody outside this room. Our colleague Caninus here has every reason to believe that there are men within the city who are providing information to this "Obduro" character, and if wind of what I want you to do for me gets out we'll lose what might be the only chance we'll have to catch these people.'

Scaurus looked at each man in turn to make sure his message was completely clear. The first spear nodded, turning his gaze on Silus, Marcus, Julius and Dubnus.

'I'm detaching the four of you for some independent duty. As far as your men are concerned you'll have gone to Fortress Bonna to liaise with the First Minervia. I expect the camp to presume that I've sent you in search of reinforcements, which is a good enough cover for what you'll really be doing. Decurion Silus will provide horses from the mounted squadron, and you will indeed ride east as far as Mosa Ford. When you get there, you will present papers authorising you to travel on to Claudius Colony on the Rhenus, and from there up river to Fortress Bonna. However, once you're out of sight of the Mosa Ford walls you're going to leave the road, and head south-west into the Arduenna forest. Using whatever paths you can find you will then get as close to the objective as you deem possible on horseback before making camp somewhere quiet. Silus will stay there with the horses while the rest of you will scout along the edge of the forest, quietly and methodically, until you find some sign of what I want you to look for. When you've got the information I need you'll pull back, making sure you remain undetected, and bring it back here as quickly as possible.'

'And exactly what is it that we'll be looking for, Tribune?'

'A camp, Centurion Corvus.'

Marcus turned to face the man who was waiting quietly in the deep shadow of the room, beyond the lamps' meagre illumination. Scaurus beckoned Caninus into the full light of the lamps set around the table.

'Prefect Caninus has a theory that you're going to test, Centurions.'

He gestured to Caninus, who walked over to the map on the wall, putting a finger on the north-western fringes of the huge forest on the opposite bank of the River Mosa from the city.

'It's logical to assume that Obduro and his band are operating from somewhere on this edge of Arduenna. If I were him there's no way I'd want to risk a night in the open after a robbery big enough to bring out the whole Tungrorum garrison after me. Look at this cluster of robberies, the ones we think his men carried out.' He pointed at a cluster of crosses on the map close to the forest's edge on the northern side of the Mosa. 'And this attack on the detached Treveri century that led to their mass desertion. All of them within a few hours' march of this part of the forest, and so close to the city as to defy belief.' He stabbed a finger at the forest, indicating a point roughly equidistant from the attacks. 'I'm willing to gamble that he always makes sure he can be inside the trees before nightfall, and doubtless there's a camp somewhere round here. That ease of access cuts both ways, of course, since it also makes it easier for us to find, and less of a problem to attack than a camp that's hidden away in the deep forest. The big question for me is how he's getting his men back across the river, given that the only bridges we know about are at Mosa Ford to the east, and where the road to the Treveri capital crosses the river further to the west at Arduenna Ford.'

He studied the map for a moment before looking up at the men gathered around him.

'Apart from that, a man as wily as Obduro isn't going to put all of his marbles in one bag; he'll have somewhere to fall back on if the camp on the forest's edge is compromised. It'll probably be built on a hill, almost certainly heavily fortified, the ground around it will be littered with mantraps and nasty surprises. If they've built the kind of stronghold I'd expect, five hundred men could probably face off ten times their number in the absence of any artillery to batter the walls down.' He paused for a moment, and Marcus saw the look of frustration that crossed his face. 'My bitter experience with bands like this one is that the moment they see soldiers coming they'll scatter in a dozen different directions, and fall back into the deep forest. And, once they've disbanded, catching them will be like trying to nail piss to a wall. If we give them time to run they'll be snug inside their fortress, wherever it may be, long before we can find it and bring our strength to bear.'

Scaurus stepped forward again.

'Which means that the secret of our success has to be in surrounding them with a nice thick ring of troops *before* they get the chance to retreat. And that means that we'll need to find this camp at the edge of the forest, but without them knowing we've done so. If we can manage that smart trick, then when we attack the camp we should be able to feed a cohort in behind them before the rest of the detachment marches up and knocks at the front door.'

Julius nodded to the tribune.

'At which point they'll make a dash for the back door, only to find it locked and bolted. After that they can either surrender or die on our spears. Neat. And all we have to do is scout the edge of the forest until we find them.'

'Indeed, Centurion.' Caninus raised an eyebrow. 'But do you think you can manage that delicate task? These are men who have had years to get used to the forest, whereas you, with no disrespect intended . . .'

Dubnus spoke, his voice sober yet powerful.

'I was raised in the great forest that runs down the spine of Britannia. I am a woodsman and a hunter, and when *I* go into the forest I move in silence. I will find your bandits and they will never know of my presence.'

Caninus nodded.

'Good. Although I suggest that I provide you with a local guide, a man who has called the forest home for as long as he's lived.'

Scaurus raised an eyebrow.

'Isn't there a risk he might be their man in your camp?'

The prefect winced.

'He's one of the very few men of whose loyalty I am absolutely sure, and I implore you not to mention any such idea in his presence. His family were taken by this gang last summer while he was serving me as a tracker, and he does not know whether they still live. I'd advise you against making an enemy of him, but he does know every path through the forest, and if you treat him well I'm sure he will be an asset to you.'

Scaurus looked at the first spear, who nodded his agreement with a shrug.

'Very well, Prefect, we accept your offer of guidance.'

Caninus pointed to the city's west, running his finger along the road into Gallia Belgica.

'In that case I'll take my men away on a sweep down the road to the west towards Beech Forest tomorrow morning. That way, if Obduro's spy is one of my men, I can at least make sure he knows nothing of your departure to the east, no matter how innocent it may appear at face value.' He looked down at the map and nodded. 'You may just provide us with the one small piece of luck I've been waiting for these last few months.'

The news that the three centurions were heading east to the fortresses on the Rhenus inspired more than one comment in the Tungrian cohorts' makeshift officers' mess that evening.

'Don't worry, brothers.' Titus, commander of the 10th Century, formed from the biggest men in the cohort and equipped with the heavy axes only they had the strength to swing in battle, leaned over the three men as they sat enjoying a cup of wine, his voice a baritone rumble. 'Your secret's safe with me.' He winked at them. 'Uncle Sextus told me all about what you're going to be doing while you're away.'

'He did?'

Julius shot him a surprised glance, and Dubnus shook his head at Marcus in disbelief.

'Oh yes, he told me about it in great detail. It was a load of rubbish, of course. I could tell from the look on his face, that one he always gets when he's not being entirely straight with whoever it is he's talking to. All that stuff about talking to the legion's fortress supply officer about equipment? All nonsense. I know what you're really doing.' The three men stared at him in consternation. Never the brightest of the cohort's officers, Titus's main value lay in his ability to command the respect and quite frequently the abject fear of the biggest and often nastiest men in the cohort. If he'd already worked out their mission from a shifty first spear and simple deduction, there was no chance of their delicate task remaining a secret. 'Yes, you're going to find out all about the Fortress Bonna vicus. Every bar, every whorehouse. You're going to visit them all in readiness for our next move. I'm right, aren't I?'

Julius's incredulous stare hardened to a sly grin in the instant it took him to grab the big man's misconception and run with it.

'For Cocidius's sake, Titus, keep your *bloody* voice down! If the other officers find out why we're really going east there'll be a mutiny! As far as everyone else is concerned we're going to talk to the Fortress Bonna stores officer, and that's the way it needs to stay.'

Titus guffawed, slapping his colleague on the shoulder and rocking him sideways.

'Of course it is, brother, of course it is! Here –' he lowered his mouth to Julius's ear conspiratorially – 'I was talking to a trader on his way through to the west yesterday when I was on guard duty, and he was telling me about a one-toothed whore—'

'*Enough!* We'll give you a full briefing when we return, only spare me any more of your speculation. I don't want to hear another word about it until we're back. You keep our little secret, and I guarantee to tell you all the details myself.'

By the time they'd had another cup of wine the story of their impending trip to the east and its 'secret' purpose was all over the camp, and as Morban addressed his centurion on the subject Marcus found himself admiring the first spear's genius in managing to generate such artful misdirection with a single seemingly innocent conversation.

'Off to Fortress Bonna, eh sir? Off to see the *lay* of the land, I hear. I'm told there's a one-toothed whore who'll stick her—'

'Standard Bearer?'

The razor edge in his centurion's voice silenced Morban in an instant.

'Sir?'

'Hold out your hand.' Squinting at his officer in discomfort and puzzlement, Morban extended his right hand, the fingers curled protectively into his palm in obvious expectation of a stroke from the Roman's vine stick. 'Turn it over and open your palm.'

Slitting his eyes in readiness for whatever punishment it was that he feared, Morban obeyed, only to goggle at his open palm as Marcus dropped a single gold aureus into it.

'I negotiated a discount on the boy's armour. You get a hundred sestertii back to do with as you see fit, and Arminius is holding the other aureus in expectation of future expenses. After all, we can't have him wasting time trying to wring money out of you every time young Lupus needs a new pair of boots. Dismissed.' The standard bearer turned away in a daze, still staring at the gold coin. 'Oh, and Standard Bearer?'

'Sir.'

'The one-toothed woman? Apparently it's true, although whether she really performs the act for which it seems she has become infamous among the men of this cohort is less than clear. We'll know for certain soon enough though.'

He turned away, leaving Morban staring open-mouthed after him. Morban waited until Marcus had turned the corner and was away to his own quarters before muttering quietly to himself, shaking his head in disgust.

'The next thing I know he'll be taking over my book as well. I think I preferred the other version.'

Julius waited until the last of the soldiers on an evening pass had returned to barracks before setting off into the city, this time dressed in his uniform with both sword and dagger strapped to his belt. Skirting around the Blue Boar to the east he found the streets deserted, and walked quietly up to the shrine to which Annia had directed him, his hobnails muffled by rags tied about his boots. Looking up and down the street to ensure that he was unobserved he reached into the shrine, feeling about behind the goddess's statue until he found a narrow horizontal slot through which to insert the key, a long rod with a two-pronged anchor-like device at its end. Turning the key from vertical to horizontal he jiggled it gently until he felt the anchor's metal tips engage a pair of holes in the bolt holding the hidden door closed. Pulling the rod to the right he felt a gentle click as the bolt disengaged from its keep, and with only a little pressure the heavy door opened easily on well-oiled hinges. Sliding through the narrow opening he closed the wooden door, which was cunningly faced with a stone cladding to blend seamlessly with the wall, and in the darkness he slid the bolt back into place by touch.

A patch of dim light appeared above him at the top of a flight of stone stairs, and a figure stepped into the meagre illumination, beckoning him on. Mounting the steps with one hand on his dagger and ready to fight, he realised as he drew close to the top that it was indeed Annia. Dressed in a light tunic and with her cosmetics removed, she hugged him enthusiastically.

'I thought you weren't coming!' Her whisper was so soft as to be virtually inaudible, and she put her mouth to his ear to be heard better. 'Take those swords off and come inside.' She ushered him into the room, lit by a single lamp, and pulled the door closed before rearranging the wall hanging that concealed it. Gesturing to a couch, she poured him a cup of wine and came to sit along-side him. 'The secret door was already here when I took the place over. The Boar's been a brothel since it was built thirty years ago, and whoever designed it had an eye to the future. Not only are all the rooms observed from secret passages, to make sure that any pillow talk of value is overheard by the guards and reported back to Petrus—'

Julius started with surprise.

'*Petrus?*'

She put a finger to his lips.

'*Shhhh!* There's no guarantee that he doesn't have a man outside this room with an ear to the door; it wouldn't be the first time he'd had me spied on. I'm his property, Julius, and he's a jealous master. If he found out about the door to the street he'd have it sealed up the same day.'

'But Petrus is the procurator's man. How would he be . . .'

He stopped talking and thought for a moment, then shook his head at how obvious the truth was once it was in the open.

'Petrus is the real power in the city. He's the man that controls the gangs, and Albanus is so deep in bed with Petrus that when my master tells him to jump the only question he's allowed to ask is how long he has to stay off the ground. I knew from the second I saw you that I still feel exactly the same way about you that I did fifteen years ago, but I didn't dare to let you know it, because if you saw it so would they. And once Petrus knew, he'd have had you dealt with, quickly and quietly. And then he'd have told me all the details while he was grinding me into that bed, taking his pleasure from my despair. It was far safer for his musclemen to tell him that I was indignant and aloof. I'm sorry.'

The Tungrian put a protective arm around her.

'It doesn't have to be that way any longer. Come with me now; bring whatever you need and leave for good. You'll never have to whore again, or suffer that arsehole's attentions.'

He stopped talking, his eyes fixed on her shaking head.

'If I walk away from here I have to leave the city *now*. You may think you could protect me, but I know that he'd have my life in a matter of days as a lesson to anyone else contemplating the same idea. I can only leave this place under one of two circumstances. Either you need to be marching away, and have the means to take me with you, or Petrus needs to be dead along with every man that might seek revenge for him in order to prove himself as Petrus's successor. Unless you can make either of those two things happen tonight, then tomorrow I shall still be the mistress of the Blue Boar.'

The small party rode east at dawn the next morning, Marcus, Julius, Dubnus and Silus all mounted on cavalry horses while a mule laden with several days' worth of food followed Silus's mount. If his comrades found Julius's demeanour even more dour than they were accustomed to, they made no mention of it.

'He went into town again last night,' Dubnus had confided to Marcus while they were waiting for Silus to arrive with the horses on which they were to carry out their mission. 'He clearly thought he was keeping it to himself, but one of my lads was doing double guard duty as a punishment for that squabble with the legion, and he told me he saw the stupid bastard walk off towards the forum once everyone had turned in for the night.'

The two men had exchanged uneasy glances, knowing that by rights such behaviour ought to be reported to the first spear, and knowing also that neither of them would do any such thing.

'He'll tell us about it in his own time, and until he does we'll just have to watch his back.'

Dubnus had nodded unhappily at his friend's decision, and it was only Silus who had carried on with the usual banter once they were on the road. Even he had quickly sensed the reluctance of his comrades to indulge in the familiar routine of insult and rebuttal, and so it was a quiet party that found Prefect Caninus's man waiting for them by the roadside once they were safely out of sight of the city walls. The scout joined the small group with no more ceremony than a sketchy salute to Julius, and the surrender of a small wax tablet signed by Caninus and marked with his seal as proof of the man's identity.

The scout was slightly built, with a face that was deeply lined and seamed, giving him the weather-beaten appearance of a man who had spent his entire life working in the open. A hunting bow was slung across his shoulder, and a quiver of heavy iron-headed arrows hung from his belt, while the only sign of ornamentation he carried was an intricately tooled leather scabbard containing a long hunting knife nearly the length of an infantry sword. Introduced in the prefect's tablet as Arabus, he quickly proved to be taciturn in the extreme, and Marcus's attempts to engage with him were met with monosyllabic answers. No attempt at conversation would elicit anything more than a nod, a shake of the head or a terse, grunted answer where a simple yes or no would not be sufficient. Julius and Dubnus rode up alongside Marcus, Dubnus tipping his head to draw his friend away from the guide, keeping silent until the three centurions were out of earshot.

'You'll get nothing more from him. I've met the type before, men who have known nothing other than the forest since birth, and nothing you can do or say will get him to open up before he feels the time is right. Mind you, I'll tell you one thing that makes me smile.'

Marcus raised an eyebrow.

'Go on.'

'His name.'

'What, Arabus?'

His friend grinned, shooting a quick look at the guide.

'In the Gaulish language I believe it means "witty". And if he was the witty one in the family, I dread to think what his brothers and sisters must have been like!'

Julius nudged Marcus, having seemingly thrown off his reverie, and held out a hand.

'Come on, then, let's have a look at that pretty new blade you've bought.'

Marcus unsheathed the patterned sword and passed it to Julius. His horse's ears pricked up at the sound of the blade's gentle metallic rasp against its scabbard's throat, and Marcus leaned forward, affectionately ruffling the close-trimmed hair on top of the beast's head.

'Not today, Bonehead. Today we're just covering ground.'

Julius looked closely at the blade, then swept it down to his right in a practice cut that hummed past his own horse's head.

'As light as a feather. And what did Uncle Sextus say when you asked him for that large a withdrawal from your saved pay?'

Marcus smiled at the memory.

'Let's just say the first spear wasn't exactly delighted to have fifty aurei taken out of the pay chest all in one go. And then when he saw the sword he spent so long looking at it I was convinced he was going to pull rank and buy it himself.'

He took the weapon back from Julius, who waited until the vicious blade was safely sheathed before speaking again.

'You think Frontinius would pay that much for a sword, when he can get an issue weapon for a tiny fraction of the price? Mind you, there'll be a bit of a rush if you should happen to stop a spear while that nice little toy's strapped to your waist. One of us will be wearing it before you're cold, you can be assured of that!'

Dubnus shook his head at the older man with a smile, a wry note in his voice.

'You can put any such idea out of your mind, Julius! Our colleague has already agreed that I'm the right man to inherit such a weapon. In my hands it would be treated with the expertise it deserves, whereas to end up in the hands of an exponent of stab and punch like yourself would be a sad end for such a fine blade.'

Julius raised an eyebrow at Marcus, who shrugged equably, and the big centurion grinned triumphantly at their colleague.

'It doesn't look to me like you've got any such agreement, Dubnus. It looks to me like it's first come, first served.'

Dubnus shrugged in turn, the smile creasing his face taking on a calculating aspect.

'Fair enough, the first man with his hands on the weapon gets to keep it, in the unlikely event that there's anyone out there good enough to leave it ownerless.' He squinted slyly across at his friend. 'Anyway, Julius, I meant to ask if you ever got round to buying that whistle you were looking at while our colleague there was spending a soldier's pension on his new toy.'

His friend nodded, fishing in his pouch and holding up his brightly polished whistle. Dubnus looked at him for a moment, clearly struggling to keep a straight face, then turned back to the road, leaving Julius frowning at him in puzzlement.

'There's something I'm not getting here, isn't there? Why are you grinning like a standard bearer who's discovered an extra hundred denarii in the century's burial fund that no one else knows about, eh? What have you . . .?' He looked harder at the whistle in his hand, his eyebrows suddenly shooting up as he realised that it was the one he'd believed lost. Looking up he found that Dubnus was holding his new whistle in one hand. 'You crafty bugger! Did you know about this, Centurion Corvus?'

Marcus fought to control his laughter, his face contorting with the effort.

'I was aware that your loss was not entirely what it seemed. At least you have a nice new whistle as a result, and a beautifully crafted one from the looks of it. And there's Mosa Ford – I can see the fort's walls through the trees. It's time to start acting like a party of professional army officers again, I suppose.'

Julius snorted derisively, giving his old whistle a long hard look of reappraisal before tucking it away in his pouch again. Dubnus waited until his hand was in the pouch, then tossed the new whistle to him, forcing him to whip the hand back out and catch it in mid-air. Shaking his head, he held up the shining brass instrument with a look of disgust.

'Ten denarii for something I didn't even need? And you suggest that *I* might want to start looking like a professional? Here, you haven't got one of these yet, have you?'

He passed the whistle to Marcus, who raised an eyebrow.

'Thank you. But shouldn't you be keeping the new one?'

'No, I've had this one since I was commissioned; it would be bad luck to abandon it now.' He gave Dubnus a hard look. 'And besides, giving you that *definitely* gives me first call on the pretty sword.'

The party passed easily enough through the scrutiny of the legion detachment guarding the bridge over the river. Tribune Scaurus's written instructions to them to proceed to the Rhenus fortresses were clear enough, and the impressive seal attached to the document more than proved their bona fides, but Julius found himself being drawn aside by the duty centurion once the fort's western gate was closed behind them and the sentries had returned to their patrols along the wooden palisade walls. Marcus walked alongside the two men as they paced through the fortified settlement towards the bridge, listening quietly as the guard officer muttered his advice in the Tungrian's ear.

'. . . and you want to be careful of that dark-faced little runt you've brought along for the ride. I've seen enough of his kind to know that he'll mean trouble soon enough.'

Julius raised an eyebrow, his face darkening.

'His kind? You mean we can't trust him because he's a *local*?'

The duty officer shook his head dourly.

'No, the local people are decent enough. I mean you can't trust him because he's from in *there*.' They had reached the bridge's western end, and Marcus looked out across the river, its surface broken by the stones that marked the shallows which had made it such an obvious bridging point for the road to the Rhenus fortresses. The duty officer pointed to the forested slopes that rose above the small settlement clustered round the bridge's eastern end, and spat over the bridge's parapet. 'Laugh it off if you like, but if you'd served as close to that bloody forest for as long as I have you wouldn't be laughing. It's only four hundred paces from here to the tree line, but by the time you've walked five hundred you might as well be five hundred miles away. There are men living in that place who don't see the light of day from one end of the year to the other, half-savage hunters without any of the values that make us the civilised people that we are. We see them sometimes, watching the fort from the edge of the trees, and we used to send patrols in to try to get hold of one, but it was like trying to catch fucking smoke. And it scared the shit out of the lads.' He looked into the distance through the open gates for a moment before speaking again. 'I stopped ordering patrols after we lost a man last year. One minute he was there at the back of the column, the next he was gone, disappeared in broad daylight without either trace or echo. We never saw him again, but that night some of the lads reckoned they could hear him screaming, just a faint sound on the breeze that only the young ones could make out, but they swore it was there.'

He spat on the ground and made the warding gesture to the guide's back.

'No, that's one of them all right. If he'd turned up here alone I'd have had his throat cut and chucked him in the river, but since he's under your protection all I can do is warn you. Where are you going from here?'

Julius pointed a hand to the east.

'Claudius Colony, then Fortress Bonna.'

'Straight to the Rhenus, eh? Fair enough. You should be fine as long as you stick to the road and don't go into the forest. Just watch the little bastard, all right?'

He stood and watched as the party remounted and rode away up the hill to the east, and Julius waited until the fort was completely out of sight before raising a hand to halt their progress. He stared at the densely packed trees for a moment, then turned to Arabus.

'Time for you to start earning your corn. You've been briefed on what we're supposed to be doing?'

The scout returned his gaze for a moment then looked at the forest, drawing in a deep breath through his nose and sighing as if in satisfaction.

'Yes, Caninus told me what I am to do. You wish to search the edge of Arduenna, from here down the river's bank back to the west until we find any sign that the bandits have a camp.' A look of serenity touched his face as he contemplated the place he clearly considered to be his home. 'Come, then. Follow me into Arduenna.'

He led them across the hundred-pace-wide strip of ground between road and forest that had been cleared of trees years before as a defence against ambush from the forest. The barren ground had clearly been tended by a gang of local labourers recently, to judge from the absence of any vegetation other than grass and small bushes. On reaching the trees Arabus paused, inhaling deeply as the scent of pine trees washed over them on the breeze.

'We will lead the horses until we find a track. Watch your footing.'

He pushed forward into the dense undergrowth, moving with deliberate caution, and the centurions followed him into the trees, looking about them in interest. The light dimmed slightly as they walked away from the forest's edge, taking on the ethereal green shade with which they were all familiar, but apart from that Marcus was unable to discern any difference between the Arduenna and any other forest in which he'd walked. Arabus padded forward, leading his horse through the trees with his gaze on the ground until, after a few minutes' walking he turned back and beckoned the centurions to him. A faint track bisected the forest floor, and they looked down its visible length to the point where it vanished into the dense undergrowth fifty or so paces to what Marcus could only presume was the south-west. Arabus pointed to the path with a smile of pride.

'As I expected, this is a hunters' track. I have not hunted this part of the forest for many years, but my memory still serves me well enough.'

Julius looked up and down the track.

'If we follow this path surely we must run a risk of meeting other travellers?'

Arabus shook his head.

'I will scout ahead on foot while you ride a hundred paces behind me, and leave my horse tethered to your mule. I will hear anyone coming up this path before they hear *me*, you can be assured of that.'

And so the party spent the rest of the day working their way along the hunters' track, moving at Arabus's cautious pace and with one man always watching the path behind them, until the light shining through the canopy above them started to dim. The guide stood waiting for them as they crested a low ridge, then pointed up the low hill's spine, deeper into the forest.

'It will soon be night. We must make camp, and gather firewood before it is too dark to see clearly. Follow me.'

He led them away from the path, climbing until they reached a bowl-shaped clearing high on the hill's side.

'Here we can light a fire without the risk of it being seen; once darkness falls it will conceal any smoke.' He pointed to the ground surrounding the clearing. 'There should be plenty of wood on the ground. I'll go this way.'

He walked away up the hill, his eyes on the ground hunting for dead wood that would burn easily, and Marcus looked at the other centurions.

'If Silus tends to the horses, I suppose the rest of us should spread out.'

They nodded agreement to each other, and Marcus headed off down the slope to the right of the clearing. Finding himself confronted by a thick belt of impenetrable thorns, he diverted to the left, and started to climb the hill again, only to find another belt of hawthorn blocking his path. A fat branch was poking out of the long grass, and he went down on one knee to examine it, wondering if it was sufficiently aged to snap into more manageable pieces. As he weighed up the bough's condition his attention was caught by a faint noise from further up the hill, and looking up he saw a vague, dark shape moving downhill behind the cover of the trees, crossing his field of view from left to right. Reaching to his belt he drew the patterned sword, the blade scraping fractionally against its scabbard's metal throat and sending a rasping note across the otherwise silent hillside. Whatever it was that was moving down the slope took fright at the faint noise, and bounded away from him in an explosion of movement that left him frowning, unable to give chase through the thorn bushes.

As the commotion of the hidden animal's panic-stricken progress through the trees died away Arabus stepped out of the trees to Marcus's left, his bow held with an arrow nocked and drawn, ready to shoot. Marcus found himself looking down the missile's shaft and into the scout's empty eyes, and he involuntarily tensed himself for the missile's impact as Arabus stared down the arrow's length at him. After a long moment the scout eased the string's tension and tucked the arrow back into his quiver, slinging the bow across his back. He strode down the slope to meet the young centurion, shaking his head in apparent amusement. It was the first time that Marcus had seen the dark-faced man smile, and he re-sheathed his own blade as he waited for the guide to reach him. Arabus put both hands on his hips, looking about him for any sign of a threat.

'I heard a sword being drawn.'

Marcus nodded, bending to pick up the branch he'd been considering when whatever it was that had caught his attention had broken cover.

'I saw something moving through the trees.'

Arabus smiled again, his seamed face twisting in amusement.

'Yes, it was a wild boar. I was readying myself to venture an arrow at it when it heard you draw your sword. It ran before I could loose the arrow.'

Marcus shook his head disgustedly.

'A boar? I mistook it for a *man*.'

Arabus raised his hands.

'There is no shame in such a mistake. A momentary glimpse through so many trees would deceive the best of men. I had a clear view of the beast, and from the size of it we would have had days of good eating had I managed to bring it down. No matter, it will be dried meat for us tonight, rather than wild pork.'

Marcus snapped the fallen branch into three pieces and resumed his search for more wood, and the guide walked away up the hillside to collect his own bundle of wood. Waiting until the sun was no more than a distant pale gleam on the horizon Arabus quickly and expertly lit the fire using flint and iron, blowing gently onto the kindling until it was well alight and then adding twigs and small branches to feed the small blaze. With the fire burning properly the five men wrapped themselves in their blankets and chewed in silence on their ration of dry meat, hard cheese and bread. The hunter drew his long sword and took a piece of the local whetstone from his pack, spitting on it before passing the blue stone down the blade's length with a harsh metallic scrape Marcus watched for a moment, admiring the intricate decoration that adorned the blade's scabbard; it depicted a charging boar ridden by a female figure wielding a bow.

'That's a fine piece of leather work.'

The guide replied without looking up from his task, working the whetstone with the delicate care of long practice.

'I made it myself. Hunting the forest at night gives a man a lot of time to practise such craft.'

The Roman nodded, looking about him at the surrounding starlit ground and the dark bulk of the trees gathered around them.

'Is the woman riding the boar your goddess?'

Arabus nodded, glancing up briefly.

'It is. I made two of these, one for myself and one for my son.' He paused for a while, his eyes misting over with the memory. 'I honour Arduenna every time I draw my blade, and every time I return it to the leather.'

Marcus looked across the fire at him.

'You speak of the forest as if it is a person. You call it "Arduenna", as if you were speaking of a woman rather than a body of trees, and I noticed that Prefect Caninus did much the same yesterday. Do you all feel the same way about the forest?'

Arabus looked at him for a long moment, as if attempting to divine whether the Roman were serious, or making fun of him, but when he saw no hint of levity on Marcus's face he answered the question with a solemn expression.

'Arduenna is different things to different people. To you Romans, men not born under her shadow, she is simply a forest. You look at her and all you see are trees, and the animals that live under their protection. You do not feel her spirit, nor hear the slow beating of her heart.' He fell silent, and stared into the dark ranks of trees without speaking for so long that Marcus was on the verge of prompting him again. 'For me, and every other man who has lived beneath her canopy for as long as they can remember, she lives and breathes, and we worship her. Which aspect of the goddess a man perceives depends on his origins. To those who live under her protection she is a powerful huntress, fair of face and riding a boar through the forest in search of her prey, which she brings down with her bow. We worship her, and offer her thanks for our success in the hunt.'

Marcus trod carefully, wary of inadvertently insulting the guide despite his desire to know more.

'Do you offer her . . . sacrifice?'

Arabus's eyebrows lowered in a disgusted frown.

'Do you take me for a savage? Do you hope to hear tell of altars deep in the forest where men are put to death in worship of the goddess?'

The Roman shrugged apologetically in the face of the guide's apparent anger.

'There are rumours . . .'

The guide bridled at the suggestion, gesturing angrily with his hands.

'All lies made up by *your* people to explain their fear of what they do not understand! We offer a small part of any game we kill to the goddess, no more!'

Marcus smiled gently.

'And I apologise. You were saying that the local people see her as a benevolent spirit. So how would an outsider perceive her?'

The guide's eyes flashed, and for that second Marcus knew he was staring into the man's soul.

'As vengeance.' Arabus's voice was as hard as his expression. 'She rides down the unbeliever who is foolish enough to venture into the dark woods, and many are her weapons. Other men like you have ridden into Arduenna to hunt in her kingdom without paying her the appropriate respect, and they have never been seen again. You are fortunate to be accompanied by a believer, to shield you from her anger.'

With that he fell silent again, and after a moment Marcus felt compelled to offer an opinion, glancing round the fire at his colleagues and finding their faces set as sceptically as his own in response to the guide's impassioned words.

'There could be . . . other explanations?'

He was about to suggest other causes for a man disappearing in the forest when Arabus spoke again, his voice harsh.

'Yes, they could have become lost and starved, or been taken by wolves; those things could happen. But I told you, *many* are her weapons. If you knew Arduenna the way that I do, you would not look for complicated explanations for the disappearances when the simplest answer is also the most obvious. We know the goddess, Centurion, we know what she can do, and we choose to respect her power where men like you blunder into her kingdom and pay the price for their lack of caution. But you are lucky. While you are under my guidance and protection you will be safe, as long as you follow the same rules that I follow. Now I suggest that we sleep.'

Julius stirred, shrugging off his blanket and standing up, warming himself in the fire's glow.

'I'll take first watch.'

Arabus frowned.

'There is little need. We are quite safe here out of sight, and—'

The heavily built officer shook his head and turned away.

'We have our routines, friend, and they don't vary. One of us will be on guard at all times until we leave this forest and return to the city.'

He walked away over the clearing's rim and into the darkness, and the other soldiers bedded themselves down in their cloaks and blankets.

Felicia left the Tungrorum hospital two hours after sunset, having been delayed longer than she'd intended by the treatment of a soldier from the legion cohort who had suffered a deep cut to his thigh in training. Depressingly, the man's wound had started to smell, with the fetid aroma of infection so horribly familiar to her, as if sepsis were setting in. After scrubbing her hands, she had dosed him with a mixture of wine, honey and the dried and ground sap of the poppy, and then set to work on the wound with her surgical equipment, working to cut and scrape away any hint of dead flesh, ruthlessly sacrificing healthy tissue in the hope of saving his life. It had been with a heavy heart that she had finally bandaged the wound and left him to sleep off the opiate mixture.

Stepping into the street she pulled her cloak about her, feeling the thick wool tight over her gently swollen belly. The baby was getting heavy now, and already her gait was slightly changed to accommodate her increasing weight and the feeling of ungainliness that the pregnancy was inflicting upon her. Taking a deep breath of the cold air she put her head down against the wind's icy caress as it funnelled down the narrow street, pushing forward doggedly against the blast. A voice spoke from the shadows, making her start at the unexpected and unseen presence.

'Here we are! I told you that good things come to the man with enough patience to wait for them.'

A dark shape detached itself from the darkness of the hospital's stone wall, the faint light of the hospital's torchlit entrance revealing a man wearing a legionary's white tunic. Felicia took one look at his face, the nose and mouth masked by a strip of dark material, and recognised the intent in his palely gleaming eyes. She turned back to the hospital entrance less than twenty paces distant, but then froze as another man appeared out of the building's shadow in front of her, his face similarly concealed.

'You were right; she's well worth waiting for.' She could see from the set of his eyes that he was smiling at her, although she doubted that the expression would be particularly pleasant were it not concealed by the mask. 'We'll soon warm you up, darling. A little bit of compensation for your lot getting us banned from the city four days out of five, eh?'

She felt the first man's strong hands grip her arms from behind, and knew that even if she'd been carrying Dubnus's knife it would have been impossible to use the weapon in such close quarters.

'I'm pregnant.'

The second man laughed disparagingly, his voice no more troubled than if their would-be victim had announced that she had red hair. Reaching out he flicked her cloak aside, then, with a leer the mask did little to conceal, he cupped her breasts.

'That doesn't matter, darling. It won't bother us, and let's face it, if you weren't already baking a loaf you soon would be once we've all been up you a few times.'

Her eyes widened in horror, and as she felt the grip on her arms tighten the man behind her leaned forward and whispered in her ear.

'Oh yes, darling, *all* of us. There's another six blokes waiting for you in our barrack, and we're going to show you a right old time. In fact we're going to fuck every—'

A shout rang out from the far end of the street, and the man standing in front of her spun to face the source of the noise, pulling a dagger from his belt. A cloaked figure was charging towards them along the hospital's wall, and as the man ran he unsheathed a sword, its long blade flashing gold in the light of the torches burning at the building's entrance. The soldier behind Felicia pushed her away, turning to run as his comrade sprinted past him and dropping his dagger in his haste to escape. Felicia fell to her knees, one hand stopping her fall while the other clutched instinctively at her stomach. Her rescuer ran past and then, realising that the two soldiers were outpacing him, he abandoned his pursuit and sheathed the sword, turning round with a brisk bow to help her back onto her feet.

'Madam. Are you . . .?'

'I'm fine, thank you, whoever you are.'

'Caninus. Quintus Caninus. I am the prefect of the city's bandit-hunting detachment. And you must be the Tungrian cohort's doctor?' She nodded, relieved that the pain she was feeling was from skinned knees rather than in her abdomen. 'Those men, they were soldiers?'

'Yes, Prefect. Legionaries with a grudge against my husband's cohort. They were planning to abduct and rape me, or at least that's what they—'

Caninus gaped at her.

'*Rape?* I thought they were robbing you! And you're sure they were legionaries?'

Felicia pointed at the dagger hidden in the building's shadow. 'That might help?'

Caninus bent to pick up the weapon, frowning as he held it up to the light.

'It looks like army issue. Come along, I think we need to show this to your tribune. A grudge I can understand, but this . . . this is beyond my experience, or my understanding, for that matter.'

Marcus took the second watch, smiling to himself as Julius rolled himself up in his blanket and was asleep within seconds. He looked around the camp in the fire's meagre glow, watching Arabus closely for a moment, but the guide was soundly asleep and snoring gently. He put some more wood on the fire before padding out into the darkness, then he climbed up the hill until the fire's gentle crackle was lost in the wind's hissing passage through the branches above his head. Settling into the shadow of an ancient oak he listened to the noises of the night-time forest and watched the stars above his head, following the training that Dubnus had imparted to him months before and giving his senses time to adjust to the ambient noise. Allowing his thoughts to stray, he mused on impending fatherhood, and the responsibility of bringing a child into the world whilst he and anyone associated with him were still under the threat of a death sentence, and subject to an imperial manhunt driven on by the vengeful Praetorian Prefect.

A tiny sound reached him, almost too gentle to be heard above the wind's susurration; it was the crack of a twig breaking somewhere not too close but still within earshot. Waiting with his breath held he heard another sound, again almost too quiet to be heard, and he turned his head slowly towards it, avoiding any sudden movement that might alert whatever had made the noise. Another sound came, slightly to the right of the first one, and Marcus reached for his sword's hilt, easing the blade out of its scabbard with a care to avoid any repeat of the noise that had betrayed his presence earlier that day. The sword's blade shone in the moonlight, and he held it upright behind his back to avoid the bar of reflected silver giving his position away.

Easing back down the slope, testing each footfall with delicate care before putting his full weight down, he slid back into the clearing's hollow bowl and touched Dubnus on the shoulder. His friend woke instantly, his eyes flicking open to find Marcus kneeling over him with a finger to his lips. The big man rolled silently to his feet, nudging Julius with his foot, and he too rose from the ground, shedding his blanket and drawing his sword without a sound. Leaving Silus and the guide asleep, the three men climbed out of the clearing, their swords shining in the moonlight. Marcus pointed with his left hand held flat, indicating the direction from which he felt the sound had come, more or less the same place where the wild boar had taken flight earlier. They spread out a little, advancing slowly and silently into the night's gloom, their senses alert to any tiny sound or movement. From somewhere behind them an animal grunted disconsolately into the cold night air, and a moment later another replied from the opposite direction.

'*Go!*'

Julius's urgent whisper sent them forward at a faster pace, sacrificing silence for speed as they weaved through the trees in a rustle of grass and snapping twigs, but after thirty paces he held up a hand to halt them, listening hard in the renewed quiet.

'*Nothing.*'

Dubnus nodded his head in agreement with Marcus's whisper.

'If there was anything out here, it's gone to earth. We'd have heard anything of any size if it had run.'

Marcus looked out into the darkness unhappily.

'There was something out here. I know that much.'

They returned to the clearing and found Silus and Arabus still asleep. The guide awoke when Marcus touched his shoulder, blinking his eyes open and staring up at the Roman in a moment of incomprehension.

'What?'

Julius sank back to the ground and reached for his blanket.

'There was something moving around out there.'

Arabus grimaced, sitting up and rubbing his eyes.

'The boars hunt at night sometimes. You can hear them digging for roots when it's quiet, and grunting and snorting at each other. It was probably the same animal we saw earlier. You see how Arduenna already has you all jumping at shadows?'

Silus opened an eye to squint at the men standing over him.

'It's a good thing I've got all you big strong infantrymen around to make sure that nothing sneaks up on me while I'm busy dreaming of beer and women. The only problem is that I don't seem to be getting much dreaming done.' He yawned hugely, then turned his back on them and nestled into his blanket again, muttering a last comment from beneath the rough fabric. 'And I'll bet not one of you dozy buggers has even thought to check the horses.'

Tribune Scaurus, predictably, was incandescent in his anger at the night's events, hammering the point of the discarded dagger deep into the polished wood of the basilica's wooden table. The knife remained there, standing upright and wobbling slightly from side to side in front of Belletor, as Scaurus walked away from it to the far wall, leaving the horrified tribune staring at the weapon. Turning back to face his colleague, white-faced with a rage he had fought to control ever since Caninus had brought Felicia to his quarters the previous night, Scaurus spat his fury at his incredulous colleague with the pitiless force of a fully wound ballista.

'I've seen all manner of brutal and bestial acts in the last ten years, but I never thought I would see the day when a Roman soldier would offer violence and the threat of rape to a respectable matron, a military doctor, and a pregnant woman, to boot!

I find myself more than amazed, Tribune; I am quite literally revolted by the idea that allegedly civilised men would stoop to so base an act by way of revenge! Were it not for our esteemed colleague Quintus Caninus's timely return from his day's patrolling, my doctor might still be suffering the unwanted attentions of an entire *fucking tent party*!' The last words were roared at the top of his voice, and he advanced on the seated Belletor with such malevolence in his eyes that the usually aggressive tribune froze in his seat. First Spear Frontinius gave his colleague Sergius a meaningful glance and limped out from his place to put a restraining hand on his superior's arm, his hard, cold grip enough to arrest Scaurus's advance and switch the furious tribune's attention from Belletor to himself. He leaned close to his superior, muttering into his ear in low tones intended not to be overheard.

'This will not undo what has been done, Tribune, and while offering violence to this man might seem appropriate to you now, you will regret it in the days to come.'

Refusing to bend under his superior's ferocious stare, he nodded to Sergius, who stepped forward and wrenched the dagger from the wood's grip, leaving a deep scar in the smooth surface.

'This is one of ours all right; it's standard issue. Ah, the soldier in question seems to have been stupid enough to use his own weapon for the crime.' He held up the dagger, turning it to the light to display letters and numbers formed out of patterns of tiny holes punched into the handle's metal. 'See? "Julius, VII II IV". Soldier Julius, Seventh Cohort, Second Century, fourth tent party. The man's as good as condemned, unless he can prove that the weapon left his ownership before the crime was committed. With your permission, Tribune?'

He looked at Belletor, who dragged his gaze away from Scaurus and distractedly waved an assenting hand. Sergius saluted, nodded to Frontinius and left, the weapon in his hand.

'First Spear Sergius will know the truth of it soon enough, I expect. In the meantime I'd suggest that we put these hostilities to one side. Not everything is as simple as it seems.'

Scaurus stared at his first spear for a moment, knowing that the older man's cautionary words contained a core of wisdom that he would be unwise to ignore. At length he put a hand on Frontinius's and gently freed himself from its grip, switching his pitiless gaze back to Belletor.

'Agreed, First Spear. But when we discover the truth of these events there will be a reckoning with whoever is brought to justice, and as they suffer their death sentence I will look into the eyes of the men who would have defiled a pregnant woman. And *you* –' he pointed a finger at Belletor – '*you* would do well to avoid lecturing me in the period between then and now. Make sure that the rest of your command knows that I have detailed a guard to the doctor, four veteran soldiers to be at her side at all times, some of them men who have recovered from battle wounds under her care. I have told them that they have orders to take whatever action they see fit, should they suspect any threat to the doctor. Any man who approaches the doctor with anything but the greatest circumspection can expect to find himself looking down the shafts of their spears, and to find unfriendly eyes behind them.'

5

The party was back on the hunters' track at first light. Marcus's eyes were red-rimmed from lack of sleep, which had refused to return after the night's disturbance, despite the absence of any further sign of the nocturnal intruder that he resolutely maintained he had heard.

'There was something else I heard, apart from the sound of breaking twigs, but I can't say what it was. It didn't sound like any noise a pig would make though.'

He pondered the fading memory as they made their cautious way along the track in the morning's grey light, at length shaking his head and deciding to put the whole thing to the back of his mind. By the time the sun had reached its highest point they had covered another five miles by his reckoning, and he was starting to contemplate the stop for lunch when Arabus ducked into the cover of a gnarled elm, raising a hand to beckon them in but in such a manner that a silent approach was clearly required. Leaving a muttering Silus to hold the horses the centurions closed up on their guide in silence, squatting down in the cover of the tree and waiting for him to speak. Leaning forward to whisper, he pointed a finger at the path beyond the elm's shelter.

'I heard something. Not loud, but not natural. It might have been a man's voice raised to shout, but it was so distant that I couldn't be certain. We need to leave the path and scout forward.'

Julius nodded, and whispered his instructions in the same quiet tone.

'Swords out, brothers. This ground's so thick with trees that there'll be no warning of any trouble. Marcus, go and tell Silus to get the animals into cover, and to wait for us here. Tell him the watchword is "Tungria" – and if he hears men approaching without using it he's at liberty to make a break for it. If we get into trouble out there I'd rather the tribune knew something rather than nothing at all.'

Marcus briefed Silus, who promptly led the horses and mule off the track and away into the forest's cover, unable to resist the temptation for a whispered parting shot at his comrade.

'Never fear, Centurion, the first sound I hear without one of you lot bellowing the watchword and I'll be on my toes without a second thought. Watch out for yourself, young Corvus, and try to avoid being attacked by any bad-tempered pigs, eh?'

The four men scouted forward in an extended line, keeping within sight of each other as they eased cautiously through the undergrowth. After a few minutes, and as the initial nervous energy prompted by the guide's warning started to seep away from his muscles, Marcus found himself shivering with the day's chill. He hunched deeper into his cloak as he slipped through the trees and bushes, the forest's silence broken only by the gentle sigh of wind through leaves. He lost sight of Dubnus, the next man in line, as his friend moved silently down into a dip in the forest floor, and in the moment of distraction, as he glanced away from the thick undergrowth to his front, a pig burst from its cover in an explosion of movement and raced away across the soft ground. An instant later a man leapt through the bushes in pursuit, a spear raised in one hand held ready to throw.

Sergius reported back to the two tribunes after an hour's swift investigation, his face sour with frustration.

'The knife was stolen from the legionary named on its blade yesterday, while the man's tent party were on fatigue detail. He reported it as missing early yesterday afternoon, and his centurion supports that claim. It's fairly obvious that it was stolen for the purpose, as a precaution against its being lost, but that doesn't provide us with any clue as to who it was that assaulted the lady last night. For what it's worth, I've spread the word that there's a reward on offer for information leading to the apprehension of these men, but I'm not holding my breath on a result. Nobody in the tent party in question is going to say a word, and they're likely to have kept their plans to themselves.'

Scaurus paced across the room away from him, turning when he reached the wall, and his voice was hard-edged when he spoke.

'To be expected, I suppose, and it leaves me without a means of identifying these soldiers, presumably as intended. I'll not pursue justice against men that can't be identified, but I will nurture my hunger for retribution for as long as it takes for them to make the mistake that will lead me to them.'

Prefect Caninus nodded firmly, picking up the knife from its place on the table's scarred wooden surface and lifting it to stare hard at the blade's glinting line of sharp iron.

'I'm with you there, Tribune. One way or another we will have justice.'

The spearman stumbled to a halt and gaped in amazement at the uniformed Roman officer standing before him, his face distorting into the beginning of a scream as Marcus swept his sword round in a blurred arc that whipped the blade through his neck and sent his head spinning to the ground. The man's body stood stock-still for a moment before slumping sideways to the forest floor, a jet of blood spurting from the corpse's neck as it fell. From close by a man called out in the native tongue, and the Roman flattened himself against the nearest tree as the second hunter's footsteps thudded softly towards him across the forest floor. As the man appeared to his right, his spear held loosely over his shoulder, Marcus kicked out with his right leg; he hooked the hunter's feet from beneath him and pitched him onto his back, putting the sword's point to his throat and looking down at his captive with a finger to his lips. The prostrate hunter swallowed, feeling the steel's cold kiss against the skin of his neck, and froze into immobility while Arabus and the other centurions gathered around him.

'*Kill him!*'

Julius put out an arm without even looking at Arabus, ignoring the threat of his long knife and taking a firm grip of his throat, hissing a warning from the side of his mouth.

'Put the knife away before I'm forced to take it off you.'

The guide stared at him for a long moment, his knuckles white on the knife's handle, before he realised that Dubnus had the point of his sword a fingernail's width from his exposed armpit. The big centurion leaned in close, touching his knife to the soft skin with sufficient force to indent the vulnerable flesh.

'Do as he says, or you'll end up as a meal for those pigs you're so fond of.'

Arabus slowly lowered the blade, sliding it back into the leather scabbard and stepping away from the terrified prisoner, but his face remained twisted in an expression of hatred and disgust.

'He's one of *them*.'

Julius grinned wolfishly.

'You mean he's a bandit?'

The guide nodded, not taking his eyes off the prisoner. His voice was cold, and as dead as his eyes.

'He's one of the men that took my woman and my son. Give him to me.'

The big Tungrian shook his head, shooting Arabus a warning glance.

'No. Not yet, at least. I want to know what he's doing here before anyone gets to play any revenge games with him. And I want to know one thing before we start.' Stabbing his sword down into the soft earth he reached down and took a firm grip of the spearman's sleeve, then he pulled out his dagger and opened up the coarse fabric with a single pass of the evilly sharp blade. He stared down at the man's flesh, shaking his head slowly at what the knife's pass had revealed. 'And what do we have here, eh? Who's a naughty boy?'

He tapped the skin of the man's shoulder with the weapon's point, indicating a tattoo crudely inked into the flesh; it was a unit identifier similar to that on his and Dubnus's left arms. Dubnus leaned over and stared at the marking for a moment, a smile creeping across his face.

'Well, now. Second Treveri, are you? Which means, for a start, that you speak Latin, so don't bother playing dumb with us.' The bandit stared back up at him with a mixture of fear and hatred, and Julius prodded the tattoo with his dagger again.

'It also means that you know all too well the penalty for the murder of your prefect. I think we'd better take this one back with us to Tungrorum and allow military justice to take its brutal course, eh lads?' He turned back to Arabus. 'Your prefect told us that your family went missing, what, a year ago?' The guide nodded reluctantly, his eyes still locked on the prisoner. 'Well, these boys mutinied only last autumn, so you can forget about taking that knife to this one; he wasn't part of whatever it was that happened to them. I still want to know where that camp is, so you and my colleague here –' he pointed to Dubnus – 'can go forward to find it, while Marcus and I stay here and have a gentle chat with my new friend here.'

Dubnus put a brawny arm around the guide's shoulder, turning him away from the prisoner.

'We can't be far from their camp now, so you and I should go forward and leave these two to watch the prisoner. Are you coming, or do you want to stay here and glare at him too?'

The guide shot a last venomous look at the captured bandit and walked away, speaking quietly into the forest's silence.

'Follow me. I know this ground as well as I knew my wife's body, before *they* took her from me.' He vanished into the trees, his passage no noisier than a gentle breeze.

Julius winked at Marcus and the two men watched their friend pad into the forest in Arabus's wake, his axe held ready to fight. Then Julius leaned over the prisoner, who was still lying on his back.

'Well, Second Treveri, now that we have some peace and quiet, and that vicious little man isn't fingering his knife and staring at your throat, perhaps we can have a civilised conversation. Let me make this easy for you. Either you answer every question I ask you quickly, honestly and in a way that doesn't make me think you're trying to be clever with me, or I'll be forced to start carving bits off you, starting with this.' He gripped the man's ear with a lightning-fast move, resting the dagger's cold, minutely jagged edge against the point where ear and scalp joined. 'In your own time . . .'

The bandit's eyes rolled helplessly.

'What do you want to know?'

Marcus squatted down in front of him, shaking his head in mock sadness.

'What do we want to know? Isn't that obvious, soldier? We want to know *everything*.'

Dubnus and Arabus moved noiselessly across the forest's sun-dappled floor, the big centurion mouthing a silent curse as he wove a sinuous path around the shafts of light lancing down through the forest's canopy high above them, staying in the shadows to avoid the blink of sunlight on metal. The guide appeared to have got over his anger at being denied the chance to take sharp iron to their prisoner, and led him on with a deft eye for cover, seemingly determined to ensure that their progress would remain undetected. The centurion smiled to himself, reflecting that Julius would have been noisier than both of them put together, but his expression changed abruptly as a hint of putrefaction reached his sensitive nose. He hissed to Arabus, flaring his nostrils to indicate the unexpected smell. The guide padded carefully across to his side, whispering in his ear.

'We're close to their camp, I think. They have a habit of using cages to scare off any hunter that stumbles across their hiding places. I've found them before, after the bandits have abandoned a camp.'

Dubnus shook his head uncomprehendingly, but the guide simply gestured him on, putting a finger to his lips and moving with exaggerated care, each footstep slow and delicate as they weaved through the undergrowth, and Arabus paused with increasing frequency to ensure that they were unobserved before moving across even the smallest of gaps in the foliage. At the top of a small rise Dubnus realised what he had meant a few minutes before when he had referred to 'cages', as a tall arrangement of stout branches, which had been formed into a cylindrical structure, resolved itself out of the surrounding vegetation. The horizontal bars were provided by thickly interweaved strips of bark which were placed to provide a clear view in and out of the cage as much as to anchor the branches together, and the whole thing was secured to the forest floor by deeply buried pegs, each one the width of a man's thumb. Dubnus stared at the construction with an unhappy certainty as to its contents.

'*Surely not?*'

Arabus turned back to him, nodding grimly at his expression of fascinated horror and whispering fiercely in his ear.

'What else were you expecting? This man Obduro understands the power of terror on men such as these. And on us, for that matter. Come on.'

He led the Tungrian closer, and with every cautious pace the stench worsened, until by the time they were close enough to see into the cage's shadows it was almost enough to choke Dubnus, despite his experience of battle, of terrible wounds and of bodies left to rot. A corpse lolled back against the bars, its sightless eyes staring at Dubnus's revolted gaze. The exposed portions of the body were rippling with maggots, and it was only an act of will-power that kept him from throwing up onto the forest floor. Arabus watched as he mastered the urge, his whispered comment harsh with emotion.

'This man's fate is a warning, both to his own people and to outsiders. If we are caught approaching their camp we will certainly suffer in exactly the same way.'

He stared at Dubnus with a level gaze, as if waiting for the Tungrian to indicate a retreat, but the big man simply nodded, gesturing to the ground before them. Shrugging, the Gaul turned away from the cage and, bent almost double, led him forward again, his pace even more cautious than before. After fifty more paces he turned his head, putting a hand to his ear.

'Do you hear that?'

Dubnus listened, concentrating and ignoring the rustling of

leaves in the early afternoon's breeze. The faint sound of men's voices reached him, their words unintelligible but their tone easy enough to understand. He nodded to the guide, indicating that he should stay where he was squatting, then he flattened himself against the forest floor, worming slowly forward towards the voices, carefully picking up and moving aside anything that might betray his presence by making a noise. The sounds got louder as he crawled closer; a group of men were talking without fear of being overheard and individual words started to make sense. He stopped and listened, guessing that he was still twenty or thirty paces short of them, but the discussion remained impossible to follow and, taking a deep breath, he squirmed forward again, now moving so slowly that his approach was quite literally without noise. The wind rustling the leaves high above his head died away for a moment, and the voices were suddenly disconcertingly clear.

'. . . and I'm fucking telling you that there's no way they'll ever catch us here. *He'll* make sure of that; he'll get them to come at us the long way round, and even if they did find the crossing we'd still be safe on the hill before they were even across the river and ready to fight. And there's no bloody infantry cohort been raised that could kick us out of those defences, not without artillery, and that legion cohort doesn't even have a single ballista. They're clearly not to be trusted with the heavy stuff.'

Another man laughed.

'You should know about trust and the army!'

Dubnus nodded to himself, having already guessed that the first speaker was another of the Treveri cohort's deserters. The reply was calm enough, although Dubnus thought he could hear an edge in the man's voice, and a hint of distaste for the comment.

'Perhaps I should, if you put it that way. But *he'll* make sure we get plenty of warning of any attempt to attack us, and there's just no way they're ever going to suspect that he's . . .'

The wind picked up again, and, apart from a few isolated words, the rest of the sentence was lost in the rustle of leaves. After a moment the men's audience laughed, and Dubnus realised that there had to be at least twenty of them, from the sound's volume. He grimaced at his proximity to their camp and started to retreat slowly backwards, sliding away from the danger of discovery as quickly as he dared. Once he had gone fifty paces or so he got cautiously to his feet and retraced his steps to where Arabus still crouched. He tugged at the guide's shoulder as he passed, pulling the other man along in his wake.

'It's time we weren't here.'

He led the guide back to where the other two men were waiting with their thoroughly cowed prisoner. Julius looked up questioningly as the scouts slipped into the clearing.

'Find them?'

Dubnus nodded grimly.

'Yes. And it doesn't make good telling. No time now though, we need to be . . .' He put a hand to his belt. 'Fuck. My bloody dagger's fallen off my belt. The strap must have finally rotted away.' He gave Julius and Marcus a significant glance. 'I've been complaining long enough about the quality of that kit, and now of all times . . . I'll go and find it, and you lot can head back to meet up with Silus. Wait for me in the same place as we camped last night, and I'll join you there.'

He turned round without allowing any time for any of them to react, creeping back through the trees until he found the dagger where he'd quietly dropped it during their retreat from the bandit camp. Waiting for a moment to ensure that he was unobserved, he turned north, towards the river, and silently slipped away into the undergrowth.

That evening, with the torches already lit and the streets of Tungrorum emptied of its citizens, Marcus walked wearily up the road from the barracks clustered around the east gate and halted in front of the bandit hunters' headquarters. The spear-armed man standing guard on the door showed no more curiosity at the presence of a uniformed centurion standing before him in the torchlight than he might have displayed with the arrival of a butcher's delivery boy. He stood aside and saluted, pointing the way into the building.

'Prefect's inside, Centurion.'

Marcus nodded and walked past him into the entrance hall, glancing around at the statuary decorating the room, their shadows seeming to flutter and twitch with each flicker of the torches that lit the open space. An impressive bust of the emperor took pride of place on one side of the door that he presumed led into the building's main room, while on the other side his eye was taken by a towering female figure mounted on a charging animal, a bow in one hand, the other reaching over her shoulder for an arrow from a painstakingly detailed quiver. Stepping closer, he marvelled at the skill of the man who had conjured the minute details of each arrow's fletching and the delicate lines of the bow from the solid marble.

'Good, isn't it? You could almost wonder why he didn't carve a bow string to match.' The Roman turned to find Caninus standing in the open doorway to his office, a slight smile on his face. 'Everyone that lays eyes on that statue does exactly the same thing. They all lean close enough to almost rub their noses on the arrows in the quiver, then look at the curves in the bow with just that expression you were wearing a moment ago. Whoever it was that sculpted this from bare rock must have been a true master. It was here when I arrived, and I keep it here to remind me of the forest's terrible power to punish the unwary, even if I prefer the mysteries of Our Lord myself. And, I suppose, to serve as a constant warning of my enemy's often stated and apparently implacable intention to see me die on an altar dedicated to her.'

Marcus looked back at the statue, realising for the first time that the huntress was mounted on a wild boar. He spoke with his eyes locked on the goddess's face; it was a classic study of a female divinity that somehow managed to capture both the subject's beauty and her ferocity in equal measure.

'I'd taken her for a representation of Diana, but now I see the truth of it. She's truly magnificent, Prefect, worthy of an imperial palace.' He turned to face his host, making a formal bow and holding the position for a moment longer than necessary to indicate the nature of his business. 'This visit is strictly a private matter, Prefect, but the gratitude I must express on behalf of myself and my wife is no less fervent for lacking an official sanction. I heard of your gallantry in rescuing Felicia from a miserable and degrading assault when I came through the gate this evening, and once I had assured myself that she is well I came straight here. I don't have very long – there's a centurions' briefing shortly – but I couldn't ignore my duty to offer you my thanks.'

Caninus made a slight bow in return.

'Your thanks are hardly necessary, Centurion Corvus. Any decent man would have done the same. Will you take a cup of wine with me?'

Marcus smiled, nodding.

'After a long day on the road your offer is more than welcome.'

The prefect turned back into his office and gestured to the Roman to follow him into the brightly lit room. He poured a generous measure of wine into a cup and handed it to his guest, then poured another for himself and raised it to meet Marcus's.

'To safe returns.' They drank, and the prefect raised a hand to indicate the map of the area painted on the wall. 'And now that you have experienced Arduenna at first hand you will understand better the respect in which we hold the forest, I suspect.'

Marcus smiled wryly.

'Quite so. Your man Arabus was insistent on the subject.'

Caninus's smile was equally sardonic.

'I thought he might be. It was one of the reasons for sending him with you, if truth be told. He's a believer, and I felt that you gentlemen needed to gain some understanding of the fanaticism that drives these people on. These aren't just bandits like the men you've encountered so far; these are men sworn to a jealous and vicious religion, one that tolerates neither argument nor interference, and which is harsh even with its most devoted followers.'

Marcus took another sip, regarding Caninus over the rim of his cup.

'And yet you choose to oppose them in the most public way possible, and despite their repeated threats?'

The other man shrugged.

'What else can I do? If I walk away from here I must thereby accept defeat, and in doing so I will be diminished not only in the eyes of my peers but, worse, in my own estimation. I doubt that I could live easily with such a painful burden. But come now, we'll not discuss even the hint of such a possibility. Your mission was a success, I take it?' He raised a hand to forestall a reply. 'No, I know it's not your place to tell me any of the details, I simply ask if you felt the journey worthwhile. Did my man Arabus perform as required?'

Marcus smiled, raising his cup for another sip.

'He did indeed. I also have reason to be grateful to him for not putting an arrow into me when I blundered into his path while he was hunting a boar.'

Caninus raised an eyebrow.

'Indeed? You were lucky. He's not the fastest man to loose an arrow, but once he's committed the shaft it invariably hits what he's aiming at. Perhaps Arduenna chose to smile on you for that moment.'

This time, Marcus noticed, there was no trace of amusement on his face.

The two tribunes walked out into the gathering of their centurions with the look of men whose fellow feeling, if it had ever existed in the first place, had long since evaporated. Scaurus paused in the doorway for a moment with a cup of wine held in one hand, listening to the babble of conversation.

'It's nice to get a decent cup of red for a change, and not that cat's piss they've been serving since we . . .'

'There were four of them, I heard, all gagging for a piece of uniformed dick . . .'

'And he's paid a hundred in gold for a bloody *sword*! You ask me, that young man's got . . .'

The two first spears stepped forward, each of them barking an order for his officers to stand to attention. Scaurus waited for the echoes of their orders to die away before speaking.

'At ease, gentlemen!'

Tribune Belletor stood by his side with a face barely the right side of disgruntled, and Julius leaned closer to Marcus, ignoring the first spear's warning glance, to mutter in his ear.

'Their tribune looks like he's lost a gold aureus and found a copper quadrans. I heard that Scaurus very nearly pulled his iron on the man and was only . . .'

Scaurus spoke again, looking round the gathered officers with a determined expression.

'Centurions, it's good to have all of you gathered in one place. If we're going to work together then we'll need to break down some of the barriers that traditionally separate auxiliary troops from the legions. I believe that it is these barriers that lead to misunderstandings, and as a result to the kind of unacceptable behaviour that we saw the other night. Behaviour, I will remind you, that had our colleague Prefect Caninus not intervened, would have left an innocent, pregnant woman repeatedly violated, and our cohorts at each other's throats.'

Scaurus paused, passing a slow gaze across the faces turned attentively towards him. He'd said much the same to Belletor a few minutes earlier, when expressing his disappointment that the legion cohort's centurions had not yet managed to unearth the guilty men. Even Frontinius, who found himself cast in the unusual role of peacemaker alongside his colleague Sergius, had commented privately that he would have found the culprits in less than a day.

'Honey and shit, that's the way it works. Nice and nasty. Rewards for the men that turn the bastards in, and collective punishment for the whole bloody cohort until they come to their senses.'

Belletor stood alongside Scaurus in unhappy silence while his colleague explained to the centurions what it was he planned for their combined force. He pointed to the map of the area on the wall of the basilica's main hall, a map which he had requested for the evening's briefing with a studied mannerliness that had left Procurator Albanus with little option but to agree. The civilian administrator was standing off to one side, and clearly fighting to contain his irritation at seeing a host of army officers in the building where he usually conducted his business.

'Centurions, we're here to safeguard the supply of corn to the legion fortresses on the Rhenus. Without that supply their existence becomes precarious, which makes our task of the utmost importance. Exterminating the bandit threat in this part of the province is also going to be of benefit to the local inhabitants, of course, but first and foremost it is about preserving the empire's north-western flank. As you can see from this map, our destruction of two of the opportunist bands that were troubling the roads to the city means that the most obvious remaining threat to the supply routes to the legions comes from here.' He slapped his pointer onto the dark green mass of the Arduenna forest. 'The forest is currently host to the largest of the bandit gangs, perhaps as many as five hundred of them, and they must now be our main focus. When we find and destroy their base of operations, kill as many as we can and scatter the rest, when we have their leader's head on a spear point . . .' He paused and looked around the gathered officers with a wry smile. '. . . with or without his famous mask, then we will have broken the back of this problem! And make no mistake, there's nothing mystical about the man, or his followers. He's just another thug, for all his fearsome reputation, and his gang are no more than that. I don't know about you, but my experience in my younger days was that when you take down the leader of a gang its members tend to lose heart. When they see the strength we muster, they'll pretty soon decide to put survival before profit, you can be sure of that! Intimidating civilians and suborning poorly led local auxiliaries is one thing, but facing up to two cohorts of battle-hardened infantry is quite another.'

He took a sip of wine before speaking again.

'So, tomorrow morning we'll muster at dawn and march west. A brisk morning's march will take us to the junction with the road south to the city of the Treveri, and then we'll turn south and cross the River Mosa. By the end of the day I expect us to be within spitting distance of the forest's edge, and we'll camp under full wartime conditions just in case they see us coming and try to take us by surprise. The day after that, we'll start probing towards their camp, which, thanks to a scouting party from the First Tungrian Cohort, we now know is here, close to the river.'

He pointed to the map behind him, and Marcus flicked a glance around his colleagues to find Titus staring back at him with a knowing expression. His brother officer had walked up to Julius with a wry smile moments earlier, putting a massive hand on Marcus's shoulder and muttering, 'A one-toothed whore, eh? Smart work, brother.' Scaurus continued, his face hawk-like in the torchlight.

'It was always logical to assume that Obduro and his band are operating from somewhere on this edge of Arduenna. They need to get back into the forest's cover as soon as they can once they've carried out a robbery, but now we actually know where to find it. There it is.' He tapped the map. 'Only a few hundred paces of the river and astride the main forest path that leads west until it reaches the road south to the Treveri capital. That ease of access cuts both ways, of course. It makes their lair easier for us to find, and less of a problem to attack than a hideaway in the deep forest. That's the good news. The bad news is that they must have another camp further into the forest, and on higher ground, which they can fall back to if the first one is compromised. It'll probably be built on a hill, almost certainly heavily fortified, and very likely with the ground around it littered with mantraps. It's likely that once they realise we're coming they'll scatter in a dozen different directions and fall back into the deep forest. And once they've disbanded catching them will be like trying to bottle smoke. What we have to do is surround the camp with a nice thick ring of troops before they get the chance to run for it, and get them bottled up and ready to either surrender or die. Either of which will suit me very well. So this plan must remain confidential from anyone not in this room until the time comes to make it work on the ground. That is all, gentlemen. Go back to your centuries and make sure that your men are ready for battle when we march tomorrow. And now, let's have a toast.' He raised his cup. 'Shared victory!'

The centurions echoed the sentiment and raised their own cups, every man in the room draining whatever remained of his wine. One of the legion centurions spoke in the silence that followed his words.

'Ready for battle tomorrow, Tribune? I thought your aim was to engage the bandits the day after that?'

Scaurus nodded grimly, fixing a hard smile on the centurion.

'Indeed it is. But our experience of warfare, no matter who the enemy is, is that they come to fight at the most inconvenient times. We may well find ourselves in battle tomorrow whether we like it or not.'

'Typical fucking army. We sweat our bollocks off for a week building barracks to keep out the rain, with our tents falling to pieces, and then just as we finish the job, they decide that a few days' campaign in the open is a good idea. Whichever genius came up with this idea needs his fucking head looking at. I reckon . . .'

Scarface snapped to attention as a tall figure leaned over his shoulder and a quiet but authoritative voice spoke softly in his ear.

'And I *reckon* that you would be better advised keeping your opinion to yourself, soldier. For while it is the right of every man to complain as often and as long as he wishes, this rule only holds true for as long as he takes good care not to be overheard. If I were actually to hear such a complaint, it would be necessary for me to deliver the appropriate discipline to you.' Scarface stood in flushed and rigid silence, his gaze locked on the line of new barracks before which the cohort was paraded. It was common knowledge that the Ninth Century's chosen man was not the happiest of men that morning, given the biting cold that had taken a grip of Tungrorum overnight, and the veteran soldier was experienced enough in the ways of his superiors to know when the time had come to wind his neck in. 'As it happens, soldier, and despite your much-vaunted mission to keep our centurion from harm, on this evidently rare occasion I happen to know a little bit more about the reason for our excursion into "the open" than it seems you do. Shall I enlighten you?'

He walked along the rear of the century's line with his brass-knobbed pole resting on his broad, mailed shoulder until he came to its end, then retraced his steps along the unit's front, speaking as he went.

'It is Tribune Scaurus's opinion that the time has come for us to deal with the bandits who hide in the Arduenna forest. And that is *his* decision, not the centurion's, not mine and most certainly not *yours*. Very shortly now you will be inspected and briefed in more detail by Centurion Corvus, and then we will march to join the other cohorts outside the city walls. Given our orders to be ready for battle, soldier, you would be better questioning yourself as to whether your sword is sharp and your arm strong, since you may have need of both before the day is ended.'

'Cheeky Hamian b—'

Scarface bit off the last word of his muttered imprecation as Qadir's pole swung out from his shoulder with surprising speed, and he winced as the brass knob struck his helmet's iron plate with a heavy clang. The pole was more usually employed to push a century's rearmost men into action should they prove reluctant to advance, but Qadir was as handy with its secondary use, as a forceful instrument of his authority, as any other chosen man in the cohort. He paced down the row of men with his face set in a neutral expression, although the abashed Scarface, despite the fact that he was concentrating on the barrack in front of him with as much force as he could muster, knew only too well that the Hamian's eyes would be burning with barely suppressed anger.

'I'll pretend I didn't hear that, since you're a senior man. The next time you challenge me to ignore a casual insult made within the range of my excellent hearing, you and I will be enjoying a swift but ugly discussion behind the barracks.' Scarface redoubled his close attention to the wall in front of him and kept his mouth firmly shut. For all his own prowess in the dirty art of barrack-block squabbles, usually settled in the first few seconds with instinctive brutality, Qadir was known to be both fast with his fists and boots and, when sufficiently roused, utterly without scruple in using them to make his point to the rare recalcitrant that chose to ignore his deceptively gentle admonishment. That the veteran soldier would give the big Hamian a decent fight was without doubt, but that he would end up on the losing end of the matter was also fairly obvious. The chosen man gazed levelly at him for a moment before continuing. 'Good. Order is restored. Since the soldier here feels the need for a better understanding of the plan for today's activity, I will elucidate, which, for those among you whose education has primarily been centred on stabbing barbarians, means that I will explain.'

The Hamian stared out across the ranks of blank-faced soldiers, his face set hard.

'In terms that you men will understand, we are marching to attack the bandits who hide in the big forest. They are currently living in a camp close to the far bank of the river, and we will be seeking to trap them there, and prevent them from escaping to their fortress deeper in the forest. If they escape into the forest it will be a bad thing, and much unhappiness will result. And unhappiness, as we all know, flows in only one direction. So I suggest that you all do what you're told, when you're told to do it! And one last thought, gentlemen. We're going to be fighting a hardened enemy, on his own ground and after several months of doing little but guard duty. And if I add up all the money that your weapons and equipment have cost, and then throw in the small brass coin each of you is worth into the bargain, it's clear that Tribune Scaurus will want to lose as few of you as possible. So keep your guards up and be ready to fight! And here, to spare us any further debate, is the centurion. Air your iron, soldiers, and let's see what sort of job you've done in readying yourselves. Present your swords!'

The twin Tungrian cohorts marched out of the city's south-west gate in a compact column, fourteen hundred hard-faced and battle-tested men whose equipment bore the scars of their previous battles like badges of honour. Whilst their shield's brass edging and bosses shone in the chilly morning's sunshine like gold, most of them were roughly scored by swords and axe blows, the laurel wreathes and crescent moons that decorated their linen-covered wooden surfaces sometimes almost completely erased by battle damage and the effects of the harsh frontier weather. Their iron helmets, whilst rust free, were frequently dented and scored by sharp iron, their brow guards deeply notched by enemy blades. In every century there were several men whose faces, while they were protected on either side by their cheek guards, were riven by crude scars that had left thick white lines through eyebrows and lips, or deep gouges in noses and cheek bones. The soldiers marched past the 1st Minervia's Cohort with parade-ground precision, their hobnailed boots rapping on the road's cobbles in perfect unison, and more than one flicked a contemptuous sideways glance at the raw legionaries waiting for them, their breath puffing out in silver plumes.

Behind the 1st Tungrian Cohort came the barbarian warriors of Martos's Votadini, their long hair and thick, brightly coloured woollen clothing at odds with the soldiers' uniform appearance. Some of the warriors were swathed in fur for warmth and all were carrying whichever weapon they favoured, swords, spears and axes as they saw fit. Where the 1st Cohort's men had confined their expressions of disregard to the odd casual glance, these ragged, scarred fighters simply stared at the legionaries in open disgust. A few of the band were carrying war hammers, including the hulking Selgovae warrior Lugos, who loomed over even the tallest of them, his weapon's heavy beak counterweighted by a massive half-moon blade with wicked points at either end with which to snag a fleeing enemy, its vicious edge rough-sharpened to inflict a grievous wound in combat.

Behind the Votadini, and in a position deliberately intended to demonstrate his utter trust in men who had been his enemies only months before, walked Tribune Scaurus, his only escort his German bodyguard, Arminius. Behind them came the 2nd Tungrian Cohort, every bit as crisply turned out and battle-scarred as their brothers in the 1st, and at their rear came the thirty horsemen of the detachment's mounted unit. Each of the animals was led out by its rider, each man marching alongside his mount and keeping a tight hold on its bridle as a precaution against any skittishness from the beasts who clearly sensed that a chance for exercise was to hand. Once the 2nd Cohort's last century had cleared the legion's line, First Spear Frontinius stepped out in front of his men and bellowed an order down the line, pointing to his left.

'Halt! Right turn! Forward march!' The order was echoed instantly by each century's centurion, and the men of both cohorts pivoted on the spot, marching the ten paces that put their formation alongside that of the legion cohort's. 'Halt! About turn! Stand at . . . *ease*!'

Frontinius looked down the road to the spot where Tribune Scaurus had stopped to wait in the wake of the marching centuries, then saluted smartly before marching to his place at the point where his two cohorts joined. Scaurus, Tribune Belletor at his side, looked up and down the line of silent soldiers before speaking.

'Men of the First Minervia and the Tungrian Cohorts! This is the day when we move onto an offensive footing against the bandit leader Obduro! Today we march to a position close to their forest encampment, and the day after that we will attack. You must stay alert to anything unusual, for these are not ordinary opponents in any sense of the word. They may only be a few hundred strong, but they have local knowledge, and many of them have military skills. I expect that they will fight like animals to avoid capture and execution, and you may find that you must attack with equal ferocity to best them even though we ought to have superiority in numbers. That is all. First Spears?'

Frontinius walked forward again, exchanging nods with Sergius, who stepped out in front of the legionaries.

'Forward . . . *march*!' Their combined bellow of command set the three cohorts into movement, and as the long line of men reached the road they shouted another command. 'Halt! Right . . . *turn*!' Within seconds the three cohorts were lined up along the road, while Scaurus, who had stepped back off the road's surface to avoid being caught in their mass movement, turned a sardonic grin on his colleague.

'Ready to march for a while, eh Tribune?'

Belletor raised an eyebrow.

'March? *March*, Rutilius Scaurus? Why would we be *marching*?'

His colleague smiled knowingly.

'Some senior officers, Tribune, like to match their fitness against that of their men, to see if they can keep pace with the old sweats through a long marching day. And besides, it's such a lovely day for a stroll.'

Belletor's snort of disbelief dripped with his incredulity at the suggestion.

'A lovely day for a stroll? I shall be riding my horse, and I'd suggest you do the same unless you want to be taken for one of those men that seek the favour of their soldiers by attempting to emulate them.'

Scaurus laughed and turned away.

'And you, Tribune, might want to consider walking for a while, unless you want to be taken for one of those men whose feet aren't hard enough to sustain the pace. I can assure you that there are worse things than being taken for an officer who respects his men well enough to share their hardships.' He raised his voice to parade-ground volume. 'Shall we be on our way, gentlemen? This Obduro isn't going to wait around forever!'

Frontinius raised his vine stick above his head, stepping to one side of the long column to be seen by as many men as possible.

'First Cohort! At the standard march . . . *march*!'

As the leading centuries strode out down the road Prefect Caninus turned to Scaurus, gesturing at his men who were waiting alongside their horses, and speaking in a quiet tone intended to keep their discussion private.

'I wish you good hunting, Tribune. As agreed, I will take my men away down the road to the west again, to ensure that there's no chance of a traitor in their ranks alerting the bandits to your approach.'

The tribune nodded.

'Thank you, Prefect, I'll certainly be happier knowing that we don't have to worry about whoever it is Obduro might have planted on you. My own mounted detachment will go forward alongside you as far as the junction where the road to Augusta

Treverorum branches off to the south, and will then report back to me that the road is clear of any sign of Obduro's band. It will be good exercise for their horses, and a nice change for their riders from having nothing to do except brush their animals and shovel away their droppings.'

Caninus nodded his understanding, then turned away, shouting orders to his men. Scaurus raised his arm and signalled to Decurion Silus. The decurion saluted and signalled to his men, who promptly mounted and trotted their horses up the column, with Caninus and his detachment following them. Scaurus looked back at Belletor, gesturing to the road stretching away to the west.

'Your last chance, Tribune. Will you accompany me for a while? Perhaps we might share a discussion about Rome. I'm sure you miss it as much as I do.'

The other man shook his head dismissively.

'I'll be riding, thank you. By all means come for a chat when you get tired of slumming it with your soldiers.'

Scaurus turned away with a wry shake of his head.

'The company of my men is likely to entertain me for longer than you might imagine possible.'

Silus reined in his horse alongside the 9th Century's marching men, grinning down at Marcus and raising an eyebrow in question.

'The usual offer is open, Centurion. You could always scout forward with us this morning. I'm sure your chosen man is more than capable of looking after these soldiers.'

The young centurion shook his head.

'Not today, I'm afraid, Silus. Much as I'd like nothing better than to ride along with you, my duty is here with my soldiers. And besides, to deprive whoever's riding that monster Bonehead of his mount today would be to condemn him to a day rubbing his feet raw and listening to our full repertoire of songs about cavalrymen and your close relationships with the local wildlife.'

One of the younger soldiers marching beside him was unable to contain himself, and raised his voice above the rattle of hobnails.

'And sheep, Centurion!'

The century's watch officer, a one-eyed veteran universally called Cyclops whenever he wasn't listening, promptly stepped out of the rank ahead of the miscreant and marched next to him with his face inches from his victim's, bellowing admonishment and imprecation at the top of his voice, much to the young soldier's dismay and Silus's pleasure.

'*Don't* you dare to interrupt the young gentleman when he's talking to another officer, you nasty little man! I'll have you shovelling shit on latrine duty for the next month!' Marcus raised an eyebrow at the decurion, rolling his eyes at the vehemence of the tirade. The watch officer caught a glimpse of the expression from the corner of his eye, but misinterpreted the cause and redoubled his verbal assault on the visibly wilting soldier. 'And now you've upset the officer, you worthless excuse for a soldier. He thinks you're a prick, the decurion thinks you're a prick, and I'm fucking certain you're a prick, which makes you what? Eh?'

'A . . . a prick?'

'A prick, *Watch Officer*! Come with me!' He dragged the soldier out of the ranks, putting a booted foot into his backside. 'Run, you fucker! Let's see how long you can keep up with the horses, shall we?'

'Ah, the enjoyment of watching an experienced professional in action. I see man management is still a strong point with the infantry.'

Marcus shook his head in resigned amusement, waving Silus away.

'You'd best be off to see what's going on over the next hill. And I'd better rescue that soldier before Watch Officer Augustus puts his severed head on a spear to encourage the rest of my men. Enjoy your day's scouting!'

The decurion shot him an ironic salute and moved away to rejoin his men, shouting a command and nudging his horse into a fast trot. As the scouts headed for the horizon Marcus turned his attention back to the hapless soldier, already fifty paces up the road with Cyclops in vigorous and noisy pursuit.

'Hold this for a minute. I need to dig my cloak out and put the bloody thing on.'

Morban passed his standard to the trumpeter marching at his side and reached for the heavy woollen rectangle, thanking the foresight that had made him roll it up and wrap it around his belt. The younger man smirked down at him as he tugged it about his barrel-shaped body with a grunt of satisfaction.

'Feeling the cold, are you?'

The standard bearer answered in a voice loud enough to be heard over the clash of hobnails, never taking his attention off the brooch's stubborn pin.

'Bloody thing won't close. I knew I should have got this seen to while we were in barracks. The pin's too short, and the bloody thing's bent in the middle.' He shot the trumpeter a vindictive glance, then turned his head and raised an eyebrow to the soldiers marching behind them. 'A bit like your cucumber, from what I could see of that rather unpleasant act you were performing last night when I walked into the barrack without knocking and giving you time to hide it away. Now have you had enough, or do you want some more, tiny bent cock?' Morban waited for a moment to be sure that the abashed trumpeter wasn't going to scrape together enough wit to come back at him with any one of the retorts he would have mustered under the same accusation, then shook his head in genuine disgust. 'Soldiers with less than ten years' service should be seen and not heard, I'd say.' The veteran marching behind him nodded his agreement, his voice a gravelly rasp as he rose to Morban's game.

'I knows. Give 'em a few months and they loves to play with the big lads, but they goes all quiet and runs away the second you gives 'em a proper smacking. Shouldn't be allowed to join in with the fun and games until they've done their ten and learned to stand up for themselves. And to hold their beer . . .'

He winked at Morban, who gave the trumpeter a significant

glance. The younger man started to protest, but swiftly closed his mouth again as Morban raised an eyebrow at him.

'I wouldn't, if I were you. Just make do with starting a conversation about something that can't be turned against you.'

'Such as?'

'Such as the weather. See, when we set out this morning the sun was all bright and shiny, and you were thinking about a lovely warm day for marching, but now the sky's the same colour as . . .'

The trumpeter opened his mouth to suggest something that matched the western sky's dull grey, but was beaten to it by the soldier behind him.

'. . . as his face when he'd done puking all over his boots the other night?'

'That's it, just the same colour!' Morban smirked at the younger man for a moment before taking pity on his expression of bemused fury. 'Now, now, don't you go getting all hot and bothered. Look, there's trees on the horizon; that's the forest we're marching to conquer!'

'So that's this Arduenna the locals all worship, is it?'

Tribune Scaurus looked across the farmland that stretched out before them to the forested hills in the distance, their dark slopes blending with the overcast sky.

Frontinius was marching beside him with a slight limp, the legacy of a sharp-eyed barbarian archer's arrow at the battle of Lost Eagle the previous year. He nodded without breaking step.

'Yes, Tribune, that's the Arduenna. If the maps are right we're only a couple of miles from the forest edge, although that might as well be twenty given the river that runs between here and the hills. A hundred paces wide and more, and apparently deep enough to be unfordable, other than across the shallows at Mosa Ford. If Dubnus has it wrong then we'll have to go all the way west to the river bridge on the road to the Treveri capital, then march back to the east along the river bank.'

He stopped talking, raising an eyebrow at the tribune, who was gently shaking his head.

'We'll just have to hope that your centurion's eyes weren't deceiving him, then, won't we? Ah, here come the mounted scouts now. You can stop the column for a rest, First Spear; let's see what your man Silus has to say for himself.'

The decurion rode up and dismounted, saluting smartly to the tribune and the two first spears, who had gathered to hear his report.

'We went all the way to the bridge, Tribune, without any sign of movement. There's a couple of carts a few miles down the road, but nothing to interest us. Prefect Caninus took his men away to the west, as agreed.'

Scaurus nodded to Frontinius, who returned his gaze with a questioning look.

'As we discussed it, Tribune?'

Opening his mouth to confirm the order, Scaurus was silenced by a voice from behind him.

'As you discussed *what*?'

Scaurus turned to find Belletor, still mounted on his horse, close behind him. He looked up at the bemused tribune with a tight smile and pointed in the direction of the river.

'We're leaving the road and marching south for the Mosa. Once we're off the road we'll deploy into formation for an approach march, and your men can bring up the rear.'

Belletor frowned down at him.

'But I thought . . .'

'. . . that we were heading for the road bridge over the Mosa another ten miles to the west? Indeed, you did, along with the entire population of Tungrorum, I'd imagine. But one of my centurions has discovered a little secret, a piece of tactical intelligence I personally rate as pure gold, so we're going to try something else, something not even Caninus and his men know about.' He turned away from the baffled tribune, gesturing to Frontinius. 'Whenever you're ready, Sextus.'

Frontinius limped away, shouting for his centurions and quickly gathering the officers around him in a tight group. First Spear Sergius tipped Belletor a quick salute and sidled across to join them, while soldiers on all sides stared at the gathering with undisguised curiosity. Scarface stared at the cluster of armoured men for a moment and then turned away, shaking his head and reaching for his shield and helmet.

'Best get your gear on, lads. The last time I seen Uncle Sextus looking that serious was before the battle where the Sixth Legion lost their eagle, and I ended up fighting off the fucking bluenoses for the rest of the afternoon. Got a nasty gash down one arm and lost both my best mates, one dead before he hit the ground, the other one coughing up blood for half a day before his eyes closed. This'll end up with us out in front, if my guess is right. And it looks set to fucking rain.'

In the heart of his gathered officers, Frontinius looked around the intent faces that surrounded him, nodding his recognition of their solemnity.

'Yes, you've all guessed it; we've got a direct route to the enemy camp and we're going straight in. Dubnus found what looks like a way across the river while he was out scouting with Centurions Julius and Corvus, so we're marching south to the Mosa at speed. We'll get deployed over the river as fast and as quietly as possible, and then go for an encirclement of the rebel camp before they even know they're under attack, never mind who's behind the spears. And if we put this lot in the bag then our job here really will be done, and we can enjoy some well-earned peace and quiet. Once we leave this rest halt we'll deploy into approach march formation.' He looked around the group again. 'I'll have the Ninth Century out in front in extended order looking for trouble all the way to the river, fast and light-footed. Try to keep it inconspicuous, Centurion Corvus. I don't want them to know we're coming until we're across the river at the very earliest, and preferably not until we've got their camp surrounded by enough spears that they'll just go straight to the bit where they throw down their iron without even considering a fight. Think you can manage that?'

Marcus nodded silently, already rehearsing the orders he would issue to his men. Frontinius recognised his preoccupation and moved the briefing on.

'Good. Dubnus, you'll be out in front with the Ninth. I need you to take us straight to the place in question without any risk of it turning into the scenic route, your chosen man can look after your men in your absence. Following up behind the scouts I want a three-century front, one solid wall of shields if the need arises, so keep the formation as tight as you like. Centurions Clodius, Caelius and Otho, your lads ought to find that well enough to their liking.'

Julius snorted his laughter into the intent silence.

'The Badger, the Hedgehog and Knuckles all in a row. You really do mean business.'

Marcus winked at Caelius, watching as his brother officer rubbed self-consciously at the spiky, brush-like hair that had led to his nickname, smiling to himself at Julius's praise. While Clodius and Otho were brutal, bombastic leaders, continually goading their men in competition for the unofficial title of the cohort's most dangerous century, Caelius was a quieter man by comparison, until, that was, the enemy were within spear throw. Then, and only then, did he seem to swell beyond his usual size, and become a leader whose simple example could encourage bravery from his men where words might fail.

Frontinius nodded at Julius with a determined expression.

'If by some chance we're in action before we reach the river I want to be up and in their faces the instant they show themselves. So you three had better be ready for anything.'

Julius nodded knowingly.

'And since the Ninth will all be dead or dying, you want these three to overrun them and rescue that pretty sword, eh First Spear?'

His superior smiled grimly.

'Well, you won't be in with any chance of recovering it, Julius, because you'll be leading one of the wings. We'll have three centuries on your side of the line, ready for an envelopment once the front three have got the enemy fixed, when and if we bump into them. The left wing will be commanded by you, Julius, and will consist of your Fifth Century with the Eighth and Second behind you, and the right will consist of the First and Tenth Centuries, led by Titus.'

The hulking commander of the Tenth Century spoke up, his voice a bass growl as he pointed a finger at Julius.

'Be ready to bring your girls running if we take the brunt of an attack, eh little man? Two centuries might struggle to hold back five hundred mutineers, even if the two centuries involved are the best in the cohort.'

Julius, himself a hulking brute of a man even if he was a head shorter than his colleague, grinned at him wolfishly before turning back to his old friend Frontinius.

'And you, First Spear, where will you be if I've got your boys alongside mine?'

'Me? I'll be accompanying Centurion Caelius, as close behind the Ninth as we can manage. Now, Second Cohort . . .' Their sister unit's centurions stepped forward, their faces every bit as grim as those of their colleagues. 'We all know that the legion cohort isn't experienced enough to stand alone against a determined attack – no insult intended, colleague.' Sergius nodded graciously to show that none was taken. 'So I'll have your lads close up behind us to provide fast reinforcement.'

'You're sure you know where to find this crossing?'

Dubnus nodded grimly in response to Arminius's question, his head thrown back to suck greedily at the cold air as they followed the 9th Century's extended line at a pace closer to a jog than a march.

'As sure as I can be, given that I only saw the place from the opposite bank, and that was with my head six inches from the ground. Like I told your lads that have run forward to scout the river bank, the only real landmark I could see was a bloody great tree on this side of the river, as I recall it, bent over almost double and with its branches trailing over the water. When we find that, we've found the crossing.'

Marcus and Qadir had already decided to add even more pace to their advance by sending forward the half-dozen fastest distance runners in the century. The men in question had dumped their shields and spears on their mates and hared forward in front of the Ninth's already rapid progress across the open ground between the road and the river, briefed to look for the landmark that Dubnus had described to them. Looking back, Marcus could see the shields of the centuries following them, a good half mile behind.

'It's getting so cold that my bloody fingers are starting to go numb.' Dubnus clenched his fists, trying to get more blood into them, and sniffed the air dubiously. 'If it wasn't already the middle of Aprilis I'd swear there was snow on the way.'

They looked unhappily at the heavy grey wall looming over them out of the western sky, and Marcus shook his head with a look of unease.

'Whatever comes out of that cloud, it isn't going to be warm.'

Arminius looked across at Marcus, who was staring up at the towering mass of dark grey cloud with a bemused expression.

'This happened every now and then in my home village. We knew well enough to find shelter and not come out until the storm had passed. When the rain starts we won't be able to see any further than the ends of our fingers.'

Dubnus shrugged.

'Nobody made you come forward with us. You could have been safe back there with the tribunes if you hadn't been so determined to keep us company.'

A brief smirk lifted one side of the German's face, and he shook his head dismissively, waving a hand towards Marcus.

'I'm not here for you, Dubnus, for all that you make a decent sparring partner on occasion. I'm here for *him*. I still owe the centurion here a life, and when the tribune sees fit to send us forward into the teeth of a spring storm to hunt army deserters I expect that my chance to repay that debt might be to hand.'

A sharp-eyed Hamian soldier striding along in front of Marcus pointed and shouted something in his own language to Qadir, who stared for a moment before calling to Marcus.

'One of the runners is waving back to us. They see the tree!'

Taking the 9th Century within two hundred paces of the river bank, Marcus advanced down the ground's gentle slope to the Mosa's meandering stream, then waved the soldiers into the cover of the scattered bushes and long grass. He made his way forward with Dubnus and Arminius until they were crouched in the shelter of the bent tree, using its trunk to protect them from the wind's biting chill. The scout who had spotted the landmark, one of the century's Hamian archers, huddled alongside them wrapped in his cloak; he eyed the river's hard, cold water with a disconsolate expression.

'You're sure it's here?'

Dubnus nodded at Marcus's question, unlacing his boots and unwinding the leg wrappings that swathed his calves, before rolling up his rough woollen leggings. Hanging the boots around his neck, he turned back to the Hamian.

'Give me your spear.' The scout handed him the weapon with a curious look which the centurion ignored, turning back to the river bank with eyes narrowed in concentration. 'Watch this.'

He stepped cautiously forward into the open, using the scout's spear to prod at the shallow water lapping along the river's muddy bank, while soft mud oozed up through his toes. The spear sank into the water with each prod, and the soldier frowned without realising it, thinking of the polishing that would be required to return the weapon to a state that would satisfy Qadir's notoriously strict views on his soldiers' equipment. Then, without any apparent reason, the iron blade stopped dead with less than half of its length in the water. Dubnus turned back with a triumphant grin, then stepped forward into the river, his feet barely submerged under the cold water. The scout gaped, pointing at the water flowing around the centurion's ankles with a look of amazement.

'Look, Centurion! He's . . . he's walking on the water!'

Marcus shook his head with a smile.

'No he isn't. But there's something there strong enough to support his weight.'

He waved the man back towards the waiting century.

'Fetch the first spear. Tell him we've found the bridge and bring him here.'

By the time Frontinius limped up to join him, a cluster of

centurions in tow, Dubnus was a hundred paces away across the river and lacing up his boots. The senior centurion stared across the river at his officer, shaking his head in disbelief and speaking quietly to Marcus.

'I can hardly believe it, but Dubnus was right. There it is, a stone bridge beneath the water's surface.' He looked hard at the far bank, but there was no sign of any movement in the trees that lined the river, except for Dubnus. 'Get your men across there and join him, Centurion Corvus, then set up a fifty-pace perimeter, and in Cocidius's name keep it *quiet*. By all means scout forward, but I don't want them waking up to our presence here with the cohort only part deployed or it could turn into a massacre of everyone that's already reached the far side. Get moving.' Marcus turned away, beckoning Qadir and Arminius to him, and Frontinius turned back to the 1st Cohort's gathered centurions. 'Right then, in the same formation as before, advance to the river at the march. When you get here the first three centuries are to follow the Ninth across, while the flank guards will stay in place on this bank to make sure we keep possession of this side of the crossing. If we feed Second Cohort through straight after that we'll have fourteen hundred men on the far bank. First Spear Sergius?'

'Colleague?' Sergius stepped forward from the group of officers, and Frontinius took a moment to weigh him up, mindful of Scaurus's concern with the man's appetite for battle. The legion cohort's first spear returned the gaze with a slight smile, his facial scar twisting with the expression. 'Wondering how much fight we've got in us?'

Frontinius nodded, deciding to address the issue bluntly.

'Yes, colleague, I am. If I send your men across the river and they get on the wrong end of a bandit counter-attack they could well break and scatter into the woods. And nobody's going to thank me if I lose an entire cohort of legionaries, are they?'

'Agreed. And yet they have to learn their trade somewhere. Why not let me set them in defence of the bridge on this side? In the unlikely event that you have to fall back from the bandit camp we'll hold the crossing and stop you getting cut off. It's nice simple duty for my lads but still a useful role, if you take a minute to think it through.'

He stared at Frontinius, and something in his expression swayed the Tungrian.

'Done. I'll make sure my tribune and yours play nicely with the idea. It's about time we all started acting like adults.'

Sergius nodded and turned away, his helmet's crest riffling with the wind's intermittent but powerful gusts, and Frontinius turned back to his centurions.

'Right, get on with it. I want the leading centuries across the river and setting up a perimeter, so get your boys moving!'

The 9th Century crossed the river, moving across the submerged bridge with exaggerated caution at first, groping forward with their bare feet ankle-deep in the Mosa's cold, swift-flowing water. With every man that crossed successfully, however, their confidence grew visibly, and by the time the century was almost fully across the river the last men were moving with easy confidence, their feet gripping the roughened stone slabs that had been laid across piers of blocks piled onto the river's bed to make the bridge's submerged surface. Marcus and Dubnus huddled in the cover of a large bush, waiting as the soldiers crouched close to the ground and pulled their socks and boots back on, rewinding the heavy woollen leg wrappings around their damp ankles.

'They must have built it in the middle of the summer last year, when the river was lower.'

Marcus nodded at Dubnus's words absently, looking back across the Mosa and then turning to peer into the trees that reached almost to the water's edge.

'It's simple enough when you think about it. Obduro's found a shallow point in the river, still too deep to be a foot crossing like the one beside the bridge at Mosa Ford, but shallow enough for his purposes, and he's used local stone to make the bridge. There's no way anyone can sail up the Mosa this far, not with the shallows and the bridge blocking the way at Mosa Ford, so there was never much risk of anyone finding this crossing point.

If you hadn't overheard his men talking about it we'd never have been any the wiser. Uncle Sextus wants us to push the perimeter out, and allow some room for the rest of the cohort, and I need to know what might be waiting for us in the trees

He signalled to Qadir, and the Hamian made his way down the century's line, bent almost double to avoid any chance of his being seen.

'Centurion?'

'Push the century forward, but slowly and quietly, and only for another hundred paces. I'm going to take Scarface and his tent party forward to do a little scouting.'

The Hamian saluted, looking up as the wind whistling through the trees above them gusted enough to drop a light shower of twigs across the waiting century.

'Yes, Centurion. And if we come under attack?'

'If you come under attack you blow your whistles and we'll pull back to the rest of the cohort. I'll not lose another century the way the Sixth got cut to pieces at the battle of the Barbarian Camp, and I haven't got enough trained centurions to throw away two good officers and my best chosen man.'

They turned to find First Spear Frontinius lacing up his boots at the river's edge, one eyebrow lifted in mock exasperation as he lifted a hand to wave Marcus and Dubnus away. 'Well, don't just stand there staring at me, get on with your scouting. And don't worry, there'll be three centuries in line behind you as soon as I can get them across, and two full cohorts queuing up behind them. I'll keep an eye on the Ninth for you.'

Marcus and Qadir shared a quick glance, the Hamian bowing his head slightly to indicate his understanding of his orders. The Roman beckoned to Scarface, who was, as usual, lurking close to his officer.

'Soldier, gather your tent party and follow me.'

The veteran looked to Qadir, whose brisk nod was part command and part warning, then turned and whispered hoarsely at his comrades.

'Come on, lads.'

The soldiers picked up their shields and waited for Marcus to lead them off into the trees, taking position to either side of their officer in a tight formation. Dubnus and Arminius exchanged wry smiles at the men's familiar protective behaviour towards 'their young gentleman', falling in behind the small group with their swords drawn. Groping forward quietly into the forest's bulk, Marcus was struck by how quickly the light filtering down through the trees changed to a washed-out green. He squinted into the forest, frowning with the realisation that it was impossible to look into the wind-rippled foliage for any distance without everything seeming to blend into a blurred green wall that rendered even his sharp eyesight close to useless. As the men beside him paced slowly into the trees, the Tungrians taking their lead from the two experienced Hamian hunters among their number, he turned back to speak with Dubnus. His friend raised a questioning eyebrow at him, and Marcus leaned close to whisper in his ear.

'How do you manage to see anything in this?'

Dubnus nodded, muttering his reply in a tone so soft that it was almost lost in the wind's steadily increasing moan through the tree tops.

'Don't try to focus on any part of the forest, just look at the whole thing.' Marcus frowned at the advice, and Arminius leaned in to speak with an amused look.

'It takes a hunter years to perfect this, my friend, and here you are trying to master it in the space of a two-hundred-pace stroll. Trust your Hamians; they are masters at seeing the slightest movement in places like this.'

The Roman shrugged and turned back to his section of the line feeling none the wiser, sensing his friends' gazes following him. The tent party edged forward pace by pace, heads lifting with increasing frequency to look up at the wind-lashed trees, until one of the men to his right sank into cover with a hand raised. As the soldiers to either side followed his example in a ripple of hissed warnings Marcus went forward quickly, a hand on the hilt of his spatha, and knelt alongside the Hamian.

'What did you see?'

'It is their camp, Centurion.'

Raising his head a fraction, the Roman looked over the bushes and found himself staring into an encampment constructed in a large circular clearing fully a hundred paces across. A curved row of crudely constructed wooden huts stretched around the clearing, and thin lines of smoke were rising from several recently extinguished fires. Frowning, he turned his head slowly in a futile attempt to find any trace of the bandits' presence.

'Nothing?'

Marcus turned his head slightly, keeping his eyes fixed on the clearing

'Nothing. But they were here recently, or the fire wouldn't be burning. I—'

He stopped in mid-sentence as a single fat snowflake danced past his face, watching as it fell onto the forest's floor and disappeared in an instant, melting away as if it had never existed. Looking up, the two men watched as a curtain of snow descended from the treetops high above them, its sudden onslaught all the more shocking for the bitterness of the wave of freezing air that washed over them at the same moment. Scarface turned a bemused gaze upwards, shaking his head.

'Here it fucking comes.' He raised an eyebrow at Marcus, tugging his cloak tighter about him. 'What now, Centurion?'

The Roman stared up into the descending snow, momentarily uncertain as to the right thing to do. He turned back to Dubnus, seeing his own uncertainty written across his friend's face.

'We could retreat to the bridge.' He paused and shook his head, imagining the first spear's reaction to a retreat in the face of a snow shower. 'No, we'll go forward, slowly and carefully, and for the time being we'll ignore the snow. It may be no more than a temporary inconvenience.'

Scarface nodded with pursed lips and turned back to his men, waving them forward with another whispered command.

'Come on now, lads, nice and easy. An' keep your fucking eyes peeled!'

The young centurion stepped through the tent party's line and was the first to break cover from the forest's edge, the patterned spatha drawn and ready in his right hand, the weight and feel of its carved hilt comforting in his moment of uncertainty. The snow was falling more thickly than before, and the clearing's far side was already almost invisible behind a barely opaque white curtain that seemed to descend with the weight and speed of rain. The ground beneath their feet was covered in a thin layer of crisp white flakes that yielded a hobnailed boot print when a man lifted his foot, and with a sinking feeling Marcus realised that the snow-fall wasn't likely to stop any time soon. Turning back he found Dubnus behind him, his head shaking and his face set against the snow being blown into it by the storm's intermittent gusts. His friend had to raise his voice to be heard over the wind's howl, but the look he gave Marcus was eloquent.

'We'll have to turn back. This isn't a quick squall; it's a full blizzard, a freezing storm!'

'But the bandits . . .'

Dubnus shook his head, pointing at the clearing's far side, now entirely lost to sight in the blizzard's shifting white wall.

'They're gone. Either they had a warning or they might just have pulled out when the storm started getting close. Either way you need to pull your men back, Marcus; this is only going to get worse. We need to get back to the—'

Something moving behind the wall of snow in front of them caught his attention, and as he squinted into the white murk a flight of arrows hissed out of the barely visible trees. One of the soldiers fell to his knees with blood pouring from his throat, his hands scrabbling at the arrow that had transfixed his neck, then pitched full length in a dark, spreading pool. Sanga, the soldier closest to Marcus of all the tent party, had the presence of mind to step in close and hold his shield across both their bodies with just enough speed to defend him against the second volley, and the Roman watched as a pair of iron heads slammed into the layered board with enough force for their points to protrude through the wood by a finger's thickness. The soldier looked round at him with a shocked expression, then dropped the shield and slowly went down on one knee with a grunt of pain, another arrow protruding from his leg just above the knee. Marcus's eyes narrowed as he reckoned the odds.

'Dubnus! Get them out of here!'

He grabbed Sanga's arrow-studded shield from the ground where the soldier had dropped it and sprinted forward across the clearing, weaving from left to right with missiles flicking past him to either side, protected from the archers by the thick, shifting curtains of snow. Without warning a figure holding a bow appeared from the storm in front of him, revealed by a sudden gust that whipped away the snow's white curtain, and without pausing in his rush Marcus hammered the shield's battered brass boss into the bandit's face, hearing the crackle of breaking bones over the storm's demonic scream. Spinning away from the felled archer he saw a line of bowmen to his left, still unaware of his presence as they loosed another volley of arrows into the snow's murk. Dropping the shield, knowing it would be more hindrance than help at such close quarters, he drew his gladius and ran at the bowmen through the trees. Raising the spatha in readiness to strike, he was upon the closest of them as the archer fumbled with numb fingers to nock another arrow, only realising he was under attack as the Roman tore his throat out with a thrust of the long blade.

The man beyond him dropped his bow, his attention caught by his comrade's choking death throes, drawing a sword and reaching for the small shield at his feet as his attacker lunged in without breaking step. Marcus raised the spatha horizontally across his body to hack at the raised shield with a backhand blow, smashing it aside and ignoring the small blade's ineffectual rasping slither across the surface of his mail, gambling that the weapon's point would not snag one of the shirt's rings and rip through its protection, then rammed his gladius up into the bandit's chest to stop his heart. The dead man's corpse sagged into his arms with a gasp of expelled breath, and Marcus held him there, ignoring the hot blood running down to splash across his boots, and staring over his victim's shoulder as the archers arrayed behind the man loosed their arrows into their comrade in the hope of killing their attacker. Three times the dead man's body shivered with the impact of their iron heads, and Marcus felt three hard taps against his armoured body as the points tore through the dead man's body and spent their remaining power against his mail's rings.

He shoved the corpse away from him to his left and sprang away to the right again, counting on a moment of indecision before the remaining archers realised which of them would be next. Ducking round a tree he ran past the first man, chopping a deep wound into his thigh with the gladius and leaving him staggering in howling agony, then he charged on to his next target, dodging one last, panicked bowshot and lowering his shoulder to charge the archer, punching the air out of him. Spinning away from the winded man he threw the gladius at the last of them, forcing him to duck away from the blade's tumbling flicker of polished iron and giving Marcus time to sprint the last few paces and hack the longer blade across the man's exposed neck. The patterned sword's lethal edge slid through flesh and bone as if he were cutting smoke, and the archer's head spun away to land on the snow-covered ground while his body slumped away like an unstrung puppet, blood pumping from the severed artery. Spinning back, Marcus put the blade's point to the winded man's throat, gesturing for him to drop the bow hanging uselessly from his right hand. The bandit obeyed without hesitation, compelled by his captor's wild stare, and he eased away into the snow's protection with his hands raised from the knife at his belt.

Marcus turned round and found his gladius, dropping it back into its scabbard.

'*Marcus!*'

The shout sounded distant, muffled by the snow, and he realised with a sinking feeling that he had run too far and too quickly to be sure in which direction he should look to find his men. As he opened his mouth to call out a reply a handful of men stepped forward from out of the falling snow, each of them carrying a standard-issue auxiliary shield and hefting a long spear, the points all aimed squarely at him. As he stood, balanced on the balls of his feet and ready to attack, no matter what the odds, a voice spoke from behind him, and he spun round to see another figure materialise out of the swirling flakes of ice, with more spearmen standing at his sides. The snowflakes falling past the polished metal of his face mask were so thick that they made the shining metal appear as white as the blizzard itself, and as Marcus stared at the apparition before him the man behind the mask spoke.

'Put up your sword, Centurion, and we'll let you live. I need a messenger to carry my words back to Tungrorum, and you'll suit my purpose just as long as you kill no more of my men. Or we could just spear you here and now, and leave you for the storm, an offering to appease Arduenna's wrath at your invasion of her sacred ground.' Marcus stared at him for a moment longer before holding his arms out, the sword dangling limply from his open hand. As the spearmen stepped forward to disarm him he heard his name called again, the sound even fainter than before although whether this was due to distance or the sheer volume of snow falling into the forest, he could not tell. 'Wise, Centurion, very wise. You shall be my guest for the night, until the goddess's anger abates, and this snow stops falling. Bring him.'

A pair of spears prodded him firmly in the back, their points jabbing at him through his mail's thin rings, and Marcus knew that he was without choice or alternatives. He was a prisoner of Obduro.

6

'We either get them across the river or they'll die here, it's as simple as that!'

First Spear Sergius squinted unhappily through the afternoon's premature gloom at the Mosa's black water. He looked to his tribune for orders, but Belletor was looking up into the falling snow with the face of a man overtaken by events.

'But if we get our tents up? Surely that'll be enough protection.'

Frontinius shook his head impatiently, pointing back at the submerged bridge.

'I didn't come back across that bloody thing at the risk of drowning myself to chat about this for a while, Sergius! Can you hear that?'

He put a cupped hand to his ear and tipped his head in question. Sergius nodded, his eyes thoughtful.

'Axes'

'Yes, axes! My pioneer centuries are across the river and chopping down trees as fast as they can. Look around you, man! On this side of the river there's nothing, no shelter, nothing to burn other than a few bushes and saplings; everything else has been torn out and then grazed flat. Over there we've got their camp, which is surrounded by trees, which means fuel for fires and some measure of shelter from this wind.'

Sergius frowned in disbelief, waving a hand at the snow falling around them.

'How will you get anything to burn in this?'

Frontinius raised both hands in imprecation.

'Fucking Cocidius, help me! Tribune?'

Scaurus glanced at Belletor, and then stepped forward, his black cloak made grey by the snow sticking to it. His voice was edged with urgency.

'We've learned a few things in the last year, First Spear Sergius. Please trust me when I tell you that lighting up these trees isn't going to be a problem, not once we've got a flame. There'll be enough heat and light for every one of us even before we're all across the river, but we have to get the men moving now, or we'll risk losing hundreds of them to the cold if this blizzard keeps up.'

Sergius looked to his own tribune again, but found the man's face a study in prevarication. He came to a decision, nodding his agreement with his colleague's proposal.

'Very well. I've got enough rope in our carts to put a line across the river for the men to hold onto.'

Frontinius clapped him on the shoulder.

'Good man, that's the spirit. With a bit of luck we'll get this lot across the river and into the warmth before any of them die of the cold. Julius?'

His deputy stepped forward, his face turned away from the blizzard's force.

'First Spear?'

'You're in charge on this side. Get the legion troops across first, then the Second Cohort, then what's left of the First. You'd better tell them to keep an eye on the mules too, and to butcher any that don't survive the cold before they go stiff. That way at least we'll have something to cook once we get the fires lit. You get this lot moving, and I'll go back over there and make sure the men that are already across are still in one piece.'

He eyed the river's black water for a moment before stepping back onto the bridge's slippery submerged stone, then turned back to shout one last instruction.

'Martos! I'll have you and your warriors across the river, if you please! Bring that jar with you, and in the name of whatever god it is you pray to, don't drop the bloody thing in the river or we're all as good as dead!'

*

'Blindfold him, Grumo. And make sure he's not going to offer any more resistance.'

Having surrendered his helmet to one of the spearmen, Marcus stood in silence while a huge man dressed in brown walked out from behind the hedge of bandit spears and approached him with a hard look in his eyes. Even the knowledge that the blow was coming did little to help him ride its power, and he reeled back several paces at the force of the giant's punch. The bandit's massive fist had smashed into his temple in a blow calculated to addle his wits, and the Roman stood helplessly with his hands on his knees and watched through pain-slitted eyes as his assailant flourished a blindfold before tying it roughly over his eyes. Another man stripped away his weapons with swift, deft movements before gripping his arm and pulling him out of his slumped position, putting the ice-cold point of a blade up the sleeve of Marcus's mail to prick at the soft skin of his armpit, only a single swift thrust from killing him. The weapon's wielder jabbed his knife into the Roman's defenceless flesh, sending him an unspoken warning that left a runnel of blood oozing into the tunic beneath his armour.

'Keep still, you fucker, or I'll jam this in to the hilt.'

He guessed it was the archer whose life he'd spared, doubtless still raging over both his easy defeat and the death of his comrades.

The flat, distorted voice spoke again from behind him, its tone peremptory.

'Easy, man; he's not going to offer us any resistance. And make sure his weapons don't vanish on the way back to camp. I'll not be party to theft from a guest.'

The knifeman snorted amusement.

'A *guest*, is he? Him that's already killed three of my mates? Those swords are worth a fortune, and I don't see—'

The faint scraping of a blade on the throat of its scabbard silenced the argument in an instant.

'You know my rule. Once this blade has been drawn it must taste blood, or its spirit will be offended to have been woken to no good purpose. I can still drop it back into the scabbard, but any further discussion of this subject will require me to be sure that I am in control here, and not you. Choose.'

The blindfold was secured in place, and Marcus felt the big man step smartly away, probably getting himself out of the way of any sword play. The tightly knotted cloth was aggravating the ache in his head, but he knew better than to comment into the tense atmosphere, and had to be content with standing rock still in the blizzard's freezing blast while the silence stretched out. At length the knifeman stepped away from him, and Marcus braced himself to dive for the ground if he heard the masked man's blade whisper free of its scabbard. The distorted voice spoke again, its tone unchanged from the conversational manner in which, not a moment before, he had offered his man the choice between backing down and fighting.

'Very wise. You would have been even wiser not to argue with me in the first place, but wisdom isn't granted to all men in equal measure, is it?' There was an instant's pause, and then, in the very second when Marcus thought that the moment for violence had passed, he heard the dreadful rasp of a sword being drawn. Instinctively shrinking away from the archer, he heard a flurry of movement, followed by a sudden grunting gasp. The Roman heard his would-be killer's slow exhalation of breath harden to a bubbling croak as he fell to the ground with a soft thump. Obduro spoke again into the hush that followed, his voice raised to a harsh shout.

'Nobody questions my judgement without paying the going price for that brief moment of pleasure, a price that only I can decide! *Nobody!* Now, does anybody else want to ask the same question, or might we head for the fortress and get out from under Arduenna's divine intervention?' A moment's silence spun out, with only the faint sound of snowflakes hitting the men's helmets to break the quiet. 'No? Very well, let's be away from here. You can leave him to lie where he fell, and the animals can have his corpse as an offering to the goddess. Get his cloak around the prisoner and let's get moving. Storm or no storm, his comrades are still searching for him, and I'd rather not risk them finding us. *Let's move!*'

A heavy weight settled on Marcus's shoulders, the stink of wet cloak wool a momentary and comforting reminder of his men, and then a hand gripped his arm tightly, pulling him in the direction of their travel with a steady but irresistible strength. Obduro's unearthly voice spoke quietly, close to his ear.

'Well, I couldn't let him live, now could I, Centurion? You of all people will understand the confidence trick that is leadership, the art of convincing those who follow you that you are a man to be feared. I lead these men as you might command a pack of dangerous dogs: I throw them scraps to keep them quiet, and I punish with a fist of iron any of them who decide to challenge me.' Marcus nodded his understanding, and the bandit leader spoke again, guiding him to the left with a gentle pull of his arm. 'Let's not have you walking into a tree, eh? I want you conscious to witness what I have decided to reveal to you. You are to be privileged, Centurion; you are to see a part of Arduenna that no man not already pledged to our cause has ever seen without dying in agony as a sacrifice to the goddess. Today is clearly your lucky day.'

Frontinius found the Tenth Century's centurion standing in the middle of the bandit camp, the freshly cleared ground beyond its edge studded with the stumps of felled trees. With a rending tear of splintering wood another tree on the clearing's edge arced into the open space, and two tent parties of the bearded pioneers fell on it in a flurry of axes, working swiftly to trim off the branches, which in turn were dragged away by waiting soldiers from the other Tungrian centuries already across the river. The remaining axemen set about the long trunk with practised strokes, hacking the sixty-foot log into sections short enough to be grappled by a team of soldiers and carried away to the growing pile of wood in the clearing's centre, while other men laid the resin laden branches as the foundations for more fires.

'Your boys are making good progress, Titus. I'll soon have more labour across the bridge than you'll be able to supply with work.'

The huge centurion nodded, casting an experienced eye around the clearing.

'There's space for three, maybe four fires. Enough to keep us all alive until this snow stops falling.' He pointed to the first pile of wood. 'This is tall enough to burn for hours. Leave me to start building the next fire, and you get that one alight.'

The first spear nodded and turned away, calling out into the clearing's frenzied activity.

'*Martos!*'

The barbarian prince stepped out of the pack of labouring soldiers, an earthenware jar tucked under one arm, while on either side of him a pair of his warriors fended off any man who ventured too close.

'First Spear. Has the time come for your fire miracle?'

Frontinius nodded.

'It has.' Martos made to put the jar at Frontinius's feet, but the first spear raised a hand to stop him. 'No, hold it a little longer, if you will. It's harmless enough sealed up in that container, and I need fire ready to use before I can release it to work its magic.'

Martos grunted, flicking snow from his long hair and turning to his men.

'"Fire", he says, as if the lighting of a fire in a snow storm were the easiest thing in all the world. Aerth! We need a flame!'

One of his warriors came forward from the group gathered about their leader, an older man with a deeply lined face. At his side a younger man carried a bundle of some kind wrapped up in his cloak. Aerth fished in a belt pouch, waving several more of Martos's warriors forward with a grumbling, gravel-throated command in his own language.

'Make the shelter.'

Four men knelt together in a huddle, three of them placing their shields to form a small curved wall against the wind, the fourth placing his board over the others to complete the enclosure. Snow no longer fell inside the tiny space and the blizzard's wind was no more than a swirl of air. Aerth now knelt on the tiny patch of ground and bent his head, growling another command.

'Kindling.'

The young warrior knelt beside him, opening his bundled cloak and spilling an armful of twigs and dead bracken into the shields' protection. The barbarian tested the kindling with his fingers, shaking his head at the results.

'Still damp.' He reached into his bag and pulled out a piece of rough wool, the untreated woven fibres thick with the natural waxy grease that soldiers treasured as waterproofing. Frontinius smiled darkly at Martos, ignoring the snow whipping past his face.

'Your man seems to know his subject. That's from one of our cloaks, I presume?'

The Votadini leader nodded wryly, his one eye narrowing in a smile.

'You know how it is, First Spear. A man must take his opportunities to gather the materials required for his expertise wherever he can. And your soldier will not have missed such a small piece of his garment.'

Aerth stared up at the two men for a moment and then turned back to his task, his face a mask of concentration. Using a small knife he shredded the oil-encrusted wool into thin strips and reduced each one to its constituent fibres, then his nimble fingers wove them into a ball of kindling. Seeing Frontinius's frown, Martos leaned forward and spoke quietly into the Tungrian's ear.

'He is a master at this. The secret lies in achieving the right mix of dry and damp material to sustain a flame.'

As he spoke the kneeling warrior looked up, his grating voice barely distinguishable from the blizzard's howl.

'And knowing which of the gods will answer my prayer.'

He stared up into the grey clouds briefly, his lips moving as he muttered an invocation to whatever deity it was that guided his hands, then he bent forward and struck a hard blow at the flint in his left hand with the rough iron haft of his dagger. A shower of sparks spat down into the kindling, and he bent so close to the ball that his nose was almost touching it, then blew softly onto the tiny spots of light. The men around him held their breath, but after a moment he knelt back on his heels with a grunt, raising his head to stare into the sky and repeat his invocation for divine assistance. Flint and iron met again, and again the barbarian bent over his kindling and blew with the delicate care of a man tending his firstborn, but again he sat back with a slight shake of his head. 'The forest goddess is strong, and she forbids the flame in her kingdom.' He lifted the dagger and pulled back his left sleeve to reveal a forearm crudely scored with cuts. Most of them had long since healed to white scars, but a few were fresher, their marks a livid red on his pale flesh. Martos leaned close to Frontinius, muttering in his ear.

'Sometimes the gods want blood as the price of their assistance. *This* is his secret.'

Frontinius nodded solemnly, watching as Aerth dragged the dagger's shining blade down the length of his arm, the cut finely judged to be more than a scratch yet not so deep as to require stitching. A dark red rivulet ran down his arm to his fingertips, and, once more intoning the vow to serve his gods, the barbarian flicked his fingers three times, shooting drops of blood into the kindling's entwined wood and leaves. Bending to his task again he lifted the dagger to strike, muttered a final word of entreaty, and hammered the iron home, sending a shower of sparks into the ball. After blowing gently on the kindling he turned his head away to breathe, then blew again, a little harder this time and with an intent focus on one of the few lingering spots of light. At first the spark remained no more than a hint of fire, but then it blossomed, taking hold of a scrap of greasy cloak material and swelling from spark to tiny flame. Aerth turned the ball in his hands, seeking to play the infant fire onto the best of the kindling, then looked up at Martos with a decisive nod. The one-eyed Votadini chieftain gestured urgently to the mound of wood and foliage.

'Now is the time, First Spear! The fire will quickly burn through that much fuel!'

Frontinius reached out to take the jar and pulled its stopper. He turned to the dark mass of wood, pouring a generous measure of the liquid onto a thick limb that protruded into the clearing,

its branches thickly coated with dark green needles, then he ran
a trail of the pungent fluid along the limb and into the centre of
the fire. An acrid smell filled the air, making his eyes water as he
stepped back.

'Light that. But keep your face away from it. When it ignites
it will burn like fury.'

Aerth stepped forward with no sign of having listened to the
Roman officer's words, his eyes fixed upon the ball of kindling
whose heart was now ablaze between his cupped hands. He
stooped to hold it beneath the outstretched branch, playing the
growing flame on the reeking wood. In an instant the flame found
fuel, igniting the evaporating spirit with a loud whump and an
explosion of fire that sent the barbarian back on his heels. He
raised a hand to protect his eyes from the fire as it roared from
infancy to full adulthood in a heartbeat, greedily chasing the trail
of liquid laid by the first spear into the centre of the bonfire. The
Votadini watched in amazed silence as the man-high pile of fresh
timber went up in a pillar of flame, the pine needles laid beneath
the logs giving up their stored resin in gouts of flame strong
enough to take hold of the green timber

'For the secret of this fire, I would give everything I have, and
cut myself one hundred times.'

Frontinius turned to find Aerth at his shoulder, his eyes fixed
on the blazing pile of wood, his eyebrows no more than a memory
and the residual stench of burnt hair. He unstoppered the jar
again and held it up for the other man to sniff, watching with
dark amusement as the barbarian recoiled at the eye-watering
vapour rising from the container's wide neck, replying in the
man's own language.

'There is no secret, brother. This is naphtha, a natural liquid
which can be purchased for more coin than you and I could ever
imagine spending on the simple task of lighting a fire. Even the
small amount that lit this blaze cost my tribune enough gold to
pay eight soldiers for a year.'

Aerth nodded, staring deep into the fire's heart, and Frontinius
realised that he was fascinated by the flame, drawn to it by

something deep in his being. He clapped the barbarian on the shoulder and turned away, handing the jar to his century's chosen man.

'Put a guard on this. Two good men . . . no, *four* men that you could trust to defend your woman's honour. The contents are worth enough money to pay the century for a year, and there will be more than one man with his eye on that jar now the power it contains is known.'

He looked about him in the bonfire's flickering light, bellowing an order over the swelling flames' angry roar.

'Centurions, to me! Let's get some more of these fires burning!'

'Perhaps you Romans will see the sense in leaving Arduenna well alone in future, eh? Many are her weapons, and this untimely snow is simply another example of her ability to deal with any intruder bent on defiling her sacred groves. She has shown that she will not tolerate your boots on her soil in sufficient numbers to defeat us, and we can wrap ourselves so deep in her protection that you might never find us in a month of searching. A little to the right here . . .'

The path along which Marcus was being guided began to flatten out after its long climb, and after another moment of walking, still being guided by Obduro's hand on his sleeve, the Roman felt a sudden change in the air around him. The snow was no longer being whipped into his face, and he felt stone underfoot. When the bandit leader's hollow voice spoke again its note was subtly different.

'Down these steps . . . that's it, feel for them with your feet and take it slowly, we don't want you going down them head first. And here we are. That's better.'

Marcus heard the sound of a cloak being shaken, then felt hands on the knot of his blindfold, while the point of a weapon dug sharply into his back and froze him in place. The rough woollen strip was pulled clear of his eyes, and he found himself blinking in the light of a blazing torch held by one of his captor's men, while Obduro himself stood barely an arm's reach from him, apparently examining him closely from behind the anonymity of his mask. Despite his readiness for any attempt at intimidation by his captor, Marcus was nevertheless taken aback by the experience of finding himself face to face with the bandit leader. Where he had been expecting a big man, capable of dominating his men with brute force, the bandit leader was of no better than average height and build. What caught the breath in Marcus's throat was the mask attached to his cavalry helmet; when viewed from so close, its perfect shining surface reflected the scene around them.

In the reflection's foreground were two figures, his own and that of the hulking bandit who had stunned and blindfolded him in the forest. The big man Grumo was lurking behind him with a spear held ready to drive through his armour's rings and deep into his back, a slight smile on his coarse-featured face. Around them, its reality distorted by the mask's curves, was a cave, every feature thrown into stark relief by the light of a dozen torches attached to the walls. Looking around him Marcus saw nothing to change his first impression, of sandy walls and a rock floor swept clean of any sign of previous occupants. The cave was twenty paces across and forty deep, and in a deep recess at the far end he could see a heavy wooden chair. Looking back at Obduro, he realised that the proximity of the blazing torch to the man's masked face was deliberate, making his eyes quite impossible to make out in the dark shadowed pits of the mask's apertures.

'This is the lowest level of our refuge, the place where we bring our prisoners for interrogation.' The bandit leader's voice took on a different quality in the confined space, adding a booming echo to the unearthly quality granted to it by the mask. He waved a hand at the men standing to either side, and they moved smartly into what appeared to be a well-practised routine, lifting the torches that lit the cave from their places on the walls and carrying them down the length of the underground room into the recess at the far end. Fitting the brands into iron loops set in the rock, the bandits quickly transformed the cave's far end from deep shadow to a blaze of light, surrounding the wooden chair with an arc of fire.

'Leave us.'

Waving the guards away, Obduro beckoned Marcus with his hand, drawing his sword as he walked through the cave at a leisurely pace, and dropping into the chair with the blade across his knees.

'You may sit, Centurion. I dare say you're used to more comfort, but I can assure you that you're having a very easy time of it by comparison with the last man I brought to this place.' With an arc of torches arrayed behind him the bandit's aspect was changed again, the arc of fire rendering even the helmet's gleaming surface almost invisible, and presenting Marcus with nothing more than a darkened silhouette. 'I usually feel safe to remove this helmet's uncomfortable burden at this point, for two reasons. One is that all this light behind me makes my face impossible to see. Can you guess the other?'

Marcus spoke after a moment's deliberation, making the swift decision not to back down in the face of the bandit leader's supreme self-confidence.

'Why worry, when it is your intention to kill your prisoners?'

'Right in one. My men in the city told me that you were a bright one, Centurion Corvus, and I can see why.'

The Roman shifted in surprise.

'You know my name?'

Marcus instinctively knew from the set of the other man's head behind the mask's inscrutable features that he was grinning behind the shining metal.

'Better than that, Centurion. I know *both* of them.'

'So when did he go missing?'

Dubnus shook his head unhappily.

'We found the bandits' camp, as expected. It seemed to have been deserted only a short time before, and we were in the act of checking it for any sign of them when the snow started falling. A moment after that they started shooting arrows at us from out of the trees. One of the men took a shaft in the leg, and Marcus charged into them to give us time to get him out. I went back for him, but the snow was so bloody thick that I could have been twenty paces from a fortress wall and never known it was there. I called his name several times, but there was no answer. I shouldn't have turned my back on him, not for a second.'

He stopped talking, and watched his superior's face as Frontinius stared at the forest's snow-covered floor, then back up at his officer, raising his voice to be heard over the blizzard's constant moan.

'So he's either dead or captive. Either way there's nothing I can do. Look about you . . .'

Most of the three cohorts were gathered round blazing fires built of felled pines while the remainder were working in tent-party-sized gangs, using torches fashioned from branches to hunt the surrounding forest for anything that would burn. All of them were huddled into their cloaks, every man wearing every piece of clothing he had carried from the city in an attempt to keep the storm's cold at bay.

'I know. We've next to no chance of finding the same spot in this weather, and sending men out in this might just be their death sentence.'

Frontinius nodded grimly.

'And in any case I've got work for you. Round up a couple of tent parties, borrow some axes from Titus and get about cutting down some more trees. It looks like this weather's set in for the night.'

Marcus stared at the masked man, fighting to keep his face expressionless while his captor rammed home his advantage over his captive.

'I know everything about *you*, Centurion. I know how much you paid for that pretty sword, I know when your wife's baby is due to be born, and I know who you really are and where you come from. Secrets are my currency, Marcus Valerius Aquila. Secrets are my bread and butter. Secrets are what put food on these men's plates, and what keep us *both* from the imperial executioner. I know things about the men who rule Tungrorum, both officially through the power of the emperor and unofficially through the strength of the gangs that control the streets, things that would see them executed within a day were I to make them known. I have access to most of the official documentation and messages that pass through the offices of those men, and there's usually a tiny nugget of gold in every cartload of that shit. And to judge from the look on your face I'm making somewhat better use of it than that fool Caninus, eh? *Prefect* Caninus? The man's a joke, as incapable a thief-taker as I might have wished to be set on our trail. When the time is right I will kill him, as well he knows, but for now his inadequacy is perfect for my purposes.'

He sat in silence for a moment, then spoke again, his voice softer.

'But never mind our mutual friend the prefect, let's talk some more about you, shall we, Centurion? You are, as we both know, Marcus Valerius Aquila, the son of a murdered senator and a fugitive from the emperor's hunters. The despatches from Rome say that you are believed to have taken refuge with one of the cohorts that patrol Britannia's northern wall, and that the reward for your capture has been doubled since the disappearance of both a Praetorian centurion and a corn officer sent to capture you, adding murder of imperial officials to your original crime of treason. You're a dangerous man, it seems, and, in the absence of any living family, a man without any vulnerability to exploit, if I ignore your wife and unborn child.'

He waved a hand dismissively at Marcus's hardening face.

'Never fear, I don't make war on women or children, any more than you would. And besides, why would I feel any need to threaten a man who has so much in common with me? I too am a fugitive from the empire's version of justice, as so ineptly administered by Prefect Caninus. I too would like nothing better than to return to my home and live in peace, but, just like you, I'm left with little choice but to fight for survival, taking what I can when I can. You and I, Valerius Aquila, we should be fighting together against injustice rather than crossing swords as enemies.'

He stood and walked towards Marcus, eclipsing the torches behind him as he stood in front of the Roman.

'Consider my words, Centurion, and give them time before rejecting the idea. You and I would make a combination that no man could bring down. With Arduenna's favour we could hold this forest against any force the governor could send against us, and build an army that would hold the survival of the German frontier garrisons in the palm of one hand. Join me, Valerius Aquila, and you and I will decide the fate of this whole province, and take revenge on those men who have wronged us. Or does the life of a fugitive centurion, living in constant fear of discovery, and the murder of all those who have aided and befriended you hold such an attraction? You are my guest for the night, for this storm will not blow itself out before the sun rises again, which means that you have more than enough time to think on my words. Consider my offer carefully, Valerius Aquila. I will seek an answer from you in the morning.' He turned away to the cave's entrance. 'Grumo!' The big man appeared in the archway, and Obduro gestured to the Roman. 'Set four spearmen to guard this chamber. We don't want him getting any ideas about escape.'

'It seems to be easing off.'

Julius followed Dubnus's pointing hand, looking up into the night sky.

'The flakes are a little smaller, I'll give you that. And about bloody time, I've had about as much snow as I ever want to see in this lifetime.'

He waved a hand at the clearing's dimly lit scene, and the hundreds of men listlessly clustered around the fires' glowing remnants. Their boots and the fires' warmth had quickly reduced the snow-soaked ground around the fires to ankle-deep mud, and made the task of dragging fresh wood from the clearing's edge an exhausting struggle against both the weight of their burden and the sticky ground's resistance. The axemen had long since handed their weapons to fresh hands, their bodies exhausted and their hands cut and blistered despite the calluses developed over years of service. Their replacements' rate of work with the heavy axes had proven so slow that Frontinius had eventually decided to cut his losses and stop the work.

Dubnus pointed again, tapping Julius on the arm.

'Look, I can see stars. The cloud's breaking up.'

The dawn confirmed his expectation, revealing a sky free of any cloud, as if the heavens had been swept clean by the storm, and as the sun rose it lit up the clearing with a rosy light that stained the remaining snow gold. Frontinius and Sergius conferred briefly, then set their men to taking a swift breakfast in preparation for the march back to Tungrorum. The first spear gathered his centurions.

'It's time for some pragmatism, gentlemen. There's no way we'll be able to find Obduro's gang after that heavy a snowfall, never mind fight them. Once the sun gets up and melts all this snow the forest will turn into a quagmire, and I see no point in our wallowing round in it while they sit in whatever fortress they've built and laugh at us, or, worse still, pick us off as we blunder about on ground they know intimately. Have your men eat whatever they've got left and then get ready to march. We're cutting our losses and marching for the city.'

Julius raised a hand, his usually jocular approach to such gatherings replaced by a look of such solemnity that Frontinius, knowing what was coming, forestalled his request.

'No, Centurion, you may not take a small party into the forest looking for any sign of Centurion Corvus. You wouldn't stand much chance of finding him, and in the unlikely event that you did you'd most likely find him in the company of several hundred bandits. Either way it's not a risk I'm minded to take. I'll worry about our missing centurion once the odds are a little less stacked against us.'

Marcus woke in darkness, and for a moment imagined that he was in his own bed next to Felicia. The hard floor beneath him and the stiffness in his back reminded him where he was, and with a groan he sat up, propping himself up against the wall. After a moment a light appeared at the far end of the cave, as a guard carrying a torch came through the opening that led to the rest of the bandit encampment.

'Follow me.'

Stretching the stiffness out of his limbs, the Roman got up and walked towards the light. As he reached the cave's opening he found himself faced by a pair of levelled spear points, and behind them stood Grumo, the big man who had blindfolded him the previous evening. He shot the Roman a long disparaging look, his tone a mixture of hatred and contempt when he finally spoke.

'Obduro wishes to speak with you. I would have slit your throat, but he's ordered that you be spared. Come this way.'

He walked away to the steps that led up into the open air, but Marcus paused and looked about him before following, his curious gaze darting down the corridor to another opening in the rock wall. One of the guards prodded him in the back with the point of his spear, then they both fell in behind Marcus, their weapons still levelled at his back as he followed their leader up a flight of crudely hewn stone steps and out into the bright sunlight, blinking and raising a hand to protect his unprepared eyes.

'*Bring him to me!*'

He turned towards the sound of Obduro's voice, and he realised that he was in the very heart of the bandit fortress, a wide enclosure bounded by log palisades that reared fully twenty feet off the ground, with wooden buildings huddled under the walls to provide the gang's men with shelter. Men stood around him on every side, many of them still clad in the remnants of their imperial uniforms, the remainder in simple woodsmen's clothing, but every man was armed with a spear, sword and shield, and many had bows strung across their shoulders. The men guarding him pushed him towards their waiting leader, and as the throng of men parted Marcus saw that Obduro was standing before what appeared to be an altar. As he drew closer the Roman realised that the stone block, long and wide enough to accommodate a man's body, was intricately carved with images of Arduenna riding through the forest on her boar. In every scene men were dying at her hand, pierced with arrows and hewn with a variety of weapons, their death agonies apparent from their contorted bodies. A variety of offerings were hanging from hooks carved into the stone, and amongst their clutter he saw something that made him frown momentarily with a spark of recognition, even though he was unable to put a finger on what it was. Mistaking the frown for disapproval Obduro spoke, a mocking note in his voice.

'This captive finds our altar distasteful, my brothers, although I can't think why.' His voice rang out across the silent camp, and the men gathered around them hissed their disapproval. Their leader half turned to the stone slab, waving a hand at its decorations. 'See the fine carvings that illustrate our devotion to the goddess!'

Marcus nodded.

'I've seen the artist's work before, I believe. It's certainly of a high quality. Which makes it a shame to cover so much of it with this . . . *ephemera.*'

The bandit leader turned back, shaking his helmeted head as if in sorrow.

'Each item here belonged to a man who met his fate on this altar, his blood drained and collected for our ceremonies. We keep them to remind us of their sacrifices.'

Marcus looked closer at the stone slab, seeing for the first time that it was covered in an intricate pattern of grooves that resolved into a number of deeper channels, which in turn merged to end at a single lip at the altar's edge. He raised an eyebrow at the bandit leader.

'I thought that the blood sacrifice had been stamped out across the empire.'

Obduro stepped forward, putting a hand on Marcus's chin and lifting his head to expose the skin of his throat.

'You have the look of a man who would bleed well for us, Valerius Aquila. You may be under my protection, but any word that besmirches our goddess would leave me no choice but to add the strength of your life to ours, and your body to the bone pit.'

Marcus kept his face devoid of expression.

'I meant no disrespect to your goddess. Her powers were demonstrated to me all too well yesterday. I was simply surprised to find that the practice has survived.'

Obduro snorted with laughter, releasing his grip on his captive's face.

'How very *Roman* of you! Your empire declares a thing to be forbidden, and we savages are expected to change the ways that have served us well for as long as we can recall. We never stopped the practice, Centurion, we simply moved it to places where the empire wouldn't be troubled by it! And where there will never be any danger of the empire intruding upon our privacy. For as you can see, Valerius Aquila, we are more than ready for any attempt to dislodge us from this hilltop. Our palisade is twenty feet tall, but each log is also buried ten feet deep in the earth, and they are secured to each other by cross beams and good strong Roman nails taken from the convoys that supply the army on the Rhenus. A legion's catapult would struggle to make much of an impression on walls that thick, even if such a burden could be dragged through the forest and up this hill. Our gate has inner and outer doors, and any force that managed to open the outer gate would pay a heavy price for the pleasure of facing the thick wood behind it. You will not see the slopes around this fortress, since you will be leaving us as blind as when you arrived, but I can assure you that no aspect of modern siege warfare has been overlooked in our preparation to resist any attack by the forces that would dearly like to end our independence from your subjugation.'

Marcus realised that the bandit leader was speaking as much to his own men as to his captive, and he looked about with a genuine interest. When he spoke, he pitched his voice low and soft, forcing Obduro to lean closer to hear his words, momentarily blocking the sunlight that was making the Roman squint at him through half-closed eyes.

'I've seen stronger walls fall.'

Obduro leaned back, a chuckle rattling out from behind the shining mask.

'I'm sure you have, Centurion, but I'd bet good money that they fell with the assistance of a push from inside, eh? No man here would be foolish enough to consider such betrayal, not given his likely swift reward by wood and nails once the fight was over. I believe the penalty for brigandage is still prompt execution, carried out without exception?'

He turned to the encircling warriors, raising his voice to be heard.

'The centurion here believes these walls can be toppled, but I think we know the truth of the matter, you men and I. First they have to find us. Then they have to reach this hill in a fit condition to fight. And then they have to batter in our gates, or come over our walls, and do so in the teeth of our resistance. And our teeth are very sharp! The goddess clearly favours us, as she demonstrated yesterday as soon as the first of the unbelievers set foot in the forest. We are too well hidden, too well protected, and too well defended for their efforts to end in anything other than slaughter and defeat.' The bandits stood in silence, their gazes locked on Marcus, and Obduro turned back to face him. 'Let us get to the point, shall we? I spared you, Valerius Aquila, in the hope that you will choose to join with us against a common enemy. You have suffered as great an injustice as any man here, and I would be honoured to have you stand alongside me. What is your answer?'

Marcus shook his head with an expression of polite regret, wondering as he did so how the apparently ruthless bandit leader might react to his rejection.

'Thank you for your offer. I am, however, forced to decline your generosity. I cannot accept the offer of service against my own people.' He paused for a moment, compelled to shoot a glance at Obduro's shining face mask despite the futility of seeking any reaction. 'I still serve the empire.'

Obduro turned away, shaking his helmeted head in disappointment.

'A shame. I had hopes of you, Valerius Aquila. No matter, you can still serve as a messenger. So take this message back to

Tungrorum! Your spears may have done for every other bandit in this entire province, but it would take a legion and more to dig us out of this place, and even then at a grievous cost in dead soldiers. And before I have you escorted to the edge of the forest, let me show you one more thing. Bring me his weapons!' A man came forward with Marcus's swords, and Obduro waited while he strapped the belt about him and hung the weapons' baldricks over his shoulders. 'You have a long sword of local manufacture, I hear, a fine weapon for which you paid a high price. May I see it?'

Marcus drew the pattern-welded spatha, conscious of the spear points waiting within inches of his back, and handed it hilt first to Obduro. The bandit leader tested the weapon's balance and peered closely at its dappled blade, nodding his appreciation.

'A fine weapon indeed, and worth every moment of the smith's labour. I would call it the finest sword I had ever seen, were it not in the shadow of this . . .' He handed Marcus the spatha and waited until it was sheathed, then drew his own blade and presented the hilt to his captive. 'Be mindful that my men will kill you if you so much as look at me in the wrong way while you hold this weapon. They have seen the havoc that it can wreak upon the best-armed men.'

Marcus gingerly accepted the sword, holding it with one hand on the hilt and the blade resting across his arm, admiring the workmanship but frowning at the weapon's metal, a darker shade of grey than any sword he had seen previously, its entire length dappled with a pattern so dark as to be almost black. Obduro chuckled.

'Let me spare you the trouble of asking the question. You look at the sword and you wonder from what manner of iron it has been wrought. The answer is that even I do not know for certain, although the man from whom I took it boasted that it had been forged in Damascus, in the distant east, with iron brought along trade routes which run far beyond the empire's frontiers. He called it his "Leopard Sword", and claimed that it had magical properties bestowed upon it by the gods.' The masked man laughed darkly. 'As to whether it is so blessed is not clear to me, but whatever divine properties it may possess clearly did not extend to the man from whom I took it. Such a blade may make an expert swordsman unassailable, but he was nothing of the sort. But in the hands of a master, like myself . . .'

He held out a hand for the weapon, and Marcus handed it back to him with a final long stare at the marvellously patterned blade. Wielding the sword with a flourish, Obduro called out a command to his men, three of whom stepped forward to face him with their shields raised, drawing their swords and slapping the blades against the brass shield edgings in a challenge to fight. Reaching out to take a small round shield the bandit leader sidestepped towards his practice partners, allowing them to edge around him until he was surrounded on three sides. Speaking over his shoulder to Marcus he hefted the sword, ready to fight.

'Even the best swordsman would consider this situation a challenge worthy of his years of practice, but even now this blade gives me such an unfair advantage that were this a real fight these men would already be standing corpses, even if they did not yet know it. They have orders to fight me as they would a real opponent, and they know that I will not harm them if I can avoid doing so . . . a fair test of a swordsman's prowess, I think you'll agree.'

He lunged towards the man waiting before him, inducing a quick defensive back step from his opponent, then turned quickly and attacked the bandit behind him and to his right, striking hard at his opponent's sword and, to Marcus's amazement, effortlessly cleaving the blade in two and dropping a foot of pointed iron into the melting snow. Backhanding the blade back across the hapless bandit's body, he hacked the man's shield in two with a slicing cut that seemed to rip cleanly through the layered board and its brass rim as if it were no thicker than paper. As the disarmed bandit stepped back, raising his hands in surrender, the other two stamped in, seeing their chance to best their leader before he turned on either of them to repeat the trick, but Obduro was too quick for them, ducking under one swinging blow and hooking the man's back foot with his own leg to dump him on the ground, then raising the mottled blade to drive it down through the length of the other's shield from top to bottom, splitting it in two to leave him defenceless. The bandit screamed out a curse and dropped his sword, clutching at the hand that had been gripping the shield's horizontal handle as a thick stream of blood gushed from between his fingers, and Marcus realised that the fearsome blade had hacked a deep cut into his hand between the middle knuckles. The last man put up his sword, unwilling to suffer a similar wound, and Obduro shrugged, looking at his weapon's blade and wiping the blood from it with a rag before dropping it back into its scabbard.

'Sometimes it is necessary to make a small sacrifice to demonstrate a point. He will be well cared for. And you see my point? In the hands of an average swordsman this weapon is formidable, whereas in mine it is given speed and purpose that make it invincible. This demonstration was for your benefit, Centurion Aquila, to ensure that you don't get any ideas about attempting to find this place and seeking to use your undoubted skills upon me once you are healed. We may be equally blessed with the ability to throw iron around, but even the beautiful workmanship of your blade would be no match for this.' He held the darkly dappled sword up to the light, turning his masked face to stare up at it. 'And now it is time for you to perform the purpose for which I have spared you, Valerius Aquila. Go and tell your tribune that on this occasion he would be well advised to leave us alone. Your welcome here is now at an end, and the next time I see you I will be looking down the blade of my Leopard Sword at a standing corpse. Grumo.'

He nodded to the big man standing alongside Marcus, and as the Roman turned to see what he meant the bandit's huge fist smashed into his jaw, dropping him to the ground with his face on fire with pain. A pair of boots stepped into his field of view as he knelt in the snow, and without looking up he knew that Obduro had moved to stand over him.

'Forgive me, Valerius Aquila, for this last indignity. I can hardly release a man whose skill at arms is the match of my own without taking some small step to remove him from the forces ranged against me, can I?'

Blindfolded once more, and little better than semi-conscious, Marcus was led out of the bandit encampment and down the hill, then out into the forest. The big man walked him in silence, speaking only to communicate changes of direction, and after what seemed an age of half walking and half staggering, he muttered a single word of command.

'Stop.'

The faint tang of wood smoke was in the air, carried on the breeze, and in the forest's deep silence the Roman wondered whether he could hear, at the very edge of his battered senses, men's voices barking orders. While he stood still, unsure as to whether Obduro's command that he was to be kept alive was to be obeyed, he sensed the bandit moving around him. The big man gripped his injured jaw with one hand, its hold so fierce that it was all Marcus could do to stop himself groaning with the pain, and tore the blindfold away with the other. Keeping a tight hold of his prisoner's face Grumo leaned close to him, his sour breath warm on the Roman's skin in the morning's chill. Swaying, and struggling to focus on the looming shadow, part blinded by the sudden sunlight and blinking fruitlessly against the effects of the blow he'd received, the Roman stared back at him, completely defenceless.

'Look at you.' The big man hawked and spat at his prisoner's feet. 'The mighty Roman conqueror? I could do you with my eating knife. If I didn't know the chief would find out I'd butcher you here, and leave you for the pigs. You killed three of my men yesterday, and the next time I see you I won't be waiting for anyone's permission to finish the job.' He released his hold on Marcus's jaw, putting the flat of his hand on the Roman's forehead and sending him staggering away to land on his back in the melting snow. 'Away with you! Come back any time . . .' He turned away, calling a final comment over his shoulder. 'I'll be waiting!'

*

The three cohorts had crossed the river in an orderly fashion, the first men across spreading out in centuries to provide security for those following, although in truth the soldiers were more interested in soaking up the morning's sunshine than in any unlikely threat, now that they were back on friendly ground. The remaining force on the river's southern bank had been reduced in strength in an orderly manner under Frontinius's close control, the withdrawal of each century from the line defending the bridge's southern end being matched by a contraction of the bridgehead, until at length there were only two centuries left.

'Take your men across first, Dubnus. Julius and I will follow once your last man's on the bridge.'

Dubnus saluted the first spear, turning away and barking orders at his chosen man and watch officer.

'Move your arses, Eighth Century! By tent party, get across that bridge and reform! Smartly, mind you, you've got an audience!'

He stalked away towards the river, upbraiding his men for the state of their dress with a vehemence that brought a grim smile to Julius's face.

'It sounds like our colleague is about as happy as I feel this morning, sunshine or no bloody sunshine.'

Frontinius grunted his agreement, sweeping the trees around the clearing's scene of devastation with one last, long stare, then he turned to watch as the 8th Century started to cross the river.

'We might have been lucky only to have lost two men, you know. It looks to me as if they knew we were coming.'

Julius nodded morosely.

'But to have lost Marcus of all men. Someone will have to tell his w—'

A man in the front rank of his 5th Century interrupted with a hoarse shout, pointing out into the trees.

'Man coming in! Looks like one of ours!'

Both officers spun to follow his pointing arm, and Julius's jaw dropped at the sight of a bedraggled centurion struggling out of the trees. He ran for the clearing's edge, waving his men forward.

'*On me!*'

The century sprinted forward in his wake, splitting to either side of the exhausted Marcus as he collapsed into Julius's arms. Frontinius limped up behind them, bellowing for them to form a line and staring into the trees for any sign of pursuit.

'Get some shields around him!'

With the 5th Century covering them, Frontinius and Julius lifted their semi-conscious comrade between them and walked him towards the bridge, exchanging unhappy glances as he tottered on his dragging feet despite their support. Julius eyed the river's width uncertainly, giving Marcus's bruised face and slitted eyes an appraising stare.

'He'll not make the crossing unaided, and if he falls in we'll lose him.'

Frontinius shook his head.

'He won't need to. Look.'

Lugos had cast his war hammer aside and was striding across the bridge, a determined look on his face. He strode up to the two officers and looked down at Marcus, who lifted a weary hand in greeting. Without saying a word the Selgovae warrior bent to examine the Roman's face, his hands surprisingly gentle as he touched the bruised jaw. Shaking his head he waved the two centurions aside, then squatted onto his haunches in front of Marcus, put his shoulder into the exhausted man's stomach and straightened his legs, hoisting the Roman and his equipment into the air like a tired infant at bedtime. He turned back towards the bridge without a word, and Frontinius watched him step onto the submerged bridge with exaggerated care, speaking to Julius without taking his eyes off the giant warrior and his burden.

'We'd best get him on a cart and away to Tungrorum. If that bruising on his face is what it looks like then he's going to need all his wife's skill to put that jaw straight again.'

Felicia took one look at her husband as Dubnus and Julius carried him through the surgery door, and pointed to the operating table that dominated the room.

'Lift him up there, please, gentlemen.' She examined the swelling bruise that was distending the right side of his face with slow, careful hands. Marcus leaned forward and muttered something in her ear, and she looked round at his colleagues with an expression only a little the right side of distress, shaking her head. 'He's clearly concussed, although I don't suppose you need me to tell you that. His jaw's badly hurt, from the feel of it. Perhaps not completely broken, but certainly fractured. He won't be able to eat solid food or speak for at least a fortnight, probably longer. Undress him, please.'

The two centurions pulled Marcus's armour over his head while he sat and shivered with the pain, his eyes dull and unfocused. Dubnus grinned at him, looking critically at the swelling that had doubled the size of his jaw on one side.

'We'd better stay for a while, eh? Your woman will need a pair of big strong boys to hold you down if she decides to amputate. And if you die, don't forget I'm first in line for that pretty sword.'

'The first person in line for that pretty sword will be me, Centurion, given the amount he spent on it.' Dubnus bowed to the doctor as she re-entered the surgery with an armful of jars.

'Of course, ma'am, it's simply—'

'Soldiers' humour. I know. But since my husband is all but unconscious with the pain I'd say the person you're amusing most is yourself. And it's hardly you that's in need of reassurance, is it?' She put the jars down and bowed her head over them for a moment before turning and taking the abashed centurion's hand, her eyes wet with tears. 'Forgive me, Dubnus, no one's made any greater sacrifice for Marcus and me, and I thank you for it. I'm just . . .'

The big man raised his hand to silence her apology.

'I know. Work your magic on him and ignore my prattling. How can we help?'

She turned back to the jars, rapidly dispensing two small quantities of powder into a cup of wine before stirring honey into the mixture, then passing the concoction to Dubnus.

'Get him to drink this. It may be bitter even with the honey, but I can't work on the injury until he's drunk it all. Here –' she passed him a thin tube made of glass – 'he can use this to avoid having to open his mouth for the cup.'

Marcus winced at the mixture's taste, but saw the look on his wife's face and lowered his head obediently to sip at it again. Julius leaned over and smelled the cup, wrinkling his nose at the odour.

'What's in the drink?'

Felicia replied over her shoulder while she laid out her equipment.

'It's a mixture of the dried sap of the poppy and something I've been reading about recently: the dried and powdered root of the mandrake plant. The imperial physician Galen recommends its use for the sedation of a patient to whom the treatment must inevitably cause pain. Make sure he drinks it all.'

Waiting until Marcus's eyes closed, and he failed to respond to a hard pinch of the soft skin on the back of his hand, she took a gentle hold of his jaw and palpated the bruised area with her fingers. When he failed to react she took a firmer grasp, and delicately put pressure on the bone, pressing it with the flat of her hand. Letting out a sigh of relief she nodded to the centurions.

'As I thought, the bone isn't shattered. Whatever hit him either only caught him a glancing blow, or, more likely, wasn't made of iron. A fist, perhaps? I expect that there's a crack in the bone though, so I shall give him the only three treatments that are available to me. Pass me that thread, please, Dubnus.' She took the reel of thread from the puzzled centurion. 'Now hold his mouth open for me, as gently as you can.' Looping the slender cord around one of her husband's front teeth, and tying a tight knot to secure it, she wound the thread around the tooth behind it, carefully pulling it tight, then repeated the act with the tooth behind that. 'Now, this is the important one. I suspect that the crack in the jawbone is between this tooth and the next, so I need to pull it closed by using the teeth as anchor posts for the thread. Open his mouth as wide as you can, please.' She reached deeper into Marcus's mouth, slipping a noose around the tooth in question then tugging it tight, with a small smile of triumph. 'Got it.'

Winding the thread tooth by tooth back to the original anchoring point, she tied it off and stood back from her unconscious husband, reaching behind her for another jar. Pulling out the container's stopper she dipped a finger into the off-white paste inside and rubbed it gently along the line of Marcus's swollen jaw.

'This is knitbone, a flowering herb that has been boiled in water and then ground into a paste and incorporated into this salve. Rubbing this ointment on his face twice a day will help the bone to knit more quickly. And now . . .' She selected a long bandage and looped it around Marcus's head, tying it loosely across his jaw. 'Tight enough to provide some support to the bone, not tight enough to force the crack open again. And that, gentlemen, is the limit of my abilities. All we can do now is leave him to sleep off the treatment, and offer whatever prayers we feel might help the gods to smile favourably on his recovery. I believe there's an arrow wound for me to deal with, now we've done all we can for this officer, and after that there's a case of frostbite?'

'There's little enough to tell, Tribune. We rode west until the snow started, fortunately close enough to a farm to take shelter in their barn, and waited it out overnight. Anyone stuck out on the road will have had a miserable time of it. Once the snow lifted we rode straight back here to find out what had become of your raid into the forest.'

Seeing Julius and Dubnus standing in the doorway of the administration building, Caninus stopped his account of the last day's events, and Scaurus, turning to find his centurions waiting for permission to enter, waved them in impatiently.

'Gentlemen, you have news of our colleague?'

Both men marched in and came to attention, and Julius saluted before speaking.

'The centurion has a fractured jaw, Tribune, and will require at least two weeks before returning to duty. Possibly longer.'

The tribune nodded.

'We can be grateful for small mercies, then. Mithras was watching over him, no doubt about that. I've seen broken jaws before, teeth smashed and the man in question left with a deformed face for the rest of his life, invalided out of the service in extreme cases. So who's to lead his century, First Spear?'

Frontinius cocked an eyebrow at Julius. His senior centurion spoke without hesitation.

'His chosen man is a good man. Very good, as it happens. He's been a bit morose of late though, which is a bit of a concern. I'm just wondering if he's the right man to pick up Centurion Corvus's lads, given their devotion to their officer. He's been a temporary centurion before, of course, when the Hamians were shipped into Arab Town, but never led a century in combat.'

Frontinius nodded decisively.

'It's make or break, then. If Tribune Scaurus is in agreement you can inform Chosen Man Qadir that he's appointed to lead the Ninth Century until Centurion Corvus is fit for duty. And you can impress upon him the fact that I'll be watching him very closely. After all, we still need to rebuild the Sixth, once we can find another eighty men to reconstitute it, He might well be the right man to build a new century, if he can hold his men together for the next few days. Tribune?'

Scaurus nodded his agreement.

'As ever, First Spear, I'll defer to your judgement when it comes to managing your people.' The two centurions saluted and turned to leave. 'Centurion Julius, I'd like you to stay and take part in our discussion as to what happened in the Arduenna. I don't believe we can determine our next steps until we work out just what it was that went so badly wrong. Whether it was betrayal or divine intervention, I'll not put my men back into that forest until I know I can take the fight to this Obduro character without fear of finding an arrow protruding from between my shoulder blades.'

★

Marcus awoke to find himself lying in a hospital bed, still bone-weary from whatever it was that had been done to him while he was under the influence of Felicia's potion. Content to lie in silence with his eyes closed as his mind surfaced from its long, deep dive into darkness, he gradually became aware of his surroundings: the scratchy feel of a blanket laid across his naked body and the hard frame of the bed beneath its thin mattress. A man groaned close by, and Marcus forced his eyes open, blinking painfully at the light of a lamp placed by his bed. Whoever it was alongside him was muttering quietly to himself, his stream of invective and profanity apparently inexhaustible.

'Fifteen years! *Fucking* bandits! Fifteen bloody years keeping the bluenoses in their place and never anything more than a scratch, then some robbing, whoremongering, goat-fucking deserter puts an arrow through my bloody knee.' The soldier was attempting to struggle to his feet with his back to the recumbent centurion, his left leg swathed in heavy bandages from thigh to calf and splinted to remove any mobility from the knee joint. He subsided onto the bed, his back still towards the now more or less wakened Marcus, and he was looking down at the wounded leg with evident disgust, to judge from his tone of voice. 'If I could just get this fucking stick off, then I could bend the bastard enough to walk on it.'

You'll be sorry if you try that, Marcus mused, *knowing the doctor and her temper as well as I do*. He tried to speak, but the combination of bandage and pain prevented him from making any sound other than a grunt.

The soldier turned as best he could, whipping up a hand in salute.

'Sorry, Centurion, I didn't realise you was awake! I suggested you might be better off in your own room, but Centurion Dubnus reckoned you'd be happier with some company. Here, I'll get the orderly. *Orderly!*' He bellowed the summons at the top of his voice, and quick footsteps hurried down the corridor. Felicia appeared at the door, taking in the scene in an instant.

'Get *back* in your bed, Soldier Sanga! And if I see you out of it without an orderly in attendance at any time before I give you permission to get up, I'll have your centurion put you on punishment duty once you're fit and well. And keep your hands off that splint; it's there to stop you bending the leg and undoing all my good work in getting the arrow out without having to cut lumps out of your knee.' Sanga raised a hand, and the doctor shook her head in further admonishment. 'I'm not your centurion, Sanga, so you don't have to raise a hand to speak to me. What is it?'

'Need the latrine, ma'am.'

'Is that all? Manius!' The orderly put his head round the door, clearly as much in awe of the new doctor as the abashed Sanga. 'This man needs to use the latrine. Front or back?'

'Eh? Oh. Front, ma'am.'

She nodded to the orderly, who came into the room and pulled out a pan from beneath the bed. He helped Sanga to roll over until he could direct his urine into the pan, and the soldier emitted a long sigh of relief as he emptied his full bladder. Manius took a long hard look at the contents, then put his nose close to the surface and inhaled deeply, ignoring Sanga's surprised expression. He passed the pan across the recumbent soldier's body to the waiting doctor, and Felicia repeated the routine.

'This seems healthy enough. Thank you, Manius.' She passed the pan back to the orderly, and he carried it away down the corridor to the latrine, for disposal. 'So now, Soldier Sanga, with your bladder safely emptied, you can lie quietly while I attend to the centurion here.' With a practised eye she bent across Marcus and examined the swelling along the line of his jaw, then gently rubbed some more of the knitbone salve into the bruised flesh. 'You mustn't try to speak, or even open and close your mouth, until I tell you it's safe to do so. We'll feed you with soup through a tube, and you can use this to communicate.'

She passed him a hinged wooden writing tablet, its interior surfaces coated in soft wax. Marcus thought briefly, then took the stylus and wrote busily for a moment.

'"When will I be allowed out of bed?"' Her face creased into a smile. 'That's my husband. When I say so, Centurion! I want you to rest and get your strength back, what with the beating you took and the effect of the drugs I had to give you. Not for a day or two, at least. Now sit back and keep still, and you'll be asleep again in a few minutes. From what I've read, the effects of the mandrake don't wear off completely for a day or so.' She kissed him on the forehead and turned to leave, only to find Sanga's hand back in the air. 'Yes, soldier?'

'Ma'am, begging your pardon for being crude, but what should I do when I need to do –' he paused, searching for a word that wouldn't offend the lady – 'you know . . . the other?'

She looked at him in bafflement before making the connection.

'Do the other? Ah, you mean when you need to open your bowels. Orderly Manius will bring you the pan, you will defecate into the pan, and then the orderly and I will have a good look at the results to ensure you have no problems in that respect either.'

Sanga's face creased in incredulity.

'You're going to look at my sh—?' He shook his head, clearly too bemused to express his amazement. 'Oh well, if that's what you have to do. Oh, and ma'am . . .?' His face recovered a little of its usual cockiness. 'Do I get a goodnight kiss too?'

Felicia's face softened.

'Of course you do, soldier.' Sanga raised an eyebrow, too startled at having his bluff called to do anything as the doctor came round Marcus's bed. She paused at the doorway, raising her voice to call down the long corridor. '*Manius!*' The orderly put his head round the door again. 'The soldier here needs a goodnight kiss.' As she disappeared out of the door her last words on the subject floated back over her shoulder. 'In your own time, gentlemen.'

When Marcus woke again there was daylight streaming into the room, and Sanga was sitting up in bed playing with a set of knucklebones.

'Morning, Centurion!' He saluted, then tossed a bone into the air, deftly flicking another into the space between the fingers of his other hand as it rested flat on the bed, before catching the falling bone. 'All the horses are in the stable. Again.'

He sighed, with the expression of a man who had been playing with the bones all morning. A noise at the door made them both turn their heads.

'And what have we here? One rather soiled-looking centurion, temporarily forbidden to speak on pain of having all domestic privileges removed . . .' Dubnus, standing in the room's doorway, raised a hand to forestall any attempt on Marcus's behalf to speak. 'No you don't! I'll not have your woman coming down on me like a chosen man with a sore arse just because you're too dim to follow instructions. And a soldier with a hole in his knee, forbidden to walk and so reduced to sitting in his bed and playing children's games. *Scarface!*' Sanga's comrade appeared round the doorframe with another of Marcus's men behind him, and Dubnus pointed to Sanga. 'I've received permission from the doctor for these two to pick you up and take you outside for some fresh air, while Qadir and I have a chat with the centurion here.'

'Best news I've had all day.' Sanga beamed at the prospect of escape from the room's confines. 'Drop me off at the latrine, eh lads? I've got the turtle's head as it is, and if I can avoid that bloody orderly picking through my crap I'll be a happier man. The bastard was sniffing my piss last night . . .'

Scarface bustled into the room and grinned at his mate, taking in the knucklebones lying on his bed.

'Bones, eh? Used to be right handy with them as a lad. Perhaps we can have a little contest, all in the interest of entertainment o' course.'

He scooped up the bones and nodded to the other soldier. They lifted Sanga up, each with an arm over their shoulders, and carried him from the room, and the three centurions smiled to each other as they heard Felicia admonishing them not to allow him onto his feet for any reason, and Scarface's reply.

'No danger of that, ma'am. I don't want him trying to leg it away from the losses he's going to take once we get these bones jumping!'

'That's better, eh, a little bit of peace for you?' Carrying a bowl of hot water and a cloth Dubnus advanced into the room, followed after a moment by Qadir. 'Your wife asked us to get you cleaned up, since all you've done since we brought you in is lie about snoring.' He set to with the wash cloth, and within minutes Marcus was sitting up with his writing tablet, while Dubnus and Qadir sat on either side of the bed. He wrote on the tablet's wax, holding it up for them to see.

'"Thank you for bringing me back"?' Dubnus laughed. 'You might not be thanking me in a week's time, when you're still not allowed to talk. How's your head?' Marcus rubbed the wax smooth and wrote his response across the clear surface. '"Better. Headache gone. Face still hurts." And it'll go on hurting for a few days. What hit you?'

In a series of one-line statements on the tablet's limited writing surface Marcus explained what had happened. At length he sat back, already tired by the mental exercise. Dubnus, recognising the signs of his rapid exhaustion, asked one last question.

'So their camp's pretty much invulnerable, they reckon?'

Marcus nodded, smoothing the tablet's surface again and writing a last comment. Dubnus patted his friend on the shoulder and stood up, pushing his chair back against the wall.

'You look all in. Get some more sleep, and we'll come back and see you tomorrow, eh?'

Qadir bent over his centurion, muttering a few quiet words. Marcus wrote a reply on his tablet, turned it for Qadir to read and raised his eyebrows in challenge, wearily lifting a clenched fist. The big Hamian looked at him for a moment, before solemnly tapping Marcus's fist with his own. Then Qadir turned and followed Dubnus out of the door. Outside in the warm spring air they found Scarface and Sanga in the middle of a gathering of their tent party. Sanga was just about to toss the bones for what appeared to be the deciding throw of whatever wager had been agreed, to judge from the men's intent expressions and the small pile of coins between them. The Hamian put a hand on Dubnus's arm and shook his head silently, restraining him from either action or comment. He padded silently up to the group, unnoticed by the soldiers until he whipped out a broad hand and caught all four of the bones in mid-air. Sanga opened his mouth to protest, closing it again when he saw the expression on his new centurion's face. The soldiers started to rise from their crouching positions, but Qadir's bellowed command beat them to the punch.

'As you were!' Looming over them, he grimaced down at the two competitors. 'You, Scarface, should know better than to wager on the bones with a man who's had all morning to practise. And you, Sanga, should know better than to be caught wagering when there are officers about. The only way this could be any worse for you would be if Morban had already come by and fleeced you both.' He put out his hand and dropped the knuckle bones onto the ground between them. 'Reclaim your stakes, soldiers, and be grateful I'm not making you donate them to the burial club. And away with you, all except you two; you need to be carrying this damaged soldier back to his bed. *Don't* wake the centurion, or the two days of extra duties you've both just earned will miraculously turn into four.'

The two centurions watched as Sanga's mates carried him back into the hospital, Dubnus smiling widely while Qadir scowled back into their indignant glances.

'Well done, brother.' Dubnus slapped his colleague on the shoulder. 'Word will get around quickly enough, and those men who were minded to test your stomach for the centurionate will wind their necks back in. But what was it Marcus wrote on the tablet for you?'

The Hamian raised an eyebrow, deciding to put another marker down as to his changed status.

'Not that it's any business of yours, *colleague* . . .' He allowed the silence to stretch for a moment before continuing. 'He wrote "Make it yours."'

Dubnus nodded, a slight smile on his face as he absorbed both

Marcus's advice to his deputy and the manner in which Qadir had swiftly re-established their relationship.

'Good advice. Come on, then, Centurion, let's go and give Uncle Sextus the report he's waiting for.'

Later that day, with the evening sun slipping towards the horizon, the first spear went to brief Scaurus on the two cohorts' condition, and the information that Dubnus and Qadir had elicited from Marcus. He walked up and down the room as he spoke, coming to his conclusion with a sour face.

'So pretty much all Corvus was able to tell us was that Obduro is physically nondescript, that he wears a mask at all times unless he's alone or with a very few trusted men, that he's got a heavily fortified camp somewhere in the forest, and that Centurion Corvus is predictably burning with the urge to find him and send him to meet his ancestors. In short, nothing we didn't already know or couldn't have guessed. He might remember more when he recovers from his whack on the jaw, but until then it's all he can give us. He did ask to see you when you have a moment, by the way.'

He looked round at Scaurus, who was sitting in a chair and staring up at a copy of Prefect Caninus's map of the land around the city. After a moment the tribune shook his head and stood up, keeping his eyes on the map.

'You missed out a point in your summary. Centurion Corvus confirms that our opponent seems to harbour a deep-seated loathing for our colleague the prefect. And two questions spring to mind with the reaffirmation of that admittedly old news. First, why should a bandit chieftain be so fixated on a relatively minor official like Caninus, especially if he's apparently so ineffective as to attract the man's derision? And if that's really the case, how have their paths crossed? What is it that the prefect isn't telling us?'

Frontinius shrugged, shaking his head in disinterest.

'I'll leave the intelligence work to you, Tribune; my interests are purely military, and right now that means getting our cohorts ready to go out there again. I've got a century's worth of soldiers whose boots have fallen to pieces, and more than a few men missing shields because other soldiers seem to have thought it might be funny to throw their boards onto the fires when they weren't looking, although of course nobody actually saw anyone else actually perpetrate the crime. I've even got a centurion from the Second Cohort with a mild case of frostbite. The idiot decided to march out without his socks on.'

Scaurus turned and gave his first spear a hard smile.

'Then you'd better send out some officers and make the city's tradesmen happy, hadn't you? I want both cohorts fully combat-effective immediately. Starting tomorrow we'll be sending patrols up and down the main road, and generally getting back up onto our feet and into Obduro's face. Doubtless the men are all still rolling their eyes and muttering to each other at the way his goddess sent snow to frustrate us, and I'll not give them time to brood on that thought. Every grain convoy from the west will have to have an escort once it's a day's march out from the city, and Decurion Silus and his mounted scouts are going to have their work cut out making sure that Obduro doesn't get his men out of the forest unobserved. And you'd better send some men south, with ropes, to rip out enough of that bridge to make it useless for any further attempts to cross the Mosa. The legion cohort can make damned sure that Procurator Albanus's grain store stays secure, and garrison the city while we invest some boot leather in preventing Obduro's men from taking one single bag of grain more from the convoys. I'll have his deserting Treveri scum eating acorns by the time autumn's here, and then we'll see just how their goddess decides to feed them. Carry on, First Spear, I'm going to pay a visit to Centurion Corvus as requested. Who knows, he might have remembered something that will help us?'

7

Marcus woke again to find Sanga lying asleep on his bed, and he quietly climbed off his own mattress, standing still for a moment to allow the slight feeling of dizziness to pass. Walking quietly on bare feet, he made his way up the corridor to the latrine, then went in search of his wife. Felicia was delighted to see him on his feet, despite her immediate concern for his well-being, which were quickly dispelled when he waved her away and turned a full circle with his arms out.

'Well, you seem to be spry enough that I think we can assume the effects of the mandrake have completely worn off. You won't be able to speak or eat solid food for some time yet though.'

'And that's why I brought this for him.' They turned to find the tribune standing in the doorway with a smile on his face, a small iron pot dangling from one hand. 'There's a food shop at the end of the street whose proprietress was only too happy to lend me the pot in the likelihood of getting your business for the next few weeks. Pass me a cup and I'll pour you some.' Marcus found his glass drinking tube and took a sip at the soup, nodding his thanks to the tribune. Scaurus sat in silence until the cup was empty, watching as the hungry centurion consumed the soup as quickly as its temperature would allow.

'That's better, eh? There's more in the pot for when I'm gone. I'd imagine you'll be spending another night in here just to be sure you're over the worst of it, but that ought to keep you going until morning. And now, Centurion, to business? First Spear Frontinius tells me that you passed a message requesting a conversation with me, although from the look of things most of the speaking will be done by me.'

Marcus nodded, reaching for his tablet and writing several lines of text. He handed the wooden case to Scaurus, who read the words and stared back at his centurion with his eyebrows raised in astonishment.

'*Really?* You're sure of this?'

After thinking for a moment, Marcus held out his hand and took the tablet back. He smoothed the wax and wrote another statement. Scaurus looked grimly at the text, shaking his head.

'You got that close to him?'

Marcus wrote in the tablet again. Scaurus read the text aloud, a wry smile on his face.

'"Take a tent party with you." A tent party? I'll need a damned century if he's as dangerous as you say. And the nastiest, most bad-tempered officer in the First Cohort. Do any names spring to mind, Centurion?'

Julius was on the point of setting out into the city, the key to Annia's secret door tucked away in a pouch on his belt, when a knock sounded at the door of his barrack. Opening it, he found one of the men assigned to guard duty waiting with a small scroll in his hand.

'Delivered to the duty centurion just now, sir, with your name written on it.'

Julius frowned, taking the scroll and turning it over to read his own name in tidy handwriting.

'Delivered? Who by?'

The soldier shook his head.

'Just some kid or other running an errand for a coin. He gave it to the men on the gate and legged it before anyone could ask any questions.'

Julius nodded, dismissing the man with a distracted gesture. By the light of his lamp he unrolled the paper, squinting in its dim illumination to read the short message.

You are no longer welcome in my establishment, Centurion. Do not visit again, or it will end badly for you and for the woman. This matter is now closed.

Shaking his head, the hulking centurion muttered angrily into the room's silence, his fist clenched around the paper.

'*Closed?* Not by a long way it's not. You've just signed your own death sentence . . .'

Squaring his shoulders he turned to the door, only to be brought up short by another knock. Wrenching the door open he drew breath to bark out his irritation, finding himself toe to toe with the tribune, dressed and equipped for battle. Snapping to attention he stood under his superior officer's scrutiny for a long moment before Scaurus spoke.

'Interesting, Centurion. I thought I'd have to get you out of your bed, given the hour, and yet here you are fully dressed and ready for duty, from the look of things. And you seem to have a piece of paper screwed up in one hand.'

He held out a hand, and Julius reluctantly surrendered the note. Smoothing out the paper, Scaurus turned to read it by the light of the nearest torch.

'It seems that your liaison with the mistress of the Blue Boar is at an end, Centurion.' Julius frowned, his puzzlement evident, and Scaurus laughed dryly at his bemusement. 'If you were first spear of this cohort, Centurion, you'd be very sure to know anything and everything that might compromise the performance of your officers, wouldn't you?' He waited for Julius to nod before continuing. 'Exactly. So when Sextus Frontinius received reports of one of his centurions heading off into the city after lights out, and not returning until the small hours, you can be assured that his interest was sufficiently strong to override your colleagues' initial reluctance to enlighten him as to exactly what business you were about. And whilst the company you keep in your own time is your own business, when it starts to affect your performance in the role for which the empire pays you a quite generous amount of money, then it becomes *his* business, wouldn't you agree? Not to mention mine.'

Julius nodded again, his face stony under the tribune's scrutiny.

'So, all things considered, it shouldn't be any surprise to discover that your attempts to regain what you lost when you left the city are known to your superiors, should it? And for the time being at least, whoever wrote this note has the right of it. If, as it appears, you were about to head off into Tungrorum on a one-man mission to hack your way through the Blue Boar's doormen and rescue the woman in question, then I've arrived at just the right time. You are absolutely forbidden to go anywhere near that blasted place, on pain of reduction to the ranks and enough administrative punishment to keep your head down in the latrines until the end of your term of service. Is that understood?'

Scaurus stepped closer to his centurion, his hard stare forcing a blink from the otherwise stone-faced Julius.

'Is. That. *Understood?*'

'Yes, sir.'

The tribune smiled tightly and stepped back, looking him up and down.

'Good. Because I'm not minded to lose my best centurion just because he can't recognise when he's beaten, even if only temporarily. Apart from anything else, if you as much as show your face at Petrus's door he's more than likely to punish you by killing the woman.' Something in Julius's eyes must have betrayed his surprise, and Scaurus laughed again. 'Yes, Centurion, we know all about Petrus's real place in the governance of this miserable city. The First Minervia have been here long enough for Sergius to have worked it out several months ago, and unlike his tribune he's not a man to keep useful information to himself. When the time comes I'll deal with Petrus, and if you can hold onto your temper until then you'll be a part of putting him in his place, but for now we've a bigger and more immediate problem.'

Prefect Caninus's face was a study in perplexity, a frown of incomprehension greeting both the unexpected sight of a full century of soldiers filling the street outside his headquarters and the peremptory tone with which the Tungrian's tribune addressed him.

'Tribune Scaurus? I was just going off duty for the night. Perhaps we can—'

Scaurus stepped forward and cut him off with a raised hand, his voice stern and uncompromising.

'Bring your men out and disarm them, Prefect! I won't ask you twice! My soldiers are still frustrated after that debacle in the forest, and they'll do the disarming for you if I slip their collars. But it won't be pretty.'

Caninus spread his hands in a placatory manner, looking to either side at his bodyguard, then he gestured to the soldiers surrounding his small party, their spears glinting in the torchlight.

'Best to do as the tribune says, gentlemen. I don't want your blood on my hands, or my own, for that matter. Stand your men down, Tornach, and drop your weapons.'

His deputy grunted an order and unbuckled his belt, easing his sword down onto the cobbles at his feet. His men followed suit, then stood in silence as a pair of soldiers came forward and picked up the weapons. Scaurus stood where he was, pointing to the prefect himself.

'And your own weapon, Quintus Caninus.'

The soldiers tensed, visibly readying themselves to fight, and with a wry smile Caninus drew his blade, placing it on the road's surface.

'Have a good look, Tribune. I think you'll find it to be standard issue, and nothing more dangerous than the sword you carry. The man you're hunting for carries something a good deal more exotic, I believe?'

Scaurus ignored him, nodding to Julius, who was waiting for instructions beside him.

'Accommodate the prefect's bodyguard for me, if you will, Centurion? There'll be no need for any rough behaviour unless they offer resistance. And you, Prefect, you can accompany me inside. I have questions for you that won't wait until morning. And post some men to guard the door please Julius, I'll call if I need them.'

Caninus turned back to the doorway to his headquarters and

entered the building, followed by Scaurus, who had taken a torch from one of his men and kept one hand on his sword's hilt. The prefect lifted fresh torches into the iron loops set in the wall to hold them, and Scaurus followed him around the room, lighting each one in turn. With the room lit, Caninus turned to face his colleague, his quizzical expression replaced by a look of growing anger.

'So now, Tribune, what is it that's so important we have to discuss it at this time of night, and with your sword very nearly kissing my throat?'

The tribune shook his head, his voice level and dangerously calm.

'Too little too late, I'm afraid, Quintus Caninus. The time for righteous indignation was back there in the street, when I humiliated you in front of your men. Simulated anger doesn't fool me, Prefect, so you can drop the act and assume the demeanour of a man who's been caught out in a lie before I decide to call my centurion in here and have it beaten into you. Believe me, I'm sure there's very little that would give Julius any more pleasure than a few moments of toe to toe with you, given the way his friend Centurion Corvus was so cruelly knocked about in the forest.'

The prefect stepped back, his face sliding from bemusement to horror in the space of a heartbeat.

'You actually think . . .?'

Scaurus dismissed his incredulity with a wave of his hand.

'No, Caninus, I actually know. I *know* who you are. I say "Caninus", but perhaps I'd be better to start calling you by the name your men have given you. What do *you* think, *Obduro*?'

The other man shook his head slowly, his eyes widening in shock.

'But I'm not—'

'You took my centurion prisoner in the Arduenna, and then you spent the night telling him how terrible an enemy you are, how much you despise the prefect of Tungrorum, and how your bandit gang can never be defeated. But your disguise slipped by a tiny fraction when he fooled you into coming close enough for him to see your eyes in the daylight through your mask's eyeholes. He's a bright young lad is Centurion Corvus, and he recognised you instantly. Green eyes like yours are distinctive enough, but when you add in the squint they're unmistakable. You're the man behind the metal, I'm sure of that much, and through your vanity you've nailed yourself to the cross I'll have my men put up for you in the morning.' He paused while the other man turned away, his face blank. 'Nothing to say?'

Caninus stared up at the ceiling for a moment, then lowered his gaze to look defiantly straight back at Scaurus, answering the question with four terse words. The tribune's eyes widened, and his usual aristocratic reserve vanished in an instant, replaced by something much harder, that he usually managed to keep concealed.

'He's fucking *what*?'

Caninus continued to look at the tribune, his jaw set hard.

'You heard me right the first time, Tribune. He is my brother. Obduro is my *brother*. My identical twin, as it happens.'

Scaurus stood open-mouthed and stared at Caninus for a long moment, then lowered his head and put both fists on the table between them, his knuckles white against the wood's age-darkened surface. When he looked up, his face was dark with barely controlled anger, but his voice was calm and steady.

'And, assuming that I can make the huge leap of faith required to swallow this story, you'd seriously have me believe that this wasn't worth telling me before?'

The prefect shrugged, his expression downcast.

'If I'd told you at the start you would have removed me from all of the discussion and the decision-making, without a second thought.'

Scaurus laughed hollowly.

'You're not wrong there! It won't surprise you to know that's exactly what's going through my mind at the moment, even if you are telling me the truth at long last.' He shook his head. 'So, from the beginning, tell me the story of how you and your twin end up in such violent opposition. And on such very different paths. in life, for that matter.' He picked a chair close to one of the torches illuminating the room and sat down, his eyes so deep in shadow that they were impossible to read. 'And this had better be spectacularly convincing, or you'll be feeding the crows by lunchtime tomorrow.'

Caninus leaned back against the wall behind him and rubbed his tired eyes with a finger and thumb.

'It's a relief to tell someone, if I'm honest. I've been keeping this from the men around me for so long that it's started to eat into me. His name is Sextus. He was born less than a hundred heartbeats after me, and for all practical purposes we're identical, right down to the squint. You can prove it easily enough; just have a copy of the relevant census records delivered from the governor's office and you'll find us both. We were born here in the city, just over thirty years ago, so we'll be detailed in the census that fell between then and the day we both left to pursue our separate destinies.'

He gestured to a chair, and raised his eyebrows in question. Scaurus grunted his assent, his hand still firmly placed on his sword's hilt. The prefect slumped into the chair, leaning back with the air of a man relieving himself of a heavy burden.

'Thank you. We were just like the twins you read about in the histories as we were growing up, closer than two peas in a pod and just as indistinguishable. Our mother had pendants made for us when she realised we were identical, discs with our numbers punched into them on chains left deliberately short, and by the time we were of a mind to exchange them they were impossible to remove without breaking the links. And she always told us there'd be hell to pay if that happened.' He pulled down the neck of his tunic to reveal the circle of metal hanging at his throat, holding it up for Scaurus to examine. 'You can see the number five punched into the metal. It's not pretty workmanship, but it is my only link with my mother. The plague took her a few years ago, although I expect it was only taking advantage of all those years of backbreaking work she put in to keep the pair of us fed.'

He shook his head, tucking the pendant away beneath the tunic's smooth wool. 'She was right to take the precaution, and to drum into us that breaking those chains would bring us more grief than any fun we could have by pretending to be each other. We were forever proving our mutual bond by exercising the same stupidities and getting into the same trouble, but for all that we were a good pair of lads, more or less. We learned to fight early, of course, our squints made sure of that, although he was always better at it than me, whereas I was the one who always managed to turn around whatever wit was thrown at us and throw it right back, only harder. That got me a few hidings, as you can imagine, so by the time we were ten we were a right pair of hard little bastards, but harmless enough. Harmless enough until our balls dropped and the hair started sprouting, and I was first at that as well, even if it was only by a few weeks. Before that happened we were inseparable, and you'd never see one of us without the other; but as we began to enter manhood that closeness started to cool off. We were looking for our own paths in life, I suppose, and we started to push each other, competing where we used to cooperate. Inside a year we weren't "the cock-eyed twins" any more, we were Quintus and Sextus, each with our own friends and our own ways of doing things. He was the real hard man, whereas I was the smoother of the two of us, with more of a way about me, and while I was never what you'd call a religious man, he turned to the worship of Arduenna with all the zeal of a forest hunter. We still knocked about together, of course, but we were developing different ways of getting what we wanted, him with his fists and me with my wits. Gods, what a team we'd have made; we'd have gone through the local gangs like shit through a goose long before now, but it wasn't to be. It was a girl that ripped us apart . . .'

Scaurus nodded his understanding, his initial incredulity cooling towards curiosity.

'Just like the histories, eh? What was her name?'

'Lucia. I forget the family name, although it wouldn't be hard to dig out of the records. She was the daughter of a wealthy family but she liked to slum it with the poor boys, if you know what I mean, and we both certainly qualified for that description. She liked the hint of danger, I guess, although she ended up getting rather more than she'd bargained for. We both fell for her, you see, and for the first time in our lives there was something we both wanted that couldn't be shared. She made a choice, and that choice was to be with me. It wasn't much, only a few nights when she could sneak out of her family's house, but she was my first proper love, and so of course I was convinced we'd find a way to be together for the rest of our lives. I expect she would have dropped me soon enough, and broken my heart for a few weeks, but she didn't get the chance.'

He paused for a moment, looking up at the ceiling again, and Scaurus prompted him in a gentler tone of voice.

'Your brother found the pair of you?'

Caninus nodded.

'Yes, he hunted all over the city until he found the place I used to take her to, a disused stable on the east side where I was sure we'd have privacy. Perhaps he followed me, perhaps someone sold the information to him, I'll never know. He burst in on us and pulled a knife on me, already furious that I'd lied to him, but beside himself with rage when he saw the proof that I'd won her, and that he'd lost. As she jumped up with her hands out to stop him, he put his foot through a rotten floorboard, and in falling he put the knife into her thigh up to the handle. She bled to death in my arms, while he raved at me about how I'd betrayed him and I shouted back for him to kill me if that was what he wanted. I think he would have done it as well, if I hadn't already been covered in her blood. In the end he calmed down enough to realise what he'd done. It wasn't just the murder of an innocent girl, enough to see him dead on its own, but it looked horribly like the abduction, rape and slaughter of the daughter of a wealthy citizen. We both knew that her father paid protection to the most powerful of the city's gangs, and that he wouldn't hesitate to call them in to take revenge for her, not to mention to save his face by avoiding the admission that she'd strayed from his protection. And there's nothing that gang leaders like more than having a chance to turn their thugs loose in a cause in which the common people see them as the deliverers of justice, rather than as the robbing scum they are. Since our relationship wasn't exactly a closely guarded secret I knew that I'd be the one they'd come looking for first, and no matter how loudly I might protest my innocence all I could do would be to condemn us both to having our throats cut in the city square, once the bastards had broken every bone in our bodies, of course.'

He shook his head.

'We were both doomed, unless we got out of the city before she was missed the next morning, so we both knew that we'd have to go under the city wall and make a run for it, once we'd buried her body under the floorboards and packed it tight with some old sawdust to keep the smell down. The River Worm flows into the city through an arch in the south-eastern section of the wall, and we both knew how to lift the gate that defends it. Once we were through the arch he told me that the next time he saw me he'd kill me without hesitation, and I saw from his eyes that he meant it. I nearly went for him then and there, to finish it one way or another, but something stopped me. Fear, possibly. He was so much better in a fight than me. Or perhaps it was some trace of the closeness we used to enjoy. Anyway, he slipped off into the night, and after a few minutes I said my last farewells to Lucia and made a run for it too.'

Scaurus stood up, stretching his weary body.

'I'd say you've done pretty well from an inauspicious start, *if* what you've told me has been the truth. Although I'd be very interested to know exactly how a man with that sort of price on his head became an imperial official, especially in a city where he's presumably still wanted for murder?'

Marcus had just finished the last of the soup, reheated for him by the orderly over the hospital's cooking stove, when Scaurus walked in, returning his centurion's salute briskly and taking a seat by the bed. Sanga froze to attention on his mattress, and the tribune looked across the room at the heavy wooden crutch propped up at his side.

'Can you use that crutch, soldier?'

Sanga, unused to speaking to the person closest to a god in his narrow world, spluttered out an answer, red-faced and staying at attention despite the fact that he was lying flat on his back.

'Yes, sir, Tribune, sir! Bit wobbly though . . . sir.'

'Well, then, it sounds to me as if you could do with some practice. Off you go. Take a few turns up and down the corridor until I tell you to come back.'

The soldier obeyed with alacrity, hobbling out of the room with a sickly smile of embarrassment on his face, and Scaurus sat back, looking around the room's featureless walls.

'Are you bored of this place yet, Centurion Corvus?' Marcus nodded, the look on his face bringing a smile to the Tribune's lips. 'I rather thought you might be. You're not one to sit around and do nothing, are you? Anyway, your time of boredom is about to end. I have a new task for you, Centurion, a job where you'll find your eyes and ears of far more use than the ability to speak. And you've already proven yourself to be more than usually skilled when it comes to spotting those small details that matter.' Manius appeared at the door with an armful of clothing and equipment. 'I told the orderly to bring your gear, and the doctor has already signed your discharge as fit for duty. It seems she knows better than I do just how bored you'll be sitting here with only a soldier for company. So get dressed and I'll see you at the front entrance. Duty calls, Centurion, and in this case you don't need a voice to answer.'

Marcus and Scaurus stood on the corner of the street in which Caninus's headquarters was located, while the gate guards observed them unhappily, still smarting from their detention overnight. As they'd walked through Tungrorum from the hospital the tribune had recounted to Marcus the story related to him by Caninus, and he was just finishing the prefect's version of the truth.

'So the story is that they packed the girl's body in sawdust to stop it from smelling too badly, then made a run for it through the arch that lets the River Worm flow into the city. Caninus went east, skirting round the fort at Mosa Ford and scrambling through the shallows rather than risk being taken by the gate guards, and he carried on as far as Claudius Colony on the Rhenus. Once he was there he kept his head down, worked hard and established a reputation as a clever lad with a habit of delivering on his promises. He ended up finding a place with the civilian authorities as an administrator. After which one thing leads to another, and ten years later here he is, prefect in charge of the province's counterbanditry effort while his long-lost brother has surfaced as the biggest, nastiest gang leader of them all. I asked him how he'd not been recognised as the man who'd fled the city ten years before, and I have to admit that his answer was a decent enough end to the story, whether it's true or not.' Marcus raised an eyebrow, and the tribune waved an arm at the surrounding city. 'It's obvious enough, if you look about you. There should be two or three times the number of citizens in Tungrorum, given the size of the place.' The young centurion nodded slowly, his lips pursing as he too recognised the potential truth in Caninus's story. 'Exactly. The plague. The same bloody pestilence that's been ravaging the empire for the last fifteen years broke out in the city about five years ago, he tells me, here and in all the forts along the Rhenus at much the same time. And if it was vicious enough to kill the last emperor in the safety of his palace, why would it spare any of its victims here? Caninus reckons at least a third of the city died during the outbreak, and a lot more took their possessions and fled, for all the good it would have done them. So, when he was sent here to serve as prefect there was simply no one left alive that recognised him. And on top of that the girl's family are all dead, and without them there's no further call for justice. That, and the fact that he purged the official files of all trace of the murder, or so he says.'

Marcus wrote in his tablet, holding it up for the tribune to read.

'Proof? The local census records were all destroyed in a fire during the plague, when some fool set light to a building full of dead and dying victims of the infection and managed to burn out a whole block of the city, including the records storage building. Caninus tells me that the stable in which the girl died went the same way, which means we won't get any validation of his story that way.'

He nodded at Marcus's raised eyebrow.

'I know. Convenient, isn't it. A story that "proves" his innocence, but without very much in the way of hard evidence. So, do I believe it?' He paused for a moment. 'In all truth, yes, I actually want his story to hold up, and may Our Lord judge me if I'm mistaken. He tells it with the right mixture of desperation and fatalism, like a man who knows that he's dangling over the drop into Hades but doesn't deserve to take the fall. Mind you, I'm not entirely trusting of this new version of the man, so I've sent away to the governor's office for a copy of the relevant census entry. At least that way we can see the truth of this "twins" story. As to whether I really trust him, that, as I told you in the hospital, is where you come in. I'm going to set you down in the heart of his command, without giving him the option, and you can observe him for a few days and tell me what you think. If this whole story is just a lie then the point must come when he lets up his guard, even if only for a moment. And if he really is Obduro, then having him under such a close watch will prevent him from taking any further action against us. Whether or not he's innocent, and simply the victim of his brother's lust for power and revenge, I can't think of a better way of finding out – other than the rather extreme expedient of torturing a potentially innocent man half to death – than setting a bright young lad like you on him.' Marcus nodded, looking at the prefecture building while Scaurus continued speaking. 'But for Mithras's sake, be careful. If he's not the innocent party in all this, then he'll probably be looking for an opportunity to strike at both of us. Watch your back, Centurion, and I want a daily report from you every evening. I've told Caninus that if you fail to appear at evening roll call I'll take that building apart brick by brick and summarily execute him and every man that gets in my way!' Marcus drew himself up and saluted, and Scaurus raised a hand in return. 'Very well, you're dismissed. May Our Unconquered Lord watch over you.'

The guards on the prefecture's main entrance snapped to attention as Marcus approached, pulling the heavy wooden door open. Their weapons had been returned to them once Scaurus had decided to make an open show of trust in their master, at least for the time being, and Marcus noted that neither of the guards chose to meet his eye. Inside the building he found the prefect's whip-thin deputy, waiting for him. Tornach nodded to him impassively, opening the door to Caninus's office and stepping back. The prefect was seated at his desk with both hands flat on the wood, clearly just sitting and waiting for Marcus to arrive. He stood, advancing round the table and stopping in front of the Roman, snapping to attention as the door closed.

'Centurion, I am at your disposal. Tribune Scaurus has informed me that my continued freedom to perform my role is dependent on your presence in my headquarters, and so I think the simplest way to approach the situation is to be honest as to the limitations to be imposed on my actions. I place myself in your hands.'

Marcus smiled gently, tapping his still swollen jaw and pointing at the chair from which Caninus had risen.

'I understand. Talking is . . . *difficult* for you at the moment?'

Marcus nodded, pointing to the chair again, and this time Caninus relaxed, returning to his seat. The young centurion passed him the wooden tablet on which he had written several lines of closely spaced text, watching as the prefect held it up to the light in his broad-fingered hand.

'"I am to watch you, but will do so as your friend. I am still grateful for your rescue of my wife."' Caninus bowed his head. 'No gratitude is required, Centurion, but your open mind is appreciated more than you might guess. Anyway . . .' He turned back to the tablet. '"I will observe, nothing more. Continue with your duties as if I were not here."' The prefect smiled wryly. 'That's an easier task for you to instruct than for me to perform, but I'll do my best to ignore your presence. And then you ask what I have planned?' He stood, pointing to the map behind him. 'I have two main objectives at this time . . . but perhaps you should take a seat before I explain any further? I still have to assume that my prefecture has been compromised by Obduro's spies.'

Marcus sat, gesturing to the prefect to continue.

'My first, and most obvious target, is clearly Obduro himself. I have my scouts out in Arduenna, hunting for their hiding place, for our first concern must be to find that encampment's location. You were there, Centurion Corvus, even if you were blind-folded and injured. Can you give me any better idea of where to look?'

Marcus wrote on his tablet for a moment, then handed it across the desk. The prefect looked at it, nodded his understanding and passed it back.

'I understand. You were knocked half-conscious, your jaw was broken, and doubtless they did everything possible to disorientate you. I can see how you say that you might have been walking for one hour or three. Nevertheless, there may be some small clue you can provide? Look at the map. If you had to take a guess as to where it might be, where would you place the location?'

Marcus stood, walked over to the map-covered wall and, after a moment of deliberation, pointed at a spot to the south-east of the submerged bridge. He shrugged helplessly, turning back to Caninus, who inclined his head with a grave smile.

'I understand. Nevertheless your guess is better informed than any that we might make. I'll have my scouts thoroughly explore that part of Arduenna.'

Marcus nodded, opening his hands in a gesture for Caninus to continue.

'I mentioned a second task. In truth it's something I've not shared with a soul outside this office.' He leaned across the desk, lowering his voice to a conspiratorial murmur. 'If any hint of my suspicions with regard to the matter I'm about to outline to you were to become generally known before the time is right then I have no doubt that the evidence would be lost within hours, and the man I suspect of gross fraud against the imperial treasury would have me in his power.' He sat back in his chair with a speculative eye on the man facing him. 'But I suspect you know what I'm talking about. Perhaps you and I can form an alliance in this matter. You might just make the perfect investigator.'

After concluding his session with Caninus, Marcus explained that he had a personal task to attend to and left the prefecture, walking briskly down the street to the food shop where Scaurus had purchased his soup the previous evening. A brief negotiation carried out in sign language, and the exchange of enough money to pay for a week's supply of food, quickly persuaded the proprietress that her new best customer was to be provided with two pots of soup a day, and the flavours were to be varied as much as possible.

His next stop was the smith from whom he'd purchased his new spatha. Unlike the food shop's owner, the sword maker had his letters and was able to read Marcus's handwritten instructions, albeit in a slow, laboured manner.

'So you want a new helmet, Centurion? Did you lose the old one when you got that lump on your face, eh?' Marcus nodded patiently. 'You want an exact copy of the one you lost, but made in the same way as that cavalry helmet I showed you? Ah, you want the iron layered, do you? You're a clever man, Centurion; you won't get any better protection than one of my helmets. Now, what else . . .?' He squinted at the tablet, frowning at the next item. 'A shield?' He frowned at the Roman. 'I didn't think you officers carried shields?' Marcus raised an eyebrow and tapped the tablet. 'Yes, sir. And you want it . . .' The smith's frown deepened as he read on. 'What use will that be, Centurion? It'll be the wrong shape for a start.'

Marcus took the tablet out of his hand and held it up, pointing at the lines inscribed on the wax with a meaningful look before tapping his purse. The smith shrugged, nodding his agreement.

'You're the customer, Centurion. If you want a shield that'll make you look like a throwback to antiquity and be a complete bastard to use, who am I to argue? So, a spear, a helmet and a shield all made to your very particular specifications . . . shall we call it ten in gold?' Marcus scratched a fresh line onto his tablet and passed it over the counter for the smith to read. '"Yes, but only if . . ."' The smith shook his head ruefully. 'For a man I had down as my best customer in years you're driving a very hard bargain, Centurion.' Marcus shrugged, took the tablet from his hand and turned for the door, prompting the smith to hurry around the counter to block his exit with a speed that belied his size. 'I didn't say it was an impossible bargain though. Here, have a seat. Are you allowed to drink wine with that bandage round your face?'

With the deal agreed and toasted with a cup of the smith's rather watery wine, Marcus walked back to the hospital with a thoughtful look on his face, collecting a fresh pot of soup on the way. He kissed his wife, then walked down the corridor until he found the room he was looking for, occupied by a single man in a centurion's uniform. The patient got painfully to his feet when he saw Marcus in the door's frame, and put out a hand in greeting.

'Centurion Corvus! It's been a long time since we had the chance to talk. I saw you lying in the room next door when they brought me in, but I've not been able to walk until today, and even now it's a bit ugly.' He turned up the sole of his left foot for Marcus to examine, and the younger man winced at the huge black blisters. 'They don't hurt all that much, and I'm allowed to walk on them if they're bandaged up, but I won't be fit for duty for at least a week.'

Marcus looked back at him with a smile of genuine affection, and went through his now practised mime of tapping his swollen jaw and handing over his tablet for the other man to read. While Tertius deciphered the lines of closely packed script, his lips moving as he read, Marcus's mind went back to their first meeting in the officer's mess at the port of Arab Town at the eastern end of the Wall, and Tertius's swift discovery of his true identity and fugitive status. The 2nd cohort centurion had had ample opportunity to profit from the knowledge, but had chosen instead to work against his prefect's plans for Marcus's exposure and execution. Rumours had circulated among the men of the Tungrian cohorts for months after Prefect Furius's mysterious death, despite the official opinion at the time being that it had been the result of natural causes. Furius, it was speculated, had been the subject of a revenge plot, murdered by a 2nd cohort centurion whose soldier brother had been crucified on his orders. No proof had been forthcoming, however, and Tertius, as the centurion in question, had stoically ignored all invitations to comment.

He looked up from the tablet with a thoughtful expression.

'You want me to do some work for you, something connected with the hunt for this Obduro bastard. It needs doing quickly, and it might be dangerous.' He grinned confidently at Marcus. 'I'm your man, and you can forget *that* . . .' He waved his friend's hand away from his purse. 'That bastard Furius crucified my brother, and you gave me my revenge. May Cocidius praise you long and loudly for it. Whatever it is that you need doing can be considered a part payment of my blood debt to you. And if there's fighting involved, so much the better.' He reached for his sword and patted the battered metal scabbard. 'Although from what you've written here, I may have more need of my other sword.'

'Your business is all done, Centurion Corvus?'

Marcus nodded at Caninus writing on his tablet and then passing it across the desk with a rueful look.

'That much? For a helmet? Gods, but that smith knows how to charge a man! For that much coin he should be making you a helmet from gold.' He shook his head, passing the tablet back across the table. 'So, let's discuss the lesser of my two targets. I'm pretty sure you've guessed who I have in mind, but for the avoidance of any doubts I'll spell out my suspicions. Procurator Albanus was appointed to his post by Governor Julianus a good time after I arrived, and so I have been able to watch and listen as he has subtly changed the mechanisms by which the grain supply to the legions on the Rhenus is managed. His remit, or so he tells anyone that will listen, is to maximise the supply of grain to the army, although I've seen no more than a small increase in the number of carts going east to the Rhenus fortresses. What I have noticed, however, is an increase in the number coming in from the various estates across the province. And if more grain comes in, but the same quantity as ever goes out to feed the soldiers, something doesn't quite add up. Either some good grain simply isn't being shipped, which is unlikely as that would stick out in the records like a bridegroom's prick, or he's accepting grain into the store that shouldn't be getting into the supply system and using it to pad out the decent stuff.'

Marcus wrote on his tablet, turning it over to reveal two words. '"Mouldy grain". Exactly, Centurion! I *knew* you were a sharp one. I think the procurator is encouraging farmers to send him grain that by rights isn't fit to eat, and paying them a small percentage of the price they'd get for the good stuff. Let's face it; ten per cent of market price is a long way better than nothing at all for something that's only fit for burning. He'll dress it up under some pretext or other, food for animals, or some such, but I'll bet good money that he's mixing it in with the good stuff. If he slips only a couple of bags of the mouldy stuff in with every hundred, he's still putting ninety per cent of the value of that many good sacks into his own purse. Doesn't sound like much, does it? But you'd be amazed just how many sacks that is per year.' He pulled a scroll from his desk and passed it to Marcus. 'Do you see the numbers involved? We send six hundred thousand bags of grain to the legions each and every year, eighty cart loads every day on average. If he's clever enough to limit his skim to just two per cent, two spoiled bags in every hundred, which is low enough to be an irritant rather than a problem, then at four denarii for a bag of corn he's still grossing over a hundred thousand a year. That's nearly ten thousand in gold, Centurion. Subtract what he's paying for the bad grain, and the bribes to keep everyone involved happy, and I'll wager it's still the neck end of six or seven thousand in gold a year, and with no taxes to pay. And the procurator has been here for over two years. A couple of years at that rate of profit and a man could buy just about anything he wanted when he returns to Rome, starting with a seat in the Senate. And of course it's the perfect "victimless" crime. Nobody loses out, not unless you count the emperor, because the grain's effectively free, levied on the farmers of this province and the Gallic provinces to the south as the price of keeping them safe from the German barbarians waiting just across the Rhenus. The procurator has two nasty problems though. *Me*, and now *you*.'

The torches were long since lit, and the familiar crowd already well lubricated, when a pair of men in the rough tunics of soldiers hobbled through the low doorway of a beer shop in the city's south-western quarter, one hobbling gingerly on obviously painful feet, the other walking with the aid of a crutch. They met the questioning stares of the clientele with blank glances around the lamplit room, foot-long military daggers prominently displayed alongside the purses that bulged from their leather belts. Their clothing was simple and functional, the heavy wool crudely darned in several places where it had worn through, and their hands and faces were marked by the scars and calluses of decades of service, but the weapons' iron handles shone out in the drinking establishment's gloom like highly polished silver, a calculated and highly visible show of deterrence. Gesturing to the owner for a couple of beers, and holding up a coin to vouchsafe payment, the younger of the two helped his mate into his seat and propped the veteran's crutch against the wall. A rather obviously made-up serving girl, her tunic cut low to display breasts little better than pre-pubescent, deposited their beers on the scarred and stained table and collected the coin, looking bemused at the failure of either man to attempt even the most perfunctory of sexual assaults upon her despite the amply provided opportunity. She shook her head, putting both hands on her hips in disgust.

'Are you two a pair of tunic lifters? No problem if you are, there's a couple of boys upstairs if that's what—'

The younger man held up a hand, and she fell silent as he took a sip of his beer and sighed appreciatively, aware of the men seated around him.

'Best beer of the day, that is.' He shook his head at the girl, smiling up into her disgust at being so abruptly turned down. 'No disrespect, love, but these days when I go looking for paid female companionship my tastes run to a slightly older lady than your good self. You're just too young and fresh for me.' He raised a hand again to forestall the next offer. 'I know, you've got "older" ladies up there as well, and again, no disrespect, just probably not my type either. We're just going to sit here and drink our beer, and at some point some nice gentleman or other will tip us off to the location of an establishment capable of furnishing us with appropriate mature company. Or, in the case of my colleague here –' he pointed to his companion with a sly glance around the room to confirm that he had an attentive audience – 'a painted and strapped-up whore with tits like a cow's udders and an arse like the back end of a cart horse, who fucks like a fully wound bolt thrower and sucks cock like a Greek sailor after a week at sea.'

A chorus of muffled sniggers followed the young woman as she walked away, and the older of the two soldiers raised his beaker in ironic salute to his colleague, his voice a low growl.

'Nice fuckin' work, Tertius. You've chased away the only woman I've seen that's been worth more than a denarius all night. And I'll bet she'd a been nice and tight.'

A seam-faced man leaned across from the table next to them, his features creased in a wry smile.

'No, friend, your mate had it right. She's the best of a pretty bad bunch, and she wasn't joking about the boys either. Both of them are her brothers, and they're both younger than she is. Yeah, I know . . .' He grinned into Tertius's disbelieving expression. 'And her old mum's up there too. It's tough times, what with the gangs getting their fingers into every pie going. But if you gentlemen are looking for a higher-class of female company then pull up a chair, buy me a beer and I'll tell you what's to be had in Tungrorum for a man with a taste for the better things in life.'

The look on Centurion Tertius's face was one of weary triumph, while Sanga's expression, like any veteran finding himself in the presence of his own centurion, first spear and tribune, was one of stone-faced inscrutability.

'We struck it lucky in the third bar we visited. The men we watched leaving the grain store when the place closed for the night were all there in a tight little huddle, drinking their beer and planning a night of whoring, as it turned out. All it took was a little play-acting by myself and the soldier here, and the spending of a little coin to back up our story as to how we came to be out on the town, and we found ourselves invited along with them to the Blue Boar. When we got there it was clear that they were regular customers, because the lump who was keeping door let them in without a word, and us too once they'd vouched for our behaviour. And it wasn't a cheap place either.'

First Spear Frontinius raised a wry eyebrow.

'I presume that you were both forced to sample the establishment's services in order to maintain the fiction of being a pair of soldiers who got lucky at your standard bearer's expense?'

Sanga struggled to maintain his mask of imperturbability, one corner of his mouth twitching slightly, and Frontinius allowed a long, hard stare to linger on him, but Tertius was speaking again, his voice free of any trace of irony.

'Yes, sir. It would have been strange if we hadn't, if you take my meaning. Mind you, it didn't hurt that Morban's reputation for taking bets on anything and everything seems to have spread across the city. The whorehouse's hired muscle was in stitches when our new friends told him our little story.'

'And?'

Tertius frowned at Scaurus's question.

'Tribune?'

Scaurus rubbed his eyes with one hand, stifling a yawn with the other.

'Centurion, whilst this is all very gratifying, you've not yet got to the crux of the matter, have you?'

Tertius nodded apologetically.

'Indeed not, Tribune. To keep the story short, the prefect seems to be justified in his suspicions about the traffic in and out of the grain store. As we expected, the men we hooked up with are labourers, paid to haul the corn off the farmers' carts and into the grain store, and then to put it onto the carters' wagons for shipment to the legion fortresses. That much was evident from the first beer, since they were still in their work clothing, but it was only after we'd got a few more wets down our throats that we got a few more clues. Soldier Sanga here managed to blurt out that jobs in the store must be well paid . . .' The officers collectively winced, each man imagining the moment of uncomfortable silence as Sanga's apparently naive words had sunk in. 'But he said it in such a morose way that all they did was laugh at what they took for jealousy at the amount of silver they were throwing around. One of them leaned forward and tapped his nose, with a smile, mind you, and said that there were things that happen in the store that it would be best we didn't know about, and he rubbed his fingers together like he had a coin between them. It was pretty clear to me that they're the men that do the dirty work when there's mouldy corn to load onto the outbound wagons, slipping it in with the good bags, and in return they get a big enough backhander to enjoy themselves properly once in a while.'

'So they didn't actually tell you how the fraud works?'

Tertius shook his head at Prefect Caninus's question.

'No, Prefect, and they were never going to. They wouldn't trust a couple of men they've just met with that sort of information. It could take another month of drinking and whoring for them to get to the point of opening up that much.' He saw Frontinius's eyebrows rise in unspoken comment and quickly continued. 'But in the absence of our having that sort of time to spend, I think it's fairly clear that there's something worth investigating.'

When the two soldiers had left the room Prefect Caninus nodded to Marcus, sitting in his enforced silence in the corner.

'Well done, Centurion. I think we have enough information to wrap up this fraud with no more than a few quick raids. If we arrest all of the likely participants at the same time one of them's bound to panic and incriminate the rest of them.'

Scaurus shifted uneasily.

'And just who are you suggesting we should arrest on the grounds of some grain store workers having more money to spend than ought to be the case, Prefect?'

Caninus shrugged.

'That all depends whether we want to scare them into inactivity, and have the gains of their crime vanish into thin air, or to catch every man involved and recover the money they've been salting away. And that sum, Tribune, is likely to be large enough to put everyone involved very much in the emperor's eye.'

He watched intently as tribune and first spear exchanged glances. Scaurus shook his head slowly, his eyes locked on the prefect's.

'That's not a status I crave, Quintus Caninus. The attention of the throne can be a double-edged sword, as anyone with any experience of imperial politics will tell you. I'll settle for recovering the gold and making sure that it is returned to its rightful owner. So, whose doors would you have me send my men to kick in? I'm presuming that you want me to put on a display of over-whelming force?'

'What in Hades are you doing, Tribune? Do you have such delu-sions of grandeur that you think you can arrest me and assume my responsibilities in your ceaseless quest for power? Do you imagine that I won't . . .'

Albanus, standing under the watchful eyes of a pair of Tungrian veterans in the middle of the basilica's main chamber, was literally spitting his indignation at Scaurus, who sat before him with an expression of weary contempt. Julius, standing close behind the prisoner with his vine stick in one hand, reached out and tapped him hard on the arm with the baton. As he did so the tribune raised an eyebrow, pointing with one hand at the fuming procurator.

'The next time my officer's vine stick touches you, the force used will be sufficient to silence you. And it will be repeated as many times as necessary to achieve that objective. Bruised or unmarked, either way you'll be silent when I command it. Shut your mouth and consider for a moment which outcome you would prefer, if you will.'

The two men stared at each other in silence before the tribune gestured with his raised hand to the stony-faced Julius, who stepped back with another tap of the stick, smiling quietly to himself as the procurator flinched at its touch. Albanus composed himself, looking down at the broad flagstones on which he stood before Scaurus's chair. Lifting his head to look at the tribune, he waited in silence for permission to speak.

'Very well, Procurator, now that you've had some time to consider our relative positions in this redefined relationship, do please continue with whatever further expression of outrage you had in mind.'

When he spoke again, Albanus's previous fury had been replaced by a more calculated approach, part submission, part sardonic sneer.

'Thank you so much, Tribune, for allowing me to voice my opinion. You have my admiration for your ploy of dragging me from my bed and forcing me to stand here, while you sit in comfort, to reinforce the difficulty of my position. It's interesting psychology, Tribune, but I'm afraid—'

Scaurus cut him off before he could warm to his subject, his tone matching the look of disparagement he was playing on his prisoner.

'I am sitting, Procurator, because I've been on my feet all night organising a series of raids on multiple locations within Tungrorum. Would you like to hazard a guess at who else we might have bagged this morning? No? Enlighten the prisoner, if you will, Centurion.'

Julius read aloud from his tablet, his parade-ground-hardened voice harsh in the room's echoing silence.

'Four grain store workers, the grain store loading and unloading supervisor, two records clerks, the store manager, your deputy, Petrus, and yourself, Procurator.'

Scaurus stood up and stretched, then took the two paces that set him toe to toe with the procurator. When he spoke his voice was pitched low, but with an edge of unmistakable ferocity.

'All of you, Albanus. I've rolled up the entire organisation that was engaged in perpetrating your fraud against the empire, every man in the city with any official part in the store's management. They're all being questioned as we speak, and doubtless one or two of them will sing in order to earn a more lenient sentence. Not that we really need them to, of course, the evidence is already more than convincing. Centurion?'

Julius opened the door to the antechamber and hefted a corn sack into the room. Scaurus walked over to it, opened the top and sank his fist deep into the black, mould-crusted grain within before pulling it back out. He opened it under Albanus's nose, watching as the procurator's face creased in reflexive disgust.

'Rotten grain. Not just a dusting of mould, but actually rotting in the bag. A bag that was found, I hasten to add, in a separate granary, well away from the sound supplies. So you were still accepting sub-standard grain into the store, but it was being stored apart from the legions' supply of good corn.' He raised a hand, forestalling Albanus as he opened his mouth to comment. 'No, no need to say it. I'll say it for you. There's been no crime committed simply because your men found a bad bag, and segregated it in a separate store built purely for that necessary expedient. But the rebuttal to such justifications is usually to be found in the detail, Procurator, and so it proves in this case.

Just how many such bags do you think we found, eh? No
answer? You need to take more of an interest in the workings
of your operation, Albanus. We found seven hundred and forty-
three spoiled bags in total, most of them nowhere near as bad
as this, although not one of them would get past a legion stores
officer.'

He dropped the corn in his hand back into the bag, rubbing
his hands in distaste at the mould stains that remained on his
skin.

'Nasty stuff, bad grain. Quite unusable for anything, including
animal feed. Except, that is, for the purposes of fraud. One or
two bags quietly pulled from the back of the store and loaded
onto each cart, an irritation for the stores officer at the other end
when they're eventually opened and found to be rotten, and doubtless you've had a few letters come back down the road already,
detailing the problem and asking you to keep a closer watch on
what gets loaded, but still well within the usual incidence of
spoiling. It's a work of genius, Albanus, to ruthlessly weed out
the usual percentage of bad grain and then turn it to your own
profit. Although of course you're quite sure I have no way to
prove my allegations, aren't you?' He stared at the silent Albanus
for a moment, and the procurator looked back, his blank expression betraying his uncertainty as to whether or not the soldier
had any means of proving the allegations he was making. With a
sigh, the tribune nodded to Julius. 'Centurion?'

Julius stepped out of the room, and returned with a heavy
wooden box under his arm. Albanus took one look and blanched,
his eyes widening. The tribune met his gaze and then gestured
to the box, a tight smile on his lips.

'Yes, indeed. Your hiding place was well chosen, and quite
expertly camouflaged, but like most soldiers my men are experts
in finding hidden valuables. The flagstone under which you had
it hidden was just a little lower than the stones around it, which
was more than enough to excite their interest. And so this is the
moment when you know without any doubt that I have you, all
of you, in the palm of my hand. I've no proof of the actual

physical action of the fraud yet, although I expect that your accomplices will be singing like birds given a little vigorous encouragement, but this find has provided some very interesting evidence as to the profit you've been taking from it.' He opened the box and lifted out a scroll, unrolling it and reading in silence for a moment. 'An impressive sum, Procurator, and still growing at a rate that implies ongoing activity. But not enough to account for the full profit, nowhere close to it, even after the deduction of the bribes you've been paying to your staff. I'm guessing that you have a partner in crime, someone with control of the sale of grain, perhaps even the milling. You steal the good corn by substituting the mouldy grain, for which you've paid a pittance, then you pass it on to your business partner and he handles the onward sale into the city. The evidence is consumed within days of the theft and everyone's happy. The farmers get to sell corn with no market value, even if they make little enough on the deal, you make a healthy profit on the price you charge your business partner, and he sells on the stolen grain at market rates and makes his own turn. Yes, everyone's happy. With the exception of one rather significant party to the deal, now I come to think about it. The Emperor Commodus, Procurator, would be less than delighted at this state of affairs, if he were to be made aware of it. He's being defrauded of thousands of denarii every month, and I can assure you that no emperor has ever reacted well to having his purse lightened, even if it is by a well-bred character like yourself.'

He turned away, strolling across the chamber and taking a spear from one of the Tungrians. Walking back, he put the weapon's vicious point under Albanus's chin, a look of disgust on his face.

'And since the emperor can't be here in person to register his unhappiness with your actions, I'll just have to take his place in dispensing justice to you. Imperial justice, Albanus.' He stood the spear on its butt spike with a scrape of metal on stone and leaned closer, whispering his next words. 'Harsh justice.' He walked away across the room, shaking his head in apparent sorrow. 'A skilled executioner can nail a man up in such a way that he'll live on the cross for two or three days before succumbing to thirst, torn between asphyxiation and the terrible pain in his feet when he pushes up against the nail hammered through them to ease his breathing. And that's before we consider the carrion birds that will do their damndest to get at your eyes while you're still breathing. And how are your family going to take it when the news reaches them that you've been crucified as an example to others, I wonder? Of course the emperor may take a lenient view of your crime. He might spare your family their property, and their lives. Or he might not. He might take the view that they are fully responsible for your actions, and have the praetorians turn them out onto the streets. Confiscation of the family properties might give him some feeling of recompense, as might the indignities that I can assure the soldiers will visit upon them in the process. They get so little entertainment, you see, that the chance to make sport of fallen aristocrats is a great opportunity for them, and so much better value than simple whoring.' He walked away from the shivering procurator, speaking aloud again. 'It goes without saying that I have the power to make this all a lot less unpleasant, for you and your loved ones. I can commute your sentence to something a little less drastic, just as long as we recover the proceeds of your crime. But that can't happen unless you give up the identity of your business partner.'

He waited in silence for Albanus to reply, but after a long pause the prisoner shook his head slowly, his voice quavering on the edge of tears.

'I can't. He knows where my family live . . .'

Scaurus shook his head in a display of sympathy.

'Ah. I see. Yes, well, that is a dilemma. I presume that you mean your "partner" has taken steps to ensure your compliance? You're the junior man in all this, and he has a good firm grip of your balls to keep you from doing anything silly?'

Albanus nodded.

'Soon after we entered into our arrangement he told me in great detail about my parents' house, my brother's wife and children, every little detail to prove his knowledge of their lives. He has connections to the gangs of Rome, and he told me in painful detail what would happen to them all if I ever tried to take more than my share, or informed on him. My crucifixion would be nothing by comparison, and the risk to my family from the emperor is less certain than what he told me would happen to them if I were to talk. None of my men will talk either; they all have people here in the city.'

Scaurus nodded, his sardonic smile replaced by a frown as he sensed the frustration of his fleeting hopes of a swift end to the matter.

'I'm starting to understand your place in all this a little better, Procurator. This man approached you with the idea in the first place, didn't he? He's got contacts in Rome, and they sent him everything he needed to ensnare you into the scheme. Your own greed was enough at the start, but any ideas of getting out once you'd made enough money were never going to be allowed, were they? After all, once a supply of gold has been opened up there's never any incentive to stop it flowing in. A gang leader can never have too much money, now can he?' He looked at Albanus, his expression fading from anger to pity. 'You know that I'll have to execute you, regardless of the circumstances?' The prisoner nodded his head miserably. 'And if I tell you that I have a very good idea who your partner is, and that I only need confirmation of that last detail?'

Albanus shook his head again.

'It would make no difference. If I even hint to you where to look for him he'll know it, one way or another. It would be better for you to put temptation out of my reach by having me killed.'

The tribune nodded with a slow, sad smile.

'I can respect your bravery in this matter, Procurator. I can see that you felt you had little choice when this man made you the offer. It was one that could not easily be refused. And if I cannot spare you the indignity of a criminal's death, I can at least make it a quick one. I'll save the more protracted exit from this life for your tormentor.' He waved a hand to Julius. 'Take him back to his cell, and make sure he doesn't meet the other prisoner. It seems your moment is at hand.'

The centurion nodded, ordering his men to escort Albanus from the room and turning to follow them with a grim smile. Scaurus worked on a stack of papers as he waited for the next prisoner to arrive, briefly raising his glance as the man was marched into the room, then returning his attention to them while the soldiers herded their charge into place with spear prods and meaningful stares. Julius stepped in close once the prisoner was upon his appointed mark, looming over the smaller man with a smouldering glare as he pulled the dagger from his belt and raised it to hack away the assistant procurator's customary long sleeves, leaving his arms bared. Holding out a hand behind him he took a torch from the waiting soldier and held it close to the prisoner, close enough to scorch the hairs on the man's arms and illuminate the mass of gang tattoos that writhed up both arms. Nodding dourly he turned away and surrendered the torch, then spun back and put a fist deep into the other man's gut, doubling him over as he gasped for breath. Scaurus looked up again, dropping a scroll onto the desk's scarred surface.

'Assistant Procurator Petrus. Forgive me if my approach is a little blunt, but I've got bigger problems than a bit of petty theft to be dealing with. I promised the centurion here one good punch, just to let you know who you're dealing with now, although I have to admit I have enough sympathy with his view of you that I was tempted to let him replace the fist with his dagger, and remove you as a problem with one flick of his wrist. You're in army hands now. I could have your throat cut here and now and never fear any consequence. My men would rip through your pitiful collection of thugs and murderers like fire through a cornfield, and I could only take pride in the act of cleaning such criminal filth from the streets of Tungrorum. And don't trouble yourself with denials; your arms speak clearly enough of your status in the city.'

He waited for the wheezing prisoner to respond, and Petrus studied him from beneath half-closed eyelids before answering, his voice strained from the effects of Julius's gut punch.

'As you say, Tribune, my tattoos do rather betray the way I've chosen to make my living.' He looked down at the artwork that decorated both of his arms. 'When I was young these were a good way to intimidate the people around me, and now . . . now they serve to remind me of where I came from, I suppose. I grew up on the street, Tribune, and the first thing I learned there was that gangs are like weeds, always there no matter how hard you work to clear them away. And if you clear mine away there'll be another crop within weeks, along with all the usual fighting that accompanies such a struggle for power. There would inevitably be innocents caught up in the chaos, but then I'm sure you know that or you'd already have done exactly as you threaten. But to return to the apparent case against me . . . petty theft, Tribune? You have me at a disadvantage. Since I was pulled from my bed at dawn I've not spoken to another person, and so I have no knowledge of the matter you're describing.'

Scaurus shook his head with a wry smile.

'Of course. And you, the quiet man behind your procurator, silently and efficiently getting on with the business of the empire.' He stood up, taking the scroll from the desk and carrying it as he went to stand before the prisoner. 'See this?' Unrolling the paper he held it up before the other man. 'Procurator Albanus – I should say ex-procurator, of course – has confessed to a rather large fraud against the imperial grain supply. These numbers detail the profits he's made over the last two years, profits he tells me he has shared with a shadowy figure he refuses to identify.'

The assistant procurator turned a glassy stare on him, his face utterly immobile as he recovered his customary reserve.

'Fraud, Tribune? Procurator Albanus? I can scarcely believe it. And how much?' He peered at the paper, his eyebrows rising in apparent amazement. 'Surely that's not possible? Those sums are truly shocking. . .'

He shook his head and lapsed back into silence, eyeing Scaurus with the same neutral expression. The tribune stared back for a long moment before turning away, talking as he rounded the desk and sat down.

'Don't worry, Petrus, I won't have a confession beaten out of you. Not that I'd hesitate to have Julius set about you with enough vigour to get the shit running down your legs if I thought a nice quick admission of guilt would result, and not that he'd hesitate to beat you half to death.' Petrus flicked a glance at the glowering centurion, who was clenching his fists so tightly the knuckles were bone white. 'I am, however, still a man of principle myself, and if you're the man I think you are then you could probably hold out long enough that I could never be sure if it was guilt speaking or simply the need to stop the violence.'

Petrus regarded him levelly, his expression still steadfastly unchanging, and in that instant Scaurus knew he was guilty.

'No, I've got a better idea. I'll be assuming the temporary role of procurator until a replacement for Albanus can be found and make his way here, and in the intervening period your services will not be required. You can consider yourself dismissed from your position as of now.' Petrus bowed his head slightly and turned away, waiting for his guards to lead him from the room, but Scaurus gestured to the pile of paperwork on his desk. 'As procurator, I am of course now responsible for the maintenance of order within the city, and I have to say that order seems to have suffered rather significantly under the auspices of the last man to have held the position. In order to ensure the upkeep of public decorum I shall therefore be closing all brothels and unlicensed drinking establishments immediately. All licensed establishments will now receive army protection against the extortion of what I believe is laughably termed "protection money", with soldiers posted outside their doors night and day. And I will be making it very clear that I am doing this as punishment for previous misdemeanours, Petrus, with your name prominent in the official pronouncements. I'd imagine that this will attract a good deal of interest from your fellow members of Tungrorum's criminal fraternity, given that I'll be closing off their supply of revenue at the same time, and to facilitate their interest I'm going to place you under house arrest. My men will make sure you remain in the Blue Boar, but may not be able to deter your former partners in crime once they realise you're the cause of their misfortune . . . unless, of course, there's anything you'd like to share with me?'

Petrus's face remained as immobile as ever, and after a moment Scaurus waved a hand in dismissal, watching with a look of disgust as he was marched out at spear point. Shaking his head wearily he raised his voice to summon Sextus Frontinius, who entered by the same door that the prisoner had been escorted through, saluting as he limped into the room.

'Tribune?'

Scaurus stood, collecting together the papers arrayed on the desk before him.

'Here.' He passed the documents to his deputy. 'These are the warrants you'll require to shut down the brothels and unlicensed beer shops, and here are the records we recovered from Albanus's hiding place. If you'd be so good as to give the latter to one of your better standard bearers, I think it's high time the emperor's money was repatriated from whichever of the local money lenders are currently making it sweat for its previous owners. Tell your men not to take no for an answer. Any failure to pay up promptly is to be treated as an opportunity for swift and uncompromising action, and I want that money counted and underground in the pay chests before dark. Who will you get to calculate the amounts?'

Frontinius smiled, lifting the stack of paper.

'Who will I get to work out how much money is owed to the throne by a collection of fraudsters? Morban, of course. He'll be driven by jealousy, greed, and an eye to that elusive golden opportunity, to find every last sestertius. And then I'll have his numbers checked by two of his colleagues, just to make sure he hasn't actually found a way to scrape a little piece off the plate and into his purse.'

He left, and Scaurus called for Marcus and Caninus, greeting the latter a good deal more warmly than had been the case a day before.

'Well done, Prefect, you've uncovered theft of a scale I wouldn't have believed if I hadn't seen the evidence with my own eyes.'

Caninus bowed, his face still sombre at the events which had played out before them.

'I find it hard to take much pleasure from being proved right, Tribune, but as you say, at least we have the perpetrators, and the proceeds will soon be returned to their rightful owner. What will you do with the money?'

Scaurus shrugged.

'The simplest expedient would seem to be dropping the problem on the nearest legionary legatus. The commander at Fortress Bonna would doubtless find a good use for that sort of funding, given that he's responsible for keeping the German tribes quiet. Once it's in his hands I really don't care whether he sends it to Rome, buries it for a rainy day or just showers half the tribal chiefs in the north with it to keep them at daggers drawn with the other half, just as long as it's off my hands.'

Caninus shared a smile with him.

'That sort of money will always attract the wrong kind of attention. You'll have it away to the Rhenus as soon as you can, I take it?'

The tribune ran a hand through his hair.

'Mithras, but I need to bathe.' He nodded distractedly. 'Yes, I'll have my First Cohort march it along the road to the east just as soon as we've got all the money there is to be had. Then we can turn our attention back to your old adversary, Obduro.'

Caninus dipped his head approvingly.

'And if I might make a suggestion?'

'Yes, Prefect?'

'A rider arrived late last night to warn me that there is a grain convoy on the road from Beech Forest. Almost two hundred carts full of grain, enough to make a tempting target for Obduro. If he knows as much about our business as he purports, then he'll know that the convoy will be coming past the forest later today. Perhaps it would be an idea to send a good-sized force west to meet them, and to deter any idea of snapping up that much grain?'

Scaurus nodded wearily.

'It will also be a good chance for my first spear to get his men out onto the ground and make it clear that we rule here, not some ragtag band of robbers and deserters. I'll have him march west in enough force to put any such idea out of Obduro's mind.' He stood, indicating to the two men that the meeting was at an end. As they made for the door he frowned for a moment, then came to a swift decision. 'One more thing, Prefect?' Caninus turned back with a questioning expression, Marcus waiting at his shoulder. 'I think you've proved your bona fides more than adequately over the last day, and under some personal pressure, to boot. With your permission I'll relieve you of the company of my centurion. I'm sure he's finding the task of watching you just as onerous as it must be to find yourself under constant scrutiny. And besides, I have something else in mind for him, something better suited to his talents.'

Caninus opened his hands in agreement.

'Having Centurion Corvus helping me was never onerous, Tribune, far from it. His idea to use your wounded men to gather intelligence as to the grain store's activities was masterful. I will, however, happily relinquish his services if you have a better use for them. And I stand ready to provide any assistance that might be useful in this new task.' He raised an enquiring eyebrow, his mouth twisting in a gentle smile. 'My tracker Arabus, perhaps?'

Scaurus shook his head wryly.

'You're too sharp for me, Prefect Caninus, far too sharp. I'll leave it up to Centurion Corvus to decide what help he might need. Now, gentlemen, if you'll excuse me? The night's activities have left me in need of a damned good sweat.'

Julius walked alongside Petrus as the soldiers escorted him back to the Blue Boar, one hand resting lightly on the handle of his dagger. As they turned the corner into the street in which the brothel stood the previously silent gang leader stopped walking and turned to his escort with a wry smile.

'If you're thinking of gutting me then this is your last chance, Centurion. Wouldn't you just love to open me up and leave me to die here, slowly and in public? I wonder what's stopping you?'

The big Tungrian shook his head dismissively.

'I gave the tribune my word not to deal with you myself. I keep to my word.'

Petrus grinned evilly.

'You keep to your word? Despite my provocation? House arrest in the Boar won't be so bad, you know. I've a ready supply of wine and whores to pass the time, and enough gold to keep my men happy until you fools have marched away and left me to continue my business as if you were never here. There's one whore in particular I plan to ride on a regular basis while I'm cooped up waiting for that moment, and every time I fuck her from behind with a good handful of her hair in my fist. I'll shout your name just to remind her what she's missing!' He squinted up at the seething centurion and nodded his head in apparent admiration. 'You really do keep your word, don't y—'

A lightning-fast punch sent Petrus staggering back onto the cobbles, blinking and snorting blood from his nose, and Julius pulled the dagger from his belt and stepped over the fallen gang leader, squatting over him where he lay.

'Tribune Scaurus promised me *two* punches, the second to be delivered along with this message. If you set foot outside the whorehouse the guards have orders to spear you, and I'll make sure that the men set to watch you are the nastiest we have. But they'll have orders from me to do no more than cripple you and then call for me. And when I arrive you and I will spend your last moments in the company of my little friend here.' He showed Petrus the dagger's blade, twisting it to catch the early morning sun and send a pattern of sunlight sparkling from its rough-sharpened blade, then he lifted the terrified man's tunic and put the dagger's point under his testicles, prodding at the soft skin with a snarl of barely controlled anger. 'I'll have your fucking manhood off and make you watch while the dogs eat your sausage.' Petrus nodded slowly, staring up into the Tungrian's enraged eyes and knowing that his only option was to remain silent. 'And one more thing, the tribune told me to tell you that Albanus will be under a similar house arrest to yours, and that should anything unfortunate happen to him I'll be free to come for you with licence to inflict whatever punishment I think fit. And trust me, Petrus, I can be surprisingly inventive when it comes to men like you.'

8

Marcus took his leave of the prefect and walked back to the hospital, where Felicia had not long since started her working day. Her Tungrian escorts saluted as he walked into the surgery and he returned the gesture, temporarily dismissing them with a waved hand. They went off around the corner to give the couple some privacy, one man nudging the other once they were safely out of sight, first miming the doctor's swollen belly and then winking at his mate, bending his legs and pretending to take a handful of a woman's hair from behind. Marcus ignored their poorly muffled snorts of mirth and held his wife against his body for a long moment before releasing her, smiling down into her sleepy eyes. The doctor in his wife took charge, untying the bandage wrapped about his face and examining the bruising around his jaw line with a critical eye.

'Not too bad, Centurion. I'd say that's healing at just about the rate I would have expected. You'll be keeping the bandage, I presume?' He nodded, and she fetched a fresh length of linen with which to renew the injury's protection. 'You look tired. In fact you look worn out. Are you going back to our quarters to get some sleep?' Marcus held up his tablet, and Felicia read the neat lines of script carved into its soft wax surface with a look of resignation. 'Are you taking anyone with you?' He shook his head, pointing to a line in the tablet's message, and her eyes narrowed with concern. 'You're a diligent man, Marcus. Nobody could accuse you of lacking commitment. But doing this alone must be more of a risk than having Dubnus or Qadir alongside you. You'll have to sleep sometime or other, and if you get the reaction it seems you're hoping to provoke . . .'

Her concerns ran dry in the face of his gentle smile, and he simply tapped the hilt of his new spatha with a meaningful expression.

'One man against the world, is that it? Well, just you be sure to keep your wits about you. A pretty new sword isn't much use if you've got a spear in your back that you never saw coming. And speaking of swords, make sure you bring that one back. I'm depending on the proceeds from its sale to keep me and your child fed and warm when you finally meet someone who's better than you are with a blade.' He smiled again, then raised his eyebrows in an expression of injured amazement, forcing a laugh from his wife. 'Yes, I know. A better man with a sword than you? Impossible.'

He kissed her and turned away, and the doctor watched with a pensive smile as the soldiers retook their positions to either side of the surgery door.

'Let's hope that your customary self-confidence is justified, Marcus Valerius Aquila. I'm not yet ready to wear a widow's red again.'

Leaving the hospital, Marcus paused to watch as a long column of soldiers marched out through the city's west gate. Spotting his friend Caelius at the head of his 4th Century he waved a hand, and the young centurion dropped out of the line of march with a smile.

'Greetings, Marcus! It's good to see you looking better. As you can see, we're away to the west to make sure the bandits don't snatch up the grain convoy that's coming up the road from Beech Forest.' He looked up at the clear blue sky with a wry smile. 'And it's such a nice day that Uncle Sextus has decided to take all of the Second Cohort and half of the First along for the walk! Think of us sweating away down the road under the lash of his temper while you're idling around the city eyeing up the girls!'

He slapped his friend on the back and hurried away up the line of men to retake his place at the head of his century. Marcus watched with pride as the remainder of the long column ground away through the gate, leaving behind them only the echo of their passing and the first snatches of a marching song. Turning away from the arched entrance to the city he walked swiftly through Tungrorum's narrow streets, returning the salutes of the soldiers and legionaries he passed and ignoring the curious glances of civilians out shopping for their day's provisions. He visited one of the shops and made the purchase of a pair of matched hour-glasses before continuing on his way to the previously empty ground where the Tungrians had established their barracks. The 1st Cohort's mounted century had erected their stables at the far end of the main run of the infantry's closely packed barracks, and it was a scene of bustling activity as the horsemen finished their daily routine of feeding and brushing their mounts and made ready for their first patrol. Decurion Silus saw his friend approaching and walked out to meet him, extending a hand with a broad smile.

'We heard you'd taken a bash in the face, but I didn't realise it was bad enough that you'd be forced to cover up your disfig-urement.' Marcus smiled ruefully in return, pointing to his jaw and miming the breaking of a stick, then he leaned forward to sniff at his friend's clothing, recoiling in mock disgust. Silus put both hands on his hips and raised his eyebrows in admonishment. 'Yes, very funny. I smell of horses. Whereas you –' he leaned forward in turn and sniffed – 'you smell of a lady's perfume. And I know which of those two rides I would prefer!' He looked his friend up and down in appraisal. 'So, whilst I'm delighted to see you, I'm sure that this isn't a social visit, not with you in full armour and dangling sharp iron from both hips. What can we do for you, Centurion Corvus?'

Marcus handed over his tablet, waiting patiently as Silus read the words he'd written, the decurion's lips moving as he ran a finger along the lines of text.

'You want to borrow a horse, do you? Are you sure that you're ready for anything more vigorous than catching grain thieves?' Silus's tone was light, but his gaze was calculating, and he raised a finger to point at Marcus's face. 'If you've cracked the bone then another smack on your chin would probably shatter it, and even your lovely wife would be hard pushed to put a broken jaw back together. I've seen enough busted faces in the last ten years – men who fell off their horses and ploughed up the ground with their mouths – and it isn't a pretty sight, I can tell you. One poor bastard I remember had his jaw ripped clean off, and all we could do for him was put him out of his misery quickly and cleanly.' He shook his head grimly at the thought, and put a hand to the silver penis amulet hanging from his wrist to ward off any evil that lurked in the memory. 'Every man I ever saw bust his jaw properly ended up with a lumpy face, and most of them could only mumble like drunks. So you're sure you want to risk spending the rest of your life with your face whatever shape the bones set into, and your orders no clearer than a pisshead's mutterings?'

Marcus took back the tablet, quickly writing a fresh line of text before handing it back to his friend. Silus read the response and shrugged helplessly.

'And you think the fact you *expect* to be followed makes it any more sensible? You'd better watch your back, Centurion, that's all I can say. You're sure you don't want a few of my lads to come along and watch it for you? I'm sure the tribune wouldn't argue with the idea.' Marcus shook his head. 'I thought not. Very well, if you're determined to do this on your own . . .' He turned away and shouted a command to the men busy at work behind him, one of whom put his brush down and led forward the horse he was grooming. The animal stopped in front of Marcus, lowering its long face to nudge at his shoulder, and Silus laughed wryly, affectionately rubbing the horse's flank. 'See, Bonehead recognises a kindred spirit. He knows that wherever he goes with you there'll soon enough be an opportunity to run wild and kick things, don't you, you feather-brained bastard?'

Marcus waited while the horse was saddled, then led it away with a wave of thanks, walking the restive animal down the row of barracks until he reached the building that housed his own century. Qadir stepped out of the chosen man's quarters to greet him, and he quickly grasped what it was that his centurion had in mind when Marcus handed him one of the two hourglasses and the tablet, nodding at the carefully worded instruction. He shouted a command over his shoulder, eyeing Marcus with a grave stare.

'Cyclops! Your presence is required!' The watch officer emerged from his barrack and shot Marcus a respectful salute before turning to listen to his chosen man's orders. 'I want the five most disreputable and unsoldierly looking men in the century here in tunic order as fast as you can.' The Hamian turned back to Marcus. 'We'll need some time to get them out to the gates. Allow one hourglass to pass before you leave the city; that should be sufficient time for us to rustle up enough slovenly characters. I see that you've borrowed your usual horse from Silus, and I don't doubt that he wanted to send some men along with you, so I won't be surprised if you refuse any offer of help.'

Marcus nodded and patted his friend on the shoulder, then pointedly turned his hourglass over. Qadir shook his head resignedly before following his example, and the Roman turned away, satisfied that he had taken the only possible precaution against what he was expecting would happen once he launched himself on his intended path of action. Leading Bonehead by his bridle, he made his way to the armourer's shop, where he was warmly greeted by the smith himself.

'I have everything you wanted, Centurion, made exactly to your specifications. Come this way, and I'll have one of my men watch your horse.' In the forge behind the smith's shop Marcus found his purchases neatly laid out for examination, and the smith took each piece in turn and offered it up for examination. 'Your spear, with the head made just as you described. Although what use it will ever be is a mystery to me.' Marcus examined the spear carefully, then nodded his satisfaction and put it aside, watching as a stout leather cover was slid over the weapon's iron head to deflect the curious gazes it was likely to draw. The smith's next offering was the helmet he'd ordered, and the young centurion looked at it closely from all angles before signalling his acceptance, writing in his tablet and lifting it up for the smith to read. 'Hold it for you? Of course, Centurion. And here, just as you requested it, the shield. I had it painted with the design you ordered, and I have to say that my artist has quite excelled himself.' He pulled off the shield's thick leather cover, turning it for Marcus to examine. 'See, it is constructed just as you wanted, although how useful it will be in a fight is doubtful, given how much it . . .' His words trailed off as Marcus spun the slightly dished shield to display the artwork that decorated its face. He stared at it for a long moment, then nodded happily at the image that would face an opponent were he to use it in combat. The smith sighed with relief, pulling the leather cover back over his creation. 'And lastly, the gift you requested of me.' He handed over a heavy leather bag, indicating the strap by which it could be hung from a saddle horn. 'I trust that you find all of this to your satisfaction, and will be able to . . .'

Marcus nodded, dropped a bag of coins into his palm and took his purchases out to the waiting horse, hanging the heavy leather bag from Bonehead's saddle before slinging the shield across his back with the strap attached to its leather cover. Mounting the eager beast he rode to his last stop, the food shop where he routinely purchased his soup. The cook came out to meet him carrying a heavy water skin, whose contents were still warm, and he paused for a moment to swallow several mouthfuls of the broth before heading for the east gate, a quick glance confirming that the hourglass was close to empty. As he approached the gate he was pleased to see one of his men lounging idly against the wall of a building, dressed in a dirty tunic which was hanging below his knees in a decidedly unmilitary fashion. With a wooden-handled knife in his belt he looked like nothing more than the kind of man who could be found right across the empire: a sharp character who preferred living off his wits rather than the sweat of his labour. Sneering up at the passing officer he swept the street behind Marcus with a bored gaze, ignoring the centurion's passage out through the gate and onto the road to the east.

Marcus spurred his horse into a trot, turning the hourglass as the last grains ran out of its upper section and starting a fresh period of measurement. He rode for a mile or so, then took advantage of a low ridge to leave the road unobserved by anyone watching from the city's walls, tethering the horse to a tree far enough inside the forest that ran alongside the road as to be invisible to the casual glance. Walking slowly back down the line of trees, he paced forward until he found a spot from which the city was clearly visible but from which there was no risk of his body being silhouetted against the skyline. Taking out the hour-glass, he waited patiently for the remaining sand to run out, keeping his eyes fixed on the walls of Tungrorum and only occasionally glancing down to view the sand's slow but inexorable progress. As the last grains ran through the glass's tiny aperture he locked his stare on the city, and after another long moment his patience was rewarded. A trail of black smoke etched an arc against the sky, the burning arrow drawing a thin charcoal line across the sky to the south of Tungrorum, and Marcus smiled grimly to himself, turning back to the horse's hiding place.

Tribune Scaurus was back at his desk by late morning, refreshed by his bath and the short sleep he had allowed himself, and was patiently plodding through a stack of official documentation taken from the procurator's office when Caninus hurried into his office. The bandit hunter saluted briskly and stood at attention in front of his superior's desk, and Scaurus laid down the scroll he was reading to glance up at his colleague with an approving expression.

'The more I read, the more I realise what a favour you've done the empire by bringing this squalid fraud to its inevitable conclusion. And what can I do for you now, Prefect?'

The other man's response was crisp with urgency.

'One of my scouts has returned to the city from Arduenna, Tribune, and he has delivered vital intelligence on the subject of Obduro and his gang.' He walked over to the map on one wall of the office, pointing to a spot in the forest close to where the Tungrians had crossed the river only days before. 'He tells me that he was hunting Arduenna for their stronghold as I have ordered, and as I promised would be my main focus of effort, but instead of finding their hiding place he stumbled across the bandits themselves, marching in strength through the forest. He counted their numbers as being over five hundred men. Once they had passed his hiding place he made his way to the river, swam across and then ran to the city. His sighting is less than three hours old.' He pointed at the map again, now indicating the point where the road south to Augusta Treverorum bridged the Mosa to the forest's west. 'With their bridge destroyed they are forced to take the long way round to reach the Beech Forest road, using the path out of Arduenna's north-western edge and then across the Mosa by the road bridge. As to where they are heading in such numbers, I am forced to conclude that the city *may* be their objective.'

Scaurus stood, frowning, and walked round the desk. When he spoke, his voice was pitched low to avoid any risk of his words reaching the men guarding his office.

'Tungrorum? How could they dare to strike here, when they know we have over three times their strength? Would Obduro be that foolish?'

The prefect shrugged, his face impassive.

'My own thoughts exactly, Tribune. But consider the facts. You have sent the majority of your men to patrol the road to the west in such strength that any attempt he makes to take the grain convoy would result in disaster. And as you say, Obduro is no fool.' He moved a step closer, his voice so low that Scaurus had to strain his ears to hear it. 'We face a dilemma. On the one hand, perhaps Obduro is marching to attack the city, seeking to pull off a huge victory by raiding the grain warehouse for its contents. In that case, our logical reaction must surely be to concentrate our forces here to defeat him. On the other hand, if we make such a step on the basis of a ruse, he would then be free to snap up the grain convoy, then be back across the river and into Arduenna's safety before we realise that we've been deceived.'

Scaurus nodded thoughtfully, and paused for a moment, staring intently at the map.

'If he crosses the Mosa as you expect, then the key moment is when he reaches the junction of the roads from the east and west once he's across. If he turns left, then he's clearly going after the convoy, whereas if he turns right, he'll be pointing his dagger squarely at the city. It's ten miles from where we crossed the river to the junction, so if he marched his men out at dawn he should have them across the Mosa and ready to turn east or west by midday. They could be knocking on our gates here by dusk, and leave us having to face him in the dark, with barely the same number of Tungrians and a cohort of undertrained boys to fight men who, despite their treachery, clearly know how to fight in the darkness. And whether or not my veterans would be likely to win such a battle, losing the contents of that grain store to him would be a disaster for the empire.'

He pondered for a moment longer.

'Very well. I'll send out a party of cavalrymen to observe the junction, and tell us which way he turns. They can also find my cohorts and get them turned around and heading back this way, so that whatever he does we'll have him in a vice. He'll have to give battle against overwhelming force attacking him from both sides, either that or have his men dump their equipment and swim the Mosa, those of them that can swim and whatever happens that'll be the end of his threat.'

Caninus nodded eagerly.

'I can go one better than that, Tribune. By all means send the cavalrymen to find your detachments and bring them back east, but allow me the honour of taking my horsemen to watch the road junction. I'll send riders back to you once it's clear what he's doing, and you can sally behind me with the legion cohort and your own remaining centuries to stiffen their line. My man Arabus has given us the chance to outmanoeuvre Obduro, to bottle him up and tear his band of killers limb from limb, *if* we get this right.'

Having remounted, Marcus rode on at a fast trot, reaching the fort at Mosa Ford just as the legionaries on guard duty were taking their midday meal. The duty centurion studied him for a moment with deep suspicion, frowning as he took in the bandage wrapped around his face, and reading the pass which the tribune had written for him with infuriating slowness. But eventually he ordered the gates to be opened and allowed Marcus to pass. Following the same path along the forest's edge that the scouting expedition had taken, all the time calculating the progress required for his plan to succeed, he spurred Bonehead back to the trot once they were moving along the hunters' track, trusting his luck that the horse would be sure-footed enough to avoid pitching him off into the undergrowth. By the time another two hours had passed he had found the clearing where they had spent their first night, and where he had been so sure he had heard the sound of something or someone moving through the forest around them. Hobbling the horse, and leaving it to enjoy the grass that carpeted the forest floor after the long trot, he quickly gathered wood and kindling, and built a fire big enough to burn for several hours. Glancing up at the sun, now starting its slide down towards the horizon, he made a quick calculation and decided that the time was right.

Working briefly with flint and iron he got the fire lit and burning well, piling on plenty of green wood among the good dry material until the blaze was sending a column of thick smoke into the air. Picking up his new spear, he discarded the leather cover that protected its head and went to ground, flattening himself behind a tree on the uphill side of the clearing. For the best part of an hour the scene remained peaceful, the fire's initial fierce crackle dying away to a gentle background mutter of flames slowly devouring wood. Lying absolutely still, Marcus watched as Bonehead contentedly cropped at the grass, a cloud of small insects buzzing around its head. The horse's ears suddenly pricked up, and it raised its head warily, looking across the clearing at something hidden from Marcus by the tree's trunk. Holding his breath, the Roman waited for whatever it was that had attracted the horse's attention, the faintest of noises confirming that something or someone was moving slowly and stealthily across the clearing. An arrowhead came into view from behind the tree's trunk, followed by the bow to which the missile was nocked. Held ready to shoot, with the arrow pulled almost as far back as the weapon's tension would allow, the barbed head swept in an arc across the clearing as the archer stopped where he stood and searched the trees around the clearing for any sign of his intended victim. Hardly daring to breathe, never mind move, Marcus watched in sick horror as the arrowhead swung back towards him, knowing that at any moment the bowman would step forward and spot him, prostrate on the ground and unable to react fast enough to evade the arrow's lethal impact at such short range.

The horse snorted, pawing at the ground, and for one precious moment the hidden archer was distracted, wondering if the horse was reacting to a familiar presence. The arrow's cruel head swept away from Marcus's hiding place, and, silently thanking Mithras as he moved, the Roman pushed himself to his feet and raised the spear to throw. The archer, still hidden behind the tree's trunk, must have heard the faint sounds, for as Marcus drew back his throwing arm the bow swung back towards him, reducing both men's survival to a simple, deadly race to be the first to loose his missile. Stamping forward with sudden, blinding speed, Marcus slung his spear into the other man's body, flinching aside as the arrow, released a fraction of a second too soon in the archer's desperation, whistled past his ear. The spear smashed into the wrong-footed hunter's side with a heavy thump, and he fell to the ground clutching his ribs with a grunting, agonised groan. Marcus drew his sword and advanced cautiously down the slope, searching the forest about him for any sign that the man he had felled had been accompanied and then, seeing nothing, he put his foot on the hunter's chest and rolled him over, shaking his head as the prostrate man gasped in pain. Reaching down, he picked up the spear, nodding in satisfaction as he contemplated the padded leather cap that covered its blunt, rounded iron head, designed to stun or smash the wind out of its target rather than skewer deep into a man's body. The two men stared into each other's eyes for a moment before the Roman reached up and untied the bandage around his face, allowing it to fall to the ground. When he spoke his voice rasped from its long period of silence, but the words were clear enough.

'I don't suppose I'll need this any longer. It seems to have served its purpose, as does my fire. But you, Arabus, your purpose is far from over. You've got some talking to do before you cross the river to meet your goddess.'

Scaurus was waiting impatiently in Caninus's office, frowning at the map on the wall and considering his options when Julius hurried in, his face grim.

'Tribune, there's a messenger. It's one of the prefect's m—'

The man pushed past him into the room, utterly ignoring the centurion's anger in his state of apparent shock, his face pale and drawn. Scaurus recognised him as Caninus's deputy, Tornach, a tall thin man with watchful eyes, who had seldom been far from his master's side, and he raised a hand to forestall Julius as his centurion moved to punish the messenger for entering unbidden. As the two men watched him the bodyguard pulled himself together, holding out a grain sack with shaking hands.

'I have a message for you, sir. A message from . . . from . . .' He swallowed and gulped in a breath, as if forcing himself to say the name. When he spoke again his voice was heavy with dread. '*Obduro.*'

He reached into the sack and pulled out something heavy, holding it up for the tribune to see. With a lurch of his stomach the Roman realised that it was a human head, the features at once familiar despite the dreadful wounds that had been inflicted on them. The eyes were empty sockets, and the mouth sagged loosely to reveal gums from which every tooth had been torn to leave gaping bloody wounds. The face itself was battered almost beyond recognition.

'What happened?'

The question was barely more than a whisper. The bodyguard dropped the sack on the office's tiled floor, looking up from his master's severed head and staring into Scaurus's eyes as he answered.

'We found the bandits, or rather they found us, a mile from the bridge. They waited until we were almost on top of them and then ambushed us, showering us with arrows. They dropped most of the horses with their first volley, and after that we never had a chance. Half of us were killed in the fight, the rest were beheaded after we'd been captured. Obduro chose me to bring the prefect's head back. The faceless bastard.' The bandit hunter looked down at the floor with an expression of self-loathing. 'He made me memorise a message to go with it too, and told me how I had to say it. He told me if I got it wrong, or failed to speak it just as he said it, he'd know, and I would die in worse pain than if he'd killed me then and there.' He drew himself up and stared Scaurus in the face. '"Tribune, as you can see, I have taken the revenge I have long promised myself on this fool. He chose to live as a lackey to you Romans, rather than honouring his goddess as we were both taught when we were young. Now I have removed his stain from my family's history I will deal with the men you sent to patrol the road while they sleep tonight, then return to defeat you, and empty your grain store. The next time we meet, you will feel the bite of my leopard sword."'

He looked at the tribune, his eyes filled with misery.

'And then he killed them, every other man that wasn't already face down. He sent them to Hades one by one, laughing as they shouted and screamed and pissed themselves with fear, laughing as they flopped about with their throats cut.'

Tornach lapsed into silence, holding one shaking hand with the other as if seeking to quiet them, and Scaurus roused himself from his amazement, nodding decisively to the waiting Julius.

'So there's definitive proof that Caninus was telling the truth about Obduro being his twin brother. Take this man away and have him looked after; he's not fit for much after the shock he's had. Parade your centuries, please, and send word to Tribune Belletor that he is respectfully requested to join me, with his men ready to march in full fighting order, and just as quickly as he likes. I'll have the bastard's head for this outrage, fancy sword or not. My regret in this whole matter is that I chose not to trust

Caninus while he was alive, but I'll send his brother to Hades quickly enough that he'll have precious little time to celebrate this act of fratricide.'

Marcus disarmed Arabus, pulling his long hunting knife from the engraved leather sheath hanging from his belt, then hauled the groaning hunter across the clearing by the back of his thick woollen tunic, ignoring his grunts and curses of pain, and threw him against the trunk of a tree. Touching the point of his patterned spatha to the man's throat, he put sufficient pressure on the sword's hilt to dimple the skin, pinning him in place so that even without bruised ribs he would have been unable to move.

'It seems that my suspicions were correct, Arabus, despite all of your offers of help and friendly behaviour. You were trying to lead us into a trap when we camped here, weren't you? If I'd not heard your accomplices approaching we'd all have vanished into the Arduenna and never been seen again, supposedly as another example of the Goddess's power, wouldn't we?' The tracker scowled back up at him, his face creased with a combination of fear and pain, but he said nothing by way of reply, provoking a hard smile from his captor. 'And now you think that silence is the best answer to my questions, do you?' He stared down into the tracker's stony face and shook his head, hardening himself to do what was necessary. When he spoke again, his voice was harsh with the promise of retribution. 'I'll give you a choice. You can either talk now, tell me what I need to know and earn a swift, clean death, and I'll leave your body whole for your afterlife, or you can spend the next few days crawling on your hands and knees with your ankle tendons cut, until you're too weak to resist the pigs when they come for you. I'm told that even a small herd of the little monsters can strip a man's corpse to rags and bones in less than an hour. You can have a moment to consider which exit from life you'd prefer.'

He waited in silence, then sighed and shook his head. He withdrew the sword from Arabus's neck and moved the blade to point it at his ankles in readiness to sever his captive's tendons. The tracker raised his hands in a placatory gesture, his evident misery betraying the quandary in which he found himself.

'I'll talk. But you must understand, they have my woman and sons.'

Marcus sheathed the spatha and pulled out his silver inlaid dagger.

'You're right, unless you want to leave this life slowly, and in more pain than you can imagine, you will talk. You'll talk until you've told me all there is to know, and when I'm satisfied I'll decide what to do with you.'

Arabus shifted, grunting at the pain in his side where Marcus's blunt iron spearhead had slammed into his ribs.

'I've been in Prefect Caninus's service for two years, tracking down parties of bandits and showing him where they can be taken. He found me in the deep Arduenna, where I have lived and hunted the unmapped forest since I was a boy, and offered me so much coin to work for him that I was unable to refuse. I left my family there, with the eldest boy to hunt and provide food for them as I had taught him, and went to the city to become his tracker. I soon proved skilful enough in leading him to the bandits plaguing the city that over fifty men were captured and executed as a result of my ability to hunt them down. I felt no sadness for them; nobody made them turn to preying on their fellow men, and it is against the ways of the goddess to steal and murder. But one band always managed to avoid capture, and avoided our hunts time after time. Whenever I thought I had clues as to the location of Obduro and his men, I was frustrated by mistakes and ill luck. Even when I found the location of their fortress, deep in the forest . . .' He paused and laughed at the look on Marcus's face, his amusement turning to an agonised grunt as the pain of his bruised ribs sank its claws into him with the movement. 'Yes, I found their hiding place, deep in the forest where the altars to the goddess are as many as blades of grass in a meadow; it is a secret, forbidden place for all but her most devoted followers. I waited in silence and stillness for a day and a night, watching it to be sure it was theirs, and when I was certain I took the news back to the prefect.

But he was unable to gather enough force to be sure of success in such an attack on a defended position, and so he kept the secret to himself for fear that they would move their camp if it became known that it was discovered.'

Marcus shook his head in puzzlement.

'But when we arrived in the city Caninus would have had all the men he needed, and more besides. What was it that stopped him from taking us into the forest to defeat Obduro, I wonder?'

Arabus shook his head, grimacing at the pain gnawing at his body.

'You do not understand. If you worshipped Arduenna as we do, you would know that none of her followers would ever knowingly guide outsiders like you to the secret places where the altars to her magnificence are hidden, and Caninus is a devoted worshipper of her greatness.' He smiled at Marcus's raised eyebrows. 'You believe him to follow Mithras, your soldiers' god, but he was born and raised here, and for a true man of Tungrorum there can only be one deity: our goddess Arduenna.' Seeing that his captor's expression was still one of disbelief, he shrugged easily. 'Believe me or don't believe me, it means little enough to me. In helping your soldiers to find their way to her holy places, the prefect would have been sealing his own doom in the afterlife . . .' He sighed, and even in his agony his expression softened to something like pity as he stared up at the Roman. 'I have told you, *many* are her weapons. When I die, I expect to enter her realm, a forest like this only stretching away into the mist forever, where the hunter will never fail to make his kill, and the feasting knows no end. But if I betray her . . .'

Marcus shook his head at the thought, reflexively touching the Mithras-blessed amulet at his wrist.

'Who set you to follow and kill me?'

The tracker's face darkened.

'Before I tell you that, you must understand why I came after you. Last winter, while we were confined to the city by the snows, the prefect's deputy came to me in secret. Like me, Tornach was born in the forest and is a steadfast believer in her power, and I had come to trust him as a decent man. When others under the prefect's command tried to abuse their power over the people we encountered on patrol, looking to rob or rape them, he always ensured their discipline, without favour or exception, and always in the goddess's name. Even the non-believers were forced to accept her disciplines, and he was without mercy in punishing any man that broke her commandments. I treated him with great respect, and believed him to be a man I could follow. But that night he came to me with a hard face, and with a blade drawn and ready to use. He told me that my woman and sons were captive, held by Obduro in his hidden stronghold, and that I was to carry out his orders without fail if I wanted to see them alive again. As proof of their captivity he showed me a silver bracelet that I gave my woman when she bore my eldest son, and he threatened them with a slow, dishonourable death if I failed to obey. And from that day I was a servant of Obduro.'

He hung his head for a long moment before raising his gaze to stare at Marcus, his expression both contrite and defiant.

'You judge me. I see it in your stare. And yet you have a child in your woman's womb. In years to come, if you were held to ransom with that child's life, what would you do, I wonder?'

Marcus pursed his lips and nodded slowly.

'Yes, so do I. Now answer my question.'

'Who set me to follow you, with orders to put an arrow in you and bury any idea that you might discover Obduro's fortress? It was Tornach, of course. Caninus made no secret that he expected you to attempt another search of Arduenna. He was worried that your presence would make the goddess angry with us all, but he did not feel able to prevent you from leaving the city. Tornach took me to one side and gave me a choice, either to find and kill you here, and earn my family's freedom, or to refuse to do so and have my body dumped in a city bone pit, without the honour to earn Arduenna's favour, and bring death on Obduro's sacrificial altar to my sons. He showed me the knife I gave to my eldest son before I left the forest, the sister to the knife I wear on my own belt, as proof that he had my family in a safe place, and he promised in her name that I would join them when I had fulfilled this last task.'

'So he gave you no choice at all.' Marcus's glance lingered on the running-boar decoration adorning the hunter's empty sheath. 'And it was Tornach who planned to kill us, the last time we ventured into the forest?'

'Yes. He is the most devoted of the goddess's followers I have ever known. For him, your boots treading on this ground is an insult to all he believes. The prefect may be a believer, but he is still a servant of your empire. I do not believe he had any part of the plan to kill you.'

The Roman saw sincerity in the tracker's pain-slitted eyes. He raised the dagger again, allowing Arabus's eyes to linger on the blade for a long moment.

'I have one last question for you. It will be hard for you to give me what I need to know, I suspect, but you have no choice in the matter. If you are to live, you must guide me to the altars of Arduenna, and tell me what I need to know if I am to find Obduro's fortress.'

Arabus gritted his teeth against the pain burning in his chest before grimly shaking his head.

'I told you that I will not betray my loyalty to Arduenna. No unbeliever can be allowed to find the sacred groves dedicated to her, and it is there that Obduro has his hiding place. You can send me to Hades, but I cannot tell you what you want to know.'

Marcus held the dagger up again.

'I know. I ask you for the one thing that you know will prevent you from receiving the favour of your goddess. But you *are* going to show me where to find Obduro. Not because of this –' the Roman sheathed the weapon before leaning forward – 'but rather because of *this* . . .' He tapped the wounded man's empty sheath, putting a finger on the stylised boar carved into its thick leather, then handed him his knife, presenting the handle to him in a gesture of trust. 'You're going to help me find Obduro because today is not your day to die, but rather your day for *revenge*.'

★

Scaurus stalked out in front of the Tungrian centuries with
Arminius at his shoulder, buckling on his helmet as the five
centurions gathered round him in a silent, hard-faced group,
Prince Martos standing slightly off to one side in unconscious
reflection of his place within the cohort's world. He looked at
them in silence for a moment before speaking.

'Gentlemen. Our colleague Prefect Caninus has been
murdered along with his men, ambushed by his brother Sextus,
the man known as "Obduro". He was killed out of hand as an
act of revenge for an imagined slight from their shared past.
By now the bandits will have crossed the Mosa and turned west,
and they plan to track First Spear Frontinius and your brother
officers down the road towards Beech Forest with the intention
of striking at them after dark, when our men are camped for
the night. And under such circumstances they might just prevail.'
He shook his head, looking about him again with an intent stare,
gauging his officers' resolve. 'Which, Centurions, is not an
eventuality I intend to permit. We will march to the west behind
them, moving as fast as the men can carry their equipment and
weapons, and we will trap the scum between our shields and
those of our comrades. Martos, I'd be grateful if your men
would scout the ground before us to avoid our falling into any
trap that might be laid out for us.' The Votadini prince nodded
his acquiescence. 'Thank you. Decurion Silus will lead his
mounted century ahead of us, find the enemy and report back,
whilst also taking word of this development to the first spear
and carrying my orders for him to turn east and put Obduro
and his men into the jaws of a trap from which there will be
no escape. I'll have that man's head on a spear, cavalry helmet
and all, by the end of the day. You've got a five-hundred count
to get them ready to march, and then we move. Centurion
Clodius, you are hereby appointed senior centurion until we
join up with the rest of our force, then First Spear Frontinius
will resume his command. Centurion Julius, a moment, please.
The rest of you are dismissed.'

Julius waited stone-faced as the other centurions scattered

to their centuries, eager to make sure their men were ready for
a forced march, none of them wanting to suffer the embarrassment of causing the cohort any delay in their headlong
charge to the west. The tribune watched them go for a moment,
then turned back to the heavily built centurion with a grim
smile.

'So, Centurion, what, you are wondering, have you done to
have your expected position as Uncle Sextus's deputy usurped
by your colleague Clodius?'

Julius shrugged, his heavyset face impassive.

'The Badger's a good man, Tribune, more than capable of
leading the cohort down a road and deploying them to wipe out
a few hundred bandits. I'll admit I'm curious though. Was it
something I've done?'

Scaurus smiled, putting a hand on the big man's shoulder.

'Yes, Julius, it was something you've done. It was every little
bit of professionalism you've displayed since I took this cohort
under my command, every order given and every enemy killed.
In the absence of the first spear you're my best individual officer,
and I've got a job that needs doing here that I can't entrust to
anyone less than my *best* centurion. We're forced to withdraw our
force from Tungrorum to deal with this new threat, but there's
enough money being held in the headquarters' safe room to attract
every thief and gang leader in this whole city, what with the pay
chests and the proceeds of the grain fraud. I'm leaving you here,
Julius, you and your century, and depending on you to make sure
that nobody gets their grubby fingers on that money. I want a
double-strength guard on the vault, and the rest of your men,
whether eating, resting or sleeping, no more than a dozen heartbeats away. You can also keep Centurion Corvus's wife and the
wounded safe from harm while you're at it, and relieve me of the
trouble of carting that jar of naphtha around. As of this moment
you're free to kill anyone and everyone you suspect to be a threat
to the emperor's gold, without hesitation or fear of any repercus-
sion. If we return that gold to the throne we will be congratulated
and possibly even rewarded, but if we lose it again, having exposed

its original loss and recapture to the throne's eyes, the outcome will be altogether darker for everyone concerned. Do we understand each other, Centurion?'

'Many men came this way, within the last half day. See?' Marcus looked down from his saddle, grimacing non-committally at the ground where Arabus was pointing. The hunter climbed down gingerly from his place behind the Roman, wincing at the pain in his ribs as his feet touched the forest floor, then he squatted on his haunches and pointed at the numerous indentations in the soft ground 'Look. Boot prints.'

Marcus climbed down and squatted beside him, peering closely at the marks of men's passage in the forest's green-tinged light.

'You're right. And there are hundreds of them.'

Arabus nodded sagely.

'Enough boots for the whole of Obduro's army. And they all point in one direction. That way.' He pointed to the west. 'They were making for the bridge over the Mosa, now that their own way across the river has been destroyed. What they will do when they have crossed the river is the question to be answered.'

He looked at Marcus with a level gaze, clearly waiting for the Roman to deduce whatever conclusion it was that had already formed in his own mind.

'And if the entire bandit army has marched, their stronghold may be unguarded, or only very lightly manned.'

The tracker inclined his head in agreement.

'Exactly. And we're close to it now; I can smell woodsmoke in the air. Do you see that hill in front of us?'

The Roman squinted through the dimly lit expanse of trees, struggling to make out the feature that Arabus was pointing to. The forest was sloping gently upwards before them, and he could see several dark knots of foliage studding the wooded slope as it rose to a crest four hundred or so paces distant.

'Yes, I see it.'

'From there we will be able to see Obduro's fortress.' We must leave the horse here. If Obduro has left men to guard their strong-hold, then one unexpected sound might bring the entire band down on us. Come.'

Marcus tied the animal's reins to a tree and took the heavy leather bag from its place on his saddle horn before following the limping hunter up the long slope. He weaved around the thicker clusters of trees in the wake of the other man's shadow-like progress up the hill, and earned a scornful glance over Arabus's shoulder as he snagged a branch and flicked the leaves backwards in an unwanted burst of movement. Staring into the closest of the copses, the Roman discerned a figure hidden within the confusion of branches, something close to human but betrayed by its stark lines and unnatural stillness. Craning his neck to see better, and putting a hand to his sword's hilt, he froze as a harsh voice whispered in his ear, the hunter's approach so quiet that he had not realised the man was close behind him.

'You are in the presence of Arduenna herself, Roman, closer than any non-believer has ever come and left with his life.' The confusing image within the copse resolved itself as if cued by Arabus's words, and Marcus realised that he was looking at a man-sized representa-tion of the goddess. 'I may owe you my life, and you may be the means by which I take my revenge, if you can prove that I have been so horribly wronged, but you must show her the proper respect or you *will* pay the price for failing to do so.'

The Roman nodded, averting his eyes and muttering a swift prayer to Mithras for the god's protection, and Arabus tugged at his sleeve, drawing him away from the sacred grove with the impatience of a man whose divided loyalties were being sorely tested. Climbing behind the tracker up the shadow-dappled slope, Marcus realised that each of the copses to either side of their path was similarly deified, the trees' branches woven around statues of Arduenna. Sometimes the goddess was standing, sometimes she was mounted on a charging boar, but every one of the statues showed her wielding her bow. Remembering the sudden onset of the snow that had frustrated the Tungrians' efforts to penetrate the forest, he shivered and silently mouthed another entreaty to Mithras before following Arabus towards the slope's crest. He made barely ten paces progress before glancing into another thicket and, with a sick lurch of his stomach, discerning a pile of bones scattered around the statue's feet. In a moment Arabus was at his side again, his face hard.

'Sacrifice. Men taken in the course of their raids, those they don't kill out of hand, are led here with the promise of being brought to the goddess, and joining in her eternal glory. It is a cruel lie. Obduro leaves them bound and helpless, their arms lashed to branches from different trees to suspend them before the goddess, and they die while she watches, sending her creatures to feed upon their corpses.' He shook his head, his gaze averted from the evidence of the sacrificial victims. 'Sometimes even upon their living bodies. And every sacrifice to her strengthens Obduro's cause with Arduenna.' A note of impatience entered his voice. 'Now come, and pay no further heed to the goddess. My presence will protect you, for I am her devout follower, but she watches us nevertheless.'

Following his guide's example, Marcus got down onto his hands and knees, then slid onto his belly as they crested the ridge. He whistled quietly as the view afforded by its elevation was revealed, drawing an exasperated glance and a whispered admonishment from the tracker.

'I swear to Arduenna that the only way you would ever catch a boar would be if it were to fall out of a tree onto your stupid Roman head.'

Marcus nodded distractedly, staring out at the bandit fortress in wonder. The wooden palisade was surrounded on all sides by a slope that fell away from the hill's flat summit at a steep angle, forming a natural defence around the stronghold.

'Look at that. With a single cohort I could hold that position against a full legion.'

Arabus stared out at the fort with pride in his eyes.

'It has been a place of worship and refuge for our tribe for as long as we have lived in the forest, or so the stories tell us. Obduro led his band here several years ago, and set up an altar to the goddess inside his wooden walls.'

'I've seen it. He sacrifices men upon it, and drinks their blood.' The tracker's eyes clouded at his harsh tone, and Marcus patted him on the shoulder, rolling onto his back and reaching into the leather bag that he had carried up the slope. 'You did well in bringing me here, and I will prove to you the truth in my words, but first we have to get inside that palisade. It's time for me to take the lead, and to find out if my acting skills are sufficient to the task.'

'Petrus! The soldiers are on the move! They're marching out of the city!'

With a complacent smile the gang leader turned to the man framed in the Blue Boar's door, nodding to the men waiting around him.

'What did I tell you? I *knew* Obduro wouldn't be sitting back and waiting for them to get bored and piss off of their own accord. And while the army's away, we can have all the fun we like, starting with the retrieval of all that lovely gold they took from Albanus.' He stood up and pointed to one of his lieutenants. 'He'll have left the money behind with a few men to look after it, and to watch each other in case temptation overcomes any of them. You, send men out and find them, *quickly*. I want to know where that gold is before they get any clever ideas about going to ground with it. And you two . . .' The doormen standing on either side of Annia nodded, straightening their backs. 'You can take her upstairs and make sure she doesn't get any ideas about making a run for it. Who knows, that day you've been waiting for all these years might just have arrived. All that time spent watching her fuck other men for money but never getting any yourselves might just be at an end . . . Have the hourglass ready.' He sat down again to await further news, grinning at the horrified looks that Annia was giving him as Slap and Stab dragged her away up the stairs. 'And if life really is kind, it'll be that arsehole centurion who's been left behind to guard the gold. We'll soon see where his loyalties lie, won't we?'

Julius watched impassively from the city walls as his cohort marched out from the city and headed away down the road to the west at the forced-march pace, the sound of Clodius's bellowed orders floating back on the breeze until first sound and then sight of the marching men was denied to him by the distance being covered by the fast-moving soldiers. The man standing alongside him, a veteran of twenty years' service with whom he had long dispensed with all formality in private, stared after them and nodded approvingly.

'Not bad. The Badger might make a half-decent first spear one day.'

The centurion grunted reluctant agreement with his chosen man's comment, turning away from the view down the road to stare out at the sprawling grain store. The legion cohort's double-strength 1st century was standing guard on the depot, whose gates were firmly shut, under the command of the cohort's first spear. Scaurus had taken him aside as the Tungrians made their last preparations to march, as the cohort's centurions and their chosen men had examined each man's boots and equipment for any sign of defect or negligence that might result in one of them falling out of the crippling fast line of march. Ignoring the bellowing of an incensed chosen man less than a dozen paces away, as the assistant centurion launched into a tirade questioning whether the soldier in question had ever actually learned the art of tying his bootlaces, then provided him with an incentive to perfection by means of forcibly introducing his brass knobbed pole to the soldier's toes whilst screaming invective into his terrified face, the tribune had muttered final, quiet instructions.

'Tribune Belletor has chosen to leave his First Century behind to guard the grain store, which is good in one respect.'

Julius had nodded.

'It's his double-strength century.'

Scaurus's frown had spoken volumes as to his opinion of the decision.

'The decision wasn't anything to do with the unit's size, if I guess right, but more an unsubtle dig at his first spear for such open cooperation with Sextus Frontinius. He may come to regret the decision, if he faces Obduro's fighters across a battlefield without his senior centurion to put some iron in his men's backs. And I'm sure we can trust Sergius to stand guard over the grain store, but I have my doubts that his men will stand firm in the event that any serious threat comes up the road, so you'll need to keep an eye on them.'

Julius had raised an eyebrow, his face otherwise imperturbable.

'What threat do you think we might expect, Tribune, other than the city's gangs trying to take advantage?'

Scaurus had shaken his head, looking across his cohort's waiting ranks.

'In theory? Nothing at all. In practice . . . I don't know. This man Obduro seems to be the very model of cunning and deceit. I won't be happy until we have his head perched on a spearhead, and all this nonsense put behind us. Just be sure to keep your guard up.'

Now, deciding that he'd reflected on the conversation for long enough, Julius made his decision and turned back to his chosen man, pointing down at the grain store.

'Those children won't stand up to a sustained assault, and they're babysitting enough grain to feed the bandits well into next year. Choose five tent parties and get yourself down there, will you Quintus? Give Sergius my regards and tell him I sent you to put some backbone into his men. I'll come down for a look myself later on, once we've had time to see what the gangs are going to do now that they think the gold's unguarded.'

The first sign of interest in the Tungrian headquarters came less than an hour after the 1st Cohort's departure. A pair of hard-faced men strolled down the street past the main entrance, their eyes lingering on the four soldiers standing guard around the doorway in full armour, while Julius's watch officer, a squat plug of a man whose face bore three recent scars as testament to his front-rank status, stood with his hands on the hilts of his sword and dagger. He spat into the road behind them, creasing his face into a sneer of disdain.

'That's right, keep fucking walking! If you're planning on coming back for the gold you'd better bring some friends. That money belongs to my boss, and he'd tear me a new arsehole if I were to lose it.'

The gang scouts walked on without looking back, and the watch officer watched them turn the corner before ducking back into the headquarters. He found Julius in the chapel of the standards, staring pensively at the chests containing the money he'd extorted from the various money lenders with whom Procurator Albanus had invested it.

'Not thinking of doing a bunk with it, are you, sir?' He grinned into the centurion's look of resigned amusement, knowing that his proven worth in a fight gave him licence to indulge in a share of the banter routinely exchanged between Julius and his officer colleagues. 'Only, if you are, you're going to need some strong lads to carry that lot.'

He nodded to the chests, massively heavy both from their construction and the weight of gold they contained. Julius shook his head and smiled wryly.

'I think not. That money belongs to my boss, and he'd—'

'Tear you a new arsehole if you were to lose it? You heard that gentle warning, then, did you, sir?'

'I did, Pugio, and hopefully so did the rest of the city. If all we have to do today is stand here and stare at those chests then I'll be the happiest man in the whole of Tungrorum.'

A soldier put his head round the chapel's door, his voice urgent.

'More of them, Centurion, coming up the street from both ends.'

Julius turned away from the money, then barked a string of orders at his men before strolling out into the street, enjoying the warmth after the chill of the chapel's cold stone floor. He stood to one side as a wave of armed and armoured soldiers washed out of the headquarters' entrance, moving in disciplined silence to form two lines ten paces apart across the narrow street, one to either side of the doorway. The watch officer picked up his shield from beside the door and then shoved his way into the line, rolling his head in a brief circle as if to loosen his neck ready for combat. Drawing his spatha he bellowed an order.

'*Swords!*'

The soldiers laid down their spears and unsheathed their blades, raising their shields and dressing their line in automatic preparation for the bloody combat that had invariably followed the watch officer's command over the preceding months. A score or so gang members advanced from both ends of the road until they were almost nose to nose with the Tungrian soldiers, then they stopped, each of them picking one of the auxiliary troops and staring hard into his opponent's eyes in a calculated attempt to browbeat the building's defenders. Pugio waited for a moment until a perfect silence had settled on the two groups, then he snapped his head forward and smashed the brow guard of his helmet into the face of the man attempting to intimidate him, sending the thug reeling backwards with his nose torn and broken. The man's comrades growled in anger, but not one of them made any move in the face of their opponents' sword points, each one backed up by a soldier whose face betrayed his willingness to kill. Petrus stepped forward from the mass and pushed two of the gang's front rank aside, approaching the Tungrian line with both hands held up, open and empty, and nodding to Julius with the manner of a man addressing an equal.

'Centurion. Before this scene descends into an ugly brawl, perhaps you and I might speak as men? There really isn't any need for *violence.*'

Julius stared at him for a moment, then nodded to Pugio.

'Let him through.'

The Tungrian rank parted sufficiently for the gang leader to pass between the watch officer and the man next to him, and Petrus nodded to Julius with an apparent confidence that narrowed the centurion's eyes in calculation. Dropping his hand to the handle of his dagger, the Tungrian stepped in close and put his face inches from the gang leader's.

'So why shouldn't I gut you here and now, Petrus, given that you're in open defiance of your house arrest? What brings you to sniff around us when you know full well what I told you I'd do if you set foot outside the whorehouse?'

The other man laughed softly, shaking his head.

'That's an easy one. There's enough gold in there to make a man the master of this entire city, I've heard, and all of it stolen from the people of this province by a man imposed on us from Rome. And we want it back.'

Julius smiled humourlessly back at him, shaking his own head in turn.

'Nice try. That money wasn't stolen from the people, because it never belonged to them. It belongs to the emperor, and I'm going to make sure he gets it back.'

Petrus raised an eyebrow, lifting his arms and looking about him in a theatrical manner.

'You are, are you? How many men do you have, Centurion. Thirty? Forty? I can bring two hundred of my bruisers here, and a mob of townsmen as well, if I tell them the right story. Do you think you can stand against five hundred gold-crazed men, or a thousand?'

Julius stared at him in silence for a moment, then, without shifting his gaze from the gang leader's face, he held out a hand to the soldier closest to him.

'Spear.'

He took the weapon, glancing critically at its iron blade, polished to a bright iron shine and sharp enough to draw a thin line of blood from his scarred thumb. He turned to the gang leader, raising the point until it was inches from the other man's face.

'See this? It's just a spear. A six-foot-long pole with iron at both ends, and seems no different from any of the hundreds of thousands carried by the emperor's armies across the empire. But this spear has one small difference. Look.' He pointed to a small inscription hammered into the spear's blade in a pattern of dots. 'I Tungri. The First Tungrian Cohort, the proudest auxiliary cohort in the empire, and the nastiest. We've faced down overwhelming odds three times in the last year, we've been dropped in the shit by treason, stupidity and simple lack of men, and we've come out smelling of roses *every* fucking time. This spear has killed a half a dozen barbarians in that time, I'd guess, men just like you who couldn't see what was coming at them until it was between their ribs and killing them. You ever taken a blade?' He grinned mirthlessly into the gang leader's face, shaking his head at the tattoos that decorated the man's arms. 'I don't mean some little pricks on the arm that you got while you were off your face on cheap wine; I'm talking about having sharp iron shoved into your body so that you can feel it deep inside you, cold as ice and hot as a branding iron. That's what we do, Petrus, we don't cut and maim our victims to extort their money or ensure their silence, we just kill, quickly and without thinking. We kill and we move on, and we don't look back.'

He waved an arm at his men, apeing the gang leader's theatrics of a moment before.

'So I'm warning you, cum-stain, that if you bring violence to these men they will take it, turn it around and ram it up you so hard you'll wish you'd not been born. These men aren't just soldiers, they're *Tungrians!*' He spat the last word in the gang leader's face, and the other man flinched involuntarily at his sudden vehemence, his eyes widening as the Tungrian took a handful of his tunic. 'In fact I think I'll start early, and show your men what they have coming. Toenails, fingernails, kneecaps, eyes, balls . . . oh yes, we'll have some fun before you go to Hades!' He paused for a moment, giving the gang leader time to take in his slitted eyes and flared nostrils. 'And for the main course we'll see how far up your back passage I can get this spear. You'll look much better face down with three feet of this little beauty sticking out of your shithole.'

Petrus nodded, swallowing his fear and pushing his jaw out pugnaciously.

'I understand, Centurion. You have your orders. But for every action there is a consequence, whether intended or not. And in this case the consequences will be suffered by someone to whom I believe you were once very close. For a long time she was the mistress of my whorehouse, and occasionally my bed warmer too, when I couldn't find anything younger and fresher, but this unfortunate turn of events puts her into the enemy camp. Annia has gone from being my most valuable possession to simply being a means of leverage, I'm afraid, and if I have to use that power over you that she gives me, it isn't going to be pleasant.' He looked at Julius for a moment with a pitying expression, and the centurion's knuckles whitened on the spear's wooden shaft. 'Oh, and if you're considering ramming that goat sticker "up me" in one of your famous fits of rage, you'd best be aware that there's an hourglass running alongside the bed I tied her to before coming here. If I'm not back there in time to turn it over, then two of my most unpleasant men will start violating her in every way you can imagine, and probably a few more you can't, and they'll go at her until they can't get it up any more, at which point the next two will take over. If she passes out they'll wake her up with a bucket of cold water and start again, and they will quite literally fuck her half to death. And when they can't face fucking her any more, when her every orifice is just a bleeding pit, they'll cut her throat. The whole thing shouldn't take more than a day or two.' He glanced down at his fingernails. 'So are you going to kill me now, and condemn your girlfriend to a protracted and deeply unpleasant fate?'

Julius stared at him for a moment, then shook his head in disgust.

'Get out of my sight.'

Petrus slid through the hole that opened in the Tungrian line, and when he was behind his own men he turned back to call his parting comment.

'I'm not an impatient man, Centurion, but when I want a thing you can be sure that I always get it. You've got until nightfall to deliver the gold to me. Fail to do so and it'll be your woman wishing she'd never been born, not me.'

*

Marcus and Arabus walked up the long, narrow path from the bottom of the moat-like depression that surrounded Obduro's fortress, keeping carefully to the well-trodden route past the defences that littered the hillside. Marcus was holding his blunt-headed spear to the older man's back, in a show of being the tracker's captor. Through the eye slits that perforated the face mask of the cavalry helmet he had carried with him from Tungrorum, the young Roman could see belts of mantrap pits running away across the rising ground to either side. They were the same 'lilies' that the Tungrians used in defence: pits dug into the ground large enough to swallow a man's foot and floored with pointed, sharp wooden stakes intended to cripple the victim. Lines of heavy wooden stakes protruded from the hill's side, their points set at throat height, intended to slow any advance to a crawl and allow time for archers on the fort's wall to reap a heavy harvest of their attackers. Marcus scanned the slope's killing field and shook his head slowly, knowing that any attack by the auxiliary cohorts would have disintegrated into a costly disaster. He put the spear's heavy iron knob against Arabus's back and prodded the limping tracker hard enough to make him stagger forward with a yelp of pain. A swift glance up at the fort's walls told him that they had an audience, a pair of heads popping up to stare down at them from the parapet over the closed main gate, and he drew breath to roar a command at them, hoping that his imitation of the bandit leader's voice would suffice to keep his deception alive.

'In Arduenna's name get that gate open! I've no time to be wasting!'

The heads vanished from sight, and in an instant Marcus was past Arabus and running hard up the slope's last few paces, throwing caution aside and risking the danger of stumbling into one of the fort's mantraps in order to beat them to the gate. As he reached the palisade's wall a heavy clank of iron inside warned him that the opportunity he sought was upon him, and he pulled the spear back until the thick iron head was alongside the helmet's elegant replica of a soldier's plaited hair, poised ready to throw.

The man-sized wicket gate opened, and as the gate keeper looked through it, a look of bewilderment forming on his face at the sight before him, Marcus slung the blunt spear into his face. The weapon struck him cleanly in the forehead with a sharp crack of breaking bone, and as he staggered backwards, his eyes rolling up into the sockets to show only their whites, Marcus shouldered the bandit aside and burst through the gate, his patterned sword drawn. The stunned bandit's companion, the man whose hand Obduro had hacked open demonstrating his sword's fearsome edge, fumbled for his own weapon with a look of surprise and terror but had the sword no more than half drawn when Marcus swung his own blade in a vicious arc and decapitated him. His corpse crumbled to the ground as though it were boneless, and the Roman looked about the fort's interior, waiting for either a challenge or an arrow to fly at him from the high wooden walls.

'They're all out with Obduro. I told you so.' Arabus was close behind him, invisible to Marcus with the cavalry helmet's restricted field of vision, and the Roman swung round to find his prisoner bolting the wicket gate behind them. 'Now you must show me the proof of what you told me in the forest, so that I may pray to Arduenna for her forgiveness for bringing you here.'

The Roman nodded, wiping his sword and sliding it back into the scabbard.

'This way.'

He led the tracker around the line of the fort's walls, keeping to the shadows and moving with as much stealth as he could, until the altar to Arduenna was clearly visible. Raising a hand he pointed to the intricately decorated stone block.

'There. Obduro hung it from the altar as an offering. He takes a token from every man sacrificed upon that stone, as evidence of his dedication to Arduenna.'

He watched as Arabus moved silently across the open ground, scanning the apparently empty fort uneasily as the tracker circled round to the altar's far side, then bent out of sight behind it. When the other man remained out of sight Marcus made his way cautiously across the thirty-pace gap between wall and altar, finding the tracker on his knees with a weather-stained leather belt held in both hands, his face contorted in silent grief. The knife sheath was just as Marcus had remembered it – a perfect duplicate of the one on Arabus's own belt – and he watched in sympathy as the tracker bent over the last remnant of his son's life, his face contorted into a silent scream of grief. A voice from behind him snapped the Roman from his reverie, the harsh tone at once familiar.

'What are you doing here? I thought you'd gone to the city for the harvest? The gate guards are dead, and . . .'

Grumo's voice trailed off as the Roman turned to face him, and the big man stared harder at the cavalry helmet before raising the bow that he had lowered a moment before, pulling back the arrow already nocked to its string and levelling the missile's polished iron head at the Roman. Marcus froze, knowing that an arrow loosed at such short range would pierce his mail armour with ease. Obduro's deputy shook his head as he spoke, his voice hard with suspicion.

'If you were the man you're impersonating then that helmet would have a scratch across the faceplate from a fight in the dark a few months ago. But the helmet you're wearing is perfect, unmarked. Newly made, in fact. Take it off and let's see what we have here. Quickly, before I get bored and put an arrow in you just for the sport of it!'

Shrugging, Marcus pulled at the helmet's buckles and dropped it to the ground, looking back up at Grumo as he frowned uncomprehendingly.

'*You?* But I broke your *jaw* . . .'

The Roman shook his head with a faint smile.

'It was a good punch, but you took an age to deliver it. I managed to ride it well enough so that all I got was a bit of concussion and a bruise the size of an apple.'

The big man stepped forward a pace and lifted the bow to aim at Marcus's face, closing the range to make sure of his kill.

'And you were stupid enough to come back. I told Obduro

that we should never have released you, but he has to indulge his need for the theatrical with these messages he insists on sending back to Tungrorum.' Marcus raised his hands and stepped back, darting a glance at Arabus who was still kneeling behind the stone altar in silent grief, hidden from Grumo's view. The tracker seemed frozen in his place, his stare vacant as he continued to hold the leather belt in both hands. The bandit matched the Roman's step back with a move forward, advancing until his hip was almost touching the altar's corner.

'Backing away isn't going to help you. I'm going to put this arrow into you, and then I'm going to hoist you onto this altar and give your life to the goddess.'

Marcus stepped back again, praying that Grumo would hold his temper for long enough.

'Like all those others you've murdered on that stone? Just kill me cleanly!'

Grumo laughed harshly and stepped forward again, aiming the bow at the Roman's thigh.

'Ah yes, that hit a nerve, did it? Yes, just like all those poor fools. I'll put an arrow in your leg to stop you from running, then open your throat and let your life drain out onto the altar. You can be a sacrifice to the goddess, another of the unworthy for her to chastise in the afterlife. I'd like to think that she pursues unbelievers like you through the endless forest with her whip and bow, tormenting you the way that Rome has tormented us, but whatever it is that happens on the other side of the stone, you'll know soon enough, won't you?'

He took up the bowstring's last few inches of tension, ready to shoot the arrow through Marcus's thigh. The Roman feigned a stumble and fell to the ground, crawling backwards with his heels and elbows, and raising his voice to ensure Arabus could hear him.

'They're not all unbelievers though, are they? The tracker's boy, he was innocent of any crime against Arduenna!'

Grumo stepped closer again, and the arrow's iron head weaved from side to side as he sought an aiming point that would cripple his retreating victim.

'Arduenna demands blood! Any blood! Roman, Tungrian, it doesn't matter as long as it's shed from a living man and fit to offer! And the tracker's boy was a believer, a fine sacrif—'

With an incoherent scream Arabus came to violent life, rising from his hiding place behind the altar and leaping onto its stone surface, his body suddenly coursing with rage as the enormity of what he was hearing finally penetrated his grief. Grumo twisted his body and reflexively loosed the arrow at him, but the tracker was already in mid-air with his teeth bared in a snarl, and the missile flicked harmlessly past his ear. He jumped onto the bandit's back and wrapped his strong legs around the big man's waist, forcing the fingers of his left hand into his victim's eye sockets and dragging his head back, forcing a bellow of pain from the giant as he dropped the bow and raised his hands in an attempt to throw his assailant over his shoulder. Arabus raised his son's knife in his right hand, the blade rusted from exposure to the rain but still sharp enough to slice through flesh, and screamed a single word at the top of his voice.

'*Arduenna!*'

He rammed the ochre-flecked bar of iron clean through Grumo's neck, its point protruding from the flesh in a spray of blood, then he jumped down from the reeling man's back, raising a hand to Marcus as the Roman went for his sword.

'Leave him! Let him die in the same way that my boy went to the goddess!'

Marcus nodded, sheathing his sword and picking up the bow, nocking an arrow to its string. As he lay prostrate on his back, Grumo's mouth was opening and closing soundlessly, his breathing a rattling, bubbling rasp. Arabus joined Marcus and stared down at his victim with a hard face, kicking him hard in the side to get his faltering attention. His voice was still choked with grief, but when he spoke his words were implacable.

'When you're dead I'm going to cut you up and scatter your remains in the forest for the pigs, all but your head. That I will keep close to me, to make sure that nobody can reunite it with the rest of you. And for as long as I have it, you will spend forever in the Otherworld awaiting your rebirth. Waiting in vain.'

Marcus nodded, patting the wet-faced tracker on the shoulder.

'Stay here, then, and take this in case any more of them appear.' He handed Arabus the bow. 'I'll have a quiet look around, and see what I can find.'

He drew the patterned sword again, stealthily easing his way down the stone stairs into Obduro's underground lair with slow, silent steps, listening intently for any sound that might betray the presence of a bandit waiting to ambush him. The dungeon was lit by crackling torches, as had been the case during his previous visit, and his soft footfalls were lost in the hiss of burning pine resin. Having proven the underground room to be empty he was about to turn and leave when a faint line of shadow down one wall caught his attention. Frowning in unconscious puzzlement he slipped the sword's point into a hair-thin gap, gently levering open a concealed wooden door whose surface was painted to resemble the stone around it. The room beyond was in darkness, and he pulled a torch from the wall before entering it, starting at the sight revealed by the brand's light. A set of four shackles secured to the rock wall by short chains was holding the dead man's body in a kneeling position, as if the corpse was caught in a never-ending act of obeisance to whatever deity the man had followed in life. Marcus knelt before the corpse, holding up the torch and examining the walls and floor before taking one of the hands and staring at it intently. A scrape of leather on rock made him turn, to find Arabus standing silently behind him in the doorway, Grumo's head held by the hair in one hand.

'We should leave. Arduenna will forgive me for what we've done here, but the longer we stay the more we risk her fury. Obduro may return at any time and find us caught like animals in a wooden cage.'

Marcus shook his head, handing the tracker the torch and gesturing to the corpse.

'We need to go, and quickly, but not because there's any danger of his returning. He's led his entire army out, as you thought, but I doubt they're hunting a grain convoy. It seems to me he has a far greater prize in mind.'

9

'Mithras, but my back hurts. And I thought I was fit.'

Clodius glanced across at his tribune, grinning wryly at the look of gritty determination on Scaurus's face.

'It's one thing to keep up with the men when we're moving at the campaign pace, sir, but it's charging along at the forced march that sorts the men from the boys. You're keeping up well enough.'

Scaurus smiled tightly back at him.

'Only because I'm not carrying anything like the weight your men are burdened with. How in Hades are the Hamians keeping it up?'

Clodius grunted.

'That's easy enough to explain. The first spear made the decision to keep them in the Ninth Century, but to distribute them through the tent parties rather than let them form their own groupings.' Scaurus nodded, his thoughtful look telling the centurion that he already understood the point he was making. 'Exactly. They're surrounded by big strong country boys, farm horses to their racing ponies, and in the space of a few months they have become Tungrians. For every struggling archer there are two or three big lads who won't let them fall by the wayside, so they'll encourage them along, kick them along and even carry their kit for them if necessary. It's not the Hamians that are worrying me, Tribune, it's the legionaries. Should we drop down the column and see how they're doing?'

Scaurus nodded and stepped out of the line of march, allowing his pace to slow to a normal walk, knowing that if he were to stop altogether the effort required to get his body moving again would be agonising. Clodius walked alongside him as the First

Cohort's long column ground past them like a monstrous armoured snake, the soldiers' heads tipped back to allow them to suck in the day's warm air. As each century's centurion passed he saluted the two men with his vine stick, and Scaurus quickly realised that the sight of their commanding officers straightened backs and stiffened resolve, his men's faces hardening against the march's agony. After a few moments Titus's men, the last of the four Tungrian centuries, marched steadily past with their heavy axes held over their shoulders, then the head of the legion cohort came into view behind them.

'That's not good.'

The tribune shook his head in agreement with his centurion's softly voiced opinion. The legionaries marching behind the Tungrians were already looking like beaten men, trudging along with stooped shoulders and with only a semblance of the Tungrians' tightly ordered ranks. Scaurus's eyes narrowed at the apparent state of the legionaries.

'The bloody fool would leave his first spear behind to teach him a lesson for getting friendly with us, and now he's got no one with the balls to step up and do the man's job for him. And there's as much hope of Tribune Belletor instilling any determination into this lot as there is of him getting off his horse and showing them a good example. Colleague, how do we find you?'

He shouted the comment to Belletor as he rode into earshot, and the legion tribune waved a lazy hand in reply.

'We're well enough, Tribune.' He smiled down at the two men from the height of his saddle, raising a sardonic eyebrow. 'Enjoying your walk, are you?'

Scaurus nodded, grinning grimly in reply as he forced his aching body back up to the forced-march pace.

'I wouldn't say the word "enjoying" would be the first one that springs to mind, but it's tolerable, thank you. And an officer soon gains some measure of the pain his commands inflict on his men when he goes about his business on foot. You really will have to try it some day. Perhaps even today, if the way your horse is nodding its head is any clue. Come along, Centurion, we'd better work our way back to the front of the column. Our men will hammer away the miles at this pace all day if we don't stop them for the rest halt.'

First Spear Frontinius took a quick glance at the sun's low position in the afternoon sky as his centurions gathered about him.

'Here's the thing, brothers. We've been marching for the best part of the day, and we must have covered a good fifteen miles, and yet there's no sign of the grain convoy we're supposed to be meeting. We have two choices: either to grind away to the west until it gets too dark to march, then set up camp and wait for them to arrive, or to turn round and head back to Tungrorum. We won't be back in the city before darkness falls, but we brought a cart full of torches with us for exactly that eventuality, and a bit of night marching will be good practice. So I've decided to turn the column around and head back to the east.' The men around him nodded their agreement. 'Does anyone have a different view?' There was silence. 'Very well, get back to your centuries and get them turned round and ready to march. Just to make it interesting, we'll start off at the forced-march pace and see how long we can keep them going that quickly.'

One of the 2nd Cohort centurions, a man Frontinius had known since they were both recruits, remained behind as the other officers dispersed to their commands.

'At the forced march, Sextus? Is there something you're not telling us?'

The first spear shrugged, a look of unease on his face.

'Nothing I can put a finger on. I just know that I'll be a lot happier when we've got this many men back to the city. I might have been wrong to only leave five centuries to guard the walls . . .'

A shout from the eastern end of the column snatched their attention, and the two officers turned to see a party of horsemen, thirty-strong, riding swiftly down the road from the city towards them. Ignoring the customary hail of abuse from the infantrymen, their leader trotted his horse down the column to Frontinius's position, jumping down to salute briskly, and the first spear raised an eyebrow in greeting.

'Decurion Silus. I presume you've not been sent galloping all the way down here just to give your animals a run out?'

The cavalryman shook his head, holding out a message tablet.

'First Spear, a message from Tribune Scaurus. The bandits are in the field, and looking to take you from behind without warning from the sound of it. You're ordered to reverse your march and make all speed to join up with the tribune. He's coming west with the rest of the First Cohort.'

The first spear took the tablet, nodding to his brother officer.

'There you go, that's what's been bothering me all day.' A thought occurred to him, and he swung back to the decurion with a questioning look. 'Silus, did you actually get eyes on these bandits as you came west?'

The decurion shook his head dourly.

'No sir, nothing at all.'

'So they might as easily have got round you to the east, and the tribune for that matter, and be moving on Tungrorum. Either way we need to head east at the double! Trumpeter, sound the advance at forced-march pace.' As the horn brayed out the command for the column to start moving, Frontinius fastened the buckle on his helmet to make it tighter, winking at his friend. 'Come on, then. It'll be just like the old days, when that sour-faced old sod Catus used to beat us up and down the military road for a full day at the forced pace, and then expected an hour's spear and sword drill in the dark at the end of it. You might even think he had a point, with hindsight.'

The late-afternoon sun was warming the walls of the Tungrorum grain store as Julius strode the short distance from the city's south-western gate at the head of his century. He stopped in front of the store's gate, waiting patiently until a familiar face appeared on the wall above him.

'Centurion Julius! I thought you had orders to remain in the city and keep the procurator's gold safe from prying eyes and sticky fingers?'

He grinned back up at the legion cohort's first spear, gesturing to the cart behind him, a tent party of his century's soldiers in place of the horses that would usually have pulled the transport. Felicia was sitting alongside the boxes of coin, and she climbed down from her perch to fuss over the cohort's wounded, who were following behind in a second cart.

'I had a short but meaningful chat with Petrus that convinced me that we needed to move before he bottled us up in the headquarters building. He's got a hard-on for this money, and I can't see him taking disappointment quietly. So here we are, with a cart full of gold and nowhere else to go. Can we come and join you?'

Sergius smiled, shaking his head.

'So you bring me a few dozen soldiers and so much gold that half the city would happily tear us limb from limb to get their hands on it?' He looked up at the sky as if questioning the gods, then turned back to his men inside the grain store's compound. 'Open the gate!'

The Tungrians ran their heavy load through the hastily opened gates, and Sergius climbed down to meet them, taking Julius's offered hand with a broad smile.

'Gold or no gold, it's good to have you in here with us.' He bowed to Felicia. 'You are especially welcome, madam. In the event of an attack I fear that a lot of my men will be wounded.' He turned back to Julius, waving a hand at the store's massive, empty expanse. 'One century of men to hold a facility the size of a legion bathhouse . . .? Your tribune may be a good man, but I think he's allowed his balls to overrule his head on this occasion.'

Julius nodded.

'We'll just have to pray that the gods really have seen fit to send Obduro away to the west, because if he turns up here I can't see you and I holding this place for very long against the equivalent of a full cohort.' He unbuckled his helmet and pulled it off, grimacing at the sweat-stained arming cap nesting inside it. 'And now, if you'll forgive me, I've an errand to run in the city. You, soldier, help me out of this mail and make sure it doesn't touch the ground once I'm out of it. I don't want it covered in dust.'

Sergius watched in bemusement as his colleague unbuckled his belt and handed it to one of his men, then bent over and struggled out of his armour, dropping the heavy mail shirt into the soldier's waiting hands.

'You're going back into Tungrorum in just your *tunic*? Is that wise? And why would you take such a . . .'

He fell silent as Julius fixed him with an implacable gaze.

'A woman I loved a long time ago is being used as a bargaining counter by the local gang leader, who also happens to be our good friend Petrus. If I make any attempt to rescue her by force of arms I'll have to cut my way through a hundred or so of his men, and more than likely as many of the locals as he can bribe or threaten into my path. It'll be a bloodbath. I'll lose more than a few men, and at the end of it I'll most likely find her with her throat cut.' He fastened the belt about his lean waist, leaving his sword in the soldier's arms and taking only his fighting knife. 'One man on his own though, that's a different prospect. I can move quickly and quietly, come at them from an unexpected direction, and I have one nice little advantage that they don't know about. I'll be back within the hour, but if I'm not you'll just have to forget me. Focus on keeping this place secure. And for what it's worth, I'd be most worried about those granaries. The front wall's easy enough to defend, but they could pick any point along either of the long sides and break through the wall, given long enough, and with the numbers we've got it'd be damned difficult to stop them.' He looked about him. 'Have you got any archers?'

Sergius shook his head.

'No. Prefect Belletor doesn't believe in encouraging the use of any but the standard issue weapons. You?'

'No, our archers are all concentrated in one century. I'll see what I can do while I'm inside the walls. I've got an idea that might allow us to keep Obduro's men at bay for a while, even if it is a bit risky. It would help if you had a fire burning by the time I'm back, and some torches ready to go. There's a stack of them on the cart.'

He turned away, one hand reflexively straying to the knife's handle. Sergius put a hand on his shoulder.

'Wait. A red tunic will stand out like a horse's cock once you're through those gates. You!' He pointed to a soldier of similar build to the hulking centurion. 'Get out of your armour and switch tunics with the centurion here.' The legionary took one look at the determined expression on his officer's face and put down his weapons, gesturing to his mates to help him unfasten his segmented armour's complicated straps and buckles. Julius nodded and unfastened his belt once more, pulling off his own tunic to reveal his muscular body.

'Appreciated, colleague. A different colour will be one more thing to give anyone that comes after me a moment's pause.' He winked at the soldier busy divesting himself of his equipment. 'Mine was clean on today, so it doesn't smell too bad. And I'll try not to get blood on yours; it'll never come out of white wool.'

Julius rapped at the city's south gate with the handle of his dagger, hammering its iron pommel on the brass rivets that studded the door's wooden surface.

'Julius, Centurion, First Tungrians! I need to get back into the city! Open this door or suffer the consequences!'

With the sound of bolts being pulled back the wicket gate opened a crack, and a beady eye regarded him through the opening.

'Leaving's one thing, but letting you back in's another. We've got orders from our commander not to admit . . .'

Knowing that his mission into the city would be over before it even began if the man on the other side secured the man-sized opening, Julius acted without conscious thought, kicking hard at the door and sending it flying open, battering the man behind it with a face full of wood. Stepping quickly through the doorway he switched the knife to his left hand and scooped up the fallen gatekeeper's spear, looking grim-faced around him at the remaining two men.

'Recognise me now, do you? I've private business in the city, and you'd be wise not to get in my way!'

One of the men, dressed like his fallen comrade in the uniform of the city guard, raised his hands in recognition of the Tungrian's evident willingness to do them grievous harm, while the other backed away slowly, putting a hand to the hilt of his sword. Julius appraised him for a moment, noting the swirling tattoo that sleeved his right arm.

'Petrus's man, are you? I thought I caught a glimpse of someone just like you scuttling along behind us as we marched down from the barracks.' He stamped forward without warning, slinging the spear so fast that the gang member's sword was less than half drawn when the flying iron spitted him clean through the sternum. Julius ripped the spear free from the dying man's body as he lay kicking and gasping on the cobbles, lifting the knife to the remaining gatekeepers. 'It's time to make a choice, lads. If I find this gate heaving with Petrus's men when I come back it'll be an inconvenience, but nothing more. And if you do sell me out, then once this is all sorted I'll make a point of coming for you. And when I do, mark me well, what he's going through now will look tame by the time I'm done with the two of you.'

The city's streets were almost empty, Tungrorum's population clearly having taken fright at the threat of impending violence by the gangs that ruled so much of their everyday lives. Whether it was fear of Obduro's band or Petrus's enforcers, hardly a soul was out of doors despite the fact that there was still an hour or so to sunset. Julius walked with swift caution into the maze of streets that was the city's eastern quarter, deliberately taking a roundabout route to his objective in hopes that Petrus's men would be concentrated mainly to the west. Hearing voices from a street that opened barely twenty paces to his left he ducked into a doorway and hefted the spear, ready to fight if need be, silently cursing himself for not bringing his sword.

'. . . so it looks like Petrus missed his chance to grab the gold, and now the bastards have gone to ground somewhere in the city, so it's a shared venture. Whoever finds them only has to get the word out and make sure they don't move again, before the other gangs come together around them. They may be soldiers, but there'll be too many of us for them to hold off, and we can always burn them out if need be. So keep your eyes open for any sign of them; I'll pay a double share to the man that takes me to them.'

Julius waited in the doorway, barely breathing, and after a moment a pair of men stalked past without sparing his hiding place a second glance, deceived by the way the white tunic blended with the house's dingy paintwork in the shadowed evening light. Blowing out a long, slow breath of relief, he muttered a quiet prayer of thanks to Cocidius and, once the hunting gang members had vanished from sight, stepped back into the street with the spear held ready, shaking his head at the good fortune with which he had evaded discovery and muttering under his breath.

'Enough of this subtlety, then.'

Moving quickly, sliding along the walls of the houses on the shadowed side of the street, he made a beeline for the Blue Boar, taking shelter in doorways at any suggestion of the men hunting for gold through Tungrorum. The voices of the hunters echoed through the empty streets on several occasions, but simple luck kept them out of his path, and soon enough he was within a hundred paces of the brothel, peering cautiously round the corner at its imposing bulk and measuring the time it would take him to reach the spot he recalled from his last visit. Without conscious thought he was moving, sprinting across the empty street and fetching up against the shrine with a scrape of hobnails on stone that echoed down the street.

A voice echoed around the corner from the brothel's entrance, swelling in volume as whoever it was left their position at the main door and headed to investigate the sound.

Fumbling with fingers that felt like sausages he reached behind the tiny statue, slid the heavy key home and pulled it to the right, easing the massive iron bolt out of its stone slot just as he'd done before, then he put his shoulder to the door's stone-clad wood and heaved it into the passage beyond. Diving through the narrow gap he turned to push the hidden entrance's door closed, and slid its bolt home with a soft click of well-greased metal, breathing as shallowly as he could. After a moment muffled voices reached him through the tiny holes drilled in the shrine's wall for the purpose.

'Well, I know what I heard. And that candle I lit for Arduenna is on the ground. Someone's been here all right, and not long ago; this wax is still warm. You'd better get inside and get some of the boys out here.'

Another voice answered, unmistakably that of the man called Baldy.

'If you want to disturb Slap while he's busy giving the queen bitch a good fucking, you be my guest. Everybody thinks Stab's the dangerous one, but I've seen Slap's eyes when he goes after a man, and I know which one of them scares me the most . . .'

Julius's lips pulled back in a snarl, and he turned to pad silently up the pitch-black stairway that led to Annia's room.

'*Horsemen!*'

Scaurus followed the Votadini scout's pointing arm, squinting into the setting sun. He paused for a moment, shading his eyes with a hand and staring hard into the sun's glare, his frown deepening. 'Those are *our* horsemen. *Shit!*' He stared at the ground while Clodius stared at him in bemusement, then shook his head in barely controlled anger. 'We've been fooled! Get your men turned around and ready to march back to the city, and pass the same order to the legion centuries.'

He walked away from the leading century's front rank, stopping after fifty paces to await the arrival of the riders. Decurion Silus reined in and jumped down from his horse with a weary salute.

'Greetings, Tribune. I have to report that—'

'I know. You rode all the way west until you ran headlong into the First Spear Frontinius's command, and never saw any sign of Obduro's men. We've been fooled, Decurion, and badly! I've thrown almost every man we had left in the city into what I thought was going to end with Obduro between the hammer and anvil, and now I find that I've left him a juicy prize for the taking. How far behind you is the first spear?'

'A mile or so, no more, Tribune.'

Scaurus's face brightened a little.

'He must have turned them around sooner than I would have. Thank Mithras that at least one of us is thinking with his head today. Decurion, take your men and scout forward towards the city as fast as you can. I want to know what's happening there before it gets too dark to see.' Silus saluted and remounted, leading his men away to the east. 'Centurion!'

Clodius ran to join him.

'Tribune?'

'Tell your men to be ready for a forced march back to the city. And tell them that anyone that falls out of the column can expect to be making his way alone, in the dark, and with a long spell on extra duty waiting for him at the end of the walk!'

At the top of the hidden stairway Julius crept forward until he found the door, sheathing the knife and groping for the heavy iron bolt. Sliding it out of its keep, he eased the door away from its frame with slow patience, mindful that any movement in the wall hanging disguising its presence might alert whoever was in the room. A mewing squeal sounded in the room behind the curtain, an involuntary expression of pain as whatever was happening to Annia took a fresh turn, and a second later the sound of a flat palm slapping bare flesh rang out.

'You're loving this, aren't you, bitch, loving having a real man up you rather than your army faggot? He couldn't make you squeak like that, could he? He's run away and left you to take the heat for him.' He grunted again, and again, clearly going at the helpless woman with all the force he had. 'I've wanted to do this to you for years now, but Petrus wanted to keep you for himself. Now that he's got no more use for you I'm going to make up for all those years.'

Recognising Slap's voice, and tensed on the balls of his feet ready to sweep the heavy curtain aside and attack, Julius held onto his rage by a fingernail's width, waiting to be sure of his bearings before striking, but then another voice spoke.

'Fucking hurry up and lose your load. I've been watching you and nursing this bone for long enough. Let me have a go, and later you can take all the time over her you want.'

He recognised Stab's voice, close enough to the hidden door that if it weren't for the wall hanging Julius knew he could have reached out and taken him by the throat. He swept the tapestry aside with a flick of his left hand, snapping the blade into the wiry man's neck and leaving it buried there, smashing him aside with a flat palm. Taking two steps to the bed he grabbed Annia's rapist by the hair just as Slap realised what was happening. Heaving the big man off the prostrate woman's body, he put a hand on the struggling bodyguard's chest and threw him bodily across the small room to smash against the far wall with a roar of anger, nodding down at Annia and gesturing for her to stay where she was. While Slap lay momentarily stunned on the room's wooden floor, Julius stepped round the bed and slid home the three bolts that secured the door.

'A nice big oak plank like that ought to keep your boys out for a few minutes, until they find an axe or two, and we'll be long gone by then. With your head, of course.'

The bodyguard groaned and climbed to his feet, rolling his head and clenching his fists.

'You should have done me while you had the chance. No man's bested me with bare fists in ten years and more. I'm going to break your fucking back and let you watch while I gut your woman in front of you.'

He stamped forward, supremely confident in his physical prowess as Julius shook his empty hands and wrapped them into big, scarred fists. Pulling his head aside smartly to dodge the bodyguard's opening shot he grabbed the other man's extended left arm, pulled it down onto his raised knee by simple brute force and broke it at the elbow, drawing a shriek of pain and horror from his suddenly agonised opponent. Snapping his head forward into Slap's nose he sent the other man reeling back, his face a bloodied mess, and watched him as he staggered back against the wall next to where Stab lay inert in a pool of his own blood, Julius's knife still protruding from his throat.

'It's a pity for you that nobody with a bit more about them than your usual brainless muscle thought to educate you in the ways of real fighting. Unlike you, I've been fighting with real men ever since I left this place at fifteen, soldiers who'll leave you bleeding at the slightest provocation, whether intended or not, and I rose to the rank of centurion by beating the living shit out of anyone that got in my way. All that deference I gave you before was just my way of avoiding a fight that could only end badly for you, and then for her.'

The door to the corridor shook in its frame as whatever reinforcement had arrived in response to the bodyguard's shout attacked it with their boots and shoulders, but the sturdy timber and heavy iron bolts seemed to be resisting their assault easily enough. Julius tipped his head to Annia, who had risen from the bed and was putting on a tunic. Slap nodded slowly, then reached down with his good arm to his dying comrade and pulled the knife free with an audible sucking noise, watching as Stab convulsed for a moment and then subsided back into the spreading crimson puddle of his lifeblood. Slap's reply was tight with the pain of his injuries, but an angry light was burning in his eye.

'Fair enough, hard man. Let's see if you can do knife work as well as you can talk.'

He came forward, crablike, his wrecked arm turned away from the Tungrian while the knife weaved a deadly pattern in front of him. Julius stepped forward cautiously to meet him, swaying back as the knife hand darted for his eyes, then wincing as the blade sliced across his gut, leaving a line of blood weeping through the slashed tunic.

'Now you've done it. The soldier that lent me this tunic's going to shit when he sees what a mess you've made of it.'

He danced in fast, catching Slap's good hand in his right fist as the bruiser made to repeat the cut, holding it steady in mid-air as the bodyguard grunted and strained in a fruitless effort to break the powerful grip on his hand. Julius tensed the bulging muscle in his right arm, physically forcing the other man's hand down his body and turning the blade in towards him.

'No . . .'

Realising his intention Slap redoubled his efforts, butting the Tungrian in the face only for Julius to ball his other hand into a fist and smash it into Slap's face with a crack of bone. With a single, powerful, grunting shove Julius forced the knife's blade into Slap's crotch, sawing it to and fro while the bodyguard screamed hoarsely at the blindingly intense pain. Pulling the weapon free from the other man's failing grasp, he pushed him away, and the bodyguard tottered backwards with his good hand gripping his ruined manhood, his wide eyes fixed on Julius as blood flowed down his legs and onto the floor in thick rivulets.

'And that's enough punishment, I'd say. Are you ready to leave?'

He turned to find Annia lacing her shoes, her face turned away from the ruined bodyguard. She spoke without looking up.

'Everything I thought I had here has turned to ashes . . . and it was all a lie in any case.'

The Tungrian strode across to the door, now silent as the men outside realised the futility of their efforts to break it down with anything less than an axe.

'You men outside! Tell Petrus that I'll be back for him. And tell him that I'm planning to take more time over his death than I did with these two fools.' He turned for the hidden door, taking

Annia gently by the arm. 'Let's go, before they realise there's another way out of here.' He paused at the top of the stairs, shaking his head at Slap as the bodyguard stared at him through eyes slitted with the agony of his wound.

'Remember when you called me an amateur, and how I smiled and ate shit for the sake of seeing her? There was only one amateur in the room that night, and it wasn't me! Die slowly, *amateur*.'

Escorted away from the basilica by the city guard after delivering the revelation of his master's murder and the slaughter of the bandit hunters, Tornach had sunk gratefully onto a pallet bed in one of the jail's empty cells and quickly fallen asleep, his equipment stacked against the wall next to the tiny stone room's open door. He had swiftly been forgotten by the guards, consigned to the status of 'that poor bastard' and the subject of idle discussion as they went about their business as ordered by Scaurus, keeping the city secure against any potential attack. As the shadows had begun to lengthen in the street outside the cell's barred window he had risen from the bed and strapped his belt and weapons about his waist, walking out to the jail's front office with a sheepish wave of his hand to the officer in charge.

'Slept like a baby.'

The guard nodded sympathetically.

'Understandable. What you saw . . .'

He left the sentiment incomplete, but Tornach pursed his lips gratefully.

'That's done now, and it's time to get on with life. I've nothing else to do, so I might as well help you boys. Where do you need another man?'

The watch commander snorted a mirthless laugh.

'Where *don't* I need another man? There's twenty-five of us to secure eight gates and keep the city calm.' He looked at the bandit hunter with an appraising eye. 'Why don't you go out to one of the gates and send a man back here? That'll let me put another body out on the streets.'

He took a tablet from a stack perched tidily on his desk, wrote a brief statement of his orders into the wax and then embossed the soft surface with the engraved official ring on his right hand. He passed the tablet to the waiting Tornach, who nodded and tipped him a respectful salute and then strode out of the door with a purposeful look on his face, just as one of the officer's men burst into the office.

'There's five hundred or so men coming up the west road, and we're pretty sure they're not the lads that went out this afternoon.'

The watch commander frowned.

'If it's not the army coming back home, there's only one other man with that sort of force to command, and the gods only know what *he'll* do if he gets inside these walls.' He stood, reaching for his helmet and sword. 'If it is Obduro we'll just have to pray he's got no means of getting in. I'm going down to the south-west gate to see what he's got to say for himself.'

'*Centurion! Soldiers on the main road!*'

Sergius mounted the grain store's wall two steps at a time in response to his chosen man's call, responding more to the urgency in the man's voice than the words themselves. He stood alongside his deputy breathing heavily and staring out into the evening sun's radiance, and at length shook his head in disgust.

'I can't see a bloody thing, what with the setting sun and the fact that my eyes are twenty years older than I'd like. Who spotted them?'

The chosen man ushered a soldier forward, and as Sergius turned to speak with the legionary he realised that the boy was barely old enough to shave. He sprang to attention, saluting his centurion with a look of uncertainty.

'No wonder you've got sharp eyes, man; you've not spent a lifetime straining them to stare at the horizon in fear of what might be waiting for you just over it.' He pointed to the distant horizon. 'Now then, in your own time, tell me what you can see, eh?'

He turned back to face the western horizon, waiting as the

soldier stared out into the evening's long shadows, and watching as the sun's orange ball sank to meet the land's smooth black line.

'Not as much as I could just now, Centurion. They're soldiers, marching on the main road. I can see their shields.'

Sergius blew out a long sigh of relief.

'Thank Mithras for that. For a moment I thought they might be Obduro's men, but if they're carrying shields then they must be—'

'No, Centurion, I don't think they're ours. They're not in any sort of formation, for one thing, and they don't look . . . well, *tidy* enough to be Roman soldiers.'

Sergius stood on the wall in the dying sun's light, and as the dimming orb met the horizon it silhouetted the oncoming men, now less than a mile away, throwing them into sharp relief. The chosen man shook his head, screwing his eyes up in an attempt to make sense of what he was seeing.

'What in Hades? They're waving something over their heads, something on their spears. They look like . . .'

'Heads.' Sergius's voice was flat with disappointment. 'So much for our chances of a quiet life, eh?' He turned back to the men waiting below him in the grain store's wide expanse. '*Stand to! Let's have you up on the wall!*'

The young legionaries watched as the bandit gang marched up the road towards Tungrorum in total silence, the distant rapping of their hobnailed boots on the hard surface the only sound to be heard. Sergius stared out at them, calculating the odds as he counted their heads for a third time and came up with the same depressing answer. Turning to his chosen man he muttered his assessment quietly, unwilling to scare his men any more than they already were.

'At least five hundred of them. With that many men I don't see how we're going to—'

A screamed warning from the man to his right snatched his attention away from the oncoming bandits, and he leaned out from the wall to follow the legionary's pointing hand. A pair of figures had burst from the closest of the city's gates and were

making for the safety of the grain store's walls. The larger of
the two was propping himself up with a spear, his pace more
of a stagger than a limp, a piece of bloodstained cloth torn from
his tunic tied about his leg. The woman beside him was dragging him along by the arm and looking back fearfully at the
open gateway. As Sergius watched a small group of men came
through the arch behind them, their murderous intent clear as
they fanned out to either side of the fleeing couple, yelling
challenges and imprecations. He turned and shouted down to
the men guarding the store's entrance. 'It's Julius! Open the
gate!'

He leapt down from the wall with more agility than grace and
waited while his men pulled away the stout timber beams securing
the store's entrance, joined within seconds by Julius's watch officer
and a handful of his men. Drawing his sword as the gate started
to open, Sergius dived through the gap at the head of the small
group and ran towards the fleeing figures, still fifty paces distant,
watching as Julius, clearly unable to go any further, turned to face
his pursuers with only the spear on which he was leaning as
armament. The woman ran a few more paces before she realised
that she was alone, then she stopped and turned round, screaming
in horror as their pursuers closed in on the Tungrian. Without
hesitation the exhausted Tungrian obeyed his instincts and went
on the offensive, lunging awkwardly forward to stab one man in
the thigh with the spear and sending him reeling away clutching
at his leg. Pivoting on his good leg, he punched the spear's butt
spike through the foot of another man, who had been sufficiently
unwary in his approach, twisting the weapon's shaft and tearing
it free, flipping the spear over in his hand with practised skill and
slashing the blade across the man's throat, dropping him choking
to the turf. The remaining attackers spread out, still not noticing
the approaching soldiers in their fixation on the Tungrian, and as
Julius stood panting, the spear's blade weaving in the air as he
struggled to keep it level, one of the gang members eased around
behind him and raised his knife to strike. As the attacker stepped
forward to deliver the death stroke the woman leapt onto him

and buried her own knife deep into his back, bearing him to the ground and stabbing at him again and again in a frenzied spray of his blood, her screams clearly on the verge of hysteria. While the remaining attackers dithered in the face of Julius's exhausted obduracy and the woman's berserk attack, Sergius shouted a hoarse challenge that snatched their attention away from the fugitives and onto the oncoming soldiers. They turned as one man and ran, sprinting back towards the city's gate as it closed in their faces with a dull thud.

'Leave them!' Sergius pointed to the bandit horde's front rank, now barely two hundred paces from the grain store's walls and running as fast as their weary legs would carry them, clearly intent on cutting the tiny party off from their refuge. 'Carry him!' A pair of Tungrians grabbed the staggering Julius by his arms, one of them tossing away the spear on which he was leaning, while Sergius abandoned any pretence at decorum and pulled the blood-soaked woman off the mutilated body of her victim, catching her knife arm and disarming her as she spun towards him with murderous intent. He dragged her alongside him as the soldiers ran for the gate in a desperate foot race with the bandits. Calculating the odds as he ran, the realisation dawned on Sergius that it was a race they were going to lose, if only by a few yards. Julius had clearly come to the same conclusion.

'Leave me, and save yourselves!'

The Tungrians to either side of him kept running as fast as their burden allowed, drawing their swords and preparing to die in defence of their centurion, and Sergius nodded as he ran alongside them, reaching for his own gladius. Scant paces from the gate, and instants from being overrun by the bandits, Sergius was bracing himself to push the woman away and make his stand, when a flight of spears arced down from the store's walls, reducing the oncoming rush of men to a chaotic jumble of tumbling limbs, giving the runners just enough time to throw themselves through the closing gate. The shattered Tungrians dropped Julius to the ground as they collapsed onto their hands and knees, one of them vomiting onto the store's immaculately raked pebbles, and Sergius's chosen man bellowed orders for the legionaries to stand ready for any attempt to climb the wall. Sergius, unable to do anything more than put his hands on his knees and resist the urge to throw up his last meal in sympathy with the exhausted man, looked down at the prostrate Tungrian centurion with a wry smile. Shaking his head, he raised a questioning eyebrow as Annia, painted with sprays of blood and trembling violently, was wrapped in a blanket by Felicia and led away.

'I really hope she's worth it, this woman of yours, given that you may well never walk without a limp again. What happened?'

Julius grimaced at the pain. Felicia had offered him a linen bandage and he held it to the wound, watching as his blood stained the fabric.

'I thought we'd got away free, but a pair of them jumped us one block from the gate. One of them managed to put his spear into my thigh before I could return the compliment.'

Sergius nodded.

'You said you had an idea about defending this place? Given we've got five hundred angry-looking bandits milling around out there I'd be grateful if you were to share it with me.'

He listened to Julius speak for a few moments then raised his eyebrows in shocked understanding.

'By all the gods but that's a terrifying idea. Nobody could ever accuse you of being afraid to think the unthinkable, could they, Centurion?'

He turned away and walked slowly up the steps onto the store's wall, looking out at the ragged band assembled below him just out of spear-throwing range. A man wearing a masked cavalry helmet pushed his way through the throng and walked forward a few paces, holding up his empty hands to indicate his desire to talk.

'I could hit him with a spear from here.'

Sergius shook his head at his chosen man's suggestion without taking his gaze off the bandit leader.

'I doubt it. And I'd rather not raise the stakes that far this early.

Those men might well soon have us at the point of their spears. *That's close enough!'*

The bandits' leader stopped, keeping his open hands raised. With the sunset behind him the cavalry helmet was stained red, and his words boomed out across the open ground in a pronouncement of the legionaries' impending doom.

'Men of the First Minervia, unless there are many more of you hiding behind those walls you appear to be no more than a single century, where we are five hundred men and more. Your walls were hardly designed for a siege, and most of your compound is not even defendable. Surrender now and I'll allow you the choice of joining us or being disarmed and sent back to your legion, but be very clear when I tell you that this grain store, like this city, is now *mine.'*

Sergius stepped forward, a pair of soldiers defending him with their shields from any bowshot.

'You seem to be forgetting that there are three cohorts out there to the west, and when they come back here they'll be the ones doing the evicting. You might be best making a run for it while you still can!'

Obduro laughed loudly, shaking his sun-burnished head.

'By the time your depressingly malleable tribune fetches up here tomorrow I'll be long gone. Scaurus will be reduced to deciding whether to fall on his sword or wait for the emperor's men to do the job for him, given the amount of Commodus's gold he's about to lose. And that's before any mention of a certain Marcus Valerius Aquila reaches official ears. You did know that the Tungrians are harbouring a fugitive from the emperor's justice?'

It was on the tip of Sergius's tongue to blurt out that the gold was safe inside the grain store's walls, but he changed his mind just as he opened his mouth to reply.

'If you want the grain you'd better come and get it. But there'll be no surrender of an imperial facility while I command here, whatever that means for the timing of my meeting with the gods.'

Obduro was silent for a long moment, then shrugged his indifference.

'It means little enough to me whether you die here and now or in some other more fitting place, First Spear Sergius, but as you wish. Bring me the prisoners.'

The three gang members who had been unable to regain the safety of the city were bodily dragged out in front of him, and at a signal from their leader the men surrounding them pulled the prisoners' arms up to the horizontal, then used their feet to hook the captives' legs wide. Obduro drew his sword with a flourish, pointing it at the distant forest.

'Mighty Arduenna, grant us swift and terrible victory in our struggle to free your land from those who have subjugated your people! We offer you the blood of these unbelievers in the hope of your favour!'

He turned swiftly and raised the sword, briefly holding the position before driving the blade down into his first victim's body at the point where neck and chest met, hacking the man's body in half with a diagonal cut that exited his body at the opposite hip. The two halves of the ruined corpse dropped to the ground, and Obduro spun across to his next victim, using the sword's momentum to swing the blade up into the helpless gang member's crotch, again cleaving the body cleanly in two. The third captive stared in terror at the blood-flecked mask as Obduro stopped in front of him with the sword's point touching his chest. He paused momentarily before pushing the blade through the man's ribs and stopping the heart behind them, pulling the sword free and raising its blood-soaked length to the men on the walls.

'Soldiers of Rome, your choice is made! There will be no quarter asked of you, and none given. Your blood will be offered to the goddess, and in her name we will kill you all! Prepare to meet your doom!'

He turned away and vanished into the press of his men, and Sergius tapped his chosen man's shoulder.

'They'll be a moment or two working out how best to attack us. Call me when they show any sign of getting serious about wanting to be inside these walls.' He climbed wearily down the steps and walked across to where Julius lay, shaking his head at the apparent depth of the bandit leader's penetration of the defenders' organisation and actions. 'He even knows my bloody name, that's how well informed he is. So, we have a choice. We can either surrender, and be butchered outside the city walls, or fight it out and be butchered inside these walls. It's not much of a choice though.'

Julius, still recumbent on the gravel, grimaced back up at him.

'And I'm not going to be much use to you, am I?'

He lifted the wounded leg, and both men shook their heads.

'No, you're not. If that wound's as deep as it's long you're not going to be . . .'

As Felicia walked towards them across the store's wide expanse from her impromptu medical post in the administrative building, she called out, staring forebodingly at Julius.

'Stop waving that leg about and keep it straight!'

Sergius laughed wryly at the doctor's imperious command, leaning closer to speak quietly into his colleague's ear.

'Obduro was shouting the odds about some fugitive by the name of Marcus Valerius Aquila. Would that be the same Marcus who had the balls to marry that woman?'

Julius looked back up at him, his response pitched just as low.

'There are some things you're better not knowing, First Spear. The man in question is innocent, but his past won't leave him alone, it seems.'

Felicia reached the centurions and bent over Julius, casting a critical eye at the gash in his thigh.

'You men, pick up this wounded officer and carry him to somewhere a little less likely to be showered with spears at any second. And then, Centurion, we can have a look at that leg and see how much damage you've taken this time.'

Julius caught her sleeve as she straightened up.

'Madam, my woman . . .?'

Felicia shook her head swiftly.

'She's been raped, watched you brutally slaughter her attackers without any thought for her sensitivities, then had to run for her life and be reduced to a quite bestial act of murder, to judge from the blood she's covered with, although she's not saying much about it. I think she's going to need a good deal of delicate handling for quite a while, and that will include *your* having no expectations that she's "your woman". Just because she's a prostitute doesn't make her any less vulnerable than any other woman under those circumstances. Come on, pick him up.'

Obduro leaned close to the former centurion who now commanded the former Treveri auxiliaries that were the main part of his band, looking about him at the dimming landscape before speaking quietly, moving closer to ensure he could be heard above his men's noise.

'I want to be inside that store in less than a single hourglass, you understand?'

The hard-faced soldier-turned-brigand nodded his understanding, intimidated by the expressionless mask only inches from his face.

'It'll be dark in less than half that time. I'll have a century keep the men on the walls busy, and send two more round either side to dig our way in through the granary walls. The men inside can't be everywhere, and once we're through the bricks and into the store it'll only take a minute or so to roll them all up.'

Obduro nodded.

'Good enough. Just make sure you succeed, if you want the share I've promised you. We need to be away from here before dawn.'

He turned away, gesturing to a man waiting quietly at a respectful distance with a military trumpet in one hand.

'It's time for my triumphant return to the city. Give the signal.'

On the city walls above Tungrorum's west gate Tornach stared out into a landscape stained red by the setting sun, while the remaining member of the city guard detailed to ensure that the entry stayed firmly closed lounged on the defence's thick stone parapet. They had watched in silence as the bandit army marched up the main road to the city and its vulnerable grain store. The guard shook his head and spat over the wall.

'That lot will have the legion boys out of the granary in no time. It's just as well we've got twenty-foot-high walls between them and us, or we'd be going the same way.'

Tornach grunted his agreement and pulled a blue sharpening stone from his pack, unsheathing his sword and eyeing the edge critically. The other man looked over at him incuriously, then back out across the darkening fields beyond the walls.

'You won't need that. There's no way they'll be able to get into the city without ladders.'

The bandit hunter spat on the whetstone and rasped it down the blade's length, leaving a thin blue coating of the stone's grit along the sword's cutting edge.

'Maybe not. But the one thing I've learned from Obduro over the last year is that the worst things tend to happen just when you're least expecting them.' He spat on the stone again and turned the sword over to sharpen the other side of the blade. 'Take us. Here we are, safe on top of a twenty-foot-high wall, with the gates below us made from oak so thick and so well secured that it would take four strong men just to lift out the bars that hold them closed. And yet . . .'

The other man eyed him dubiously.

'And yet what?'

A trumpet sounded from the south, a long wailing note followed swiftly by another, and then a third. The guard shifted from his lounging position, leaning out over the parapet and craning his neck in an attempt to see what was happening around the wall's curve. 'Sounds like some sort of signal.'

He shuddered as Tornach's sword slid up into the sleeve of his mail coat, the point stabbing deep into his left armpit with expert precision. Leaping back from the wall he put a hand to the hilt of his own weapon, his eyes wide with shock as he swayed on his feet for a moment with blood pouring down his left side, then crumpled helplessly to the wall's stone walkway. Tornach stared dispassionately down at him, nodding as the truth dawned in the dying man eyes.

'And yet one man inside these walls might change all that in an instant.' He wiped the sword's blade on the dying man's tunic, a mixture of crimson blood and the whetstone's blue residue staining the cloth a dark purple, then sheathed the weapon, spreading his arms as if taking the salute of a baying arena crowd. 'All I have to do now is open the gate and my task is complete.'

The guard shook his head weakly.

'Needs . . . four . . . men . . .'

Tornach smiled again, reaching into his pack and pulling out a coil of rope.

'So it does. And here they are.'

Several miles to the west, the reunited Tungrian cohorts were storming up the road towards the city with Scaurus at their head and the legion's cohort struggling in their wake. No longer heedful of the effects of such a long march on his men he was setting a murderous pace at the front of the long column of soldiers, while behind him the three cohorts' centurions encouraged, cajoled and simply threatened their men to keep them moving at the required pace. Silus had ridden far enough to the east to watch Obduro's army making their approach to the city, further darkening Scaurus's mood and goading him to greater efforts in leading his men's increasingly painful double-pace forced march. Labouring alongside him, Frontinius glanced back down the column to the legion centuries, grimacing as he turned back to the road stretching out into the dusk before them.

'Our lads are grinding along well enough, but the legion centuries are having a bad time of it. Perhaps we ought to call a rest halt? Apart from anything else we need to work out how we're going to recognise the bandits in the heat of a night battle. It might be best to have that worked out before it gets dark?'

Scaurus nodded.

'We could get the torches lit too. Very well, First Spear, we'll take a few minutes to work all that out.'

The soldiers slumped exhaustedly at the roadside where the column came to a halt, their centurions trotting tiredly up the road to cluster round the First Spear, while the chosen men and watch officers pulled torches from each century's mule cart and readied them for lighting. Frontinius waited until the last of the legion officers had reached him before starting his briefing, ignoring the fact that Tribune Belletor had yet to make an appearance.

'Time isn't on our side, gentlemen, so I'll keep this brief. Decurion Silus's reconnaissance confirms that we've been taken for fools, and decoyed away from the city in order for Obduro to have the time and leisure to smash his way into the grain store and make his escape with enough corn to keep his men fed for the best part of a year. And we can't allow that to happen. On top of that, the emperor's gold is also in the city, and whilst I expect Julius has enough presence of mind to see off any gang interest, several hundred bandits would be a different matter. So after we get the men back on their feet we're going all the way back to the city at the double, and there won't be any time to issue orders.' He looked around the cluster of serious-faced men, now barely visible as darkness crept over the landscape. 'So you're going to have to use your initiative, and we'll depend on sheer numbers to do the job for us. Once we're within sight of the city I'm going to blow one long blast on my whistle, which will be the signal to halt the march and form up for the attack. Use the torches of the men in front of you as your guide, and we'll keep it simple, given that it'll be pitch black by then. Odd-numbered centuries will deploy to the left, even numbers to the right. Find the end of the line and anchor your century onto it. I want one long line and no gaps, or we'll have men blundering about in the dark in no time. A one-cohort front ought to be wide enough, so we'll have the Second Cohort lined up behind the First, and the legion behind them. I don't care if they run to the east, but any man trying to escape through us dies. And the tribune's put a bounty on the head of their leader. There are ten gold aurei waiting for the man that brings me the head of this man Obduro still wearing his helmet.' Eyebrows were raised around the circle of men at the size of the reward on offer. 'Yes, he wants the man dead badly enough to offer a year's pay to the man that can deliver it. And we want to avoid half of our men killing the other half, so we'll use the watchword system to minimise the chance of mistakes. The challenge will be "Mithras", the response "Unconquered". Any man that doesn't know the response should be considered an enemy, but make sure your men use some sense. The lads in the grain store won't know the response, and neither will Julius's men. Dismissed!'

Tribune Belletor, who had walked up to the group while the first spear had delivered Scaurus's orders, stepped forward with a serious look on his face as the centurions dispersed back to their men.

'Colleague, I fear my horse has gone lame.'

Scaurus nodded, his expression unreadable in the twilight.

'As I thought it might. It's been favouring one foot for most of the day.'

Frontinius realised that Belletor's voice lacked its usual bombast, and folded his arms in expectation of what was coming.

'So I'm clearly going to have to walk. Perhaps you could reduce the pace a little? I doubt I'll be able to . . .'

Scaurus shook his head, reinforcing the almost invisible gesture with an extravagant sweep of his hand.

'Absolutely not. You've got men depending on us to push through the pain and come to their rescue before it's too late, and I'll not be jeopardising their chances because you've neglected your own physical conditioning. Keep up for as long as you can, and if you have to drop out keep a tent party with you for safety, but don't expect the column to stop.' He turned away from the glowering Belletor and beckoned Frontinius closer, waving his thanks as a soldier with a newly lit torch stepped near to illuminate their discussion.

'Time to be on our way, First Spear. I wish you good fortune in the battle to come. Perhaps this time you might stay behind the line of your men? You know as well as I do just how confused a fight can get at night, and I'd hate to lose you to one of their spears, much less one of our own.'

Frontinius chuckled dourly.

'I'll stay close to you, Tribune, but for exactly the same reason. Someone has to make sure none of these idiots puts his iron through you by mistake.'

The two men clasped arms, nodding at each other in recognition of the risk they were about to take in throwing their men into the confusion of a night battle. Frontinius turned away and tapped his trumpeter on the arm.

'Sound the advance! Let's go and see just how good Obduro's Treveri are in the dark.'

'First Spear!'

Sergius ran up the steps onto the grain store's wall in response to the summons, staring out onto darkened ground between store and city. Barely a hundred men were left of the original cohort strength that had been at Obduro's back as he'd confronted the defenders moments before, their ranks illuminated by torches.

'Where are the rest of them?'

'That's why I called you, sir! The rest of them have split to either side of the store.'

The first spear turned back to the men waiting behind the wall with lit torches, and barked an urgent command.

'They're going to come over the rooftops. Get ready to kill them as they hit the ground!' The legionaries and soldiers spread out, their spears held ready to strike, but after a few moments' wait it became apparent that the expected threat wasn't materialising. Sergius stalked across the store's empty interior, waving both his own chosen man and Julius's to him. Julius, who had been sitting on the ground outside Felicia's improvised surgery with his wounded leg stretched out straight, climbed awkwardly to his feet and hobbled across to join them, using a spear shaft as a makeshift support for the weakened limb. He grimaced at Sergius, who nodded his head to recognise their shared understanding.

'Smart boys. They know we're waiting for them so they're going to hack their way into one of the granaries and then fight their way out as a group. Get your lads to listen quietly and you'll soon find out where they're working at the walls.'

The soldiers spread out throughout the store, opening the individual granary doors and listening for any sign that the bandits were attempting to dig their way through the thick brick walls. A man standing outside a granary on the store's western side waved his torch up and down to attract the officers' attention, and Sergius ran across to the spot, followed by his hobbling Tungrian colleague. The sound of men hacking at the granary's exterior brickwork was clear enough with the wide wooden doors unbarred and opened, and the two centurions exchanged a significant glance. Sergius gestured a tent party men forward, pointing into the store.

'As we discussed it, get your shoes and belt order off, and get in there. And remember, the second they put a hole in the wall you get out and make sure you leave the doors open. After that all you've got to do is run for your lives . . .'

'It seems we've lost your colleague already, Tribune.'

Scaurus turned his head to look back down the column's length, following the first spear's pointing hand to see a small cluster of torches falling behind the last legion century. He laughed bitterly through the pain of the stitch that was torturing his stomach, his face contorted by the stabbing pain.

'I've a fair idea how he's feeling.'

Frontinius patted his labouring tribune on the shoulder.

'You'll get through it. And you have to; they're all watching you . . .'

A voice from behind them spoke over the din of the soldiers' hobnailed boots rapping on the road's rough surface.

'Which side of your body hurts, sir?'

Scaurus looked back at the men following him, finding in their faces the same agony he was enduring. In the wavering torchlight he saw that one of them, a twenty-year veteran from the look of him, had his eyebrows raised in question.

'It's in my right side.'

Even the words hurt, and for a moment he found himself

wrestling with the thought of falling out of the line of march, the prospect of blessed relief from the pain mixed with the certainty that the column would disintegrate into chaos were he to stop marching. The hard-faced veteran smiled encouragingly at him, nodding his head vigorously, and while the tribune knew that his first spear would be poised to intervene, and tell the soldier to mind his own business, Frontinius was clearly holding back his instinctive retort.

'I gets the same thing every time we marches this quick! If you breathe out hard as your left boot hits the road it'll go away soon enough.'

Scaurus nodded at the soldier, consciously exhaling as instructed, and after a hundred paces he found the nagging pain was starting to diminish, only slightly at first, but then more swiftly, as the soldier's trick took greater effect. Able to speak without agony again he turned to Frontinius with a growing sense of relief that the overwhelming urge to stop marching had passed.

'I don't know what difference it makes, but that man's trick seems to have worked.'

The first spear pointed forward into the darkness beyond the small circle of illumination cast by the column's torches. As they crested a shallow ridge the city had come into view, still two miles distant but clear enough through the clear night air; the watch fires burning on its high walls were flickering pinpricks of light. Beneath the walls a cluster of lights were gathered around the spot where he estimated the grain store must stand, and the tribune's mouth tightened as he realised the depth of Obduro's ambition.

'You were right, First Spear. I can only curse myself for throwing the entire force west to chase shadows while leaving the city unprotected.'

Frontinius grunted, his attention fixed on the scene before them.

'Not entirely undefended, Tribune. We'll have to hope that Sergius and Julius can give a good account of themselves.'

★

Tornach pulled the last of the three climbers over the city wall's parapet, then led them down the stone stairs that took them to the city's west gate. Mounting the steps built on either side of the gate, two men on each side, they lifted the higher of the two weighty bracing bars that prevented the heavy doors from opening, dropping the wooden beam to the ground before repeating the action with the other. Dragging the beams away from the gateway they heaved the doors open, then stepped back to allow their leader to enter the city. Walking slowly into the city at the head of half a dozen men, Obduro stared about him with evident satisfaction.

'Close the gate!' He waited while the bracing bars were dropped back into place, securing the entrance and isolating the city from any external aid. 'And so I return. If only I had the time I could make this excrescence of a city into a name that would echo down the ages for the terror of my revenge.' He sighed, shaking his head. 'The horror that we could visit upon this place, given a day and a night in which to celebrate our worship of the goddess. The streets would run with the blood of these unbelievers.' Reaching for the cavalry helmet, he pulled it down onto his head and lowered the face mask. 'No matter. While the inhabitants of this cesspit cower in their houses we have business to conduct. Let's see just how pleased our colleague Albanus is to be liberated from his captivity, shall we?' He turned and spoke quietly to Tornach while his deputy stared into the face mask's impassivity. 'And you, my brother, you have excelled in your actions, sending that fool Scaurus away on a fruitless chase to the west and opening the city for our entry. The time is coming when we'll have no more need for deception and deceit, when we can openly rule the forest in the goddess's name, but I need one more thing from you. Go and prepare our exit from the city while I gather the prize that will set us free from this empire and its restrictions.'

Marcus and Arabus stood together a mile from the city, watching the lights swarming around the grain store from the vantage point where the Roman had watched for Qadir's signal earlier that day. Their ride from the bandit fortress had been uneventful, and the duty centurion at Mosa Ford had allowed them across the bridge once Marcus's identity had been proven, albeit with looks of undisguised enmity at the tracker sitting behind the centurion.

'You want to watch that one; he'll slit your throat and—'

Marcus had overridden his warning with an uncharacteristic lack of patience.

'I've no time to bandy words with you, Centurion. There are hundreds of bandits attacking Tungrorum and my place is there, not listening to your prejudices, no matter how well founded they might be. And you might want to consider the sturdiness of your gate, and your men. This is their most likely escape route back into the forest, I'd say.'

Night had fallen by the time they had reached the spot from which they were now watching the attack on the city, and all that Marcus could see were the bandits' torches clustered around the grain store.

'Just as he planned it. A diversionary attack to keep the defenders pinned down, and with the possibility of capturing enough grain to keep them fed for months, while Obduro himself attends to the main business of the night. All of the gates will be shut and barred, and whichever way he gets in isn't going to stay open once he's inside. We'll just have to hope that the only other way in is still open.'

'That's close enough.'

Sergius put a hand on the arm of the soldier standing next to him, restraining the man's urge to move nearer to see what was happening inside the granary. Dimly lit by the flickering light of the soldier's torch, the men inside were working frantically, half of them slitting the grain bags and upending them onto the stone floor in streams of golden corn, while others threw handfuls of the grain up into the air. The enclosed space was already thick with a fog of choking dust, and the soldiers were starting to labour at their task, slowing down as exertion and the effect on their lungs began to tell in fits of violent coughing, despite the scarves tied across their mouths.

'Is that sufficient, do you think?'

Julius stared hard at the scene for a moment.

'Send fresh men in. We need to get as much dust into the air as we can if this is going to work.'

The work party staggered out into the fresh air at Sergius's command. They were wraithlike figures, their skin and clothing coated in white dust and their bodies wracked by heaving coughs. The first spear ordered another tent party into the store, and had the stricken soldiers dragged clear. One of them got to his feet and addressed his centurion, his voice a wheezing whisper.

'Won't be long . . . First Spear . . . I could hear . . . their voices . . . through what's left . . . of the wall.'

Sergius patted him on the shoulder and turned back to the soldier who was waiting behind him with a spear gripped in one hand, a rag tied about its iron head.

'Are you ready?'

The legionary nodded, bracing his massive body at his centurion's question.

'Yes, First Spear, the legionary is ready as instructed!'

Sergius smiled wryly back at him.

'Good. Now relax. You're the best man in the century with a thrown spear. You know it, your fellow soldiers know it, and, most importantly, *I'm* convinced of it. All I need from you is one very simple thing, something I've seen you do a thousand times in weapons drill. I need you to put your spear through the doorway of that granary, clean through it and into the building, mind you. If you can do that for me I'll make you an immune, and you'll never have to clean out the latrines again. Does that sound good to you?'

The young legionary nodded eagerly, but his face clouded with a question.

'What if I miss?'

Sergius shook his head with a grim smile.

'Not likely! I've not seen you miss a man-sized target at twenty paces in all the months we've been practising with the thrown spear, so once the enemy are inside that granary all you have to do is pick one of them and put your spear into him. Julius's fire water will do the rest. Speaking of which, I think it's time to ready the spear.'

Julius's chosen man stepped forward with the jar of naphtha, liberally soaking the spear's rag adornment with the pungent fluid. The young legionary held it away from his body, wiping a tear from his eyes as the naphtha's acrid fumes evaporated into the night air. A shout from the men in the granary caught their attention, and a moment later the labouring legionaries erupted through the door, two of them dragging one of their fellow soldiers between them.

'They've broken through the wall!'

Julius took the torch from the man next to him.

'Hold out the spear!'

He waited for the legionary to level his weapon, then played the torch's flame delicately at the rag's trailing edge. In an instant the wool was burning fiercely, and the big legionary eyed it warily, his confidence draining away at the thought of actually throwing the fire weapon. Sergius slapped him on the shoulder and barked an order.

'*Ready spears!*'

The ingrained routine of a thousand training sessions took over, and the spearman braced himself to throw, placing his left foot forward and pulling the weapon back until the blazing rag was within inches of his face.

'*Throw!*'

He lunged forward one big pace, slinging the spear at the granary's doorway just as a bandit appeared out of the thick dust to stand in the opening, his sword held ready to fight. The spear spitted him straight through, and the rag's flame was extinguished in an instant as it plunged through the hapless man's body. Screaming in agony at the pain of his wound he staggered back into the granary, leaving the defenders staring in horror at the failure of their plan. Behind the dying man the hole through which the bandits were pouring into the granary suddenly flared with light, as a man with a blazing torch stepped up to the breach, the brand's fiery light turning the grain dust into a red fog. Ducking into the cover of his shield Sergius bellowed a command at his uncomprehending legionaries.

'*Shields! Get behind your shields!*'

10

'Well met, Procurator. I'll wager you hadn't expected to see me again.' Wiping the dappled blade of his sword free of the blood of the lone city guard who had been set to ensure that the disgraced procurator didn't attempt to escape, Obduro stepped into Albanus's house with an appreciative whistle. 'I have to say that you're clearly a man who knows how to live, Albanus. Look at all this . . .' He waved a hand at the furnishings. 'Opulence, that's the only word for it.' He put a hand to the helmet's face mask and lifted it away. 'It's a horrible thing to wear for any length of time, you know, but it does make such an excellent disguise. All that time we were doing business and you never had a clue how I was getting into the city past the guards and the prefect's men. And now you know!'

He grinned at the look on the procurator's face, and Albanus spluttered his amazement.

'But you're . . .'

Albanus stepped back against the wall, his face suddenly white with fear, and the bandit leader's grin broadened.

'Just worked it out, have you? That if I've shown you my face then I'm not likely to let you live? Clever boy, Albanus, even if you are somewhat late in reaching the conclusion. I know that Scaurus took your share of the profits from our little venture, although I expect that my man Petrus will have recovered it by now.'

Julius's shouted command snapped the watching soldiers out of their momentary dismay, and Sergius crouched into the cover of the shield he'd borrowed from his chosen man, snatching one last glance into the granary as the torchbearer stepped through the roughly hewn hole and into the cloud of dust. With a roaring explosion that made the watching soldiers stagger back a pace, the burning dust tore the solidly built granary to pieces like the hand of a vengeful god, sending a fireball into the night air that lit up the grain store's compound like a momentary flash of daylight. Something hit Sergius's shield hard, cracking the layered wooden board, and the spear thrower crouching next to him was smashed aside by a flying brick. When the first spear turned round to look at the man he realised that his soldier was already dead, his head bashed in by the massive impact. For a moment the senior centurion was as stunned as the men around him, and he stared out at a scene of devastation that was hard to comprehend. Where the granary had stood there remained only a gaping wound in the otherwise uninterrupted run of brickwork, and the ground around him was littered with bricks, roof tiles and the corpses of several of his men who had been too slow in taking shelter. Shaking his head to clear it, Sergius drew his sword and pointed it at the gaping hole in the row of granaries, but the command for his men to storm the shattered granary died in his throat at the sight of a thirty-foot-high column of fire raging out of the ruin.

Albanus's house trembled, and the sound of a powerful explosion reached the two men through the thick walls. The door opened and one of Obduro's men put his head round it.

'A mighty flash to the south, my lord, close to the walls!'

The bandit leader nodded, waving the man back to his post. He turned back to Albanus with a wry smile.

'As I was saying, I expect that Petrus will have reclaimed your share of the fraud from the Tungrians by now, and my next stop will be the collection of that rather large sum of money, less the commission we agreed in advance. After that all that remains for me to do is to retrieve my own share from its hiding place, and the stage will be set for my disappearance into history. Once I'm across the Mosa and into the forest the entire Rhenus garrison won't be able to find me. I'll quietly re-emerge somewhere to the south with a few picked men and enough wealth to deal with any difficult questions. You *did* hide my money as instructed, I hope? Your family in Rome really are most horribly vulnerable to a man possessed of as few scruples as myself.'

Albanus nodded frantically, putting up his hands in a feeble gesture of self-defence.

'It's all there, just as you instructed!'

Obduro nodded his approval, drawing his sword with a loud rasp of metal in the silent house.

Good. Now, then, let's get this over with. If you behave yourself I'll make sure it's as quick and painless as I can.'

The former procurator shrank away from him, babbling helplessly at the sight of the sword's dappled steel.

'There's really no need for this. I can assure you that I won't talk! There must be something I have that you want!'

Obduro lowered the face mask over his features, its emotionless face regarding the trembling Albanus with a pitiless gaze. He spoke again, his voice rendered flat and hollow behind the thick sheet of hammered metal.

'But of *course* you have something I want. Something only you can give me.'

'Anything, just name it! I'll give you anything if you—'

Obduro stepped forward and rammed the point of his sword up into the gabbling procurator's throat, twisting the blade as he withdrew it to release the stream of gore that flowed down his victim's tunic. Choking on the blood running down his throat, the dying man sank to his knees, staring up mutely at his murderer.

'And there it is. Your silence, Albanus. That's all I came for.'

He turned away, calling to his men as he left the house.

'That rather loud bang sounded like it might have been a problem, if it was what I suspect it was, so I'm advancing our schedule. You, run to the Blue Boar and tell Petrus that I'm coming for the late procurator's money. Go!'

Marcus and Arabus looked up at the city's wall from the banks of the River Worm, and the Roman walked forward to the point where wall and river met. In the moon's dim light he could see the stark lines of the heavy metal gate that filled the perfectly hemispherical arch through which the river flowed on into Tungrorum. He shook his head at the tracker, pointing at the impassable archway.

'The guard must have closed it when the gates were closed on the tribune's orders. I can't see how—'

A loud clanking noise from the other side of the wall made them both start with surprise, and Marcus flattened himself against the wall, gesturing to the tracker to do the same. Slowly, an inch at a time, the heavy iron gate was being lifted out of the water by whatever mechanism was working on it, until a rattling of chains indicated that whoever had raised it was securing it in place. The two men waited in perfect silence, listening intently as a man's footsteps padded softly along the footpath that ran alongside the river, halting for a moment as whoever it was stopped to duck under the gate's iron frame. Marcus eased the eagle-pommelled gladius out of its scabbard in a slow slither of polished iron, careful not to make a sound as the unknown man's steps drew closer. A figure appeared only a few paces from the crouching Roman, his dark silhouette obscuring the lowest stars in the cloudless night sky as he stepped out of the arch and stopped to look across the empty ground beyond the city's wall, breathing out a soft, slow sigh of relief. Marcus struck before the exhalation of breath was finished, rising quickly and sweeping the man's feet out from under him with a swift kick, then pouncing on him as he hit the ground with a painful grunt. For an instant his captive tensed to struggle, but the cold touch of Marcus's sword at his throat froze him into immobility.

Arabus stepped out of the wall's shadow, his face a mask of hatred in the moonlight, and Tornach gaped up at the two men with poorly disguised dismay. Marcus spoke quietly to the tracker, glancing through the river gate.

'Arabus, check inside the gate to see if he brought any friends with him.' While the tracker padded off reluctantly into the shadows, the Roman looked down at Prefect Caninus's deputy and shook his head in disgust. 'Yes, it is a bit of a surprise, isn't it? You send out a man with orders to kill an interfering outsider, and the next thing you know the pair of them have you at sword point. And you can be grateful that it's me holding the blade to your throat and not your man there. I showed him your sacrificial altar in the fortress on the hill, and he was quick enough to spot his son's belt hanging from it. If I leave you to his mercies you'll last either no more than a few heartbeats or no less than a few thousand, depending on whether he wants to take his revenge quickly or slowly. Either way I'd say you're not very likely to see the dawn.' Arabus came out of the shadows, and shook his head. 'You're on your own, then, are you, with nobody to come to your aid? Although why you'd be opening such an out-of-the-way exit from the city is a little hard to understand . . .' He paused, as if in thought, then nodded knowingly. 'Unless of course you're readying an exit for Obduro, a quiet and unwatched way out for a few men carrying heavy boxes, eh? Perhaps your master's less interested in the grain than he'd have us believe, and more interested in a rather large sum of money that he's got hidden in the city. The only thing I don't know is exactly where it's hidden.'

He waited in silence, holding the gladius to Tornach's throat and watching as fear and uncertainty mounted in the other man's eyes.

'What do you want?'

He smiled down at his captive.

'What do I want? From you? Nothing at all. I've got what I need. I can bring my soldiers here and wait for your master to blunder into our arms. I just thought we'd share a few moments together before I let this embittered man behind me loose on you. After all, you set him to kill me, so the least I can do is enjoy the irony of the fact that it'll be his knife ending your life, don't you think?'

Tornach looked over the Roman's shoulder at his tracker, quailing at the look in Arabus's eyes.

'Let me live. Let me live and I'll give you Obduro, and the gold.'

Marcus spoke without taking his eyes off the prostrate man.

'How's that, Arabus? You let Tornach here live, and in return you get a chance for revenge with his master?'

The tracker thought for a moment, then nodded and reached into his pack, which he'd left in the wall's shadow. He stepped forward with a length of rope, and bent to wrap it around Tornach's ankles before speaking gruffly to his former superior.

'Wrists.'

The bandit shook his head.

'I can't stay here! Obduro will—'

A twitch of Marcus's gladius silenced him.

'Obduro will what? Kill me and then make his escape from the city via this convenient little hole as planned? Find you here, and kill you as the price for your treachery? Quite possibly. So you'd better hope I pull off the apparently impossible feat of defeating him man to man, hadn't you? Hold up your wrists before I grow bored and save him the trouble of having to kill you!' Tornach glowered up at him as Arabus tied his wrists together with the rope that was securing his ankles, rendering him utterly helpless. 'That's better, now there's no risk of you overpowering Arabus here while the pair of you wait to see who comes through this arch when it's all done with.' He reached for the helmet bag and his heavy leather-covered round shield, hefting its weight and looking down at the helpless bandit. 'And since your immediate safety from his revenge depends on my success, you might want to tell me where he is. The rest I can manage for myself.'

Tornach grimaced at him with a vindictive smile.

'He was on his way to deal with the procurator, then to collect his share of Albanus's grain take from Petrus. After that he had only one more stop to make: the place where his share of the fraud is hidden. I'll tell you where it is, but you'd be better running now, while you have the chance. That shield won't protect you from his blade.'

Marcus nodded back down at him, his attention already focused on the city waiting beyond the arch's dark hole.

'Possibly so. But I might have a thing or two to teach Obduro about deception.'

*

'Open your door, Petrus, before I'm forced to open it for you!'

After a moment's pause a window on the building's third floor opened, and the gang leader leaned out, addressing the men in the street in almost conversational tones.

'Obduro! I'd bow my respect to you if I were down there with you. I simply marvel at your audacity in walking into the city like a conquering general.'

The masked man looked up at him, beckoning him down with the fingers of his right hand.

'So come down and make your bow, Petrus, and while you're at it you can hand over the money I told you to take from the Tungrians.'

Petrus's reply was heavy with irony, and he spread his arms in a gesture of helplessness.

'Nothing could have made me happier, Obduro, if only it were possible. Unfortunately word has reached me that the centurion in charge of the gold seems to have decided that it would be safer in the grain store. Your men will very shortly be discovering it for themselves, unless that loud noise we heard just now was bad news for them. And you . . . So I think I'll stay up here, if it's all the same to you. I suspect that my reward for failure might well involve iron, rather than gold.'

Obduro stood in silence for a moment, absorbing the news Petrus had related, before replying in a voice that was harder than before.

'I could burn you out, Petrus.'

The gang leader shrugged again.

'Yes, you could. You could send your men to break in and set fire to my establishment, but I give you fair warning that it's a solid old thing, this brothel, and I've added to its security since I bought it, in the event that I might need a bolt-hole if everything went wrong. Getting in might not be as simple as you imagine. And you might want to be aware that my men on the roof tell me they can see torches coming up the road from the west. A *lot* of torches. So you *might* want to be about the rest of your business and away, before a vengeful Roman tribune arrives and separates that helmet from the rest of you, with your head still in it. Just a thought.'

Obduro thought again, then turned away, calling back over his shoulder.

'You'd best sleep with an eye open from now on, Petrus. A man with as much money as I'll be taking with me can buy a lot of assassins!'

The gang leader watched him lead his men away, then called back softly into the room behind him to the leader of the heavily built and well-armed enforcers he had gathered to his side once the Tungrians had left the city.

'Quickly, away down that bitch's hidden staircase and follow him, but do it invisibly or it'll be you paying the price of failure. We'll wait until he's opened the vault, then step in and take his profits. I'll not be threatened with death in my own city and then let him get away with enough gold to buy a full century of hired killers.'

The leading Tungrian centuries deployed into line half a mile from the blazing grain store, the ground before them lit by the fire still burning on the store's south-western side. As prefect and first spear waited in silence for the remainder of the cohort to complete their manoeuvre from column into line, another tongue of fire leapt skywards, further lightening the ground before them, followed a moment later by another huge explosion that slapped at the soldiers' ears.

'Whoever's in command in there seems to be using his head well enough.'

Frontinius nodded dourly at the tribune's comment, his seamed face ruddy in the light cast by the store's blazing fires.

'Indeed, if it's still attached to his shoulders. And anyone within a hundred paces of that explosion won't be hearing anything for a while.' He looked about him, searching for the raised century standards that indicated that his centuries were in line and ready to advance. 'The First Cohort's ready, Tribune. I was going to wait for the second and third lines to be formed, but given what's happening over there I suggest we get moving before Obduro's men recover from their nasty surprise and make a run for it.' Scaurus gestured his assent, his attention still held by the twin conflagrations before them. Frontinius pushed his way back through the first century's line, bellowing an order at the closest centurion of the Second Cohort, whose line was still only half formed as each of its centuries split from the line of march to either side. 'We're attacking now. Follow us in once your line's complete!' He stepped back to his own front rank, pointing to his trumpeter. 'Sound the advance to battle!'

At the trumpet call, its notes repeated by each century's trumpeter, the Tungrians stepped forward holding their spears ready to strike, then they walked steadily towards the wrecked grain store. A man wearing the mail armour of an auxiliary soldier ran towards them out of the smoke, then, seeing the line of advancing soldiers coming at him out of the night, he turned and fled in the other direction, screaming a warning to his fellow Treveri. A spear arced out from the Tungrian line and took him between the shoulder blades, its heavy iron head punching through the mail's rings and dropping him to the ground. As the line went forward the soldiers marched over debris thrown out from the explosions; at first it was scattered single bricks and splinters of wood, but as they drew closer the wreckage thickened until it was almost a carpet of rubble.

'They're falling back! Do you think we should pursue? Or should we let them go and round them up later?'

Frontinius shook his head.

'Now's the time to deal with them, not when whoever's managed to get away has had time to sort themselves out. Otherwise we'll be digging them out in ones and twos for the next six months.'

Scaurus nodded his agreement.

'You'd better set your dogs loose, then; they're not going to stand and fight.'

At the first notes of the signal for general pursuit the cohort's line shivered and broke, men streaming forward, eager to kill, the weariness of their long march forgotten in the promise of monetary reward for the capture of bandits. They went forward in teams of two and three men, all focused on finding those bandits too stunned or stubborn to have run for the shelter of the night. Tribune and first spear walked past a surrendering Treveri auxiliary dressed in the tattered remnants of his uniform, Frontinius ostentatiously ignoring the heated debate between the two soldiers standing over him as to just whose captive he was. The grain store gates opened, and First Spear Sergius stepped through them to greet the two officers with a broad smile. Scaurus shook his hand, slapping the legion officer on the shoulder.

'You seem to have done a very effective job of seeing off Obduro's men, First Spear, even if you have reduced an imperial grain store to rubble and burned half its contents.'

Sergius saluted, then tapped his ear, shouting his response.

'I'm sorry, Tribune, but I can't hear a thing! That second explosion seems to have taken my hearing! Sorry about the damage, but we do seem to have seen off the bandits! Mind you, I can't take much credit for beating them; the trick of setting fire to the grain dust was all your centurion's idea!'

Scaurus nodded his understanding, speaking quietly to his first spear.

'That will doubtless suit Tribune Belletor very nicely when the account for this destruction is tallied up. Ah, and speaking of Centurion Julius . . .'

The big man was hobbling towards them with a spear shaft for a support, his face wearing the same slightly baffled expression as Sergius's. At that moment, with all eyes focused elsewhere, the two soldiers and their captive Treveri mutineer passed within a few feet of the officers, the Tungrians still bickering as to which of them had captured the man. Momentarily ignored, and not yet restrained by anything more than the threat of his captors' swords, he snatched at the fleeting opportunity, grabbing up a spear from the ground and lunging forward, aiming the weapon's blade squarely at Scaurus's back with a berserk scream of incoherent rage. The only man to react quickly enough was Frontinius, stepping forward empty-handed to defend his superior. Grabbing at the spear's head he pulled hard at it, his eyes widening as the bandit, rather than fighting him for control of the weapon, and as the soldiers around him stepped in with their swords raised to strike, thrust the spear through his mail and deep into his chest. A stab to the back felled the bandit, and another to the back of his neck killed him instantly, but as the first spear sagged to the debris-strewn ground it was clear that the damage was already done.

Obduro walked quickly down the temple's steps with a torch held in his right hand, grimacing at the moisture coating the ceiling and walls of the tunnel-like staircase.

'Two of you, down here now! There's a heavy weight to move.' He advanced on the altar, sizing up the massive stone frieze as a pair of heavily built men, clearly selected for their strength, came down the steps and joined him in contemplating the ornately carved slab of rock. He waved a hand at the altar.

'Time to earn all that corn that's gone down your necks in the last few months. I need that thing lifted off the turntable.'

The two men took up positions on either side of the frieze and gripped it at the base, their big hands searching for purchase on the heavy piece of stone. Nodding at each other they strained at the lift, their heavy muscles flexing and tensing as they heaved the frieze off its rotating plinth and half carried, half staggered away to put it down on the floor, leaning it against the temple's wall. Obduro gave them a moment to recover from the effort, then gestured to the platform on which the frieze had rested.

'Now that. Careful with it – it's solid iron.'

They repeated the lift, grunting at the iron disc's weight and lifting it to reveal a cylindrical stone-lined hole beneath the frieze's usual resting place. Obduro pointed down into the concealed hiding place, and was about to speak when a voice from the other end of the temple cut him off short.

'What in the name of our Unconquered Lord are you doing here, desecrating a holy place?'

The temple's pater stood at the foot of the staircase, bristling with indignation. Obduro shook his head at his men, walking round the uncovered hole and barring the priest's way through to the altar.

'Usually you can expect your word to be the law in this place, I suppose, but today, priest, you are reduced to the role of bystander. I've come to reclaim the gold that has been hidden here. You did know this day would come, didn't you? After all, why else would we have spent so much perfectly good coin building a shrine to a god that none of us believe in?'

The priest frowned, shaking his head.

'But I was told that the money was intended to spread Our Lord Mithras's word, when the time was right . . .'

He trailed off, suddenly intimidated as Obduro bent close enough to him that his own face was reflected in the mask's surface. The bandit leader lifted the mask, watching as the priest recoiled in amazement.

'I know you were, priest, because it was me that gave Albanus the lie to feed to you in the first place. I came to your celebrations of this false god with a smile, and encouraged you to see me as a devout member of your congregation, but all the time I was secretly worshipping Arduenna, and waiting for the right time to reclaim what is mine. Can you really see me leaving enough gold to make me a senator to a deluded old fool like you? You labour in the service of a false god from the east, a god served by the soldiers and emperors who enslaved my people. Now get out of my way! You two, bring the gold!'

He pushed the priest aside and lowered the mask again, gesturing to his men to pull the chest of gold from its hiding place. With an indignant yelp the reeling pater stumbled over the raised feasting platform behind him and fell heavily, banging his head on the stone surface. He lay still, with a trickle of blood staining his thin hair. Obduro's men bent back to their task, then started away from the hole as a man stepped out of the robing room at the temple's far end, with a drawn sword and raised shield. The newcomer was wearing a cavalry helmet almost identical to that on Obduro's head, and his round shield was decorated with an exquisitely detailed rendering of the goddess Arduenna riding a monstrous boar, her bow drawn to shoot an arrow at her foe.

'Leave now, unless you all want to die in this holy place.'

The speaker's voice was muffled by the helmet's lowered mask, and Obduro tipped his head to one side in bafflement.

'They do say that the imitation of a thing is the most sincere of compliments, I believe. In which case I suppose I should feel myself thoroughly complimented by whoever it is that you are. You've adopted my style of headgear, you have my goddess on your pretty little shield . . . Yes, all in all you're quite the image of *me*. Although of course you're not *me*, are you? So let's see how good you are. You two, you ought to be enough. Take him, and let's see who's beneath that helmet.'

The big men drew their short swords and advanced on the waiting figure, who stepped forward to meet them with his sword raised. Nodding to each other they attacked simultaneously, one of them lifting his blade to hammer at the painted shield while the other charged in with the point of his sword levelled. Parrying away the man on his left with a firm punch of the shield, he flicked the other's blade aside with a deft twist of his own blade, lunging forward on a bent knee to run him through with the long sword's point. With a shriek of pain the bandit fell back from his intended victim, clutching at his stomach, and the mysterious figure turned to his other assailant, whipping the blade in low as his remaining opponent jumped back in to attack him again, severing the man's leg at the ankle.

Obduro shook his head in disgust, drawing his own sword as the stranger stepped past his defeated men and regarded him dispassionately through the eyeholes of the cavalry mask.

'It seems that I'll have to deal with you myself.' The bandit leader stared at his opponent for a moment longer before speaking again, his voice a mixture of assumed superiority and curiosity. 'I've always found it easier to fight man to man without the constraints imposed by this frankly ludicrous disguise. And to be honest, not only am I curious to find out just who has the courage to face me, given my justified reputation with this weapon, but I'd like to see your face as I send you to meet Mithras, or whichever god it is that you serve. What do you say? Shall we lose these awkward helmets?'

The other man nodded, and the two men lifted their face masks simultaneously, staring at each other before Obduro broke the silence.

'Well, now. Centurion Corvus . . . or perhaps I'd be more accurate to have said "Centurion Aquila"? It seems that your enforced necessity for disguise has become a bit of a habit, doesn't it? And that jaw seems to have healed quicker than might be deemed feasible.'

Marcus smiled thinly back at him.

'Disguises come in many forms. When you told your man to put me out of action I decided it might be a good idea to allow you to believe you'd succeeded. A whisper in my wife's ear was enough to have her play along, and so, as far as Tungrorum knew, my jaw was broken. But nobody died to foster that illusion, whereas you, *Obduro*, seem to have elevated the knack of spending other men's lives to conceal your identity to an art form. And that's the last time I'll use your somewhat over-regarded title. It seemed to me at first that you were at least genuine in your desire for freedom from the empire, but now I can see you're just another honourless robber with no concern except to escape with the fruits of your violent trade. There never really was a plan for you to defy the empire from the forest, was there, *Sextus* Caninus?' He waited for a moment, while Caninus stared back at him with an unfathomable expression. 'Yes, I called you by your real name. It wasn't a girl called Lucia you left to rot in a disused stable all those years ago, was it?'

The other man nodded, raising an eyebrow as an indication of respect.

'Well done. How long have you known?'

'That you killed your brother Quintus in a fit of jealousy over something or other before you hid him under a floorboard and ran for your life? I've known that for certain since you admitted to it just a moment ago. Before then it was no more than an educated guess. How long have I known that you're not Quintus? For a matter of hours, since I found a dead body in your fortress earlier today.'

Caninus attacked without warning, stamping forward and swinging the leopard sword in a deadly arc, but Marcus had been waiting for the onslaught all the time he'd been talking, and he lifted his shield in defence rather than going blade to blade with the bandit leader, knowing that even his patterned spatha could never hope to trade blows with the fearsome damascened steel. With an expression of glee Caninus chopped his sword into the round shield's rim, but rather than hacking cleanly through the layered wood and linen, the blade's fearsome edge bit deeply into the bowl's edge before stopping dead against something beneath its painted surface, sticking fast. Knowing that if Caninus managed to wrench the blade free he wouldn't be fooled a second time, Marcus used every ounce of his arm strength to twist the shield violently, wrenching the sword out of Caninus's hands, then tossing it aside behind him. Without a second's hesitation the bandit leader lowered his face mask and leapt forward, moving so fast that he was inside the Roman's defences before Marcus had a chance to use his own sword. Holding his opponent's sword hand aside, Caninus pulled his head back to deliver a powerful head butt, but realising what the bandit leader intended Marcus dropped the sword and grappled with him, pushing him off balance and preventing the blow from landing. Forcing his opponent to the right, the Roman hooked a foot behind the struggling Caninus's right leg and then reversed his grip, using the struggling bandit's own strength to throw him into the stone frieze propped against the temple's wall. Caninus saw his chance, and kicked his body off the frieze's surface to lunge full length across the floor, grasping for the hilt of Marcus's discarded sword and raising the blade to hack it into the Roman's legs and end the fight. But, unbalanced by his kick, the heavy stone slab fell away from the wall, landing squarely on his feet and legs. The bandit leader screamed and dropped the sword, twisting desperately in a futile attempt to free himself from both the stone panel's massive weight and the agony of his shattered feet and ankles. Marcus pushed the sword away from him with a booted toe, then bent and picked it up, sheathing the weapon. He bent down again and pulled off Caninus's helmet, revealing a face twisted in agony and hatred. The bandit leader stared up at him helplessly, still writhing in pain. His voice, when he spoke through gritted teeth, was harsh with hate.

'You have the favour of the gods today, it seems! Kill me!'

Marcus shook his head, standing up to stare down at his prostrate enemy.

'There was no luck involved. You brought your blasphemous blood cult into this holy place, and Mithras dealt out your punishment in the way he saw fit. And you'll die soon enough, you can be assured of that.'

He tugged the damascened steel blade from his shield, looking down at Caninus in a mixture of pity and contempt for a long moment before raising the shield and lowering his face mask ready to fight, stepping cautiously up the steps that led to the outside world. A score and more tattooed gang members stood waiting for him with Petrus at their head, and Caninus's remaining men were scattered across the square where they had fallen in what looked to have been a brief and one-sided combat. Marcus waited in silence as the gang leader stepped forward and drew himself up to speak.

'Obduro, put down your sword and accept the terms I offer you, or I will send these men at you, too many for even *you* to kill. I have promised them each a share of the gold waiting for us in the temple, to them if they live, or to their families if they die, and all stand ready to take you down if you refuse to surrender!'

Raising the helmet's faceplate, Marcus smiled into Petrus's astonishment.

'The man you call Obduro, former imperial prefect Caninus, awaits the emperor's justice in the temple below us, having already been judged by Mithras and found wanting. This temple is holy ground which I am sworn to defend with my life. If you want the gold, you will indeed have to come through me . . .'

He lowered the faceplate again, readying himself for the inevitable onslaught, then turned to face the source of a fresh voice.

'And me!' Julius was hobbling across the square with a spear as a prop, and he took his place alongside his comrade with a wink. 'I've come to offer you the chance to surrender, Petrus. If you give it up now you'll be treated far better than if you make us work for it.'

Petrus's smile broadened.

'Just when it doesn't seem as if life could get any better, the last piece of the puzzle falls into place. The soldier who invaded my business, killed two of my men and stole a valuable item of my property presents himself to me on a silver plate with an offer of "*the chance to surrender*".' He wiped an imaginary tear of mirth from his eye, shaking his head at the grinning centurion. 'Surrender? Really? To quote your words back at you, I'll have your cock and balls fed to *my* dogs, Centurion, and I'll do it while you're still alive to enjoy the sight. Right lads, let's have—'

Julius held up a hand.

'Before you set your men on the pair of us, there's just one thing.' He put a shiny brass whistle to his lips and blew a long shrill blast. For a moment the men around him heard nothing other than the echoes of the whistle's note dying away, but just as the smile was returning to Petrus's face, and with a sudden rattle of hobnails, a century's strength of soldiers burst into the square from several directions, their shields and spears raised to trap the gang members where they stood. Julius raised his eyebrows at Marcus, who raised his cavalry helmet's face mask and grinned out at the men of his own century as they herded the captives into a tight knot and forcibly disarmed them at spear point. A hulking gang member scowled down at the diminutive Hamian confronting him, only to find himself with the point of the easterner's dagger pressed firmly into his crotch.

'Move it or lose it, arsehole.'

The soldiers around the Hamian nodded approvingly, and more than one gave the big man a look that promised there was worse to come were he not to obey the command promptly. Qadir strolled across to Marcus with a quiet smile, looking his centurion up and down with a slight smile.

'Is there any way in which we may be of service, Centurion Corvus?'

Marcus shook his head, wearily resting the Greek shield's rim on the square's cobbles.

'Apart from telling me how you knew I'd be here, no.'

'You will recall that you asked me to set a watch on the city's gates yesterday, and to send a fire arrow over the wall to tell you if someone came after you, and in which direction. The same man walked into our lines while we were mopping up those bandits who had not been blasted to their gods, with one of Prefect Caninus's men at knife point. He told us that Caninus would be here to retrieve his gold, and that you would attempt to prevent him from leaving the city.' He gave Marcus an appraising look. 'Shall I have one of our men carry that shield down to the barracks?' He reached out and lifted the shield out of his friend's hands, pulling a face as he raised it to the fighting position. 'This is remarkably heavy, presumably largely due to the unusual amount of iron welded onto the rim. Here, you . . .' He passed the shield to Scarface, who took it with only a minimal display of bad grace. 'Take this to the centurion's quarters. And take a man with you; the streets aren't entirely safe yet.' Scarface gathered a mate to him by eye, and the pair set off towards the Tungrian barracks with a conspiratorial look. Qadir turned back to Marcus. 'That way you won't have to put up with him hanging about you for the next hour or so, since I expect them to duck into the first beer shop they find with the door unlocked. Perhaps your wife would appreciate your presence at what's left of the grain store, given that she's not sure if you're alive or dead?'

Marcus nodded, and then wrinkled his forehead as he remembered one last thing.

'You might want to send a tent party and your watch officer down into the temple. Respectfully, mind you. It seems that Our Lord's not in the mood for misbehaviour. There are two of Caninus's men down there with fairly nasty injuries, plus the man himself pinned under the stone frieze, and a large chest full of gold that needs uniting with the one that we took from Procurator Albanus. In fact perhaps you'd better escort that back in person, and whatever you do . . .'

'Don't let Morban near it?'

'Exactly.'

The standard bearer frowned at the two centurions.

'That's not fair, I—'

'Resemble that comment? I'm sure you do, Standard Bearer.' Qadir shook his head at the older man. 'Just content yourself with running a book on how much coin there is in the chest.' He saw the standard bearer's face brighten. 'And no, no one's going to be allowed to open it until the tribune's present. If you're lucky, perhaps he'll let you do the honours.'

Marcus snorted his laughter.

'Not if Uncle Sextus has any say in the matter, I'd imagine . . .'

His voice trailed off, as Morban's face fell and the big Hamian pursed his lips in dismay.

Tribune Scaurus offered Marcus a cup of wine, and looked his officer up and down.

'You seem none the worse for your adventures of the last twelve hours, Centurion Corvus.'

Marcus bowed slightly, then sipped from the cup.

'Thank you, sir. I seem to have enjoyed a good-sized piece of luck.'

Scaurus raised an eyebrow.

'The more audacity we bring to this life, the luckier we seem to be when it pays off, no matter how we make that luck happen. And it seems that Mithras has smiled upon you, Centurion. Perhaps the temple's pater will reward you with the advancement of another grade, once he's recovered from his bang on the head. Caninus, it seems, will live to go on the cross if we're prompt with the punishment.' He laughed bitterly. 'And we'll be prompt with the punishment, you can be sure of that! I want Tungrorum to see all three of them pay the price for their crimes. Caninus,

Petrus and Tornach, I'll have them all crucified and the rest of their men branded as thieves and then sold on to the local farms to serve the empire for the rest of their lives. That should make Tribune Belletor happy, at least. He's been dropping dark hints that he's going to mention the destruction of half the grain store to his legatus in his next despatch, and I wouldn't put it past the snivelling little man to have a decent-sized victory go into my record as a defeat, given the chance. The real shame, of course, is that we lost First Spear Frontinius so needlessly. Yet another mistake on my part.' He shook his head. 'The first rule of soldiering, Centurion, is to admit your errors, accept them as your own and belonging to no other man, and then learn from them and never repeat them. I so badly wanted Caninus to be telling the truth that I let it blind me to the reality. One thing I would like to know though . . .'

Marcus raised a questioning eyebrow.

'If, as you suspect, Caninus left his brother dead in that stable ten years ago, rather than this apparently fictional girl Lucia, how in Hades did he send me a severed head that was so obviously his?'

The centurion sipped at his wine.

'That's easy, Tribune, if you can accept the proposition that the Caninus twins weren't the only boys their mother raised. It seems there was another brother a few years younger than Quintus and Sextus, and their mother logically enough named him Septimus. When I found the headless corpse of an unidentified male in Caninus's fortress earlier today, I also found the words "Septimus will have revenge on the fratricide Sextus" scratched into the wall of the cell where he'd been held, and the body's hands had that same broad-fingered look to them. And Caninus was quick enough to admit it, when he thought he could kill me and walk away with the gold. He wasn't Quintus, the older of the twins who let his wits talk him out of trouble; he was Sextus, the younger brother whose violent and ruthless nature couldn't tolerate his twin having something he wanted for himself. Caninus must have told their younger brother, Septimus, that he'd killed his twin, either to cow him or perhaps simply because he could.

When I found the headless body it was clear that Sextus, or Quintus as we believed him to be, was making his move, and intended to use his remaining brother's head to make you believe he was dead. Julius told me how badly battered it was, the eyes and teeth literally torn out?'

Scaurus nodded, unable to suppress a shiver at the memory of the brutally disfigured head Tornach had held out to them in his apparently trembling hands.

'Yes. Mutilations intended to conceal the differences between the two men, I presume. We can only hope he was dead before they set to work with the pincers.'

Marcus shook his head sadly.

'Not from the amount of blood in the sand around the corpse.'

'Indeed. The man never allowed another's pain to get in the way of making his deceptions absolutely believable. We can only be grateful that he drew the line at allowing his men to commit a genuine rape of your wife, although their use of a stolen knife to sour the relationship between you and Tribune Belletor was a masterstroke.'

The centurion shook his head again ruefully.

'Not that it needed much more souring. And no wonder Albanus was so terrified of being questioned; it was Obduro, not Petrus, who was his business partner. Petrus was no more than a gang leader with an eye to the main chance, and with the right connections to dispose of the stolen grain and to ensure that Albanus knew what would happen if he stepped out of line. And it was probably me that set Caninus off on his path to attack the city when I sent away for the copy of the census. He must have known that something in it would have betrayed him. Perhaps he feared that the existence of a younger brother would set us to thinking, or perhaps it was simply that this girl Lucia, the supposed daughter of a wealthy merchant, never actually existed.'

He sighed.

'Whatever it was that led to Caninus's last big throw of the dice, it seems that everything I've done in the last few days has turned to ashes. I even missed the clue at the execution, when that man started shouting that the real danger was among the city's officers. He must have been one of "Obduro's" men to have recognised the man's voice, and the prefect's man, Tornach, was certainly ruthless enough to kill him in order to maintain his identity as the bandit hunter. I'll be glad to see the back of this place, if it restores my judgement.' He tipped his head to the damascened steel sword, which Marcus had laid across a chair. 'Is that thing as formidable as it was rumoured to be?'

Marcus nodded, his face sober.

'Terrifyingly so. That shield I had lined with iron strips to stop the blade barely did the job. The idea worked though, and because it was round I could twist it and tear the sword from his hands while it was stuck in the rim.'

Scaurus walked across to the sword, picking it up and feeling the weapon's balance.

'What will you do with it?'

His centurion pondered for a moment.

'Part of me wants to keep it. I'll never see another sword like it – that's a certainty – but another part of me knows that the damned thing's been turned to evil once already, and that it might well serve the same purpose again. It might be better to turn it into something a little less all-powerful. I'll take it to the smith and see what he makes of it. Some knife blades, perhaps . . .'

Julius was sitting quietly with Annia in the hospital when the tribune's runner found him. The number of men who were wounded during the defence of the grain store had been remarkably low, since those close enough to be hit by flying debris had either been killed outright or died from their injuries soon thereafter, and Felicia had been able to put the emotionally traumatised woman in a private room, with a soldier on the door at all times to ensure her privacy. She had permitted Julius a visit, and whilst she had warned him to steer well clear of any reference to the events of the previous day, he'd quickly realised that Annia was not to be dissuaded from the subject.

'Of course the doctor thinks I'm still too delicate to talk about it.

She doesn't realise that what I need is a drink with a friend I can trust, and a chance to talk it through and put it behind me. I haven't killed a man before . . .' She paused for a moment, then looked at him appraisingly. 'I can trust you, Julius? To be there when I need you?'

The big man struggled to meet her eyes.

'I'm sorry. I don't know any other way to say it. I should have made you come away with me when I had the chance.'

'I didn't mean that. The rape wasn't your fault, it was Petrus's, and seeing that he's to be nailed to a cross I can hardly complain that he's not paid for it. And I've had worse things happen to me in the last fifteen years. I'm asking if you can organise some part of your life around a woman like me. I can't stay here, not now that I understand the reality of my trade. No matter how thoroughly your tribune cleans up the city there will always be gangs, and gangs will always see women like me as property, nothing more. And I won't ever be a man's property again. Can you live with me on those terms? They're all I have to offer.'

He nodded, taking her hand.

'I made the mistake once. I won't make it again. And I have my own life as a centurion, so I can't exactly complain if you choose to live the way that fits you best. What will you do?'

She smiled at him knowingly.

'I thought I might ask the doctor if she needs a volunteer orderly. She tells me that she lost her last assistant last year, and since then she's had nothing better than a succession of dull-minded soldiers working for her. And who knows, perhaps I can . . .'

She fell silent as the soldier put his head round the door.

'Begging your pardon, Centurion, but the tribune requests your presence in the basilica.'

Annia smiled at him, shooing him away.

'See, there's that life of yours. I'm going to have a bit of a sleep, and then I'm going to talk to the doctor and make her an offer of my services. Come by later on with a flask of wine, and hopefully we can drink to my new life.'

Julius marched into the tribune's office in the basilica with his vine stick under his arm and stamped to attention, guessing that the tribune had summoned him for the difficult conversation he'd been expecting ever since the cohorts' return. Scaurus glanced up at him from the desk, gesturing with a wry look at the scrolls and tablets vying for his attention.

'Stand easy, Centurion. You've got a powerful habit of getting my attention, Julius. If you're not destroying whole granaries by incinerating their contents, then you're deserting your command and running about the city rescuing female civilians who are apparently possessed of absolutely no military value whatsoever. You are a highly trained and capable officer of inestimable military value to both me and this cohort, and you put yourself at risk. You put your century at risk by leaving them under the command of your chosen man at a time when enemy attack was imminent. And, to be frank, your actions in defence of the grain store may well have destroyed what's left of my career, unless we can turn some of this stolen gold to making amends.'

Julius stared straight ahead, ready for whatever punishment the tribune chose to deliver to him, but the tribune had already turned away without waiting for an answer, pointing to a sword lying across the chair next to his desk. Julius recognised it as Frontinius's weapon, traditionally passed from each first spear to his successor.

'As if all this weren't enough, I've still got the major problem of not having a clear successor for Sextus Frontinius. It clearly can't be you, given your recent escapades, so if you've got any ideas as to who among your colleagues would make a worthy successor, then please feel free to share them with me.'

Julius thought for a moment.

'Corvus, Dubnus and Caelius are all too young. Clodius and Otho are both too brutal and Milo's not brutal enough. Titus could do it, after a fashion, but he'd not thank you for the opportunity.' He sighed, shaking his head. 'It's at times like these I miss Rufius the most. That, and whenever Dubnus starts getting uppity . . .'

The tribune walked back across the room and stood in front of him with a fierce expression.

'Do you take me for a fool, Centurion?'

Scaurus waited in silence, and Julius realised that this was one of those rare questions that – although it invited the man being asked to venture a negative opinion of the man doing the asking – he was actually expected to answer.

'No, Tribune, far from it.'

His superior kept staring at him, to the point where even the imperturbable centurion was starting to feel discomfort at the tight smile on the tribune's face.

'Really? It was the only conclusion I was able to come to when I considered our relative records over the last twenty-four hours. While I was away chasing down a non-existent threat I left you and your century to guard the procurator's gold. Instead of which you managed not only to safeguard the money, but also to free an innocent civilian, a victim of my stupidity in leaving the gold so lightly guarded that Petrus and his cronies believed it was theirs for the taking if they just applied a little leverage with your woman. I scarcely have to add that the honey in this particular cake is your single-handed destruction of Obduro's band with your inspired idea to set fire to the grain dust. I heard the storeman's warning of how a spark from a hobnail could set a whole granary alight just as clearly as you, but I'm not sure that I would have been clever enough to use that potential for destruction as a weapon.'

He sat back with an equable expression, prompting Julius to frown at his words.

'But the damage to the grain store? And your ca—'

'Career? To buggery with my career, First Spear. I'm never going to be a legatus, not unless something truly unprecedented happens to uproot the current political realities. I'm not from a good enough family, you see. Besides which, by the time we've rebuilt the store and restocked it, we'll still have enough gold to make a very favourable impression on the local governor. Have you seen the casualty figures? No? I'll read them to you. We took thirteen dead and another seven wounded, mostly as the result of stopping flying bricks, whereas the bandits had almost ninety men killed, the same number wounded and of the rest of them barely a tenth got away. Most of the men we captured were still wandering about with their senses blasted out of them. They were too close to the granaries when the dust ignited, you see, and the flying debris seems to have gone through them like a reaping hook.' He stood up, advancing round his desk with his hand extended. 'Well done, Centurion, and not just for pulling my testicles out of the fire. The day when we forget our duty to the innocents who're caught between us and the enemy will be a sad day. Your friend's profession is of no relevance whatsoever. She was just such an innocent caught between two enemies, and you did the right thing. You plan to look after her, I imagine?'

He turned away without waiting for an answer, pointing to the first spear's sword.

'You're the natural successor to the ownership of that honourable blade, and in just a minute I'm going to invite you to strap it on and take charge of the First Cohort. You can help me to choose a man to lead the Second as one of your first tasks. Being in charge of two cohorts is too much for any man in my opinion. But before I invite you to change your life forever, let's just be clear on something that's very important to me.' He looked the centurion hard in the eye. 'If you ever feel that I or any other officer in this cohort is making a mistake of the size that nearly ended in disaster yesterday, you are to tell me so, and to keep telling me until I start listening to your concerns. Is that clear?'

Julius nodded, looking at his superior with a new-found respect.

'Yes, sir. Crystal clear. Of course I'll have to discuss this with my brother officers. It's our tradition, sir.'

Scaurus smiled again, slapping the big man on the shoulder and then reaching over for the first spear's sword, putting the weapon into Julius's reverentially extended hands.

'I know that your tradition says that the cohort's first spear must be chosen by a gathering of the officers, and whilst I could override that convention I don't really see the need to do so, since I fully expect your brother officers to be as clear-headed on the matter as I am. And until that decision is made I am ordering you to assume the duties of the role on a temporary basis. Carry on, First Spear.'

The Tungrian centurions were unusually subdued as they gathered after the parade at which they'd witnessed the crucifixion of Caninus and his cronies, despite the thoroughness with which imperial justice had been administered. Whilst a barely conscious Caninus had, as expected, succumbed to asphyxiation within minutes, unable to use his shattered legs to relieve the pressure on his chest, both Petrus and Tornach had showed every sign of facing protracted deaths, despite both having been soundly scourged before being nailed into position. In perfect silence the assembled men of the three cohorts had listened to their helpless cries for mercy as they had writhed on their crosses to either side of Caninus's inert corpse, both men panting in pain and terror as the enormity of imperial justice bore down upon them. The chained and shackled line of freshly branded slaves, the only remnant of the bandit army, had filed past the crucified men in silence, their overseers punishing any sound from the shuffling men with swift strokes of their whips. It had been, the officers of the Tungrian cohort agreed, sound punishment swiftly delivered to men that deserved nothing less. Their acting first spear had ordered a gathering of his officers once their men were back in barracks, and he now stood in the middle of his colleagues with a neutral expression, waiting until the last of them was holding a cup of wine.

'Brothers, our first duty is to pay our respects to First Spear Sextus Frontinius in the time-honoured manner. Raise your cups.' He waited in silence until every man had his cup in the air. 'To Uncle Sextus! The best damned first spear I ever served under, and taken from us before his time was due! Sextus Frontinius!' He drained his cup, looking around him as his brother officers echoed his toast and did the same. 'Before we leave this city I'll have an altar to his name built into the grain store wall, to mark the place where he fell.'

He stood for a moment as the other centurions nodded their agreement. Frontinius's body had been burned the previous evening, his funeral pyre saluted by a march past of both Tungrian cohorts and a deputation from the legion cohort led by a temporarily abashed Belletor, but an altar was the accepted way for a revered officer who fell in battle to be honoured by his men, and Julius knew there would be no shortage of donations to pay for the mason's careful work.

'But now, my brothers, we have important business to discuss. The matter of First Spear Fontinius's replacement requires discussion. Whilst the tribune has nominated me, I don't—'

A deep rumbling voice interrupted him.

'We all know it has to be you, Julius. We don't need to vote on the subject.'

'Titus—'

Julius got no further with his reply, as Otho shook his head and interrupted him again.

'It's you, Julius. We all feel the same way. Now get on with it before I'm forced to beat some common sense into you.'

Julius saw that all seven centurions gathered around him were nodding agreement.

'Even you, Dubnus? You've been heard to voice the opinion that I wasn't fit to command a legion century, never mind one formed of real fighting men.'

Dubnus grinned back at him.

'That was before, when I was carrying the pole and pushing soldiers around for you, before I got the chance to serve alongside you. You'll do.'

Marcus raised a hand.

'If I might comment, brother?'

Julius raised his eyebrows and looked up at the ceiling with a smile.

'If only I'd seen Morban and placed money on a lecture from our only properly educated brother I might very shortly be a good deal richer. Go on, Marcus, but keep it quick.'

His friend returned the smile.

'Your brothers are all expressing the blindingly obvious, Julius. It *has* to be you. Dubnus, Caelius and I are too wet *behind* the ears . . .' The older centurions all nodded vigorously. 'Otho, Milo and Clodius are too solid *between* the ears . . .' He ignored the good-natured grumbling that greeted the opinion and pressed on. 'And Titus . . .?'

The massive centurion turned to face him, bending slightly to look him in the face, his eyebrow raised.

'Yes, little brother? Are there ears involved?'

Marcus kept a commendably straight face.

'Titus is simply too terrifying a prospect for any of us. After all, he is rumoured to *collect* ears . . .'

The big man nodded knowingly, while the men around him muttered their apparent disgust at his evident failure to take offence, as Marcus continued.

'You were First Spear Frontinius's chosen replacement were he to fall in battle, and there's not one of us will go against his judgement in making this decision.'

Julius looked around his fellow centurions one last time, and to Marcus's eye his face took on an expression that was almost pleading.

'You're all sure?'

'For *fuck's* sake, man, accept the sword so that we can have a bloody drink!'

Bowing to the ever irascible Clodius, Julius nodded.

'Agreed, brother Badger. But before we pour the wine again and celebrate our fallen brother's achievements in life, we have an empty slot to fill within this brotherhood. I will move to command the First Century, as is expected of me, which leaves the Fifth in need of a centurion. And in response to that need, my decision is this. Acting Centurion Qadir will assume command of the Ninth Century, and Centurion Corvus will move to command the Fifth. And look after them properly, you young pup, I'm genuinely quite fond of one or two of them.'

Heads nodded around the circle.

'And now, I think it's time to drink the rest of that rather tasty Gaulish wine that Petrus sold us back when he was just a merchant.'

Wine was poured, and the officers fell to talking amongst themselves. Marcus watched in silence as his new superior walked across to the barrack window and stared out at the city's east gate, before slowly walking across to join him.

'For a man who's just reached the pinnacle of his career, you're not the happiest soldier I've ever seen.'

Julius replied without taking his eyes off the gate's massive timbers, his eyes shining in the daylight streaming in through the window.

'I don't know if I can do it, Marcus. Fifteen years I've wanted this, and now that I have it . . .'

Marcus patted his shoulder.

'Your life has changed in more ways than you could have expected. You've seen more fighting in a year than most men see in twenty-five; you've had friends killed and wounded; then, just when you take on the biggest, most unforgiving job of your life, you have a woman to care for, one you thought you'd never see again.' He waited in silence until Julius sighed, nodding his agreement. 'In which case I'll remind you of a conversation we had in the bathhouse a few days ago. You told me that family was my main responsibility, and I'll turn that advice back on you. Except this cohort is your family and, like it or not, you're now our father. Why else do you think we all deferred so readily to your taking the sword? These men will go through torture for you, they will stand and die with you when all else is lost, but they need you to lead them, and to give them the certainty that we will always come through whatever shit we're thrown into. And if your woman doesn't understand that then she's not as astute as I make her out to be. So take a moment to get a smile back on your face and join your brothers, *First Spear*. To remind you of your own words, do it for them, if not for me.'

Julius smiled quietly back at him, took a deep breath and turned back to the room with his cup raised for a refill.

'Fair advice, Centurion. Just don't start treating me any differently. And make sure that Dubnus learns to stop stealing my . . .'

He paused, looking around the room. 'Where is Dubnus? He was here just a minute . . .' He looked about him again, his face hardening with sudden understanding. 'Bugger, Dubnus! Where's my bloody vine stick!?'

HISTORICAL NOTE

By now regular readers of the *Empire* series will understand why I've chosen this period in which to set my stories. In all honesty my first impulse to the late second century was a simple one – there was a handy revolt in Britannia which saw a Roman general dead and the north of the province in uproar, which suited my intended plot very nicely – but further reading soon opened my eyes to the possibilities in a period when the conflict was pretty much non-stop between 182 and 211 AD. Add to that:

- the climactic year 193 AD, the 'year of the *five* emperors' (take *that*, 69 AD with your miserable four rulers);
- a protracted and bloody civil war fought between three characters we'll soon be getting to know as they start their climb up the ladder of imperial power on their way to the top;
- the fabulous (unless of course you took part in it) two-day battle of Lugdunum in 197 AD;
- a string of campaigns fought around the empire by Septimius Severus from then until 211 AD;
- and the bitter emnity between Severus's sons as they grow to maturity.

So, you can see that Marcus Valerius Aquila (no reference to *The Eagle of the Ninth* intended) is going to see a *lot* of action over the next twenty-five years of history, and not all of it on the winning side.

So, how do we find the empire in early 183 AD? In a pretty ropey state, all things considered. Many commentators put the start of the rot firmly on the shoulders of the young emperor Commodus, whose accession to power on the death of his father Marcus Aurelius in 180 AD and prompt abandonment of the wars with the northern German tribes set the scene for a slump in Roman fortunes, as so vividly portrayed in the film *Gladiator*. This was the point at which the era of the 'five wise emperors' (Nerva, Trajan, Hadrian, Antoninus Pius and Marcus Aurelius) came to an end, and the principle of nominating the best man to take the throne was replaced by the hereditary principle which, as so often proves to be the case, was doomed to fail. And yet in truth the seeds of disaster had been sown fifteen years before, when soldiers returning from a campaign in the east mounted by Marcus Aurelius's co-emperor Lucius Verus brought what is believed to have been smallpox back into the empire.

The Antonine Plague ravaged the empire, killing one in every four people infected and as many as a third of the population in some parts of the empire. It also took a heavy toll on the army. Fast forward to 183 AD, and we find the army on the Rhenus (Rhine) not only still weak from the plague and the long Marcomannic wars, fought by Marcus Aurelius to keep the German tribes from occupying the northern provinces that bordered the barrier rivers of the Rhine and the Danube, but additionally weakened by another event. Earlier in the decade, as related in the first book in this series, *Wounds of Honour*, serious losses had been suffered in Britannia as the result of a native uprising. If the island province was to be held it would have to be reinforced with men from the Rhine, further weakening the army on the northern frontier. Men were sent west to Britannia, and the Rhine legions were forced to soldier on with even fewer men.

Throw in a growing number of *latrones* – soldiers, escaped slaves and simple men on the make who were turning in ever greater numbers to banditry across northern Europe as their only means of survival – and it can be seen that the empire's northern frontier was in a state of flux. This is the stage on which the fictional events depicted in *The Leopard Sword* play out, the invented story strongly based on documented historical fact.

THE CULT OF MITHRAS

The **Raven** was the lowest grade, and would have served as doorman of the temple. St Augustine tells us that at the ritual feast he wore a raven head-mask and wings, and in the Santa Prisca murals he also wears a dark red tunic. His symbols were a *caduceus* and a cup, and he was under the protection of Mercury.

The **Bridegroom** was the second grade. He was the initiate vowed to the cult. A damaged Ostian fresco shows a bridegroom wearing a short yellow tunic with red bands and carrying a red cloth in his hands. The Santa Prisca Bridegroom, also damaged, wears a yellow veil and carries a lamp in his veiled hands. The grade was under the protection of the goddess Venus and its symbols were a lamp and a veil.

The third grade was the **Soldier of Mithras**, and we know a little of his initiation. The initiate had to kneel, naked and blindfolded, and was offered a crown on the point of a sword. He was crowned, but was immediately ordered to remove the object and place it on his shoulder, saying that Mithras was his divine crown. By this act he became a Soldier of Mithras and in memory of his vow he could never again receive coronation. His symbols were a quiver of arrows and a kit-bag, and he was under the protection of Mars.

These three grades comprised the lower orders of the cult.

The **Lion** was the first of the senior grades. Initiates are described as growling like Lions, and the Konjic relief shows one wearing a leonine head-dress. The Lion had his hands washed and his tongue anointed with honey and after this (in Mithraic ritual at least) he could not touch water, for he had entered the grade which symbolised the element of fire. The grade was under the protection of Jupiter and at least one of its duties was to attend the sacred altar-flame. Its symbols were a thunderbolt, a fire-shovel and a *sistrum*, or Egyptian metal rattle much used in the Mystery cults.

The fifth grade was that of the **Persian**, who was also purified with honey. The symbols of the grade were ears of corn and a sickle, and it was under the protection of the Moon.

The second highest grade was that of **Runner of the Sun**. The initiates of this grade imitated the Sun at the ritual banquet, sitting next to Mithras himself (the Father). The patron god of the grade was the Sun.

The highest grade of all was that of **Father** (Pater). He was Mithras' earthly counterpart and responsible for the teaching, discipline and ordering of the congregation which he led. His symbols were a Persian cap, a *patera* or libation dish, a sickle-like sword and his staff of office. He was under the protection of Saturn.

If you want to know more about Mithraism I would recommend *Mithras and his Temples on the Wall* by Charles Daniels, one of the books I consulted in the process of researching Mithraism, and perhaps the most accessible.

THE CULT OF MITHRAS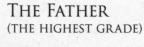

 THE FATHER
(THE HIGHEST GRADE)

 THE RUNNER OF THE SUN
(SITS NEXT TO THE FATHER)

 THE PERSIAN

 THE LION
(FIRST OF THE MIDDLE GRADES)

 THE SOLDIER
(THE LOWEST INITIATED RANK)

 THE BRIDEGROOM

 THE RAVEN
(THE LOWEST GRADE)

EMPIRE

The story began in

Wounds of Honour
Arrows of Fury
and
Fortress of Spears.

A new chapter began with
The Leopard Sword.

It continues in

The Wolf's Gold

THE WOLF'S GOLD

The horsemen rode forward for a mile or so on the road's hard surface, their horses' hoofs clattering loudly in the silence that hung over the wooded hills to either side. Silus looked back down the road to be sure they were sufficiently well ahead of the marching column of infantrymen, and then waved a hand at the wooded slopes.

'Time to get off the road and make a bit less noise, gentlemen, we're sticking out like tits on a bull as it is. Keep your eyes and ears open for anything out of the ordinary.'

The horsemen separated into two parties, each half a dozen strong, and rode their horses onto the strips of cleared ground on either side of the road before reining them in to a walk so that their hoofs would be almost silent in the long grass. Qadir steered his beast alongside Marcus's big grey, the graceful chestnut mare's finely drawn lines a stark contrast to the warhorse, while Arminius's mount fell in behind them at the German's urging. The three men talked quietly as the patrol ghosted forward up the road's margins, until Arminius suddenly frowned and wrinkled his nose.

'Do you smell that?'

Marcus inhaled deeply, discerning the very slightest edge of a familiar aroma on the air.

'Woodsmoke. And burning fat.'

Qadir nodded, waving a hand to Silus and putting a finger to his nose as Marcus bent to pull his shield from the grey's flank. As the decurion nodded his understanding an arrow flicked out of the trees fifty paces to their front, snapping past the Roman's head with a whistle of flight feathers. Flicking down the helmet's polished face mask he spurred the grey into action, dropping his spear from the vertical carrying position to point forward, knowing that the sight of its long blade would be enough to spark the big horse's customary berserk charge. A second arrow flew from the trees, its flight a blur of motion that ended with a clang as the missile's iron head glanced from his facemask's many-layered protection. The impact's force knocked his head to one side, momentarily blurring his vision. Raising the shield across his body the Roman rose in the saddle by tensing his thigh muscles against the grey's flanks, hefting the spear in readiness to throw. The hidden bowman loosed another shot, aiming for horse rather than rider this time, and Marcus felt the beast shudder with the blow, but the animal's pace was unaffected as it thundered towards the archer's hiding place. Rising to run rather than stand his ground for a final shot, the enemy scout presented Marcus with a fleeting target as the grey hammered past the spot from which the tribesman had watched the horsemen approach, but his hurled spear flew past the fleeing archer with a venomous power born of his anger at his horse's wound and missed by an arm's length.

Pulling the grey up he raised a leg over the saddle's horns to slide from the horse's back, landing on his feet and drawing hislong sword as he strode furiously into the trees behind his raised shield, acutely aware that the layered board's protection was largely illusory against a bow at such short range. In front of him the scout was still dodging through the trees, but seeming to stagger slightly as he ran, one side of his body sagging as if he were a puppet with a string missing. He abruptly stopped running, staggering to a halt and standing still for a moment, swaying on his feet, one hand clenching and unclenching around the shaft of an arrow that dangled unnoticed at his side. Marcus stepped in close, his eyes narrowed in anticipation of a further ambush, raising the long bladed spatha to make the easy kill even as he wondered at such suicidal behaviour. The enemy scout turned, his feet dragging through the fallen pine needles like a sleepwalker's, and the look on his face stayed the Roman's hand as he stared with horrified fascination. Momentarily considering the masked centurion before him with empty, glassy eyes, his mouth hanging open to release a thin stream of bloody spittle, the barbarian slowly raised the arrow he was holding until it was in front of his face and emitted a high pitched moan of distress. Marcus watched in wonder as he realised that his intended victim's legs were shaking hard enough to make his whole body shudder uncontrollably. With a long groaning exhalation of his fear and despair, the archer toppled backward onto the forest's needle-strewn floor and lay twitching, soiling his breeches as he shook spasmodically.

Bending to examine the seemingly helpless man more closely, the young centurion held his sword ready to strike as he pushed the barbarian onto his back with a booted foot. The scout's eyes were pinned wide, their pupils shrunk to the size of tiny dots as he stared sightlessly up at the Roman, and the arrow spilled from his nerveless hand, the shaft's last fingernail length painted a deep and ruddy red. Bending closer to look at something that caught his eye on the man's arm, Marcus heard the faintest of noises, the creak of a bow being drawn back, and used the split second's warning to thrust his shield forward toward the tiny fragment of sound. An arrow slammed into the board with enough power to punch clean through the layers of wood and linen, only stopping when the heavy iron head impacted on his mail shirt's iron rings with a hard rap. A powerful stench of something rotting filled Marcus's nostrils, and he rolled away from the spot into the shelter of a tree, calling out to Silus: 'There's another one here! Flank him!'

The Tungrian troopers advanced into the trees to either side, shouting to each other as they sought to trap the second archer in an enveloping movement, but in a scatter of twigs the man was up and running to Marcus's right faster than the dismounted Tungrians could follow. As the Roman watched through the trees, his ambusher vaulted onto a waiting horse and bolted for the road, looking to make his escape before the Tungrians could remount. Pushing up the cavalry helmet's facemask and fighting his way back out of the undergrowth, Marcus almost blundered into Qadir as the Hamian coolly nocked an arrow to his heavy framed hunting bow and pulled the missile back until its flight feathers were level with his ear. Qadir waited patiently as the scout's horse crashed through the undergrowth towards the road, allowing a slow exhalation of breath to trickle from his lips as he readied himself for the shot. Bursting from the trees, the rider whipped his mount to a gallop, crouching low over the animal's neck to present a smaller target, and for a moment Marcus wondered if his friend might hold back the shot for fear of hitting the horse. Qadir leaned forward a fraction, his eyes narrowing in concentration, then loosed the arrow and lowered the weapon, making no attempt to reach for another. Struck cleanly in the square of his back the barbarian scout arched convulsively, toppling over his horse's hindquarters and smashing down hard onto the road's cobbled surface.

Walking forward with his shield raised against any further attempt at ambush, his nose wrinkling at the fetid smell from the bone arrowhead still poking through a long split in the wooden board, Marcus watched the trees to either side warily. Reaching the fallen rider he prodded the man's arm with a toe, sliding it away from the long knife sheathed on the man's belt.

'No need. He's as good as dead.' Glancing up, he found Silus approaching with a look of disgust. 'It's a shame. I'd like to have shared a few quiet moments with him to discuss this . . .'

The decurion reached out and broke the shaft of the arrow stuck through Marcus's shield, pulling out the barbed head and sniffing at it. Pulling a face, he held the offending missile at arm's length and called for an empty feed sack.

'Poisoned?'

The cavalryman nodded grimly at Marcus's question, wrapping the arrowhead in several layers of sacking before snapping it from the shaft and knotting the little package closed.

'Here, it'll be a souvenir for you. Just don't cut yourself with it.' He kicked the dying man hard in the head, his face white with anger. 'No, let the fucker lie here and die as slowly as he likes. And if you've got any problem with that, you'd better go back and see the state your horse is in.'

Marcus started guiltily and hurried back to where the big grey lay rigid on the verge with its legs sticking stiffly out from its body, trembling violently and rolling its eyes in terror while Arminius and Qadir stood over it, turning to greet Marcus with shaking heads. A single arrow protruded from the horse's right shoulder, its shaft painted the same deep red as the one in the dying archer's open hand. A froth of foam was trailing from the animal's open mouth, every shallow exhalation of breath accompanied by a soft groan as the arrow's poison tore at the horse's innards. Shaking his head in sorrow Marcus squatted beside the horse's head, stroking the long face gently as he pulled a hunting knife from its place on his belt. The blade was almost supernaturally sharp, one of a dozen he had paid a swordsmith to forge and edge with metal from the Damascus steel sword he'd taken from the bandit Obduro in Tungrorum. To his brother officers' great delight he had given them all one of the resulting blades, although whether he had managed to neutralise the evil he had sensed in the sword from his first touch of its hilt by doing so, or simply distributed it more widely, he was unable to tell. Tracing a hand down the horse's throat he put the knife to the beast's sweat-slickened neck and made a single fast cut, opening the veins hidden beneath the twitching flesh and staring down with a sad smile as a stream of hot blood poured out onto the ground.

'Farewell, Bonehead. You were a good mount.'

Waiting until the horse's eyes closed he stood, wiping and sheathing the knife with a regretful sigh.

'Properly done, brother. We'll make a cavalryman of you yet.' Silus turned away from the dead animal, shaking his head at the waiting troopers standing around him. 'We won't be eating horse tonight, not unless you lot want to risk meat with enough poison in it to knock this big sod over in less than a hundred heartbeats.'

Marcus walked into the trees and found the spot where the first archer was stretched out in his death agonies, cutting his throat with a single expert pass of the knife's fearsome blade and picking up the quiver of arrows that lay beside him. Bending close to the corpse, he saw that the mark on the man's arm which had drawn his attention briefly during the fight was a scratch, the skin discoloured around the small wound. He went back to the spot on the road where the scout was slowly expiring under Qadir's impassive stare.

'Kill him. He's not going to give us anything that's not already obvious from their presence here, and if I'll do it for a horse then I owe him the same dignity.' He handed the Hamian the quiver, waving a hand at the dying man before them. 'You'd better collect his arrows as well. They may come in handy, and I'd rather not leave them lying about here. And watch out for the ones with the red paint, the slightest puncture will kill a man, from the looks of it.'

From

The Wolf's Gold

The fifth book in the EMPIRE series